Three Short Novels

Three Short Novels

THE SON
~

THE LIGHTS OF EARTH
~

CONFERENCE OF VICTIMS

Gina Berriault

COUNTERPOINT
BERKELEY

Library of Congress Cataloging-in-Publication Data is available
ISBN 978-1-61902-247-8

Cover design by QUEMADURA

COUNTERPOINT
1919 Fifth Street
Berkeley, CA 94710
www.counterpointpress.com

Printed in the United States of America
Distributed by Publishers Group West

10 9 8 7 6 5 4 3 2 1

The Son

My well loved and tender son, know and understand that your house is not here. This house wherein you are born is but a nest, an inn at which you have arrived, your entry into this world: here do you bud and flower. Your true house is another.

AZTEC FRAGMENT
The Midwife to the Newborn

1

On the night of the day she was graduated from a girls' school with twenty-three other girls in the same kind of virginal white gown, all floating under the trees with their ribboned diplomas in their hands, she demanded that her parents consent to her marriage to the brother of her father's mistress. The young man was nineteen, extraordinarily handsome and on his way to Hollywood where, with the help of a cousin who was an actress, he would become an actor. He had no money and no job other than as an occasional waiter in a big, cheap restaurant frequented by Italian families, and he could not act, so he could not, her father explained to her, ever hope for much to happen unless his beauty was so great that nothing more would be required, and this, her father said, was doubtful, for wasn't his head too large and his legs too thick, and wasn't he a bit pigeon-toed? Her father was an elegant man with a fine profile, and he made a practice, in times of stress, of deriding and condemning the enemy by referring to physical deficiencies. But swayed by his daughter's threats to accompany the young man anyway, and to bear a child to make matters worse, he consented to the marriage, and his wife consented also, and the wedding of Vivian Carpentier and Paul Cardoni took place in the Episcopal cathedral.

She had wanted as many guests as possible, for the greater the number the greater was the approval of her obsession with the groom, the more public the marriage the more assured was his future as an actor; that was the superstitious and substantive role the guests played. In Paul's old Ford they drove down the coast, stayed a few nights with the actress, then found a small apartment of their own; he went to work as a waiter in a famous restaurant patronized by the movie crowd and there awaited discovery. When she became pregnant, a month after the wedding, she looked forward to the child as a unifier of the parents. The child was to make the marriage last forever, though she had no doubt that it would anyway. But the pregnancy lasted longer than the marriage. Toward the end of the pregnancy he was troubled by insomnia, brought on, he revealed one night, by his dread of her bearing a child. The advent of a child unnerved him; he had not realized what a shock a child could be to the parents. He felt that his chance for fame was less now, he felt that he was chained to a rock. Since he revealed his feelings only one time, one night, she believed that he felt the way he described only once, as a person has a case of nausea one night and then no more. Not long after that night, however, he failed to return from his job, and nine days after his disappearance a letter came from Chicago, instructing her to return to her parents and to wait to hear from him. He was on his way to New York to try to get on the stage. He would, he wrote, send her an address when he got there, and he wanted her to let him know when the baby was born.

After riding all night on the train, she arrived just as her parents and her brother were sitting down to Sunday breakfast. She had not eaten supper the night before, having been revolted by the thought of food, and was hungry now; but hunger was not the only reason she ate with a gluttonous concentration. She felt that her parents had construed as wholly selfish her desire to marry the young man who had now deserted her, and, in their care again, she mockingly accepted their view of her by obligingly demonstrating the same kind of selfish desperation over the meal. She had been prepared for the world by her mother's celestial mauve ceilings and pale yellow satin sofas, yet here she was in her true nature: a girl with cheap, draggy pregnancy clothes given her by some neighbor's sister; her hair dried by peroxide and bleached two colors, white edged with sulphur yellow; her high heels turning under; her fingernails unclean; and too insensitive to lift her head for even a moment to say a gracious word to her family.

She sat in her mother's room while her mother spent an hour dressing and making up her face, apparently unaccepting of the reflection, patting her cheeks with rouge, twisting down hennaed curls to cover the cheeks. Vivian took cigarettes from her mother's porcelain box on the dresser and smoked them the way her husband smoked—after a long draw on the cigarette, throwing back her head to let the smoke trickle out. She crossed her knees, hooked her arm over the back of the chair, and swung her foot, while she told her mother about the actresses and actors into whose homes and pools Paul and she had been welcomed. She said that Paul had got a part in a movie that was being filmed in the Arizona desert, and she had told him before he left that she was going to visit her parents because he had been afraid she would be lonesome without him. At that point she broke into tears, sobbing so loudly she felt that she was wrenching the child out of place.

She lay limp and manageable in her mother's bed, babbling about cockroaches in the sink, grease-eating ants in the tub; blaming insects as the cause of her husband's departure because insects had been a constant irritant during a time she could not begin to examine, and because to examine the marriage, even if she could, was to see her life as she suspected her mother saw it, as a great prevalence of mistakes.

Her mother covered her with a blanket, her and the large hump of her child, and went off to church.

Four days after her return, her father drove her late one night to the hospital, and the child was born in the early morning. She named the boy David, not in honor of any relative or friend but because the name had always appealed to her for its calling up of the youth who had slain the giant and in his manhood had become king, for the eternal youthfulness of it. The child had dark, downy hair and eyes like narrow luminous beads within plump lids, eyes of a deep yet indeterminable color; his feet were wrinkled and tinged with purple as if they were two hundred years old; and everything possessed that perfectness of miniature objects of art.

She was surprised by how her body responded to the child's cry when she herself was doubtful in response, unsure of how she felt about him—whether she would grieve if he were to be taken from her or whether she would be relieved, or whether she would both grieve and be relieved at once. When the child cried to be fed, a minute ferment started up in her breasts, an activity like that which might go on inside a fruit when the hot sun concentrates on it. The milk seeped through the cloth of the nightgown, and, when she lay on her side to feed him, the trembling draw of his mouth on her nipple tugged the womb upward in a most inward, upward pulling that made the sucking a pleasure for her and almost a reason for having borne the child. At these times she would caress his small, round head and his limbs of no angles, no joints, that had a curve like a doll's rubber legs, trying with her touch to perceive who he was, what manner of person he was to be, touching with a feeling of dread the hair that lay over the soft fontanel where the soul seemed to be contained. And even when, gazing down at his small face, she was disturbed by the inanity of his hunger, by the animal simplicity of his need to be fed and of his satisfaction while he fed, by this simple demand upon her because it forecast unknowable, more complicated demands, even as she felt in her spirit a shrinking away from his demands upon her and her future, her breasts responded to his mouth, her body enjoyed the secret and yet unsecret, the known to all upward pull within, and she was pleased with his dependency on her body.

Once, toward the end of her stay in the maternity ward, as she sat in the chair next to the bed, nursing him, it seemed to her a ludicrous mistake that a man should ever be in the condition of infancy. She wondered if he might be ashamed of her later—of the time of his infancy, and look at other male infants, even his son, and be ashamed for them. The time of his infancy seemed so absurd because there was already present in his person the time when he would be of significance beyond her—the girl who held him at her breasts, her two hands spanning his length. She was so amused by the absurdity of his infancy that she lifted him high to press her laughing face into the almost weightless combination of small dangling body and soft garments.

After one week she packed her few things, nightgowns and bathrobe and slippers. Her father carried her overnight case for her and she left the hospital, holding her baby wrapped in a blanket. She was careful of her step over the elevator threshold because she was wearing very high heels and taking some satisfaction in the fact that the shoes opposed the baby, that they hinted she was not in any girlish elation over the real baby in her arms, that the time of her delusion was over. In the walk along the corridor of the main floor and down the broad steps and out through the parking lot to her father's car, she fought an urge she knew she would never give in to and yet feared— to stumble in her heels and drop the baby. When her shoe turned a little, out by the car, she clutched the child closer in terror.

2

Almost every day, for the rest of that summer, she guided the canvas baby carriage down the hill to the park and sat on a bench in the sun and the moving shade of the trees, a girl in a pastel cotton dress, her legs and arms bare, her feet in sandals. There were always small children on the grass; and mothers, each with her disarray of kits and bottles; and there was sometimes a solitary man on a bench, a different man each time, who watched her over his newspaper or watched her without concealment. Joggling the carriage with her toe, she imagined herself with the man across the path, imagined a union so amorous that her husband would be wiped from her memory. Sometimes the proprietor of the grocery store gazed at her from under the awning, a small, green-smocked figure across the street, standing watchful. Was there about a girl with her first child, she wondered, the greater desirability of a woman who is innocently pledged? She speculated on her effect as she pushed the carriage home, pausing along under the awning to examine the fruit on the sidewalk stall, catching in the dimness within the store his gazing eye or the quick lift of his head.

THE SON

The white, frilly bassinet was set up on its stiff legs and rollers in a corner of her room, and, when the child slept, she listened to the radio by her bed or read the novels that her mother bought, and the magazines, and was restless for the use of her body. The use of her body was enough; the rest of it—the belief that somebody else could know her spirit as well or better than she knew it herself—was a delusion. She lay on the bed, listening to popular songs or reading, with the fantasy of her next embrace always in the back of her mind, her body always waiting for the fantasy to claim it. She saw no ending to this time in her parents' home with her child other than the beginning of a time with another man, and in her mother's crooning and clucking at the baby she sensed the wish for another man to come and take the daughter away. The wish was in the sweet, ardent, rather weary sounds as her mother bent over the basket, in the feminine ways of her body, ways exaggerated for the daughter to see and to imitate; since the daughter was now again at home and with a child, one must assume that she had not used and was not using her ultimate powers. As for her father, if Vivian were to run off with a man, he would not miss her, she knew. He lectured at medical schools on his specialty, the heart, saw his private patients, and spent almost every evening at his club or with his mistress; his family had become like a group of patients he had treated when he had been specializing in a branch of medicine that no longer interested him but whom he was obliged to look over once in a while. Her brother, Charles, Jr., six years older than she and interning in a hospital across the bay, although he sometimes came home for a night, did not visit with her or show any interest in the child. When he did come into her room, it was usually in the few spare minutes before he left the house, and the contempt in his manner made her stand away from him and answer him grudgingly. She could not bear his loud, drawling voice, his calves bulging importantly against his trousers, and the long legs nervously shifting in professional style from one crepe sole to the other. When he asked her what she intended to do with her life, she told him, turning away from him, that she intended to take a course for charwomen.

She did, however, venture out, after a time. Her father's mistress, Paul's sister, was her good friend—a tall, almost harshly beautiful young woman, an advertising artist, who painted in oils and who had black walls in her apartment. Vivian often walked the two miles to Adele's to drink with her friends—newspaper reporters and commercial artists and actors. She sang for them one night, imitating a torch singer, perching herself on the arm of a chair, crossing her knees, languidly plucking at the drooping petals of a beige rose that Adele put into her hands. She sang again, a few nights later, for one of Adele's brothers-in-law, who owned a bar where the customers were entertained by singers and raconteurs at the piano. He had come over to Adele's apartment to hear her. She wore a dark brown silk dress that fit tightly and a long string of amber and jade beads, and her voice was insinuatingly low and warmed by the brandy.

The first night she sang in the bar, her parents came in together, hoping, she knew, that in spite of what they had learned about the lives of aspiring actors and entertainers, their daughter would be famous someday, bypassing the pitfalls. Her hair was cut short like a boy's, the shining paleness in startling contrast with her large, dark eyes; and her slender, young body affected the sensual indolence of the woman of experience, enticing yet seeming to remain aloof, waiting for the right one. The first few nights she was afraid that the patrons would suspect that she was fooling them. The gestures were not her own—she had learned them from singers in nightclubs and movies; the voice imitated that of an already famous singer, husky and plaintive with a controlled break in it; and the color of her hair was the color that was popular with movie starlets and salesgirls and carhops. As she repeated her act, it came to seem natural because the fixed, absorbed gaze of the audience and their applause led her to believe what they believed, that everything was natural with her, that everything was not a matter of trickery but of her own nature, as if she, herself, had originated all that was imitative and the others were imitating her. And when certain men in the audience became infatuated with her, this was further proof.

She became infatuated, in turn, with a big and amiable radio announcer, a widower in his fifties. He had a small gray mustache and gray curls brushed slickly back with silver brushes. She chose this man to make her body known to her again because he, among the others, seemed most affected by her. When he sat with her at a restaurant table, his fingers trembled touching her wrist and fingers, and his bass voice shook. He was not, she knew, the one who would mean more than her husband had meant, the one to rid her of the desire for others, but he was the one to break the link, her body's link, with her child. On the unmade bed in his half-empty apartment, he uncovered her breasts that had given up the mouth of the child only a month before and still felt the communion with the child; now the mouth of the man destroyed the link and, though it had to be destroyed, under the excitement she was disturbed by its breaking. Where the child had emerged, the doctor had sewn her into a virgin again, and the pain that resulted in the man's embrace seemed like an attempt of her body to repulse the stranger who was destroying the link with the child. She went up to his apartment often, and they lay in each other's arms for hours, approaching a tender respect for each other that took faults and failings into consideration; but always, when he rose from the bed and she lay watching him dress, his shirt tentlike around his hips, he became troubling to her and futureless.

No word had come from her husband since the letter written along the route of his escape, and at her parents' promptings she sued for divorce. The erotic atmosphere of the lounge was not, they implied, to be denied its possibilities. The child, at this time, receded from the center of her life. The Swedish cook and housekeeper, who lived in the servants' quarters off the kitchen, took the child to her room on the evenings that Vivian sang in the lounge, and her wages were increased for this extra service to the family. Sometimes, when Vivian had stayed out all night and slept all morning, she would go down in her robe, a sense of guilt upon her, and find the baby asleep in the bassinet in the sun filtering through the lace curtains in the woman's room, or gazing up at the canary in its cage. Although to sing and to be applauded was gratifying, and the nights with her lover exciting, she felt this was not enough to warrant her separation from the child. The separation seemed furtive, no matter how many accomplices she had. And she would make a show of love for the child, taking him up in her arms and carrying him through the house, laying him down on her bed or on a couch and nuzzling his belly and the soles of his feet; and the semblance of love passed over into the real.

3

With a grudging look of curiosity, her brother came into the lounge with a friend, a young resident doctor. She had met him, her brother told her, at her wedding, and she pretended to remember him. The young man, George Gustafsen, came in alone a few nights later and, talking with her, accidentally knocked his glass off the table.

He declared his undying love for her the first time he took her out and made the demand of her to love him as much. This declaration and demand were made while he sat apart from her in his car, then, without preparatory caressing, he threw himself upon her. She resisted him because his sudden ardor struck her as comic and because he was not pleasing to her physically—his face plump, his hips high and jutting; and he had the pomposity of her brother, as if he were emulating the other. After a few times with him, however, when he did not throw himself upon her but continued to declare his love and to demand that she marry him, she felt that his choosing her to be responsible for his happiness the rest of his life elevated her higher than anyone else had ever done, and she fell in love with him because of that oppressive honor and because a man so much in love, so possessive, so broodingly jealous, would surely take care of her forever and be true to her forever.

When she refused to go with the radio announcer to his apartment, he taunted her for her youth, predicting, with a pitiable meanness in his thick cheeks, her panic and loneliness at his age. She never saw him again. Even though she was sorry for him, some belief that no man was ever as helpless as he appeared to be, prevented her from feeling deeply about his condition. To think that a man was helpless was like thinking that the sun was helpless because it could not be other than a burning light.

The marriage to George Gustafsen took place in the home of her Aunt Belle, her mother's sister, in St. Francis Woods, the house strewn with red roses and a fashionable pastor officiating. The guests were relatives and close friends, but, reserved and small as the wedding was, Vivian felt that it was more than it ought to be, even as she had felt about the first wedding that it was not as much as it might have been. By this time she mocked all marriage ceremonies except the brief, civil kind, and made a practice of glancing derisively through the society section of the newspapers for nuptial items that told the fraternity of the groom, the sorority of the bride, the color and material of the bride's mother's gown, and for photographs of happy pairs, startled-eyed in all their trappings and suspicious of what the years were to bring in spite of blessings from God and pastors and parents and the bureau of licenses.

She gave up her singing in the lounge and sat at home evenings with her husband—the evenings he was not on duty—and with her son, who was at the time of her wedding almost two. She was again a wife, and although it was expected of her to be desirable to other men, she was to cease the overt demonstration, as in the lounge, of her desire for them. They bought a modest, two-story house in a neighborhood of narrow, stylish houses not far from her parents but not as commodious as the houses of her parents' neighborhood. She selected the decor with her mother, who was greeted by every manager in the six-story store, and in this decor, while David slept in his room upstairs and her husband read his medical journals and his *Time* and *Fortune* magazines, she sat curled up on the couch, knitting. She was acting, she felt, the role of a woman who has caused something important to happen to herself, and she was convinced that her husband was also acting; that his was the role of the young husband on his way to prominence and prosperity, content to be at home evenings with his wife, and proud that he was a loving father to another man's child. His legs were stuck straight out to the velvet footstool as if ordered in that position by some director of the scene. It seemed to her that he was like a boy imitating some perfect adult in everything he did from paring his nails to lifting the child into the air, from clearing his throat to predicting Hitler's next move. She sympathized with him, for this need of his to perform as others expected him to, but again, as with her lover, as with Paul, her sympathy was baffled by the conviction that because he was a man he was not in real need of sympathy, that he got along very well without it, and that to grant it to him was to take away some of his maleness—the more sympathy granted him the more of his maleness was taken away, and the less she thought of him. It was this troubling conflict that led her one evening to sit on his lap, for to be close against him, to be enveloped by his presence, would rid her of her conflict, and she slipped onto his lap with the innocence of a woman in the sway of her own femininity, placing herself within his arm that held the magazine and laying her head against his chest.

She pretended to be as absorbed as he in the magazine, but the close-set type in narrow columns gave her the same feeling of ignorance and insufficiency that was given her by blueprints and the financial sections of the newspapers. When he turned the page and a picture of Mussolini appeared, of his big face haranguing a crowd, she was instantly intrigued. She touched the dictator's chin with her index finger and the gesture was like taking a liberty with the man himself, repulsing him and flirting with him at the same time.

"What's that for?" her husband inquired.

"Isn't that a monster of a chin?" she asked, afraid that he had guessed her trick of access into the lives of famous men. The only way she could get close enough to them to see that they were human was to imagine them making love.

"It isn't that bad," he said.

She waited for him to say something more and knew, unmoving in his lap, that there was to be some clash to enliven their evening and that both welcomed it and were tensed by it, and yet would have preferred to let the day go by without it.

"He excites you?" he asked, his voice as strained as if the Italian dictator were their next-door neighbor.

She felt a laugh readying itself in her chest at the comicalness of his jealousy, while her mind prepared itself for the seriousness of it. "I imagine he makes love like a bull," she said placatingly.

"You've imagined it?"

She shrugged. "Don't you imagine things?"

"There are other things to think about. . . . "

"Oh, yes," she agreed.

"Let me ask you something," he said, and asked her then the question she knew he had been wanting to ask her ever since he met her. "Did you sleep with any man besides Paul?"

"No," she said, and laughed. "I was saving myself for you."

Their bodies became intolerant of each other and still she sat unmoving, hoping with the closeness of bodies to force that satisfaction in union for which they had married.

"You weren't saving yourself for anybody," he said.

She struck aside the magazine and got up. "You've been aching for me to confess ever since you met me," she cried, walking back and forth in her black satin mules, a hand on her hip, knowing how her buttocks moved in the black slacks, every movement substantiating what he suspected of her. Since their wedding she had felt a restriction on the grace of her body. He seemed, if she were graceful, if she were almost unconsciously provocative as she undressed, to suspect her of remembering someone else for whom she had learned those movements or of anticipating appreciation by someone other than he, and he would sometimes not touch her when she lay down beside him. But now in this promenading that preceded her confessing whatever little she had to confess, she recaptured her gracefulness, flaunting it because she had, for months now, suppressed it in fear of his displeasure and of his rebuff. She could not, however, confess her affair. It was the only thing she had to confess, but to confess it was to deny her right to it, to violate the secret matrix where knowledge about herself was forming like an embryo. She told him, instead, of the men she had been told about by the two dancers who had lived in the apartment below hers and Paul's in Los Angeles, but claiming those men as her own lovers. She told him the stories she had heard from the dancers who had talked endlessly of their lovers, enthralling her with not only each story but with the extraordinary powers they seemed to possess because of their profusion of men. If one man meant as much to them as to her, she had thought, what meaning there was in the profusion! And when the girls had laughed about each man's idiosyncrasies, she had wondered, and wondered now as she repeated their mockery, why they retaliated for that profusion of love. She threw herself into a chair, swinging her leg over its wide arm, to tell him in that sprawling position about her lovers, while he walked the room like a man mortally wounded and attempting to prove to himself that he was not. After a time he lay down and closed his eyes, but she knew that he still listened and would listen as long as she spoke.

She lay alone in their bed, her head filled with the surfeit of stories she had told, with the memory of her harsh voice claiming to know the frailties and prowess of men she had never seen, angry with him for imposing that surfeit upon her and the reluctant excitement of it. Almost everything she had ever done, it seemed to her now, was done at other persons' urging, whether they spoke their urging or did not speak it. The way she had walked around the room, and the way she flung herself across the chair, and the untrue confession, all were imposed by him. There did not seem to be any core within herself that was unaffected by him, by the men of her life, by her father and brother, by Paul and by her lover, and by her son.

At two in the morning she went down to shake him off the sofa. "When I didn't know you existed, why should I have waited for you?" she cried. "Why should I have waited even if I knew you existed? Can you tell me why?"—shouting down the opposing voice within her that said she ought to have waited because he had wanted her to, that all that was necessary was his wanting her to, even though he had not known her then, that his wanting was more than enough.

Upstairs, David began to wail. Unable to stop her trembling, she did not go up to him. Her husband, glad of the excuse to escape her, went up to the boy, closing the door after him.

She lay on her back, alone again in her bed, her hands clasped below her breasts, enticing sleep with that position, enticing with that innocent position a blamelessness for the use she had made of her womanness. That use of it as a weapon was not the use she wanted for it, and she was as dismayed by that use as she was by the entire eruption that followed upon her flirtatious finger on Mussolini's chin.

George wept dryly in her arms the first night he returned to their bed, after several nights on the couch in David's room, and she covered his head with kisses and confessed that she had lied and urged him not to weep, for she was unable to bear the sounds in his throat that were as unreasonable as their discord had been.

When the Japanese bombed the U.S. fleet in Hawaii, a change

was brought about in their marriage. Because they were now plunged into momentous times, swept into war and the unknown with the rest of the world, because of the imminence of separation or death, what it was that each feared in the other seemed not so fearsome, and they became inseparable. They seemed to have been mated by destiny—the condition that her husband had desired in the beginning.

In the blackouts they held hands, and, if David was still awake, they picked him up and held him and looked out the window at a dark city, imagining the suspense everybody must be feeling—the anti-aircraft men and the sailors on the ships in the bay and the people at all their windows. She was aware of the thousands, the millions of people who held one another in the dark of other cities in Europe and Asia. She was aware of tremendous armies, of the magnitude of the seas and the land, and she was alive, as never before, to the near particulars of the earth—the tree in the street below and a solitary seagull soaring, its white breast made visible by the natural light in the sky.

George enlisted in the army medical corps and was flown East for training, and Vivian and her son were left alone. Before the child went to sleep, she told him about the heroic exploits his stepfather was to perform, rescuing wounded and dying soldiers, saving every life. But as she told her tales of heroism, lying on her bed with the child, her mind was not on the absent man but, with pleasurable fear, on the encroachments of the world on her life.

In that genteel neighborhood changes took place. Late at night doors were slammed and voices were heard in the street, and sometimes she was wakened by curses and by footsteps running down the hill. She went for walks with David, who was three years old and ran ahead of her and off on tangents, up porch steps and into stores; she sat on a bench in the park while he played on the grass; they had lunch often at her mother's or at her aunt's or at her cousin Teresa's; she wrote every day to her husband and she read the newspapers; and her restlessness increased, the impatient waiting for the chaos around her to break in upon her. The country was in an uproar, millions of people were moving across the continent, whole families moving, armies moving from one coast to the other. She felt the vibrations of the city at work in the night; woke for a moment at midnight and knew that people were moving through the city on trolleys and in cars, going to and from the shipyards; heard the long convoys of brown, canvas-covered trucks rumbling through the streets in the hours before dawn; and knew, at dawn, that people were rising from their beds in rooms they had moved into the day before. It seemed to her that whole regions of people were moving into the city; she heard dialects that were like foreign languages, and strange intonations, strange pitches. Around her everything was in flux, and when she lay down beside David during the blackouts, the time of hiding in darkness with the rest of the people in the city was like a step into further mingling with them. She felt that she was using the child as ballast, as a mooring, and that, without him, if he did not exist, she might step out the door into the flood of change.

One night, before they fell asleep together, she kissed him over his face and head fervently, in need of protection from him, trying to kiss him into that condition of stability that she had desired from her husbands and that her kisses of adoration deluded her into believing they possessed. With her kissing of her son she wanted to persuade him to become at once a man and protect her from her desire to run out into the chaos. David whimpered against the fervency of her kisses, and she released him and lay back, turning her face to the window. The night was faintly illumined by the moon that was rising in that part of the sky not visible to her. She felt an exhaustion as after love and the dissatisfaction that at times combined with it, that desire for something more, as if something more had been promised her that was not yet given.

4

A friend of her mother's owned a dress shop off the lobby of one of the larger hotels, and she accepted a job there as a salesgirl. She wanted to sing again in a lounge, but that would be like an act of infidelity. Even her job at the hotel might seem like that to her husband, and when he returned for a few days before he was sent to England, she did not tell him that she was working.

The shop's windows faced the lobby and the street, both, and so the shop, with its gilded, high-domed ceiling, was like a display case for her. The hotel guests glanced in at her and she glanced out at them. She saw them as also on display, a passing display of generals and officers, industrialists, and diplomats. The hotel was like a hub for the entire war-frantic city. She saw them arriving and departing in immaculate uniforms and perfect suits, their faces not so preoccupied with their great tasks that she went unnoticed.

She sold dresses to wealthy women, some of them her friends and her mother's friends, to discontented young women and young women delighted with their lives, and to elderly women whose sagging flesh was held up by elaborate corsets. Since her own mother was slender, Vivian had never seen women's bodies compressed and thrust up, and when these women took a long time to feel cloth between their fingers, or to decide for or against a ruffle or pleat, or to turn around and around again, in gowns and negligees, before the triple mirrors, their contemplation and deliberation seemed to her so futile. The war was not their concern; their anxiety was for their reflection in the long mirrors in the dressing room, whether they grew old like queens, as if age were an accretion of power, or sweetly, to placate the inevitable, or grew old retaliatively, as if everyone were cheating them of life. Among these elderly ones she felt a species apart, herself the only one of her kind, never to grow old and never to die.

In this gilded room with claret carpet and chairs of ocher velvet and rows of gowns on black velvet hangers, in this room fragrant with cologne sprayed into the air, where she was visible from the street and the lobby, she underwent a constant shifting of emotions. Her curiosity about the men who passed through the lobby or who came into the shop to buy gifts for women was chastened by her own need for fidelity, a yearning for her husband, and this shifting itself was exciting, a constant tremor of the heart.

She felt, at this time, estranged from her son. She had hired a woman to take care of him, and the woman, Olga, lived with them—a spindly, aging woman with gray and orange hair and dark grape lipstick, who, because of an intolerance for racket, could not work in the shipyards, one among a few women, as she said of herself, not making a fortune sorting rivets and counting bolts. With no husband around who was generous with the child, as George had been, Vivian lacked the example. With no husband around to devote herself to, she had no desire to devote herself to anyone. She was with David only an hour or so in the morning and in the evening, and the impatience with him that had always been present now declared itself only as an uneasy deafness to his small, complaining voice and his screams of joy; since she was not so bound to him, she no longer felt so impatient with him.

She began to stay away evenings, serving as hostess at a U.S.O. center for soldiers and sailors. She enjoyed dancing with them, the change of bodies against hers, the many strange bodies responding to the strangeness of hers. Some of the men were appealing to her, the appeal of the few made stronger by the presence of the many. Teresa, her cousin, whose husband was also in England, took men home with her, but, for Vivian, taking a strange man to bed for one night was like taking a first step into that freedom which she preferred to titillate herself with rather than experience. Every day she wrote her letter or added to an unfinished letter. She wrote that she loved him, and she was sure that she did, but as she wrote her words of love, she imagined all the things he would condemn her for if she did them.

She was asked to supper one evening by her father's mistress, Adele, who had telephoned her at work, and, on entering the apartment, saw a young sailor stand up from the couch. The lamps, as usual, were dim, and in a moment's time she took a dislike to the laxness of his body, to the lazing pleasure the body took in its attractiveness. When he shifted weight, at her approach, from one foot to the other, an ungainliness in his legs, an overgrownness of his body, revealed him as Paul. Adele, sitting on the floor, her legs crossed, hugging an ankle with one hand and holding a wine glass with the other, jokingly introduced them as if they had never met, and they laughed with embarrassment, their laughter and voices sounding to Vivian like that of a couple who have always wanted to meet. Although, after he had left her, she had not known anyone who had meant as much to her, there was now no desire for him, only a superficial excitement. Adele served a feast despite the rationing, telling them it was done with mirrors and spices, and presided with a wide-gesturing charm that declared this young man her favorite brother and that denied she had ever ranted against him for his abandonment of his wife and child. He dawdled his fingers over the linen cloth, the arm of his chair, the silverware, as if his sense of touch had become more acute now that he was in the perceptive presence of two women who called for sensitivity; it was flattery done with gestures. He told them of his tribulations in New York; he had got a small part in a musical and found his legs rather heavy to dance around on; and with the closing of that show he had spent a year in Nassau as a companion for a very old and very wealthy man, but he had tired, he said, of reading his employer *Alice in Wonderland* every night, and then he laughed, apparently realizing Vivian was no longer naïve, that she might even have become more worldly than he and that his leaving her had contributed to her awakening.

David always came to her bed in the morning, while she reclined against the pillows and read the newspaper, and, with his legs under the covers, he ate his toast and sipped coffee and cream from her saucer and played with odd bits of broken jewelry and with a few small toys he carried in with him. Scrutinizing his features, the morning after her supper with Paul and Adele, she was pleased to find only a minimal resemblance to his father. She had known all along that the resemblance was only an undertone, but felt a desire to reassure herself about it. At four, his beauty combined the best features of her family. His hair, although resembling his father's in its thickness and its arcs of curls like the hair of Renaissance angels, was a darker brown, with a cast of amber red, like her mother's hair, a color she had always envied, for her own was the common light brown of her father's family and had always to be bleached. David's eyes were blue, but darker than his father's, and there was a broadness across his eyes that Paul lacked, and a narrowing toward the chin. Under her scrutiny, he appeared to be more perfect than ever and more her own than ever, wholly her own and not the father's, who had inquired about him with his glance slipping away as if to inquire was to confess a crime. But, though he seemed more than ever her own, the elusiveness of his father, which had contrived to make the son her own, became the son's possession also. Although she nurtured him now and sustained him, his life was to be his own, even as his father and his stepfather appeared to belong to nobody but themselves, their lives their own though they were herded into regiments and battalions, into staffs and corps, onto transports, onto tremendous gray ships, and into battles.

When George was killed at St. Vith, she forgot his faults and remembered only his virtues. It seemed to her that his jealousy had indicated not a lack of understanding of her but a greater understanding than her own. He had prized her—that was the reason for his jealousy—and, prizing her, he must have known her essential self, the innocent self, and had struggled with her other self, the heedless, all-desirous self, as if it were his deadly enemy as well as hers. Nobody else would ever love her as much and understand her as well and join with her against the enemy within herself.

5

A few months after the news reached her of her husband's death, she went up, one evening, to the room of an air corps captain who had bought a lacy slip for his wife back in Boston. In the shop he had chatted with her about the two cities, comparing this point and that, and then had invited her to dinner. In a quick breath, nervously, he told her he had some Scotch in his room and asked her to come up before dinner so they could work up an appetite. Up in his room, after the Scotch had eased his nervousness, he was able to look at her for a long moment with his eyes unclouded by his fear of her personal life.

"You got a husband?" he asked her, like a doctor who has been told that psychologizing with the patient helps in the cure. He sat on the foot of the bed and she in the chair. "Ah, somewhere?" he asked.

She saw him glancing at her legs and wished that silk stockings were still available—the rayon kind weren't so flattering. "He's dead," she said, her mouth wanting the captain's mouth. She saw that his little blue eyes were surprised. "At St. Vith. He was a doctor, he was a captain with the second division. They gave him a silver star, he has a silver star," she said, tears slipping down her face.

"Ah, that's too bad," he said, alarmed, suddenly turning his head to see what was behind him. "You want to come over here and lie down?"

She lay on her back, weeping with her face exposed as if had just received the news from this man. He lay down beside her, jolting the bed in an awkward attempt to lie down tenderly, and put his arm across her, and she wanted to relate every detail of her life to him because he had laid his arm across her comfortingly like a man who was to love her and protect her for the rest of her life. She turned her head at his prompting to enable him to wipe her face with the palm of his hand and his fingertips, and saw, above his fingers, the many intimate details of his face that was as close as her husband's had been, as the faces of the other men who had meant something to her, whom she had loved or had thought she loved; and she desired from that face, close beside hers, what all faces that lie close are called upon give. She had imagined that, since his face was temporal, she would ask for nothing, only the time together, even the eventual indifference, only the transience itself, the excitement of the transient union; but now she called for the lastingness that ought to come from the one close on the bed. She gazed above his fingers into his eyes that avoided hers; at his sparse lashes that were here and there in clusters; at the coarse skin tinged with pink, a weatherworn skin with a few small scars so faint she knew they were childhood scars; at the flat, small ears and the very short, scrubby hair and the hairline where there were some few gray hairs, hardly different in color from the rest; at the thin lips concealing thought; and, having examined the minute particulars of his face, she kissed the palm of his hand as it crossed her mouth.

With his mouth on hers, he moved his hand over her body heavily as if receiving long, difficult messages through his palm. "Well, what pretty things," he said about her garments in the way. "What pretty little things," and helped her remove them with care while she kissed his hands and his body. "Well, what pretty things. You know you had such pretty things?" holding up her opalescent slip to follow its satin glow moving up and down the folds. "Ah, the pretty things to cover up the pretty things. One pretty thing deserves another, right? Never saw such pretty things in all my life. Look at that." Even if he had a wife in Boston, he might not be getting along with her, or before the war was over his wife might leave him, or the woman for whom he had bought the slip was not his wife. A man who could undress her with consoling words must be the man who would return to her.

But when he sat up on the side of the bed, rubbing his thighs, the bed moving up and down as he nervously rocked, the intent of the evening accomplished before the evening began and his gaze muddled, she knew that he was to be for that time only. She drew the blankets to her chin and lay grieving about his temporality as if it were a surprise, a revelation, and not a conviction that had accompanied her in the rising elevator. A sudden lowering of her spirits, an onslaught of reality, the elusiveness of the men she had loved, Paul elusive by running away and George by dying, all brought on a need for grieving under blankets. She watched this one as he walked around the room, pouring Scotch—his bare, very muscular legs, his short body and broad back, his bristle haircut and small, flat face, his eyes narrowing to appear wise when he came to the denouement of the story with which he was bombastically entertaining her.

Afraid of other temporal lovers, she fell in love with him to transform him into the lasting lover as he hopped around the room, pulling on his trousers.

She clung to him in the taxi. She ran her lips up and down his face and told him that there had never been anyone so good to her, even her husband. She would not release him when the taxi drew up at the curb before her house and made him sit with her for half an hour while she begged him to return to her. The taxi driver, a woman, got out and took a stroll down the middle of the street, her hands in her trouser pockets.

Alone in her room, she removed her clothes that seemed soiled as though from several days of wear because she had already removed them twice that night, once before supper and once again after, and felt a rage take her over, a rage against the man who had left her at her door. She knew he would never write to her and never return to her, that he had rubbed his mouth against her face and promised to write only because the promising and the rubbing were part of the joke that he always seemed to be laughing at to himself and that he could not tell her, and she felt rage against herself for clinging to him, for exaggerating her wish beyond the true degree of it, when the truth was she wanted nothing to last, when she wanted to be as he was, elusive as he was. Wrapped in her negligee, she smoked one after another of the canteen cigarettes the captain had given her because so few were available to civilians, smoking them as though they were a glut on the market.

6

Her father escorted her one evening to a small lounge in one of the large hotels on Nob Hill. The manager sat down with them; he was a patient of her father's and deferential to him, ordering a cognac for them, chatting with them, and watching them put the glasses to their lips. Over in a corner a slight, blond man was pounding a baby grand piano, smiling over its dark, slanting wing at the men in uniform and their women, who crossed their knees when he sang at them, their short skirts slipping up their thighs. While she was glancing away at the couples in the dim light of the carriage lanterns, stirred by the crowding of bodies, the manager clasped her wrist and asked her to sing. He escorted her to the pianist, who seemed delighted, who said he remembered her, and she sang, picking up the tricks again, toying with her beads, coddling her voice in her throat, combining the skills of her voice and her body. She was hired to sing several nights a week, and she and her father drank together with the manager to celebrate. She knew that her father would be delighted by his daughter's becoming a famous singer as much as—or more than—he would be by his son's becoming a physician who was summoned to the bedsides of presidents. He was attracted to theatrical people, to artists, especially to bizarre artists of any field if they were elegantly bizarre, not imitative, not tawdry. He never missed a first night at the Opera House or a society ball, and even his everyday clothes had the touch of the actor—his dark gray form-fitted overcoat and his black homburg.

David liked to watch her prepare herself to go out and sing. He sat cross-legged on her bed with his head thrown back against the head-board, his mouth open because he was bemused by her and, since it was nine o'clock, half asleep. His eyes shifted from the glitter of the buckles on her shoes to the glow of the dress where it curved over the hips and the breasts to the fall and sway of the long string of beads. He did not often look at her face, he was used to her face and was, instead, intrigued by the animation of inanimate things. But some-times she sang to him as she dressed, and he would watch her face then, as if it too were inanimate and the words and the tune made it flicker and change, as curious about the mechanism in her throat that made the low, strong whisper of a voice as he was about the central mystery of a performing toy; and while he gazed at the lively spirits in her garments and in her face, she was transfixed by him, in return— by the particulars of his beauty, the sturdy shape of his legs, his half-closed eyes and open lips, by the vitality evident even in repose. At this phase of his life, although all he could convey to her was what he perceived, as a five-year-old, of the workings of the world, she was more tolerant than she had ever been, more humoring, and more demonstrative of her love, because she was in touch with the world now, because she sang to those who were involved and who com-prehended the world. All around the earth, armies battled and cities were bombed, and she sang to the salesmen and the manufacturers of everything necessary to the prosecution of the war; she sang to the generals and the admirals and all the uniforms of the services of the country in a hotel on a hill in a great port city.

She stood before the long, oval mirror, with imperious flicks of her fingers pressing the rubber ball in its golden net to spray cologne over her bare arms, watching her son, acting as an empress for him. Then she sprayed the air, high up toward the ceiling, pretending to wield an antiaircraft gun, and he laughed, still with his head back, his arched throat jumping. When she played with him during the day, he was often at odds with her, but in the evening, in this hour in which she felt no boredom because she was to leave him in a matter of minutes, she enjoyed the playing. During the day he was absorbed in his own self and she was his accomplice in that absorption, but now he became an accomplice in her self-absorption. When she pantomimed for him, acted silly for him, she felt that the audience later in the night was already gathered around her, enthralled by her entertaining her son.

"Olga!" she called, "did you make the bed?" And to him, "Never mind, we'll dump you in anyway." She held out her arms to him. "Come on, then. You want to fly into bed? You feel like a bird? If the war's still going on when you're eighteen, you can learn to fly. You can fly a plane."

He leaped into her arms, causing her to stagger in her high heels. With his arms clasping her neck, a leg on each side of her waist, and his face looking back over her shoulder, he was carried into his room.

"Up, up you go," she said, boosting him onto the dresser top. From there he jumped, arms outspread, onto his bed.

She threw back the covers, pushed and joked him under, and kissed him on the mouth when he was settled in. When he called to her while she was in her bedroom again, slipping her coat from the hanger, she called in turn to Olga to go and see what he wanted. With her coat slung over one shoulder, she passed his open door; Olga was sitting on the small chair, attempting a low, singsong voice that induced sleep. Vivian went down to the kitchen and stood drinking black coffee while she waited for the taxi horn, glancing at her dark red fingernails, turning her head to see the back of her knee just under the black dress, to see the high satin heel of her shoe.

7

The day that Roosevelt died she took her son for a walk to share the shock of the death with the people in the streets. She and her son went hand in hand along by the shops, and in every shop people were talking about the death, and the ones inside and the ones waiting to cross at corners all had a look of shock that— because it was not for anyone close, for father or brother or husband, for anyone they had spent a lifetime with, but for a great man—was touched or tainted with a sense of privilege: that they were granted a time beyond the life of the great man was like a sign of favor. The sorrow that she felt over the President's death became an encompassing sorrow for the millions of others dying, the anonymous others dying, and her husband dying, and for everything that went on that was tragic and that was not known to her. But as little as she knew, she thought, her son's knowledge was only a fraction of her own. He was not even aware of nations and their governments, of the year and the era, and much less of the irretrievability of the dead; but if he did not have the comprehension now, he would have it in a few years. In a few years he would have more than she had at this moment, a great man himself, perhaps, about whose death—when he was seventy or eighty, and she was already dead a long time—everybody would be informed by newspaper and by radio. They walked slowly because that pace was suited to the day of mourning and to her son's small legs; yet, after a time, the slowness began to annoy her. There seemed to be too much imposed upon her in that slowness, the dependent age of the child and the tremendous death of one great man.

In the evening, among the patrons of the lounge—among the men who, although they were subdued by the death, were nevertheless bathed and shaved and manicured and brilliantined and brushed and polished, and anticipative of pleasures that night with the women beside them or women waiting somewhere else—she gave herself up to the exciting paradox of the living opulently mourning the dead, and something more came into her consciousness of the magnitude of the world. At night in the bar with the changing patrons, the changing faces in the dimness moving in and out of her vision with more fluidity, more grace, because of the solemnity of the night, she realized, more than earlier with her son, the extent of a great man's effect upon the world, the extent of the power he seemed to have even after his death, the extent of power over death that all these men seemed to have. She sang the president's favorite song, and the pianist played it over and over again, pounding it out like a dirge while the solemn drinking went on at the tables.

Her father came in with Adele and with the actress who was to have helped Paul into the movies, a woman small and delicate, with a broad, flat-boned, powdered face, her shoulders emerging tense and arrogant from her ample fur coat. With her was the actor Max Laurie, a tragic comedian, always in each of his movies in love with the hero's woman. A civilian at the table next to them, whose shoulder was near to Max's, leaned over between him and the actress, gazing with a pretense of idolatry from one to the other, amusing his two companions, two men, with his intrusion into the glamorous company.

"It's a sad day," he said to Max. "You agree with me it's a sad day?"

"We agree," said the actress.

The man turned his head to look at the actress appealingly, a flicker of ridicule crossing his face. "Anybody who disagrees is a dog," he said.

"Nobody disagrees," said the actress.

"You ever met him?" the man asked. "They say he liked the company of actors and actresses. Banquets and entertainments, he liked that. Like a king, you can say, with his jesters. I thought you might have met him."

"Never did," she said, turning her back on him, drawing up her fur coat that lay over her chair so that the high collar barred his face. Then she turned abruptly back, as she would have on the screen, while the man's face was still surprised by the fur collar. "Are you envious because you won't die great?" she asked him.

"I'm living great, that's all I want," he said, and his companions laughed. "If you want to know another fact of life, because you don't know all of them, it's this: If you're living great, the odds are you'll die great. Like in the arms of some beautiful woman, right smack in her boodwah." And while his companions laughed, he looked around at Max and at Vivian and at her father, and since they were not regarding him with annoyance, he looked again, boldly, into the face of the actress.

"He was a wonderful man," said Max, his rich voice conciliatory, simple. "I met him myself. A bunch of us were out making speeches for him, can't remember if it was his first term or his twelfth." He had a way of lowering his eyes when everybody laughed and glancing up with a smile that suspected, shyly, that he was lovable.

"What was your name?" the man asked.

"Max Laurie," he said.

"Is that Jewish or is it Scotch?" the man asked and everybody at both tables laughed. "He loved everybody, didn't he?" he went on, striking their table with his palm. "Regardless of race, color, or creed. He had no discrimination—is that the word?" and overcome by his joke he bowed back over his own table, in silent tussle with his laughter.

Vivian left the table to sing again, and when she returned, the actress had moved to the chair Vivian had vacated, and she sat down in the actress's chair, nearer now to the intrusive man, and saw that he was observing her, his face that of an outsider, desirous, recriminative. "I guess he thought he was going to live forever," he said to her. "You could tell he thought so by the way he smoked that cigarette in the longest holder I ever saw outside of the movie queens back in the flapper days."

"You saw his picture when he was at Yalta?" she asked him, repeating an observation she had heard earlier. "He looked sick then, his face looked as if it got the message he was going to die. He had a blanket or an overcoat around his shoulders."

He patted her wrist. "You're sweet," he said.

"How do you know?"

"Because you got nursey eyes. 'He looked sick at Yalta.' Did you hear that?" he asked his companions, who were no longer listening to him. "You got nursey eyes." He took her hand between both of his, caressing it between his palms, attributing to her, with that pressure of his hands, a sympathetic knowledge of all men. "Go on."

"Go on what?" she asked.

"Tell me some more."

"More of what?"

"Oh, they got so much on their minds they don't take care of themselves. More of that. You know when a man gets a lot on his mind what happens to his body? Look at Gandhi—that's what's the matter with me. I'm as skinny as Gandhi only more because I'm twice as tall as he is. I think big thoughts. My head is big, see, but all my hair has turned white and my body is skinny."

"What big thoughts?" she asked him.

"We all got a stake in it," he said. "Those who stayed at home as much as those who laid down their lives. Got two factories going day and night, one down in El Segundo, out near the beach where the aircraft factories are. We make a small part that you girls would call an itsy-bitsy part, but without it the plane couldn't fly. It couldn't fly. Got another factory up here, feeds the shipyards with another itsy-bitsy part. When the general goes marching through the surf up to his neck, we're right along with him, you and me. You and me, we're right there when he delivers the coop de grace. The coop de grace belongs to you and me."

He brought their clasped hands into her lap and, opening her hand, he began to smooth it flat, palm up, insistently smoothing out her fingers that curled again after his hand passed over them.

8

On the night when the lights of the city came on again, she walked several miles before she hailed a taxi, elated by the glitter and glow of the signs, by the suffusion of colors, by the colors pulsing through the tubes, crackling and humming; by the animation of the signs whose borders ran in a demented pursuit of themselves, or each letter of the letter before it; and by the lights reflected on dark windows and gliding along the windows of passing cars. She saw the change of colors upon her white coat and upon her legs as she walked and knew that her face was tinted with the colors that she walked through as were the faces of other strollers, and this coming on again of every light was like an absolving of everyone in the city and like a mindless promise of further experiences that might call for further absolving.

The Manufacturer—she called him that, amusing herself with the anonymity of it—appeared again in the lounge. He brought no friends with him and he spoke to no other patrons. Their first night, when everyone had left her alone with him, she had gone up to his room and she had been delightedly aroused. Yet, after, she had wanted to seem uncaring if he were not to return, she had wanted to seem as elusive as she expected him to be, and with that she had brought him back to her. When they lay together again, his hands caressing her seemed to be discovering her for the first time, not having truly known her that other time.

He stayed four days in the city and promised to return in two weeks. Now that the war was over, he said, he would be in the city more often, conferring with his brother-in-law who was an investment banker. She no longer called him, jokingly, the Manufacturer. His name was Leland Talley, and she bought him six fine handkerchiefs with his initials in blue silk thread, and read her intimate knowledge of him in those fancy letters that could be felt under her thumb.

When he returned in two weeks and telephoned her from the hotel, she asked him to come to the house. It was early afternoon and David was home from school. He stood up from the floor, where a number of his toys were set about in some inviolable scheme, and shook hands with the visitor. Talley's manner with the boy was brusque and affable, his eyes veering away, distracted by other things; he seemed to resist being charmed by the boy's beauty, as though to be charmed by it was a sign of weakness on his part and the boy's also. David engaged in a fervent telling of an involved and unfollowable tale, his voice high and nervous and monotonous, his face without expression as he talked on and on intrusively, as if he had gone deaf and could not hear her and her visitor talking between themselves, as if he saw their mouths moving without voices.

Up in her room she dressed to go out to supper with her lover, who sat on the bed, his drink in his hand, watching her every move—the lifting of her arms for the slip to slide down, her hips within the slip as she walked to the chair, and the extending of her leg as she drew on the stocking with a graceful working of her fingers. Whenever she glanced at him as she talked, he narrowed his eyes, as if caught at some speculation that she was not a party to. Was he thinking that a serious affair with her might break up his marriage? She resented his hardheaded thinking about it, and yet was pleased that his resistance to her was falling away in her presence.

While she was brushing her hair and he sat watching her lifted arms and the pale curls springing back from the brush, David slipped in through the half-open door and, speaking at once, bowing his head over a toy he carried, he walked directly to the man on the bed. Something was wrong with the toy, he said, some wheel, some part was lost or stolen. "Right here, right here," he said, his voice high and hypnotized, "here, here. It's a clock. The lost wheel pushed the blue wheel. It was a red wheel but it got lost. The hands don't go. The big one—it was yellow—fell off and this one is loose, the little one, the green one. The wheel is gone on the other side. Right here, you see? The red wheel is gone." His complaining voice was a high, driving chant that, possibly, could endure to the end of the night. She called to him, but he failed to hear her. She called his name again, but he would not look at her or come to her. Instead, he sat down on the floor, his head still bowed over the clock. "Right here, right here, it used to be a big yellow hand. It used to go around when you wound it here. You could make it any time you wanted, you could make it any time of day." He went with them down the stairs and to the front door, the clock left behind on her rug, warning them about the dog next door, instructing them as to what they were to do if the dog attacked them.

After that day, the appearance of her lover, every few weeks, did not result in her son's acceptance of the man. Instead, David avoided him, apparently ashamed of his behavior that first time, or not ashamed but brooding over some other way of appeal. He kept apart from them and was not inquired after by her lover, who brought a gift for him occasionally but left it lying on the sofa or on a table. And in the early months of her desperate love for the man, she could not, she knew, be tolerant of her son's intrusion if he were driven to intrude. In the time between her lover's visits she was consumed by her longing for the man. She thought of him incessantly, and on his visits underwent a complete abandon at the first touch of his hand. She lay in his hotel room for hours while he went out into the city to attend to his appointments, waiting for him to return to the bed and to her body.

She no longer sang in the hotel lounge because the time there sometimes interfered with his visits. The months—almost without her consciousness of them, because the present was a combining of longing and fulfillment—ran on through the first year, and each last day and last night of his visits were always for her the peak of that combining. It was understood, at the beginning, that his wife was ailing and that he could not, now, approach her about a divorce, and that, since his factories were in a state of upheaval with the end of the war and his plans were to move with his wife to San Francisco and to become a partner in his brother-in-law's investment firm, for a time their love must await the stabilizing of the other factors in his life. Over supper tables and in his hotel room or her bedroom, he talked a great deal about his factories, about conversion. There were complications in his reports that were unsolvable for her, and yet she felt that he was not really attempting to establish the truth, the reality, for her, because he thought it too much for her to comprehend, that he was not telling her much of anything, only the skimming, only the jokes repeated by the clerical help, only the froth that rose from the turbulence of the business, from the heavy maneuvering. But this was enough, it was all she wanted to know, the rest was his domain.

With the diminishing of the intensity of their times together, in the second year, some certainty of the future had to compensate for the lessening. When he and his wife moved up to Hillsborough, a few miles from the city, his constant proximity, then, was a substitute for that certainty, was an approach to it. And yet, as the months went by, that proximity of both himself and his wife in a colonial-style home upon several acres of landscaped grounds served to make the certainty grow more distant.

He was as aware as she of the slow abating, but he was not apprehensive of the end; he did not appear to believe that the end was approaching simply because the zenith was passed. He was now involved with his brother-in-law in plans for investment in Japan and the Philippines, and something of his optimism was transmitted to their affair.

"Listen, there's going to be big things in Japan," he told her. "Got to start their exports going, got to help them rebuild. I'm going over and take a look around. You want to fly over with me?"

The invitation to go with him to Japan was an intimation of something more, a return to the zenith, even a promise that she was to be his wife; it served for several months as proof of the constancy of their love. Then he left without her, promising to take her along the next time, explaining that this time was to be for a minimum of days.

She drove him to the airport, and as they stood together in the corridor he said to her, to the crown of her head as she was fingering the buttons of his overcoat, "You know why we're crazy about each other? It's because we're apart so much. If we go on like this, it'll go down in history, won't it? With those great passions? If we lived together, some of that crazy wildness might get lost, and I don't want to lose a fraction of it. We've got something I don't think anybody else ever had."

She looked down at him crossing the ground to the plane, ready to wave should he look up at her in the window of the waiting room. He seemed a man designated to bring about a prosperous future for all concerned, and his stride appeared so quick and purposeful she wondered if he might always be worried about missteps. The morning wind was flapping his trouser legs and lifting his white hair in tufts. He bent his head to enter the plane, a habitual bowing in doorways that were high enough.

When he disappeared into the plane, she was seized by fear, convinced the plane was to fall from the sky, plunging into the ocean. Out in the parking lot, trapped in the roar of planes flying in low and planes rising and vanishing into the high fog, she asked herself if she would want him to die rather than leave her willfully. Then she wondered how much she loved him or if she loved him at all, if such a question could cross her mind. Dismayed by her own mind, she wandered the parking lot, lost, unable to recognize her own car.

9

On the way to her room, at midnight,
she entered her son's room. The window was up a few inches and a
cold wind was stirring the curtains. Out on the bay the foghorns were
sounding, expectantly repetitive, like a deep-spoken word. She sat on
the edge of his bed, shivering in her negligee, watching him, his face
plump with sleep, his arms flung above his head. If now, at the end of
the affair, she doubted that she had loved, if her life was spent in seeking and pleasing some man, if her life was spent in need of his need of
her, was love nothing but desperation passing for love? Was the only
love that was not a delusion her love for her son?

The confusion, the terror she had experienced out at the airport
returned and she began to weep, wanting to waken him with her
weeping, wanting him to come up out of sleep to a consciousness
of her. She lay down on his bed, facing him, facing his small, awake,
alarmed face. After a time, realizing, perhaps, that her weeping was
not caused by him, was not his fault, he began to stroke her hair and
her cheek. Her love for him was not a delusion. He was the person
in whom reality was posited; he was abiding, he was constant. Since

the room was cold and she was lying on top of the blankets, he threw the top quilt over her, smoothing it around her so that it formed a cocoon, and she slept that way for a time.

Olga had left them, returning to Idaho some months before, and Vivian, rising early in the morning, went down to prepare breakfast for her son. After she had called him several times, he came down, still in his pajamas, and she saw his sullen resistance to her, a stubborn contesting with her, as if too much had been exacted of him the night before. He sat at breakfast with his eyes down, and when she asked him if he were going to school in his pajamas, he told her he was not going that day. When she tried to tug him upstairs to dress, he went limp, and, unable to drag him, she left him there, a small figure in blue and white striped pajamas, lying on the stairs. He remained all day in his room in his pajamas, coming down for his meals and going up again and closing his door.

The following morning she forced him out of bed by pulling down the covers and dressing him herself. He ate his breakfast and permitted her to slip his yellow raincoat over his back and over his limp arms and jerk the hood of it over his head. In the moment before she thrust him out the front door, she saw his small face, smaller within the yellow hood and paler in the gray light of outdoors, gaze out with a failing of his resistance to her, enthralled for that moment by the mingling of fog and rain, by the change of weather. The first rain of fall made the streets and sidewalks dark and glistening, and the leaves of the slender trees in their wire enclosures by the curb were moved erratically by the drops. She thrust him out, and he sat down on the steps. At ten o'clock, looking out the round glass in the door, she saw him still on the top step, throwing pebbles from the potted plant. The drifting rain, slow and unabating, glistened on his yellow raincoat and hood from a long accumulation. The small, stubborn figure forecast a future of contesting: they were to be alone together, and whatever was to trouble her would be for him only a reason for contesting. She called him in from the neighborhood's sight and, when the door was closed, turned him to face up the stairs and struck him across the back. With no retaliation, no anger, he went up the stairs, and the paradox of the fragility of his very young body and the power of his will led her to strike him again across his back.

The next day he got ready for school, ate his breakfast, and left, all with the casualness of a habit that had not been broken. Some time in the days that followed, before Leland's return from Japan, the conflict that had gone on between herself and her son roused her to an awareness, more than ever before, of the boy's separateness. He was someone unknown. And she acknowledged the pleasure for her in that unknownness. She took pleasure in his strong will. In those days of her lover's absence, she grew fascinated with her son's beauty, with the slender shape of his bare feet, with the thick, dark hair with its cast of amber red, with the hard blue of his eyes, with all the particulars of his face, the pliability of his lips. He had grown shy about his body without her realizing it. When the shyness had begun she could not recall, but her awareness of it now led her to become less concealing of her own self. With only a negligee around her she drank her coffee at the table while he ate his breakfast, the translucent, ruffled garment falling away from her breasts; with the door to her room open, she undressed or drew on her stockings while she sat in her slip; and she returned from her bath to her room with the negligee clinging to her body.

On the day of her lover's return from Japan, he telephoned at midnight, speaking to her with a teasing, insinuative voice, and in another twenty minutes he was there, roving his voice, which he seemed to have realized on his trip might be a means of arousing a woman, over her neck and down over her breasts within the white negligee she had bought a few days before. They went up the stairs together, his hand moving over her back under the negligee. In her room, her lover sat down on the velvet bench, drawing her to stand between his knees as if she were attempting to escape him, delighting her with that vise. She put her hands on his head to brace herself against the languor that was pulling her down, against his unbalancing of her as he moved his knee between hers to open her thighs.

She closed her eyes, sensing that her son was in the doorway and must be driven out, and, opening them again, saw him there, his small figure in pajamas, gone before her lover could turn to see what had caused her to push him away. She hid her face, clotted with shame and anger, cursing her son for intruding upon the heart of her privacy, yet knowing that neither shame nor anger was as strong as she was making it appear. With a twist of the brass knob she locked the door and lay down on her bed, stricken silent by the commotion within her.

Leland, still on the bench, untied his shoes, laughing softly. When he came down beside her, there was a remainder of laughter in his mouth and in his teasing body, and not until after their loving did she ask, "Why did you laugh?" But he was already asleep and she already knew the answer. He had laughed because the years with her were to lead to nowhere, and so he could make light of her son's curiosity and even use it to their advantage.

With the end of the affair, the false anger she had felt against her son became true. She was angry with him because he had always baffled her conscience, and she recalled, often, the shock of his small figure in pajamas, there in her doorway. She avoided him and he avoided her; he went to school, did all that was asked of him, and avoided her, besides.

One morning, when she had not heard from her lover for several weeks, wanting to impress upon him her remorse for asking for certitude when no one's future gratification was ever certain, she telephoned him at his office and was told by his secretary that he had gone to Japan again. She locked herself in her room and wept as if someone else had locked her in. She walked the room, smoking and weeping. A woman alone was obviously a sinner, had obviously not done something right or done all things wrong, and the aloneness was inflicted upon her to bring her to a comprehension of the enormity of her sin. She longed to be forgiven by her son for the time she had struck him across the back, for if he forgave her for that, then it would serve as a forgiving of more, of all her sins, those she knew about and those she did not. He had seen her in her worst moments and in her best, and, though he was a child, she felt he sensed who she was more than any other person sensed or cared to sense. Nobody else knew her so well. Nobody else was so near, so near he could walk into the heart of her privacy, knowing that her anger could never make him less a son, less than the dearest one.

10

Up in the hills above the Russian River, her father owned a farm inherited from a bachelor uncle who had grown apples and raised sheep. He went there in the winter, taking a few friends, to hunt deer and quail. Nothing was grown with purpose anymore. The trees went on blossoming, the apples went on ripening, and there was a small grazing flock of sheep, a few chickens, a few pigeons. Everything was watched over in its cycles by an elderly woman who had been a painter in the city and who preferred the solitude on the farm, wearing old jodhpurs and hiking boots, her hair peppery gray and cut as short as a man's.

In the late fall of David's ninth year, her father suggested that she bring her son to the farm on the same weekend that he was there with a few friends; he would take the boy hunting and teach him how to handle a gun. She drove up with David a day before her father and his friends were to arrive, and in the evening they strolled out into the orchard. The sheep, wandering in the fields and under the apple trees, trotted up to them. Several were afflicted with colds and made burbling noises as they breathed, and out in the twilight and the cold she felt a sympathy for them as for neglected children. Down below, a long drift of white fog, touched by the daylight still in the sky and by the moon rising, was moving along above the river, fog more silent than the fogs on the bay that came in filled with sound, the deep and high sounds of horns on the bridges and the ships. The call of the quail was fading into the night, into the bushes and groves of trees. Strolling out with David, their sweater collars turned up against the cold, against the darkness sifting down over the low hills around them, she longed to feel in communion with him. The distance was still between them. After school he stayed away, doing whatever it was that boys together kept secret from their parents and that gave him a wordless wildness, an aura, at night, of the entire day of boys and secrecy, his face like the face of a leader recalling treason or of a follower recalling humiliation. On this stroll with him in the orchard, he told her nothing of himself, though the possibility for closeness was there in the beauty all around, the silver fog below, and the rising moon.

While David slept way up in the attic, she sat with the woman in the parlor. The wood-burning stove sent out its waves of heat, and the large parrot hung upside down in his cage and hid behind the tasseled shade of a standing lamp, curling his claws and tongue in a cawing, clucking, moronically cunning flirtation. The woman was knitting a red sweater; under the yarn her thighs were heavy in the faded jodhpurs. She had been gregarious in the city, a ponderous raconteur over cheap wine, a good friend of Adele's; but in the four years up here on the farm she had become a hermit. For an hour Vivian leafed through several magazines, chatting with the woman about their friends in the city, and, going up early, she felt that the woman was not offended and even preferred to be left alone.

She went up the narrow stairs that were lit by the globe in the hallway on the second floor. The door to her room was open and the lamp on, and she could see the bed covered with a reddish quilt, and the dresser with a long white cloth, and on the cloth a hand mirror with a tarnished silver back. Reluctant to enter her room, she climbed the staircase to the upper reaches of the house to look in at her son. He might be regretting his choice of sleeping quarters and willing to accept a small bedroom of his own on the second floor. Climbing the staircase that was enclosed by age-darkened walls and lit with a dim globe for the convenience of her son, a globe that would not be lit the other nights when the woman was alone, she was afraid for herself, a fear that, someday, she, too, would be able to be alone, like the woman alone in this house.

The top floor was not partitioned, as below, with bedrooms. It was one large room under a peaked roof that came down to the row of casement windows at each side, and, on one side, under the windows, were three cots. In the middle cot she saw the small, dark hump David's body made under the olive-drab blankets. From up here, the fog along the river was seen in its dimensions; from the window it had a breadth and a depth that seethed with moonlight. Way down in the yard and out in the woods and the orchard, the silence appeared to be the moonlight, to be tangible. She crossed the bare floor to the other side of the room and leaned on the sill to look out the open window, but a low hill, its top at a level with her eyes, seemed to crowd against the house, an obstacle to the view she had expected, and the trickery of the scene increased her fear. She went down again to the parlor, hearing on the way down the woman talking to the parrot. She explained to the woman that it was difficult for her to sleep in a strange house, and she sat down on the sofa, leafing through the same magazines and chatting again until eleven o'clock, when they parted.

With her father came two friends, the actor Max Laurie and a man younger than both, whom she had not met before. The three men in winter jackets and boots got out of her father's gray Chrysler and began to cross the yard to the house. The men turned when she and David, on higher ground up in the orchard, called to them. In a row, they watched her and her son approach, and the memory of her fear, the night before, was dispelled. The farmhouse and the cold orchard and the yard in which they waited for her—everything was filled with the presence of the men as with a clap of thunder or a flooding of hot sun. When they began to turn away, because it was a long way for her to approach, and to look around the yard and lift up their faces toward the hills and the water tower, she took her son's hand and ran with him, and the running passed for a welcome from a woman unaware of herself in her happiness at seeing them. She threw her arms around her father and around Max and shook hands with the young man who, up close, was not so young, was in his late thirties, the coarse skin of his face incongruous with the young stance of his body as he had watched her approach.

She walked with him to the house, while David walked ahead of them between his grandfather and Max, and the presence of the men was the reason for *her* presence on the farm. She admired her father's build, his erect back and his elegant head; and admired the small figure of her son in the pearl-gray sweater her mother had knit for him, his straight legs in jeans; and admired the self-conscious sprightliness in the actor's body. They brought her—the three men—the excitement of pleasing them, the pleasure of pleasing them. She was glad that none of them had brought a woman. She was the only woman. The old woman in her hiking boots did not count as a woman; she was a past woman.

They had drinks together in the parlor. David drank hot cocoa and sat by Max, with whom he exchanged riddles and jokes and she, the only woman, listened to her father and Russell talk about the nightclub they were to finance in partnership with a shipping-company executive, and, engaged with them, she felt the riches of her womanness—in her gestures, in the ease of her laughing, in the appreciation in her eyes and in her body of all they told to interest her and amuse her. And she saw that the man who was new among them, Russell Maddux, was glancing at her with that alternating peculiar to some men, a desire for her and a concealing of desire that passed over his eyes like a curtain shutting off their depths.

They all went out into the woods early in the afternoon to hunt quail. She and her son were each given a shotgun, Russell instructing her in the use of hers and her father instructing David, and in a line they went through the brush and among the trees. Russell was to her left and Max beyond him, and to her right David and then her father. For the first time David had a gun in his hands, and she saw that he strove for an ease in his walk, an experienced hunter's grace, but was stiff in the knees and the elbows. The space that was between her and him; his face, glimpsed in profile, set forward timorously, transfixed by the quail that might rise up in the next moment; the awkwardness and the grace of his small, slender body; the blindness of his feet in sneakers—all roused in her a desire for him to remain as he was, the only one and the closest one, the dearest, incontestably more dear than any man who was to become her lover and who was now a stranger. While she was bound over to the lover, her son might leave her forever. Walking three yards away from him—walking gracefully because the man to her left was a few feet behind her for a moment and was perhaps noting the movement of her buttocks in the tight, trim slacks—she felt a strong desire to embrace her son and to beg him not to allow another man to lessen her closeness with him, not to allow her to give herself over to another lover.

A covey of quail whirred up, skimming over bushes, flying over the tops of the low trees. One was brought down, her father assuring David that, although both had shot at the birds, he had missed but David had not. David began a babbling prediction of hundreds of more quail brought down, and had to be cautioned by her father to be quiet. After that first shot, David's attack on quail and cottontail rabbits was almost ridiculously pompous, more confident than the men's.

They tramped back through the cold woods—in the bag four quail and two rabbits among them all—and on the large round oak table in the kitchen tossed the game down. She was standing across the table from her son and saw his face was flushed from the cold, his eyes narrowed by the intense excitement of the day, and it seemed to her that the span of years between him and the others, the men, had disappeared.

They stayed late around the table after a supper of roast lamb, of fruit preserves—the figs and plums of the hot summer—drinking brandies and smoking, talking about the division of Germany, and Russell about his experiences in the war in Europe, and Max about his entertaining the troops. David stayed with them in the parlor until midnight, listening and recalling at every chance everything about the hunt as if they had not accompanied him and were eager to hear, and when at last he fell asleep on the parlor rug, she roused him and went up with him. He fell onto his cot, too weary to undress, and she pulled off his shoes and waked him enough to undress himself, and he was asleep again the moment he lay down under the covers. As she lay in her bed, hearing below her the considerately low voices of the men in the parlor, their presence below her like depths to float upon, the sense of the loss of her son to the men seemed not so alarming, instead seemed desirable, for the presence of the men in the house, among them David, was to release her into a sleep that was like the expectation of a reward. The men came up quietly, their footsteps on the stairs a sound that in her half-sleep seemed to go on forever. She heard them in their rooms around her, the murmur of their voices, the scrape of a chair, and their number verified their strength. In each was the strength of all three and their strength was in David also, in his cot way up in the attic's vast reaches.

11

Russell unlocked the door of the nightclub, fumbled on a light, and escorted her down red-carpeted stairs to a large, cold cellar where numerous little tables and chairs were scattered around a stage. The cellar ran under a restaurant and a bar, and the pipes along the ceiling were covered with a false sky—a black cloth painted with many gold moons, both crescent and round, and festooned with gilded gauze. The seepage and the dampness had been taken care of first, he told her; everything was as dry as a bone. The sign above the door—THE CARNIVAL—would be lit next Friday night, when the gossip columnists and some local big names would be wined and dined and entertained by a stripteaser and by a comedian and by a jazz trio who were to appear for the opening weeks. He himself, he said, and her father and the other owner had nothing to do with the details—everything from the plumbing to the entertainers was taken care of by the manager, but the whole works, he said, fascinated him. He did a jig step up on the stage, then stooped down to pick up a wire, and stood gazing upward to trace the origin of the trailing wire in his hand.

Later in the evening, in a quiet bar, he told her that he had been married twice, the first time when he was twenty. His second marriage had ended in the death of his wife, Anna. She had been a very unhappy person, weeping over slights that nobody else, he said, would even think to call slights, and, for days, brooding and miserable for reasons unknown to him. After a year she had decided to have a child because she might, she had said, feel necessary to somebody. But the child, a girl, had failed to bring that certainty to her and she had grown worse, calling herself foul names and wandering away, leaving the child alone in the house. She saw a psychiatrist almost every day, and every night took sedatives to sleep. She slept alone. The child slept in a bedroom of her own and he slept on the couch in the den. One night he was wakened by the smell of smoke and had time only to run into the child's room and rescue her. That part of the house where his wife slept was already in flames. Under the soft light of the bar lamps, he removed his coat, loosened a cuff link, and pushed up his shirtsleeve to show her the long, heavy scar down his arm.

The rest of the evening he brought up a hundred other topics, his way of apologizing for the story that had checked her vivacity. There was something unlikable about him after the story. She was afraid to be close with someone who had suffered the death of a wife under those circumstances. That he had been on the other side of the burning door, that he had been unable to break through, made it impossible for her to look into his eyes. She felt that he had been marked for that catastrophe and might be marked for others, and that there was nothing he could do to prevent them, even as he could not prevent his wife dying on the other side of the burning door. Yet, later in the night, lying with him in his apartment, she kissed the long scar on his arm, wondering if her dislike of him, earlier, had been fear of another dimension of reality. Waking in the middle of the night, she drank his brandy and laughed with him over a joke. When he sat up on the edge of the bed, she got up on her knees and kissed the back of his head and his shoulders, unwilling to let him go from her even for a moment, desiring to transform him, with her kissing, into a man who could avert any catastrophe.

The wedding, in the rectory of the church her mother attended, with only Russell's aunt and her parents and David present, seemed to her the wisest occasion of her life. Her parents liked him. He was a more responsive son, a more companionable son than their own; in addition, he was, at last, a son-in-law as affluent as they were, and perhaps more so.

They moved into a home he owned near Twin Peaks, on a wide avenue of white stucco homes of early California architecture. The lawn was perfect and so was the patio with its pink hydrangea bushes and granite birdbaths. The three of them, Russell and herself and David, each contributed, she felt, an admirable self to the pleasure of the marriage. At the beginning there appeared to be an easy compatibility between David and his stepfather, and their evenings together were always pleasant, with cocktails before supper and a special grenadine cocktail for David, and the gourmet suppers she cooked for them and for their frequent guests, Russell's friends, who were loan-company executives and bank officials, and their wives. They went on trips together in their red convertible to Lake Tahoe and to the mountains to fish and up into Sun Valley to ski, and always she was aware of the picture they made of the elegant family, climbing into or springing from their car and entering the lobby of the hotel, the father or the mother resting an arm on the boy's shoulder.

Neither she nor Russell had any desire to bring his daughter, Maria, to live with them, and, even had they wanted to, the girl would have chosen to remain with her maternal grandmother, a vigorous women with a daughter of seventeen, whom Maria idolized. They sometimes, however, took her along on their trips, and they sometimes had her over for a weekend, but her presence among them was, to Vivian, like a flaw in the picture. She was a year younger than David, a slight, colorless girl with enormous smoky blue eyes that seldom lifted. She was a reminder of the tragedy because it seemed to have shocked her from her normal pace of growth. When Russell brought the girl from her grandmother's, he hustled and bustled around to entertain her, to entertain them all. His eyes were tired when he came in the door with her, tired of the visit before it began, and afraid of the child he performed for. Around the girl he was a man making extravagant amends, a weary buffoon. In the last minutes of the girl's visits, with everybody collecting her possessions, gifts and hats and gloves and candy, Maria joined in with them, gave up sitting and being done unto, and, with her participation in the search, implied that she was both gratified and sorry her visit had roused them all to such a pitch of expiation.

After the girl's visits, when Vivian was left alone in the house with her son, there was always a time of relief, in which she felt the bond between herself and David, the bond of mother and son, to be stronger than that between herself and Russell. If Russell remained away, visiting with Marie's grandmother and, afterward, drinking at the nightclub, and David was asleep, she would go in and watch the boy while he slept.

In the light of lamp he lay on his back as if flung there, sometimes clear of the blankets from the waist up, his pajama top twisted upward, exposing his pale, tender stomach. He was, at these times, like an old friend. If her husband was not that, then her son was that. If marriage was not a resolving, then some compensation, or more than that, some answer, was to be found in the existence of her son. One night she bent and kissed him above the navel, pleased by the warm, resilient flesh, knowing that he would not wake up from the kiss because he slept so soundly and in the morning always came up fathoms out of sleep.

12

Some land that Russell had inherited south of the city, near the ocean, sold to a tract developer, and almost every week, or so it seemed to her, he sold at a great profit an old apartment building or a small hotel that he had bought only a few months before with a loan and had remodeled with another loan. And everything that she did with this prosperity brought words of praise, whether it was the accumulation of exquisite clothes or of oil paintings from the Museum of Art exhibits, the selection of silver and crystal and antiques, or the artistry of her suppers for a few guests. After two years in the house near Twin Peaks, they moved to a modern house surrounded by a Japanese garden, and the combining of her antiques with the modern architecture, all the harmonious combining was like a confirmation of the happiness of the family. It was further confirmed by color photographs in a magazine of interior decoration and by the article written by one of the editors who stressed the wonderful compatibility of antique and modern that had, as its source, the compatibility of the family with everything beautiful. No member of the family, however, appeared in the pictures—only Vivian at a far distance, her back turned, a very small figure in lemon-yellow slacks way out among the etching-like trees of the garden, glimpsed through the open glass doors of the living room. It was in bad taste to show the family, she understood; they would appear to be like the nouveaux riches, wanting to be seen among their possessions. Not to show the family gave more seclusion to the home and a touch of the sacred to the family.

In the second spring after their move to the new house, it was included in a tour of several beautiful homes in the city, the tour a charitable endeavor by the young matrons' league to which she belonged. While the woman who came once a week to the house was cleaning it the day before the tour, Vivian locked up in cabinets and closets small valuables that could be pocketed, although there was to be a leaguer in almost every room to act as hostess. It was customary for the owners of the houses in the tour to be away all day, and she had planned to spend the day with her mother, shopping for summer clothes. But the night before, carefully wiping out with a tissue the ashtrays she and Russell had been using and rinsing their liquor glasses, she knew she would remain in the house—not to hear words of praise and not to prevent any thefts, but to stand anonymously by and watch the flow of strangers who had paid their tour-ticket price in order to enter into the privacy of her home.

With the other women who were acting as hostesses, she awaited the invasion. Wearing a pink spring suit and white gloves, a white purse under her arm, she was, she felt, sure to be mistaken by the crowd for one of them. The early ones, at ten o'clock, entered with a reverent step because it was their first house of the day; but the later ones entered with less reverence, commenting loudly on plants and garden lamps as they came up the front path, taking in the living room with gazes already somewhat jaded by their acquaintance with other homes of secluded beauty. She watched them as she sat on the arm of a chair, chatting with a hostess, or wandered with them through the house. They were chic women, young and old, and they were impeccably dressed men with oblique faces as if seen in attendance upon her in a mirror of a beauty salon and never in direct confrontation; they were eccentrics, one a young woman in a garishly green outfit, with a pheasant feather a foot long attached to her beret and switching the space behind her as she stopped frequently, her feet in a dancer's pose, to glance around with large, transfixed eyes and a saintly smile; and there were two seedy brothers, shuffling and gray, who had the look of small-time realtors from the Mission district. For brief moments Vivian met eyes with the invaders, their roundly open eyes, their shifting eyes, their eyes ashamed of their curiosity, their envious eyes, and their eyes desiring ruin. She caught sight of a hole in the sock of one of the seedy brothers and of their run-down, polished shoes. She mingled with them up and down the hallways, on the flight of stairs between the two floors, and in and out of rooms, following a group into the serenity of the bedroom of herself and her husband and observing with them the wide, high-swelling bed, the ornately carved bedstead and the plum silk spread, the highboy with its shining brass hardware; the lamps, one on each side of the bed, a yard high with cylindrical shades of white silk; the black marble ashtrays; and the sand-color, thick carpeting that hushed everyone's step. They were fascinated by the small photos of Russell and David in pewter frames on her dressing table, and by a snapshot of the three of them in ski clothes. They bent to see the three faces closer, and after the others had done this, she, too, leaned closer to see for herself.

13

In the summer of the third year of their marriage they bought an old, large house near Clearlake on four acres planted with fruit trees. They invited two and three couples for weekends and spent the time in boats on the lake, over elaborate breakfasts and buffet suppers, drinking at the bars to survey the patrons and reclining at home in the sun or under the trees if the sun was too hot.

David was off on his own all day. He was twelve, that year, and although she knew that his distance from them all was due, in part, to a dislike of their friends, it was also, she felt, a sullen and almost violent resistance to any tracing of him, either the tracing of him in his roaming during the day or of his present self into the past, as the eyes of their friends traced him into childhood, and as hers did, and Russell's. They saw him cruising around on the lake with another boy in somebody else's motorboat, or laughing with another boy as the two bailed out a dinghy, or they did not see him for an entire day. Sometimes he did not come in for meals and ate leftovers up in his room, wanting more privacy than was given him in the kitchen where the guests went in and out and tried to talk with him.

One night, however, he came to watch them dance in their bare feet in the parlor. He sat on a kitchen chair near the door, his arms crossed over his chest and his legs stretched out toward the dancers. The women tugged at his shirt to persuade him to dance with them, and one drew up another chair by his and stroked his hair and called him shy. When at last he danced with the woman, he danced without the hesitation and clumsiness and deafness to the beat of the music that were signs of shyness. He danced with the woman almost instructively, a glide of insinuation in his hips and a contempt and an urging of her in his gaze that he kept on her belly and legs.

The night was warm, the house warmer than the night, containing in all its rooms the heat from the day. The women wore no more than they had worn during the day, cotton shorts and halters. The woman he was dancing with, the wife of the bank manager, had loosened her high pile of red hair so that it fell in strands along each side of her face. That she was short and stocky, that her long hair and bare feet made her almost comically squat, she was apparently not aware. They danced a foot apart, each flattering the other, seductively, with every move. The days of his avoiding them, of crossing to the other side of the road, of eating alone in his room at night—all were cast off in an eruption of melancholy desire. His eyes appeared almost black, they were open wider, and there was a firmness in his hands on the woman like that of a man experienced in arousing, and the vigor in his slender body ridiculed the men in the room who were slumped earthward, who were debilitated by the sun of the day rather than enlivened by it, as he appeared to be. Vivian recalled the comic dance he had performed as a child, the uncontrolled dancing, the stomping with no grace or rhythm, the prancing that was nothing more than self-tripping. The woman cupped her breast with one hand, a gesture that she did not appear conscious of. It must be, Vivian thought, a habitual caress, probably one that she gave herself when alone. The woman was smiling at David, and since he was watching her belly and legs, it appeared that she was watching herself with his eyes. When the music was over, she collapsed onto the couch, falling into her husband's lap.

"You ought to get him in the movies," said the bank manager. His hands had gone up to protect himself from his wife's falling body; in the next moment he had removed his hands from her, jerking his leg away also. He was a tall thin man whose high, complaining voice Vivian would often hear when she stood in the marble rotunda of the bank, and once she had watched him stride from his carpeted enclosure, slam the gate that only swung noiselessly, and run up the stairs, too impatient and full too of complaints to wait for the slow elevator.

"You remember that kid? You remember that thirteen-year-old kid?" Duggan, an attorney, a small, blond man who wore sports clothes that seemed with their expensiveness to dwarf him. Even when his lips were not moving in speech, they moved with anticipation of speech. "You remember he ran away with that woman? I attended the hearing. She had six kids and was thirty-eight and I forgot to mention she had a husband too. They took her 1941 Plymouth to Tucson and shacked up there in a motel—Big Indian or Little Indian Motel—stayed for four days, I think it was, before they were apprehended. She said she loved him, she said she loved him more than her husband, she said he was the greatest lover of the century. One of her boys was two and a half years older than her lover. She was stacked, that woman, almost six feet tall. You can imagine." He was talking rapidly and loudly over the music of the record that had dropped into place.

Vivian turned the volume knob to obliterate his moist voice and, dancing, approached her son. She danced with him in a spontaneous attempt to prove to all of them that his dancing was a boy's imitation of dancing he had seen in the movies and that he was ignorant of its implications. She was a shield between him and the lascivious attorney's story. But he lost his competence dancing with her; his legs bungled the rhythm, he looked down at his feet, and when the music was over he sat apart again.

When David danced with Duggan's wife, who came up to him, he made up with wildness for his clumsiness dancing with his mother. The woman was a tall blonde, with utter vanity in the poking forward of her gaunt hips and long, bare thighs; an assumption, in her dancing postures, of a lunacy that matched her partner's. These woman had no lunacy, Vivian thought. They had no wantonness, no risk, and he was wasting on them his abandonment of himself to his sensuality, the first public display of the sensuality that would be his in years to come. With her back to the dancing couple, with her drink held up high in her right hand while with her left she riffled through the record albums on the table, she lifted her eyes to see their reflection in the French doors: the woman's turquoise shorts and white blouse with its one diagonal stripe of red, her long bare arms and legs in angular seduction, and David's small figure in tan pants and soiled white shirt, his dark hair, and his face that was pale in the reflection against the night and yet was brown from the summer sun—both figures moving across the panes to the blaring jangle of the music.

At the moment she turned to watch them, Russell slipped himself between David and the woman, holding his arms up high in exaggerated homage to her and dancing away with her in his small-footed way that was always just a beat off. David sat for a while watching them, then went upstairs while everyone was dancing. After he left, although the records continued to fall into place and the music blared on and the vocalists sang on or whispered on, there was no more dancing.

Russell mixed a drink for them all that he called a golden viper. "This'll stone you on the first swallow," he warned them. The bank manager's wife sipped with a little girl's curiosity, her eyes big over the rim of her glass. Russell, Vivian saw, made the most of this small sway over them; from the secret of the viper he went on to reveal another secret—where and for what a low price he had purchased the cut glass from which they drank, holding up his glass to the light and turning it in his fingers, conscious, she knew, that she was watching him critically. While he sat on the edge of the table, the center of the group, host and entertainer, she remembered the times she had driven him home after parties, listening while he incoherently probed his depths and deplored his friends' shallowness. The loan officials who peopled his days, he condemned when alone with her. They respected him for what they called his genius, and their appraisers overvalued the hotels and apartment houses so that the loans they made to him were larger than warranted; he ate lunch with them in the best restaurants and drank with them in the best bars, and was, she knew, always his charming, boyish, shrewd, and witty self; and at night he ridiculed them for a tie, for suede shoes, and for their very shrewdness that saw him as the one to put their money on.

While they were talking about the war in Korea, with the bank manager predicting that the Chinese were going to overrun the world, Vivian left them and went up the stairs. The heat of the day was pocketed in the upstairs hallway; all the bedroom doors, and David's door at the end of the hallway, were closed. He was lying under the sheet, the blankets thrown off onto the floor, reading under the metal lamp fixed to the bed. His head was tilted against the headboard, the pillow stuffed under his neck.

"You were the life of the party and now they're just talking," she told him, collapsing into the canvas chair and resting her feet on the bed. The room had a meager look; it was more a sanctum than his room at home. "Silly rug looks like it's eaten all around the edge by mouse teeth," she said, lowering one leg to kick up the edge of the rug. "Read a little to me," she said, closing her eyes.

"It's just about birds," he said.

"Go on, read to me if it's about birds," she urged. "I'm interested in birds."

"What part?" he asked, embarrassed, she saw, about reading aloud, knowing that her interest was feigned. He flipped through the pages to lose deliberately the page that he had been reading, leading her away from himself by leading her away from the part that had absorbed him. "The hummingbird can't glide," he said. "You want that important bit of information?"

"Ah, poor things, can't glide," she said. "Go on. But what do they need to glide for?"

"You act like a teacher," he said. "They ask you questions and spoil everything."

"Me a teacher?" she cried in mock distress. "I came in here to learn a few things and you accuse me of acting like a teacher. Baby, I'm ignorant," she pleaded. "I don't know anything about birds except they've all got feathers and go peep-peep. Go on and tell me about them. Because birds are the greatest miracle. God really outdid Himself when He made a bird. Say you and I were God, could we think up something like a bird? Never in a million years. It took God to think them up, and even for Him it was something. You go on, tell me more about birds."

"It says about migration," he began again, "that millions of them never get there, where they're going. It says it's really a big risk to a bird, the biggest risk in his life. It says that hundreds of millions of them never get there."

"Isn't that funny? I thought they all made it," she said.

For a time he read to her about the perils of migration. She recrossed her ankles, while she listened, observing the arches of her bare feet. Then, because she heard a murmur of voices in the glassed-in porch below, where the bank manager and his wife slept, and knew that the rest would be coming up the stairs and that only a short time was left her in her son's room, she lost her feigned reverence for birds. "Listen, Davy baby," she began. "I don't want you to get vain about being a good dancer or looking like the great lover Gable just because you stirred up those women down there. You're neither. You want to know what it is?" She tilted her head back, lifting her gaze to the ceiling. "It's your youth. It's because you're so young, baby." She laughed. "You look at them as if you're seeing women for the first time, and what it does to them is make them feel they're being seen for the first time by any man. You make them feel fabulous—oh, as if they've got a thousand secrets they could tell you." She laughed again, still toward the ceiling. "You know what Russell is going to say? When everybody is asleep, he'll say in a whisper, he'll say, 'Davy got out of hand tonight, didn't he? Those women will be creeping around the house all night long.'" She brought her gaze down, a humorously warning gaze. "You want to put a chair against your door?"

She saw in his expressionless face that he did not want to understand her joke. He did not want to suspect that she had come up the stairs and away from the others not to tell him about the other women but to tell him, by her presence, that nobody else could claim his enticing youth except herself, if it were to be claimed at all. He was her son; she had given him his life and his youth, his present and his future, his elusiveness, and, by telling him she knew his effect upon the other women, she was reminding him of her claim to him, if she had a claim. "Go on," she said, settling farther into her chair. "Read to me, read to me."

She heard Duggan and his wife come up the stairs and enter their bedroom quietly, while the murmuring below was borne out on the still air into the dark yard. After a time she heard Russell come up. Then the murmuring ceased and the house was silent. David read to her for a while longer and when he was tired of reading she told him to turn off the light, and she sat in darkness, reluctant to go to her husband, to lie down beside him. She was struck by the years of her accumulated contempt for her husband as by an unexpected blow to her body. Their voices muted by the darkness, she and her son talked together, finding inconsequential things to talk about. He told her about a boy he had made friends with a few days before and how far around the lake they went with the boy's uncle in his motorboat, and as he talked she listened more to the sound of his voice than to the words, feeling the sound of his young voice, his faltering, low, slightly hoarse voice reverberate in her body.

Her husband was sitting on the bed in the darkness. The light from the hallway, as she opened the door, revealed him half undressed, smoking a cigarette. Though he was not yet in bed, he had already turned off the lamp, or not turned it on, apparently wanting to reject her with darkness, and she felt that she had come from the presence of a man who was more than he. It seemed to her that Russell and the others in the house and herself were all to be left behind by her son, their lives nothing compared to what his life was to be, that this man, castigating her with darkness, sat in a cul-de-sac of a life. She felt that all of them except her son were trapped in the summer night in that house with the unwashed glasses and ashtrays on floors and couches and windowsills, with intimate, used garments on floors and chairs— everything testifying to wasted lives.

"Golden vipers," she said, low, pacing the floor in her bare feet, making no noise on the floorboards, as if she were weightless. "Always some little surprise or other, always some concoction nobody ever heard of before and that's deadly familiar. How do you manage to accomplish both at the same time?"

"Enough, enough. Every little thing. Enough . . . ," he said, breathing out the words as if someone were testing him physically to see how much pain he was able to bear.

"They all add up to the big thing."

"What's the big thing?" he asked, challengingly, unafraid.

"You. They all add up to you." She was unable to move, struck by her own cruelty.

"You don't see me right, Vivian," he said. "You've got a crazy way of looking at me. You put together things nobody notices because they're nothing to notice. You watch for everything and call it a fault."

She pressed her temples to destroy the cruelty in her head, but it was not cornered by a posture or a wish. "It's you I see," she insisted.

"Me? Me?" He kept his voice low. "You act like I misrepresented myself. I never misrepresented myself, Vivian. Besides, you're smart, Vivian. You're smart enough to know if a man's lying to you. That's not saying I'm satisfied with myself. You don't know what's plaguing me. You think I think everything's great. You think I think my life's just great. What I gripe about—this guy and that guy, some deals— you think there's nothing else that gripes me. I see the way you see me and I don't look so good, sometimes, but you can't see what I *feel*. I'd like to tell you what I feel. Or maybe I wouldn't like to. If I could tell you, you still wouldn't know." He paused. "I'll tell you," and paused again. He was rubbing his knees, trying to rub away his confusion over himself, straining to engage his being in whatever was the aspiration he could not find words for.

It was so amorphous a thing for him to tell—the thing which he hoped would make him more in her eyes—that the attempt to reveal it was almost like an attempt to confess a crime instead of to reveal a virtue.

She went over to him. There was no one else to lie down beside if she wanted an embrace against her own cruelty. He leaned forward to clasp her around her legs, drawing her down with him.

"Vivian, listen. When I first saw you, the way you ran down that hill like a kid, I said there's a woman with a heart as big as the world. So if I blow up, you're supposed to know I don't mean it. Lie still, lie still," he urged.

14

Maria came to visit more frequently at Vivian's invitation until she was with them almost ritually every weekend. Along with the diffidence, there was now in her manner almost the slyness of a spy in the enemy camp. At twelve she was ineffectually pretty in Vivian's eyes; there was no quickness, no grace, no wiles, no artifice to make persuasive the large, smoky blue eyes and fair skin; and this lack of conscious femininity, which was, to Vivian, the very soul of a woman, was not, she thought, the girl's fault, not the dead mother's fault, not the fault of the grandmother with whom she lived, but Russell's fault. The girl was evidence to her always that he had not been the man he ought to have been in that other marriage. The girl was like the dead wife's past consciousness of him as he was; she was like the wife's dismayed, sorrowing consciousness of him.

With the girl, they drove up to the mountains to ski, and Maria, who could not ski and could not learn, spent the time walking in snowshoes, and Vivian sometimes accompanied her, affected by the sight of the girl alone, her sad face surrounded by a knit cap of exultant red. In the summer, they drove to Monterey, or up into the gold-mining country and gambled on the machines in desolate saloons, or they went to Clearlake or to Tahoe to swim.

Constantly urged by Russell to intrude upon David, to swim as far, to climb as far, Maria, one day at Lake Tahoe, in the midst of Russell's badgering, stood up from the shallow water where she had been paddling around and struck out after David, who was climbing onto a raft several yards offshore. She was an awkward swimmer, fearful and rigid. Even so, while they watched apprehensively and with shame, the girl, apparently propelled by sheer anger against the man who had taunted her, got as far as midway, and then could neither turn back nor continue on to the raft. Russell ran into the water and swam after her, and, with one arm around her, helped her back to shore. Once on her feet and out of the water, Maria refused to go as far as the blanket where they had congregated before. She sat down on wet sand, facing the water, clasping her knees, not acknowledging her father's presence or Vivian's. Vivian laid a sweater over the girl's back and sat down beside her. Russell lay on his back, several yards away.

"I think he wanted me to drown," Maria said.

"That's not true." Vivian put her arm around the girl.

"It's true," the girl said.

"But he rescued you."

"I wasn't drowning."

"Then you see, it's not true," Vivian said, hugging the girl to impress upon her their humorous reasoning.

Maria sat alone, after Vivian had left her, until it was time for them to leave the lake, and on the long drive back to the city that evening she did not speak, not even to answer.

Russell returned at two in the morning, after taking Maria home, and, as was his habit, stopping by at the nightclub. He stumbled down onto the bench of Vivian's dressing table, facing her where she lay in bed. "You terribly awfully fond of her, Vivian?" he asked. "Why?"

"Why?" she repeated, half asleep.

"Why?"

"Why? Because I guess I feel sorry for her."

"You're not fond of her and you're not sorry for her and you're not fond of me and you're not sorry for me. You just don't like me. It's that simple. That's the crux of it. You don't like me and because you don't like me you fix it up so we see her every week. You use her to remind me of something you think ought to be plaguing me. What do you want to plague me with, Vivian?" He began to weep without covering his face, and his pale eyes, paler because of the deeply flushed face, seemed to have wept out their color before he returned home to weep.

She slept in the guest room after that night, and heard him come home, stumbling, slamming doors, an hour after the nightclub closed. One night he did not come home, and in the morning her father telephoned to tell her that the manager had ordered Russell from the club because he had made a nuisance of himself, complaining to the patrons that his wife refused to sleep with him. He did not come home that day and, at two in the morning, her father telephoned again: Russell had spent the evening in the restaurant next door to the club, buying drinks for a couple, buying supper for them, telling of his ostracism, that his wife forbade him to come home and his partners forbade him to enter the nightclub.

An hour after her father had called, Russell returned. "It's me, don't shoot!" he shouted, unlocking the front door. "Vivian, you hear me up there? I'm turning on all the lights so you can see it's me. You saw that thing in the papers? She shot her husband dead because she thought he was a prowler?" He came up the stairs, stamping, and into their bedroom, shaking his keys above his head with both hands.

As if he felt he required some excuse for being there, for returning, he began to undress, pulling at his tie, unbuttoning his shirt before he had removed his coat. He took off his coat and seemed surprised to find his tie gone and his shirt already unbuttoned. Then, as if he were afraid that somebody else had unbuttoned him because he was incapable of it, because he was drunk, his face flushed up in humiliation. "What's this guilt every woman puts on me? What's this bloody guilt?" he shouted. "What're you retaliating for, Viv? What're you retaliating for? You're always retaliating for something I never know I do to you."

"I said nothing," she said.

"You say nothing. What makes you think you need to say something? I get the point. And Maria says nothing, but I get the point. She's like a creditor—I didn't pay my bill, I didn't meet my obligations, or the check bounces. What's this guilt every woman puts on me? What's this bloody guilt? I been walking around with it all my life. I was sitting next to this guy and I was telling him what a wonderful woman you are and goddamn how I didn't deserve you, how I wasn't good enough for you, when he says to me, 'You got guilt on you, man. What you don't deserve is your guilt.' That man, a stranger, knows more about me than any man I call a friend. 'You got guilt on you,' he says. 'That's the only thing you don't deserve.' You hear that? Seems to be a goddamn disease that women got. They give you a dose of guilt like a whore gives you a dose of clap." He sat down on the bench, bent over to untie his shoe, his face lifted to her at the same moment that his bare back was reflected in the large, round mirror of the dressing table, and it seemed to her that his undressing was an act assuring him his words would not, after all, bring about the end. "If there were trials, if there were trials, if they could accuse you of leading your wife to her end just by being yourself, they'd do it and hang you for it. Isn't that the truth, over there? That you got me for life and what kind of life is it? You got everything invested in me and who am I? What I'd like to know is why the hell did you get into the bind? And why the hell did Anna? Why did *she?* What do you want? What do you expect? You think you're embracing the whole goddamn universe and you wake up the next morning and it's me there? It's me there? And what do you do, then? You give me this guilt. You give me this guilt when I'm spitting up my heart to do the job right."

She threw off the covers and sat on the edge of the bed, trembling. Alerted by her movement, apparently suspecting that she was about to flee across the hall to her son, he lifted his head as if he could, if he tried, hear David listening. The boy could not hear the words, she knew, but the angry pitch could reach him. "You get 'em young enough, you got 'em on your side. You get 'em in the cradle. That's it. That's a goddamn political truth, every politician knows that. Give 'em the ideology with their mother's milk and you got 'em for life. Go on in and throw yourself on him and tell him what you're suffering, tell him how I make you suffer." He slammed his hand down hard and flat on the bench. "I never did anything to you!" he shouted. "I never did anything to any woman that I have to feel guilty about. Why do you want to make me guilty?"

"I'm not Anna," she said. "Don't talk to me that way," as if he had shouted that other wife into her grave.

"You're all Anna," he cried. "You're all alike. Sometimes I start to call you Anna." He stood up to unbuckle his belt but the rage against her forced him to put on his shirt again. His hands shook as they went down the buttons.

She began to walk around the room, frightened by his accusation that she was as his wife Anna had been. She had not thought that the desperation in herself was as much as in that other woman, but this comparing them roused in her the fear that it was as much. "If I'm Anna," she cried, "then I can tell you how she felt. You want to know how she felt? Everything she said against herself was against you, because she was afraid to say it against you."

"She wasn't afraid to say it!" he shouted. "What makes you think she was afraid?"

"Sometimes I say it, but I'm afraid when I say it," she told him. "Every time I say something against you to your face, it's like a terrible falling, like I've cut the ground out from under my feet."

"That *is* the ground under your feet!" he shouted. "That *is* the ground."

"No, it's true," she said, twining her fingers. "It's true what I say. That's the way she felt, I *know*. She couldn't bear you anymore, but she couldn't cut the ground away. That's a terrible thing, not to be able to bear the ground under your feet. What do you do then but die?"

"You blame me for it?"

She gave him a look of scorn, and was appalled by the slipping away of the ground. He came toward her and she waited, unable to expect that he would strike her. He struck her and she fell to her knees, clinging to him. He grasped her arms and flung her off. When she got to her feet, he followed her. "Go on! Goddamn! Go on! Go on, faster!" he shouted. "You know the way, you know the way. Take off your goddamn nightgown. What's that on for when you run naked in the hallway? He'll think you're dressed to go out, looks like a goddamn dress to go out in." He grasped the hem of it, but she swung around, striking at him, and, missing him, fell against her son's door.

Above her, she saw her son strike Russell in the chest. The boy flew at the man, all his taciturnity released into rage, into shouting and striking. Russell flung him away, and when the boy fell against the wall, struck him in the face with the back of his hand and left them. David helped her into his room and locked the door, and they sat together on his bed, trembling, listening to Russell's sobs and his screams at the sobs to stay down, and they heard the rush of water in the basin. Then he left the house, raced the engine of his car, and roared away.

She ran down the stairs and bolted the door, afraid that he would return, afraid that later in the night, wherever he was, in some hotel room, he would be forced to return. She lay down in her bed. She was not concerned with her son; he could take care of himself and his own wounds. If he was trembling, it was with fear of things beginning, of woundings and conflicts beginning; he was not trembling with the fear of endings.

15

In the morning they packed a few clothes and left the house, wanting to be away if Russell returned. On the drive down to Monterey, David drowsed in the sun beating into the open car, his head lolling back against the seat. She glanced at his face; as dearly familiar as it was, she always found more than a touch of the unfamiliar, and now the bruise increased the strangeness. As she drove with the drowsing boy, it seemed to her that his elusiveness was an accusation that she had always, since his birth, held other persons to be more valuable than he, that all her time was spent in the company of other persons for whom she must make herself valuable, when who were the others, after all? He was to repay her in kind, she knew. It was inevitable. He was to spend his life in the company of persons whose value for him she would never be able to comprehend, and she felt a deep stirring of curiosity about that life of his beyond his fourteen years and about those persons, some not yet born, who were to rake his mind and his heart with their being.

On either side of the highway stretched rows of low, tangled vines, their green muted by the fine dust concocted of hot sun and vast open fields. For miles she drove through sun-bleached hills, ranging in color from almost white to a dark gold, and early in the afternoon she turned along by the sea. Her body felt fragile, but the sun on her bare arms and legs and on the crown of her head was a healing warmth. They found a pink stucco motel, primly neat, fronted by geometrical patches of grass and gravel, and ringed by cypress. The walls of the room were coral pink and the spreads on the twin beds were also coral, scrawled with white nautical designs. They left their cases on the beds and walked to the restaurant close by, whose enormous sign was like a lighted tower signaling ships at sea.

She walked in, aware of their complementary beauty, the young mother and her young son, both pretending an easy familiarity with the place, although his pretense, she knew, was the result of shyness. He walked behind her, yet she knew, from having turned other times in other restaurants to ask him something, just how he looked, how one thumb was hooked in his back pocket and how he glanced neither to the right nor to the left but kept his gaze down to the level of her ankles.

She was glad to see that there were waiters here and no waitresses, and to their young waiter she made evident her consciousness of him as a man in the way she rested her elbow on the table and set her profile on view, and in the way she took a cigarette from her purse and smiled at him to light it for her. She shared her graces between the waiter and her son who, because of his attack on Russell, had made the unspoken demand of him to treat him as the man he was to become; and, afraid of that demand, she required an obvious flirtation with the waiter, almost an infatuation. The waiter's eyes wobbled away when their glances met. He told them, as he picked up soup bowls and laid down salad bowls, keeping his elbows close to his sides, that the weather yesterday had been very nice, the sun up hot and early. It was time, he said, for the fog to roll in. "Is there any fog on the horizon?" he asked, like one denied the sight of the day, although the restaurant's front windows looked out to sea. She reported that they had seen no fog, nothing, and laughed with the waiter over his moody refusal to glance out the window at the clear day that others were free to roam around in.

The tide was out when they strolled down to the water, so far out it left exposed a wide stretch of wet sand reflecting the sandpipers running over it. With his trouser legs rolled up, gesturing widely, David told her that the water was drawn far out like that before a tidal wave. He seemed elated by the prospect. She walked in step with him over the firm wet sand and through cool gusts of wind raised by the breakers. The flock of sandpipers rose up incredibly swift, skimming over the waves, turning so fast in one instant, flashing white, then dark. Far up the beach, the flock curved in again and landed. On the horizon lay a slate-blue bank of fog.

"You want to bet tomorrow is foggy?" she said, hugging herself against the thought of it. "There's nothing more dreary than fog by the ocean. Let's go to the mountains somewhere. Let's do that."

Once they had canceled their room, however, and carried their bags to the car, her desire to leave the town grew less and they spent several hours wandering the streets where the smart shops were, and they stayed on to eat a late supper out on the wharf. On the drive to the Santa Cruz mountains, he talked awhile about the day's trivia, uneasy, she knew, over his changing voice; then he was silent. She asked him if he were awake and heard no reply, but she suspected that the night and their aloneness for miles forced him to dissemble sleep.

It was past midnight when she drove into the parking area of a cabin motel, and whether he had slept for hours or had fallen asleep a moment before they arrived, he woke up only long enough to carry in his overnight bag and to undress and climb into bed. She switched off the paper-shaded lamp that stood on the small table between the beds and undressed by the yard light. She lay with her back to him and the room, her gaze on the vine that webbed the screen high in the wall, afraid to move, afraid that the small sound of the turning of her body would be enough to wake him.

16

The morning was hot and filled with the chitter of birds. David was already gone from the room when she awoke; she heard him talking in the yard with a woman. She peered out through the screen. The yard was struck with sun, a shock of white space in which she could not locate him.

They ate their breakfast at a cafe near the motel and took the trail suggested to them by the proprietor, climbing up through the silence of the day that seemed to resound off the mountains in waves. Small lizards ran off the narrow trail into the dry grass, stopping to lift their heads and look back. David kept his eyes on a large bird circling so that he could name it for her; but it soared away as if it were swept off to the side by some wide current of heat. When she climbed ahead of him, he darted side to side so that his voice could reach around her, and when she came along behind him, he paused on the trail to turn and tell her something to her face, and sometimes he walked backwards. A dog was barking down below, and the sound was isolated by the silence, and magnified and like another sound, a sound she had never heard before, the barking of a beast that went by the name of dog. This discovery of the unfamiliar in the dog's barking set off an elation in her breast. A delight in the preposterous. And she was delighted with herself for running away from her husband, for running away from her marriage, for running away from everything that bound her.

She stepped off the trail into a clearing and sat down on a rock in the scanty shade of a tree, counting on the prosaic act of resting and smoking a cigarette to bring her down to the prohibitive world again. A long time ago someone had begun to erect a cabin in the clearing and had given up. Around them lay rusty chains and saw blades, a mound of yellow newspapers, pulpy and mixed with the gray stuffing of a moldy mattress; and the giving up, after hauling up the trail the materials of the future, was further cause for the ridiculous elation that the barking of the dog had set off. The sun was directly overhead, the shade was not enough, and the sweat ran down from under her breasts to where her shorts were belted in. David had taken off his shirt and was wiping his chest and face with it. Up in the tallest tree an insect was making a ringing noise, a high-pitched humming like a sound of torment, as though the sun was slowly burning its edges away.

David spoke to her, but all she heard was the waiting silence after his voice. She wanted him to know her body again as he had known it as an infant or to know her body as he had not known it, like a lover who had been unconscious of who it was he had loved, who had loved a woman for a time and yet not known the person she was; and she wanted to know his body as she had known it and claimed it when he was an infant and as it would be in the years to come when he was apart from her, and she wanted this knowledge of each other to put them forever apart from everyone else, as covertly wise persons were apart. She glanced over at him as he leaned against a tree two yards away from her. Gazing at her, he looked stricken and pale in the sun, like someone waiting to be sacrificed. She ground her cigarette into the dirt. There were dry pine needles and rust-colored leaves on the ground, and as though she were concerned about starting a blaze, she continued to grind the cigarette with the sole of her shoe, sending all the wanting down into the earth.

They went down the trail to the highway, he following her from afar. On the edge of the highway, as they walked together again, unspeaking, she placed her hand on his shoulder, needing to assure herself that she had meant him no harm.

In the motel swimming pool, in the midst of countless children, she was kicked by beating feet, water splashed in her eyes and shouts rang in her ears, and she dodged small, sharp elbows. She often lost sight of him; once saw him talking to a girl a year or two older than he, both of them holding to the edge of the pool and with only their heads above water. The girl's light brown hair in wet strands to the shoulders, the small, delicate profile, the unformed and forming spirit, brought her a moment's anguish. Surrounded by splashing young bodies, she suspected that if she were to drown she would not be missed, that she would lie at the bottom of the pool, and for hours, for the entire day under the sun, the young bodies would splash above her. Even when her body was discovered she would not be missed. So now, in the time before she was drowned, in the time before the water seeped under her cap and the chlorine turned her bleached hair green and she became a grotesque drowned woman, in the time before she was dead and revealed, she must experience a union with him that was more than with any other person on earth. It was not enough to have given him birth, it was not enough to be his mother, that union was not enough. Mothers were always of the past and never of the future. A boy rose straight up out of the water directly in front of her, bumping against her legs and breasts. For a second he looked at her with bright, unseeing eyes; then he struck away from her and was at once lost among the other shrill and splashing children. Frightened, she climbed from the pool, away from all the quick, contemptuous bodies in the water.

When she had dressed, she walked down the highway to the cafe. She slipped a morning paper from the rack and was opening it to read at the counter while she drank her coffee when David got onto the stool beside her, his body wet, his bare feet coated with the dust of the highway. Unspeaking, they ate side by side, he with his back humped and his head bent down, and shivering a little. Some water ran down his temple, some dripped from his trunks to the floor. She was pleased with his alarm—it was like an outburst, a confession—and at the same time she was afraid of it and of the pleasure that she took in it.

While he put on his clothes, she waited for him in the yard, and they walked for miles along the highway, past motels and cabins and streams. Not only the exercise but the immense, vertical, judicial monotony of the forest was tiring. She saw the forest as austere and disinterested, but she knew that, if they were to rest again among the trees, the judicial aspect would dissolve within the heat and the silence.

On the way back they ate supper at a small restaurant in another motel, sitting at a green Formica table; then they returned to their cabin and lay down on their beds, flat on their backs, with their dusty shoes still on. The air was cool with the onset of evening and the yard light in the trees began to filter into the room as the twilight deepened. He slipped off her sandals and tucked around her feet the Indian blanket that lay folded at the foot of the bed. After taking off his shoes he lay down again on his bed, watching her. In the yard a group of guests were talking together. She knew by their voices and laughter who they were—provincials, churchgoers, probably off a tour bus.

"Sounds like a bunch of fools," she said. She sat up, lit a cigarette, and, leaning back against the wall, with the red glass ashtray on her lifted knees, she comically mimicked the voices, the cackling laughter, attempting to destroy the importance of the ones who saw no reason within the unreasonable and who never forgave an aberration. But she knew that her ridicule would fail if only because she wanted it to fail. She wanted those densely stolid persons out in the yard to interfere. They were judges, a convocation of judges.

David lay gazing at her, absorbed by the suspect interplay of her low voice with their loud ones. When the group wandered away, she got up, covered him with a blanket, then lay down again under her own blanket. Later in the night she heard him undressing in the dark and lying down again. A wind was rising, rattling twigs against the roof, and she fell asleep within the mingling of darkness and wind and trees.

17

They returned to the city in the morning and found the house unlocked and all her husband's belongings gone. He had taken nothing more than his personal possessions—his clothes and his papers and his few books on real estate and his skis, but all that was left, everything that belonged to the house and to her, was less, as if most of the intrinsic value was gone. After a few days, this devaluation of the objects passed and she began to cherish each one as if each were proof of her attempt to build a sound and lasting marriage. She polished silver, fine wood, and brass, and when everything was polished and the settlement arrived at—after hours in her attorney's office haggling with Russell's attorney—and the house and its furnishings hers and the divorce filed, she was again alienated from the house. Each time a man was gone from her life she felt that the time with him had deprived her of all sorts of possibilities with another, with others. She felt that she had forfeited another kind of life for herself.

In the fall David began his first year in high school. Often he did not return home until a few minutes before supper, and after supper he wandered out again. She began going out to parties, as much to be with her friends as to avoid her son's avoidance of her, and sometimes she was the last to leave a party, coming home in the early morning.

With her cousin Teresa she opened a shop where imported craft was sold—brassware from India, sweaters from Sweden, glass from Mexico, something from almost everywhere. The shop was located in a block of other small, high-class shops—a florist and an interior decorator and a designer of chic maternity clothes. Sitting in a crimson sling chair all day, reading paperbacks, she was more bored than she had ever been in her life. With a graceful gliding down of her hands to pick up an object for a customer, with a graceful cupping of the object, stroking it as if it were alive, she attempted to engross herself in the shop, in the objects tinkling and glittering, fragile, transparent, iridescent, gilded. But the attempt failed, and she sold her interest and looked for another occupation to keep her away from the house and to engage her.

She served as a volunteer saleswoman in a shop operated by the young matrons' league to which she belonged; clothes discarded by wealthy women were sold there at very low prices and the proceeds given over to charity. The hours dragged while she fended off, with her cigarettes and mint chocolates, the stale smell of the place, of the dry-cleaned clothes mixed with the smell of shop dust. One afternoon, alone, she found the staleness unbearable. The staleness had got into the nice, clean garments that hung in rows under discarded prints of van Gogh and Currier & Ives and Chagall, also for sale; the staleness was in the shoes, worn to the shape of the past owners' feet and whitened or blackened, and with new rubber heels; the staleness was in the thin carpet whose colors and pattern were worn down to a drab gray; it was in the table on which her elbows rested, the scars evident under the coat of chartreuse paint. It seemed to her that the staleness had been present in the garments even while they were being worn by whoever had bought them first, and that it was present in everything that covered the body or decorated the house because, soon enough, the dress and the vase and the rug and the necklace would all belong to the past. A light, cold rain was falling; the Chinese paper lantern with its silk tasseled cord, hanging from the ceiling, shook a little, and the wind suddenly banged against the door with the weight of a falling body. She put on her raincoat and locked the door.

By taxi she went up the hill to the Mark Hopkins hotel and, after ordering a drink in the bar off the lobby, she telephoned the man she had spent the night with two nights before, a married man who kept an apartment of his own as a condition for remaining with his wife and two children. She wanted desperately to lie with him in the afternoon while others were at work, while others engaged in their acts of charity, while everything went on that always went on. She required his need of her in an hour when he ought to be engaged in something else, in whatever was the protocol, the ritual, the complexity of his occupation; she required the certainty that she had persuaded him to come to her for that hour and to postpone all else.

"So I ran out," she said, leaning back against the wall of the booth, her voice down low in her throat, her mouth close against the phone. "Let me tell you I couldn't get out of that smelly place fast enough. I felt like I was smothered."

"Listen, Viv," he interrupted. "I'm snowed under here."

"Me too, me too. Nicky, love, I know just how you feel." She was unable to let him go, unable to get set for the plunge down into panic. "Listen, can you drop everything for a minute and come up here? I mean we can go and sit at the top, if you want, and watch the rain come down on the roofs way down beneath us. Don't you think that'd be exciting?"

"I can't," he said, his voice impersonal suddenly. "I'd love to, but I can't."

"Well, if you'd *love* to, you've got to do it," she said. "Think of all the opportunities you've had in your life to do the things you'd love to do and didn't do. I met a man the other night whose brother just threw everything over and went to Tahiti. Thriving, really, a canning executive, just like you, only in St. Louis, can't remember, or Iowa, and never came back. Got six mistresses over there, no seven, and all that beautiful scenery. If you'd try and make a list of all the things you let yourself miss, you couldn't, you'd break right down and cry. Go on, start making your list. You don't have to write it down, just make it in your head. Go on." She gave him a few seconds and felt the loss of the hour, of the man, of whatever value she wanted him to impart to her with his acquiescent desire. "Listen, if you don't want a drink, you might want to do something else," she said, afraid that he had not understood the reason for her call. "You might want a different kind of break in the middle of the day. You want to go up to your place? You want to meet me there?"—trying with her husky voice, with the murmurous volition of her voice, to convince him of his need of her at that hour.

"There's nothing I'd like better," he said. "But there's nothing I can do about it."

"Nicky, baby. Baby, you there?" she pleaded, her voice like her voice in his ear or over his body.

"Viv," he begged.

"Listen, baby, I'll die if you don't," she said. "I'll pass out in the lobby here. That's what they pass out from, those women you see passing out in lobbies. They tell you—I mean when they're carried off and revived—they tell you they just had a tooth extracted or they ate something, but they're lying. They die of what you're doing to me."

"Viv, where are you?" he asked, when she was silent.

"You haven't been listening. The first thing I said to you," she reminded him, "was, 'Nicky, baby, I'm at the Mark.' "

"You want a taxi home?" he asked. "I'll call you a taxi to take you home."

"Nobody was ever so good to me!" she cried. "Like sit way over in his office and call me a taxi way over here. God, you have no idea what that means to me. Nobody ever."

"Viv, come off it," he begged.

"You know what I think of a man who puts a woman in a taxi? I don't care whether he's right there on the curb or a mile away. The man who puts a woman in a taxi and turns around and walks the other way has got no intimation of what's going to become of her. He doesn't know and he doesn't care. That's what I think of a man who calls you a taxi."

"Vivian, for the love of God, hang up," he pleaded. "So I don't have to hang up on you."

"Say uncle," she said.

"Oh God—uncle."

She went back to her table in the bar and sat very erect on the banquette, flushed with shame. She lived, as she had learned a long time ago, by delusion and desperation, but there was nobody worth the agony, no man, not even God, nobody worth the desperation to entice and to impress, nobody worth the delusion that she was invaluable to him and he invaluable to her. She ordered another drink, caressing the back of the waiter's hand when he set it down before her. They were friends, she knew him by name, and she knew he was prepared, if she glanced up, to wink at her consolingly. When the glass was empty, she put on her raincoat with the waiter's help and went out through the lobby to where the taxis came in under the canopy.

She called to her son from the doorstep, her harsh voice grating her throat. She had no idea of what she would do with her anger if he were home; perhaps strike him across the back as she had done that once when he was a small child, strike him with her fists while he hung his head, unwilling to prevent her because he knew why she was striking him. She called to him again when she entered the house.

David came from the kitchen, another boy behind him, both young faces apprehensive.

"Ah, you've got friends!"

"We're cooking supper," he said. "I thought you weren't coming home."

"Am I invited?" She looked past him to his friend, who stood with his thumbs hooked in his pockets, a boy who knew something about her, something told him by David. In his eyes, in his face was his expectation of her as an exciting woman, a woman who had lovers. She was pleased with that expectation, enjoying and deprecating with her own glance his germinal knowledge of her.

"Well, don't we introduce people around here?" She threw her raincoat over a chair in the kitchen, and, learning his name, she shook hands with the boy. He peeled off his sweater, wanting to hide his face from her for the few seconds the sweater went up over his head.

She ate the fried eggs and ham with more gusto than they, sitting indolently sideways at the table so that her crossed legs were around the corner from the boy, almost under his elbow; enjoying his appreciation of her as a woman who complimented him with her nearness, gauche as he was, adolescent as he was. None of the desperation remained from her encounter on the telephone, for in the presence of a stranger her desperation gave way to a charming vivacity. She laughed at the friend's jokes, told in a voice cracked with change and timidity. Then, carried away by her exuberant response to him, he told her a joke that was a joke boys kept among themselves, and she laughed so heartily that she had to hold her head in her hands, elated for that moment by his sight of her as a beautiful, laughing woman who knew boundless more than he did about the joke's meaning.

The friend was the same age as David, fifteen, perhaps a few months older, and with a remarkable symmetry of features. She could, she thought, introduce him to his manhood. She could leave her impression upon him for the rest of his life; she had only to ask him to return. But the boy was not desirable; he was desirable only in a brief fantasy because the fantasy was desirable, animating her body and alleviating the burden of her son's sulking face, that face more beautiful than any face in the world, that face deserted, left out from her involvement with his friend and sensing why it was left out.

She took up her raincoat, slinging it over one shoulder, and, as she went around the table to the door, she trailed her hand across the friend's shoulders and her son's, her touchan endorsement of their friendship that she had not intruded upon but had only fortified—she, the young mother who knew their yearnings more than other women, other mothers.

18

She brought into her home her father's friend, Max Laurie. Years ago he had played the hero's accomplice or confidant, roles that called for an actor of ambiguous looks, either handsome or homely in an attractive, manly way. She remembered him in the movies as having great, dark eyes, a broad face, and a forehead made low by the bangs of black hair; now he was in his fifties, his hair gray, his body smaller. He had been an actor with a name, and he had lost most of his money to three wives and two children. She knew that in his youth he had been virile, that he had basked in women's flirting, and that his grateful surprise with their flirting had endeared him to them. The night she had first met him, years ago during the war—when he had come into the lounge with her father, her father's mistress, and the actress in furs, the night of the day Roosevelt had died—she had been attracted to him. And after he moved up to San Francisco, she had been attracted again whenever she had met him in the company of her father or of some divorced socialite.

One afternoon she encountered him in a restaurant where she had gone for coffee and cake after shopping. He told her that he suffered from a heart condition, gazing at her with an appealing, sorrowing gleam of doubt, as if no woman could love him because his heart was impaired. Everything he did now was hesitant—shyness and hesitancy had become part of the act of the aging celebrity. Years ago he had pretended to be surprised by adoration; now he was truly surprised by deterioration. It was cancer he was dying of. Her father, who was his physician, had told her.

He lived in a small apartment, riding a slow, clanking elevator to get up to it and going along a narrow, dark hallway with mustard-brown walls flecked with gilt. Outside, the building was very white in the sun. It rose to twelve floors, way above the others around it, and had its own parking lot; the interior was a dark hive. His bed opened out from the wall; the curtains were heavy and floral, and so was the upholstered furniture. Slick photographs of himself in his most famous roles were pinned to the walls of the small kitchen.

The love she made to him in the dark apartment was tender and asked for nothing in return. Lying against him, caressing his grateful body, she invited him to come and live with her. He opened alarmed eyes: "Not an old man with a heart condition." She kissed the gray, crinkled hairs in the shape of a triangle on his belly and told him that she knew his trouble, that he had no reason to hide it from her, and that she would take care of him.

She knew that he saw her as her father saw her—uncritically, aware of her faults but amused by them, and amused by her virtues, as if she were still a child forming and growing, and it was not known how she would turn out; but she knew that he was wondering about her reason for wanting to take care of him. At no other time, with no one else, had she demonstrated self-sacrifice. Since he had always carried on a detached flirtation with her, one that an actor would feel called upon to engage in with the daughter of his best friend, she was able to convince him that she had always been drawn to him and that she was making up now for the years she had denied them the rich possibilities of an affair. When he protested that the presence in her home of a man to whom she was not married would be unacceptable to her friends, she mimicked the disapproval he was anticipating on the faces of her friends, and the mimicry roused his actor's admiration for those who put something over harmlessly and with bravura. So he gave up the apartment that he had lived in for seven years and came with his suitcases to her house, and she began to devote herself to him as if it were an involvement she had looked forward to all her life.

She saw to his every comfort, she brought him gifts, cakes of the most lavishly expensive soap, leather brushes, silk pajamas, and at night she went into his room to make love to him. She knew he continued to wonder about her, and that he found no reason for bringing him into her home and giving over her days and nights to serving him. When he was no longer ill at ease, when he no longer accepted her devotion with an edge of toleration as if it were forced upon him, she knew that he no longer wondered.

David had always been entertained by the actor, humored by him, livelier with Max than with anyone else. But now he seemed to have no memory of their friendship. Her son avoided the guest just as he avoided her, but his avoidance of her was more demanding than ever. She felt that his need of her was greater than anyone's need of her, ever, and that her need of him was a somnabulist's need beyond waking caution, and so they passed each other in the house, asking of each other something more than anyone else was able to give. He was rapidly growing tall, and they had a joke about it, the only joke left between them—that he would wake up some morning and raise the roof; and each morning she pretended that he had grown another yard in the night, and she slipped by him, cowering. He was as tall now as his father had been, not heavy in the legs or afflicted with his father's clumsiness, but slender, and there was always a calm alertness in the turn of his head, a grace in the turn of his body.

He was always alone. He brought no friends home, and she sometimes wondered if he had any, but this lack of friends did not trouble her. Instead, she was pleased about it because he seemed in his aloneness to be a more convincing figure of a boy who was to become a man sought after, a man who would make aloneness a way of life and be sought after because of it. His aloneness was proof that he would make something of his life, and she desired this with more fervency than she had ever desired anything for herself; but, passing him and wanting to touch his chest or his face or his dark head to bless him on his way, she held back her hand because she knew it could not bless him.

She devoted herself to Max with the intensity of a penitent. She saw to everything and to that desire which she thought uppermost after his desire to live. She came at night into his room, wearing a negligee or a kimono. She came barefoot down the hall, clean and fragrant from an hour of bathing and massaging herself with lotion; and even during the steep, downhill months, when he often seemed oblivious of her, she continued to come to him.

One night she lay down beside him as usual and opened her clothes in her usual way that was a caressing open. He had lain all afternoon and evening in sedated sleep, moaning and alert to his moaning, waking at the sounds with a start and a look of dread. He took her wrist and thrust her hand away, at the same time turning his face away from hers.

"It's obscene," he complained. "There comes a time when it's obscene."

She was not sure that she had heard him right. He seemed to be muttering in a dream. Wounded, unmoving beside him, she asked him if he was awake.

"God says there's a time and a place for everything," he said, his face turned upward again. "I'm awake."

"Let a man die in peace," he said. "Let a man get hold of his mind before he dies. No distractions. I never knew what my mind was for except to make a woman or a buck. Leave me alone so I can get acquainted with my mind. You act like I wait here all day thinking of you. It's obscene when it's not the right time, and the time's not right anymore for me. Last night I dreamed of earth turned over. You know, with a shovel. Or maybe I dreamed it a minute ago. I saw how it looks to God, and I don't like it that way. I'm afraid to see things that way." He sat up to cover himself with the folded blanket at the foot of the bed, unfolding it over himself as he lay down again, unconscious of his act.

She sat up, her back to him, covering her breasts with her negligee. All her life she had been expecting this castigation from men for intruding on their lives, even though they beckoned and begged.

"Viv, listen, little girl," he pleaded. "You have to remember I'm not always in my right mind. Now this way I feel, about the dream, you know, that might mean I'm out of my mind. Maybe I'm not in touch with the mighty things, maybe I'm just dreaming crazy dreams cut down to my size. I don't say no to you because I'm thinking mighty thoughts. Maybe I say no because I'm tired, I don't have the old stuff in me anymore. That's the only reason, there's no big reason. You hear me, Viv?"

She said nothing, leaving him to his dream. Someday, some year, somebody was to be left out of her last dream, no matter how much she might love that person, even more than her life.

After that night, she never came again to caress him, and never caressed him while she bathed him and changed his garments unless he caught her hand and laid it upon himself. But in the last months when he could not leave his bed, she was at his call every hour, alleviating—as her father had instructed her—his coughing and his suffering. She lost weight and neglected her appearance. She went around unbathed, her cotton dresses, her linen dresses, bought in anticipation and in enticement of the pleasures of other summers, now soiled and stained. Oblivion was an expression in his eyes; his eyes grew darker each day, more globular, the depths going back to forever, and she felt that she, too, looked that way from gazing so long into his face.

Her father visited Max every other day as the months wore on, concerned more about his daughter's condition of servitude than he was about his friend. His friend was dying, he was not the first or the last to die. When, before, her father had come once a week to play chess with his friend, he had seemed to accept her devotion to the man as something aberrant, inexplicable, and yet something he expected of her and was not surprised by. Now he was surprised at the endurance of her devotion.

One day he sat with her in the patio under the large fringed and scalloped pink umbrella she had bought just before the end of her marriage to Russell, and that now seemed frivolous. For some days her father had tried to convey to her with his deploring eyes his fear that she had lost her mind. She sat under the umbrella with him, her bare legs out in the sun. Every year at the beginning of summer she had always engaged in an indolent race with other women of her circle to acquire an early tan; now, after having denied herself most of the summer sun, it seemed to her that she had not felt the sun's warmth for years. But because her legs were responding to the sun, because she wanted to drop her knees apart, and because her feet in frayed gold mules were warmed, the arches drawing up, she turned her pink canvas chair with great effort toward the table to put herself in the shade again, to deny herself the sun that the man in the house was to be denied forever. With her elbow on the table, she held her chin in her hand, smoking, offering her pale face to her father's deploring eyes, remembering that she was intolerable to him whenever, as a child, her hair was frizzled by a permanent wave or she had grimaced or acted clumsy. On display for him now were her broken fingernails, the spots on her dress, her hair growing in darker, each separate disrepair a separate unhappiness for him because each particular of her beauty had once been so important to her.

"What's going on?" he demanded. "For a while I figured it was some old fixation, some old girlish passion you never let on about, but that's ridiculous. It was ridiculous when I thought of it and more so now as he gets worse. You want to tell me what's going on?"

"He's more comfortable here than at his place," she said.

"That tells me nothing," he said. "The reason he's more comfortable is that you're waiting on him every minute of the day and night. God, I don't know how you stand it. You're not used to anybody dying, like I am, and even I couldn't stand the continual proximity. I avoid dying people. What I want to know is why. You want to tell me why?"

She was silent, her chin in her hand, gazing away from him as if troubled by the sun around her. His mind was pat, she thought, his and her mother's and her brother's, and she waited now for him to produce a pat answer to the question he had asked her. He was, she felt, way up in the top row of the gallery, unable to make sense of her performance, straining for the simple meaning of it.

"It's punishment," he said.

"For what?" she asked him, wondering if he could, in his way, actually come upon an answer.

"It's *like* punishment," he said, more cautious.

"For what?" she repeated.

"You tell me," he said. "You tell me for what."

She cradled her face in both hands, confronting him with her full face like a child waiting for an answer to a riddle. "For my crimes?"

"What the hell crimes have you committed? If it's punishment for a crime, it's one you only imagine you committed."

"I didn't imagine my life," she said, grimacing against the tears, observing his disgust with her grimace and with her fingernails set up to conceal it. "Sometimes I *think* I imagined it."

"Oh, God," he said. "You're nowhere near the menopause and

you're wailing about what you did and didn't do with your life." He reached out to grasp her wrist, consolingly.

"You don't like to see my face when it cries," she said, pulling away from his hand. They sat for several minutes in silence.

"Maybe I'm punishing myself because I let too many men see me cry," she said. "I shouldn't have done that to them, or to me. And I don't mean just cry. There are ways of crying other than this way. There are ways like accusations, like belittling, like ways I don't want to say. If you think I'm punishing myself, taking care of Max, you may be right."

Again they were both silent. Then, veering away from the unfamiliar, her father went on. "You ought to make yourself attractive to him. It worries him that you're neglecting yourself. He told me. He feels responsible, of course. Otherwise," he said, having received no promise, no reply, "he'll figure you want everybody to know what you're doing for him. You're making something terribly public about it, looking that way."

"Nobody sees me," she said.

"So nobody comes by anymore?" he asked, derisively.

"Max's wife, his last one," she said. "That's all."

"Your son sees you," he said. "He's more important than the others, anyway. You ever wonder what he thinks—his mother waiting on a stranger day and night, looking like a hag?"

"He'll understand when he's older."

"I'm older and I don't understand."

"You're not David."

She walked beside him around the house to his car, impressing her presence upon him, her ravaged presence, so that if ever he was to have any greater knowledge of her, he would remember that she had atoned for whatever she had done in her life that ought to be atoned for.

19

The presence of Max Laurie was like a great impassable hand between herself and her son. The disintegration of the man, the constant grappling for his body by nothingness, served as a barrier between herself and her son, who was becoming, that summer of his sixteenth year, the man she had imagined for him when he was a child.

Each day of the warm spell at the end of summer she bathed Max's body as he lay in his bed. "I wish I had never hurt anybody in my life," he said to her, stroking her arm.

"How many have you hurt?" she asked, humoringly.

"Everybody I've ever known," he said. "Not deliberately. I'll say deliberately, because in the back of my mind I knew what I was doing. I used to say it was circumstance, but I think it was me. I don't know what it was. It might have been circumstance after all. But whatever it was, nobody should be hurt. They'll die too, and whatever dies shouldn't be hurt while it's alive."

"You want to be a saint?" she asked.

He frowned a deep, intolerant frown that closed his eyes, a frown that was a revelation to her of the turbulence at his core. Then, still with his eyes closed, he began stroking her arm again.

"The only reason I'm talking this way," he said, "is because I'm sorry nobody knows who the other one is, what's troubling him, what's in his heart. I don't know why you brought me here. I know it wasn't because of any great love for me. I don't know why, but you've been more than kind, and whatever it is that's troubling you, I want you to know that I wish I could help you, and that's the way I want you to remember me—that I wished I could help you."

"You help me," she assured him.

"Sometimes I feel like I haven't been tested yet," he went on, "that my life hasn't been lived yet. I feel like a boy who hasn't been put to the test yet, and I feel old, like I've been through the mill. I feel both. But I think I feel mostly that I haven't been tested yet, that more was expected of me. But what? What more? I should have done what I want others to do for me now—weep over me. It's the indifference that scares me. When so many die at once, in the war, in the concentration camps, what else can you do but be indifferent when one man passes out of the picture? Or maybe it was the indifference that led to everything. That's why I feel my life hasn't been lived yet. What did I do about the indifference? Was I supposed to do something about it?"

"I don't know, I don't know." The cloth was absorbing the heat of his body. She dipped it into the bowl of tepid water and continued to bathe him, resisting the loss he was leading her into, the loss not only of him but of all the men of her life, the men she had believed were all more than this man's body was telling her they were.

He stroked her bare arm, down from the shoulder. "I wish somebody would keep a light on for me, like my mother did for my father," he said. "It's one of those Jewish customs I forgot about. You light a candle or you keep an electric light on—every year on the day the person died. For his spirit. We had a dark hall in the apartment, we left the light on there. The way mother told it to me, it's to light his way to God. I used to think it took an awfully long time for him to find his way, it went on year after year. It's just a matter of being remembered, that's all. I did it one year for my mother and then I forgot, or I was ashamed to do it. Depends on who you're living with at the time. Maybe nobody does it anymore. Not since so many died at once. What's one light? But I think I'd like you to do it for me anyway. No promises, nothing like that," he insisted. "No promises."

20

When Max was taken to the hospital she kissed his brow and his hands in the presence of her father. She promised him, kissing his hands, that she would come by to visit him the next morning. Although he appeared to know what was happening to him, that he was being conveyed away, he did not seem aware of her kissing or of her promise or even of her presence.

In the hour following, she sat out in the garden, grieving over him, knowing that she would not visit him tomorrow or any day, that the sight of him while she kissed him had been the last sight. Around her she heard the sounds of the neighborhood's tranquility on a warm evening at the end of summer, but listened for sounds of violence and for violence without sound and for the return of her son that would deafen her to all sounds. With cigarettes falling from the package held upside down in her hands, she wandered into the living room and lay down on the sofa to wait for him. Exhausted by the heat of the day and by the countless nights of interrupted sleep, she slept, and was wakened by the fear that her son was not returning. It was night. She lit the lamp by the sofa and slept again.

"Is Max dead?"

She found she was lying on her side with her hands under her cheek, like a child. He had asked if Max was dead, she knew, because she had thrown herself on the sofa and appeared to be waiting to tell him. For no other reason would she be lying out there so startlingly.

"Where were you?" she demanded, sitting up, her question accusing him of solitude, of his young and slender body, of his response to the night, his skin paled by the night but everything else deepened— his curiosity, his innocence, his eyes. "You don't know and you don't care, that's what you think of Max." He went on toward the stairs to escape her anger, and she called after him, "David? Do you hear me?"

She followed him to where he waited by the stairs, his back to the wall. "They took him away," she cried, gripping his arms, lifting her face for him to see the spasms of grief, and he put his hand clumsily at the back of her head and pressed her face against his chest. With her hands covering her face, she went with him up the stairs as though returning to her bed to find rest and a cessation of grief and of all demands upon her, glimpsing through her fingers her bare feet climbing.

They sat together on her bed in an embrace of grief, until his consoling, his stroking her face and hands drew her down, drew him down beside her. She held his head with both her hands so that he could not elude her mouth moving over his face as if they both would die if she lifted it away, as if she were charged with the task of keeping them both alive. Against her mouth she felt his face pleading with her to save him from the world's chaos and to take him into the heart of that chaos. She undressed him and herself, his clothes among her own, as if she undressed one body, freeing them both from the flickering show of concealing and revealing that had gone on for the years of his life, and at last he lay beside her as he was to lie beside other women who were to be less now, forever less, than she, even as everyone in his life to come was to be less. She took his hands, guiding them to console her over more sorrow than he could ever imagine, guiding his body onto her body, at last obliterating the holy separateness she had given him at birth.

Stricken by the same fear, then, they were unable to move apart. The fear that someone, everyone, would discover them if they moved, that even the slightest movement would reveal them, that everyone in their life must sense their presence here together and would sound the alarm if they attempted to return into the order of things. Furtively, in stages, she unbent her legs, but he moved suddenly, arresting his body in a nightmare fall, and she held him down, warningly. The lamp by the bed was on; holding him to her with one arm, she lifted her other arm to switch it off. Then, in the dark, it seemed to her that she had never been so conscious. Never so conscious before of her dominion.

21

The hour before dawn foretold how stifling the day was to be. Although his face was only a few inches away, it seemed to have suddenly receded far into the past, lapsing into sleep, into unconsciousness to elude a comprehension as hoveringly near as her face. She drew herself away from him. She found her negligee on the floor and, drawing it around her, wondered where to go to hide from him so that when he woke he could claim he woke from a dream. But when she moved toward the door, he flung himself off the bed, falling to the floor.

The sounds of his body thrashing against the floor deafened her to her own voice calling to him. Kneeling by him, she found him very still, the stillness as frightening as his paroxysm.

"I'll sleep here, I'll sleep here," he said. But when she stood up, relieved to hear him speak of sleep, he lifted his head, coiling himself toward her feet, biting her ankle above the place his hands gripped it. She struggled to be free, wailing, and he released her, flinging himself away from her.

She went out to the garden and lay down on the canvas cot, on the scattered leaves. She lay unmoving in the warm dark that was filled with the voices of birds like the sound of daylight breaking through in many small places, and, sleeping, dreamed that she was running backward into sleep, a stumbling, ungainly, heavy backward run into sleep, escaping her son running toward her, her son at the age of three or four, in a white suit, with everything clean upon him, running toward her to wipe his face in her skirt and leave an irremovable stain.

She opened her eyes to the sunlight of midmorning and closed them again. She was lying in the sun, unprotected by shadow, exhausted by the sun and by sleep itself, by the days and nights without sleep, by the memory of the night, and unable to rise and drag the cot into shade. She slept again, this time her sleep an oppression upon her like a sorrowfully familiar body, and woke to the sun exactly overhead, her face upward to it, the negligee fallen open and her body in a slattern's torpor. Rising, she returned to the house through the dense, obscuring sun, but stood outside the door, afraid to enter and afraid to see him again, wanting never to see him again and never to be seen by him, and, at the same time, feeling the loss of him as if he had died while she slept and her grief was never to be less.

For the rest of the day she remained in the garden, by the table in the shade of the umbrella, or wandering the narrow flagstone paths, waiting for her son to come out to her and forgive her. At the end of the afternoon, overcome by the conviction that she had denied all day, the conviction that he was gone, she entered the house. The silence, and even the fact that she could not find him, did not prove that he was gone; the silence was his taciturnity that she had experienced for so long. She accepted his absence only when she stood by the window of her bedroom, looking down on the leaf-littered cot where she had lain. Sometime during the morning, she knew, he had looked down, and it was to be his last sight of her.

22

Early in the evening she went out, afraid that he might return that night. She concealed her face with cosmetics like an actress hoping to conceal herself with a false face. She put on a yellow taffeta dress she had bought a year ago when Max had come to live with her; she put on her gray calf shoes whose color was a subtle silver, also bought a year ago; and though the night was warm she put on her long mink coat that Russell had given her for her birthday, their last year together. She had the appearance of a woman convalescing, who, in haste, in terror of falling ill again, applies her beauty awry. Afraid to remain at home and afraid to go out, she drove to her parents' house. The excuse that she gave to her mother, who was home alone, was that she had been on her way to a dinner party and felt ill and, since she had been near to her mother's house, she had decided to rest there awhile.

"My God, Viv, furs. It's a warm night," her mother said when Vivian threw off her coat to lie down on the sofa. "Is it chills and fever?" She placed her small, smooth palm on Vivian's forehead. "You're tired out. You've exhausted yourself taking care of Max. Are you cold?" She laid the fur coat over her daughter, up and over the breasts in the tight, saffron taffeta cups and up over the bare shoulders. "You may have caught something from him. I don't mean what he had, of course. I mean something else—the fear. When a young person like you is around somebody who's dying, she can't help but catch the fear."

"It's something I drank," Vivian called after her mother, who was already on her way through the delicately tinted rooms to the kitchen. She lay waiting for whatever her mother would bring, gazing down the length of her body, the length of the fur coat, to her feet in the silver shoes. If any confession was ever to be made it would not be made to her mother. A confession could never be made to any woman; there was more shame in confessing to a woman and nothing to be gained by it, no forgiveness that meant anything. To confess to a man, whether it led him to despise her or to forgive her, meant more, but it was not to be made to any man, either. She drew the coat over her mouth and nose.

Her mother returned, bearing a teapot and cups on a tray. "If you'd rather have coffee or sherry . . . "

"No, no, it's tea I wanted." She swung her legs down and sat up, holding her coat up around her to her chin, and reaching around it to lift the cup and saucer from the tray.

"You're thin," her mother said. "You're thin as a rail. You ought to go to Hawaii. Teresa's there—she's always lots of fun—and some of your friends." She found her niece's letter in a novel on the coffee table, unfolded it, and read, while Vivian held the coat to her chin and sipped tea, commenting on the pleasures to be found in the islands.

"You haven't been out in so long," her mother said, apparently wondering if the year of her daughter's devotion to Max had damaged her wits so that, the day after the man was taken away, she stumbled out into the world, dressed as though on her way to a ball and going nowhere. "You look beautiful, but you've got so thin and you don't look after yourself. You ought to have gone to Nicole's to have your hair done."

The china began to rattle in Vivian's hands, and, leaning forward, she set the cup and saucer on the rug by her feet. "David ran away," she said, her head down, her fingers unable to release the rattling china.

"Vivian, lie down," her mother begged.

She lay down again and her mother drew the coat over her again.

"Where did he go?"

"At this point I don't care where he went. At this point he's on his own. At this point I don't care if he never shows up again. I never told you, did I, how jealous he was?" She threw off the coat and sat up. "What time is it?"

"Do you want me to phone and tell them you're not coming?" her mother asked.

"No, because I'm going," she said. She got into her coat with her mother's help. "You can't imagine how jealous he was of Max. Can you imagine—of Max? Not just him," she cried. "Of everybody. Of Russell. Because I don't come and tell you my troubles, you think I've got none."

"I know about them," her mother said.

"He's gone to the Pastori family at Clearlake. That's where he wanted to go. They've got a boy his age. He'll be all right. I drove him to the bus depot," she said, wanting to dispel the alarm from her mother's face, wanting no face near her that showed alarm.

She went upstairs with her mother because no one was waiting for her to sit down with the rest of the party. Her old room was immaculate, satin shining on the bed and walnut glowing. The silver-framed photograph of herself at the age of twelve in a ballet pose was obscured by the reflected light on the glass that covered it. She undressed while her mother was out of the room finding a nightgown for her, and, waiting, she covered herself with her slip, afraid that her mother would sense, at the sight of her nakedness, what use the daughter had made of her body. She let the slip fall to her lap as her mother helped her draw on the gown, a pink gown fragrant with sachets, yielding to the gown like a small girl who needs help with undressing.

"I told him to go," she said. " 'Goddamn it, go,' I said. 'What do you think, that you're going to stay with me forever, looking at me with those baleful eyes?' Isn't that what kind of eyes he has? Like somebody in a storybook? Animals and awful creatures? Mama, you remember?"

Sitting up in bed, she held up the palm of her hand submissively for the capsule her mother put there, swallowing it down with port wine from the decanter that was kept in her mother's room.

23

She waited for him with dread, and the few times she went out she expected to find him somewhere in the house when she returned. Waking in the morning or at noon or in the night, she was at once alert to the possibility of his presence by her bed. Wanting to be far away, she was unable to leave because he had no other person to return to; there was no other person from whom he had got sustenance, got love.

In the second week of his absence, a letter came from Las Vegas, from Paul, his father. Through the years, he had sent the boy a few letters and a snapshot of himself and his wife, smiling into the glaring sun of that desert city. David was with them, he wrote, and although the boy had asked them not to tell her, they were sure she was troubled by his disappearance and they thought it best to inform her of his whereabouts. And for another reason it was best: the boy was miserable, and they were trying to persuade him to return to her so that she and David could talk over their bad feelings and forgive each other for whatever the quarrel was about. A few days after the first letter a second came: David had been put aboard a bus to San Francisco.

She waited with the curtains closed. On the sixth day, when she went out to the sidewalk box to pick up the accumulation of mail, she found a letter from David, mailed from Galveston, Texas. The sight of his handwriting was like a confrontation. She could not stand, and sat down on the steps to read.

Vivian. In large letters, with pencil, her name was scrawled across the top of the scrap of paper. *I want you to die. If you die I won't have to. I hope when you read this it will be like a curse that works. Maybe you won't even get to this line.* He had not signed his name.

She left the city that day, driving her mother, and her mother's two poodles, to her parents' summer home on the shore of Lake Tahoe. She lay out in the sun on the wide deck of the house, drowsing and pretending to drowse, wakened often by the fear that he was gazing down at her from upstairs, sometimes shaken awake by her mother, who said that she had been crying in her sleep. In her mother's face she saw how her own face must appear down on the cushions. Her mother's face, bending over hers, was her own face in the years to come, the face of herself as a past woman, alone and alarmed; and she drew her mother down upon her.

At her mother's urgings she had her hair cut and bleached again, and she had a manicure and a pedicure. She bought flamboyantly flowered, very slim dresses from the resort shops, and delicate sandals with high heels and no backs, and, urged by her mother to a display of this artful care of her person, she strolled out with the two poodles into the crowds. Although she despised them for their yapping and the tension of their bodies, she reluctantly enjoyed the spectacle of herself and the dogs, whose fur was the white of her hair, all three of them exquisitely groomed.

After her mother's return to the city with the dogs, Vivian stayed on, spending her afternoons in the cool bars and in the casinos, bringing home her small winnings and sometimes a man she had chosen to sit down by. A long time ago, her first love after the birth of her son had separated her body from the infant's, but now the men she brought to her bed to obliterate her son failed to convince her that the body she lay against was not her son's, and waking with someone beside her was always a time of panic.

On her return to the city, late in October, she sold the house with its furnishings and antiques, taking with her only enough for her small apartment on Green Street in a building of four apartments signed over to her by her father shortly after the war. With her mother she sailed to Hawaii. On the boat, her mother, excited by the voyage, imagined that everyone mistook them for sisters, that her twenty-five years beyond her daughter's age were swept away by the sea winds. They stayed at one of the more seclusive hotels where they could settle down for a time without the constant bustling change of other guests and, in March, returned home by air.

She took a separate taxi, declining to go home to her mother's house. In the apartment, she sat down on the sofa, clasping herself, shivering with the change of climate as if the transition from sun to fog had taken no more than a minute. When the sound of the cab driver's footsteps, running down the stairs, was gone, the silence in the apartment, whose location and existence her son was ignorant of, became the silence that had swallowed both herself and her son.

Not long after her return, Joe Duggan, the attorney who had often visited in the time of her marriage to Russell, asked her out to dinner. He had separated from his wife; she had learned this some time ago. She disliked the man; he had always insinuated a knowledge of her and it had seemed to her that the basis for any insinuation was ignorance. She felt that he conversed not with her but with the woman he thought she was, while she sat listening to the dialogue like a third person. But, as in other times when she had been in need of someone, her criticism of her companion began to seem flimsy, and she wanted to believe he was capable of that knowledge of her most personal self. Then everything became attractive—his indisputable voice, his obviously elegant clothes, and his little blond mustache that was like a stamp of approval on his face.

In his apartment, with its leased view of the bay and the bridges, he inquired after David, and she told him what she had told her parents, that the boy was attending a private school in the East. He recalled the night at Clearlake when David had danced with all the women, also recalling that she had gone upstairs before the others. Insinuative, self-amused, he lay beside her, recalling.

"You've got everything, Viv," he said, "but one thing."

"What?" she asked, afraid.

"Something you had with Russell."

"What? What?"

"Something I couldn't have then. Now that you're with me, you don't have it anymore. All it is is what I couldn't have then." He held in his laughter; she felt the sputter against her throat. "Otherwise, you've got everything."

She could not bring herself to push him away. He knew so very little that his ignorance of her was like an unbearable vulgarity. And yet, with his lewd curiosity, he seemed to know everything, if only because he suspected everything. Lying beside him, she found that the memory of her son, the night with her son, was being reduced to what it would be in Duggan's mind if he knew about it, even as her life was being reduced to what it was in his mind. His curiosity forgave everything because everything fed his curiosity. Unresisting, she lay under him, kissing him in return, accepting his ignorance of her as if it were a forgiving wisdom.

In July, a few days before David's birthday, a letter came from him, postmarked El Centro, California, and forwarded from the house she had left. The handwriting was a barrier between him and herself, a fence beyond which all his experiences in the past year had gone on. It was written in ink, the letters neater and smaller than in the first letter. He was working, he wrote, on a date farm near the Mexican border. On his seventeenth birthday he wanted to enlist in the army, and that was why he was writing to her—because he required her consent.

She was unable, for a few days, to answer the letter or to go a notary to make out her consent. The request from her son surrounded her with the terrors of the world, as if only now she had been born into the midst of them. One night she dreamed that he was dying. He lay on her bed, in an army uniform, his head shaven. He begged her to lift him and carry him away in her arms to some place safe from death, but she was unable to approach him. She had entered the room with a group of strangers behind her, who appeared to be waiting for her to save him, but she could do nothing. The sensation of dying was in herself as it was in him.

She sought out a notary and found one in a hotel, in a cubicle off the lobby, a gray-haired woman whose eyes seemed a part of her bejeweled spectacles. In the legalistic words suggested by the notary, she gave her consent for her son to enter the army, and, after the consent was typed and she had signed it, she asked for an envelope. Then, pushing pennies across the corner of the desk with the tip of a gloved finger, she asked apologetically to buy a stamp.

Early in September, Duggan flew to Washington in the interests of a case, and from there to New York. The first few nights he telephoned her. On the fifth night he failed to call and she lay awake, reading, knowing it was too late for him to phone, but expecting him to wake up in the middle of the night on the other side of the country and remember that he had not phoned her, and in his imagination see her waiting. She fell asleep, waking at one o'clock to the light of the lamp she had left on, and, in that moment of surprising light, she was reminded of Max and of his plea to her to leave a light burning for him. She could not recall the date that he had died because she had never known the date. It was a short time after he was taken away; she had been told the day, but she had not known the date of that day and she had not attended his funeral. One night was as good as another as long as a year had gone by. He would, she felt, forgive her if she were in error by a few days.

With the light full on her face, she lay against the several pillows she had propped herself with to read, glad that there was no one around to ridicule her about the ritual or to disapprove of it, no one around to feel like an outsider in what might appear to be a most personal engagement of hers with someone not there. The light in the room seemed remote from its purpose. It was simply a light in an apartment among hundreds of lights in apartments all over the city, and how was one light to be separated from all others as the one that remembered him and lit his way? The purpose of the light was remote from the light, even as the ritual was remote from her, even as the man himself had been remote, even as all of them were remote. There was no illumination of anybody other than herself, lying alone, waiting for one of the remote ones to return and lie down beside her.

The
Lights
of
Earth

"A tremendous passion is this longing that our memory
may be rescued from the oblivion which overtakes others."

MIGUEL DE UNAMUNO

1

Years after the night of that strange little party her memory played a trick on her. Her memory set him among the others, the guest of honor who heard every word, who saw every gesture and every expression on every face. But he wasn't there. He wasn't even expected that night. He must have been still in Spain or New York or down in Los Angeles or over the continent on his way back to San Francisco. He must have been up in the sky, somewhere over all, as the suddenly famous ones seem to be.

The name of the couple whose house it was, the house where she had not been before and was never to enter again, seemed of no consequence and she didn't quite hear it. Later, when she knew the name of the wife, she was unable to say that name aloud. An ordinary name to anyone else, for her it was the shattering presence of the woman herself. The couple had asked Claud, a friend of Martin—the guest of honor who wasn't there—to bring Ilona along. Just by her presence and even without a word she might tell them something about the man who was her lover. Even though he was to appear soon, any day, their impatience threw open the door to her as wide as it would have been had he accompanied her. They must have been hoping for someone like him to come into their lives, each one's hope so ardently secret from the other that he must have seemed inevitable.

The oval glass in the oak door of the Victorian house was etched so profusely with grapes and leaves and tendrils it served as an impenetrable silver mist that with utmost graciousness denied you a view of what went on inside. A lamp or a chandelier in some far room glinted off the entwined grapes and turned them gold, now one and now another, a matter of how you shifted your feet or your eyes.

Claud had ridiculed the host on the way over, but now at the last moment the desire to be presentable forced him to comb down his hair, tossed by the wind. He wore a sportcoat with only one button missing and each pocket held a pack of cigarettes to protect him from his perverse need to smoke the couple's. Ilona had refused at first to come along. She had come only because the couple's curiosity about the man who was her lover stirred her own curiosity about something she wanted not to think about at all—a premonition of loss.

Grasping Claud's arm, shaking Ilona's right hand with his left, the host drew them inside, the three awkwardly linked. The host's jeans were faded, his hiking boots were grayed by rough use, and the most humble garment of all was his gauzy shirt from India. In those years, the early seventies, some affluent young were imitating the poor of the world. The shirt, however, failed to lessen his chest's prosperity. It was as obdurate as all other wealthy chests, narrow or broad, that she'd slipped by or asked something of, a job or simple directions, or brought something to, a tray of whatever was ordered.

Beyond the wide doorway to the dining room, the several persons lounging around the long table were like actors on a stage, made small by their surroundings and each striving to be seen and heard. Except one, who had no need to strive—the one among the women who was beautiful, and Ilona knew at once that the woman was the wife of the man who was guiding Claud and herself toward the table and knew that she was the eventual one, the one who takes away the lover, the one who is a reward in a time of rewards, and she wished for herself a time when presentiment of loss would never bother her because she would be wise enough to know that loss was as natural as breathing.

Ilona, seated across from the woman, looked instead at the couple's son, close to three years old, who sat elevated by cushions next to his mother, turning his gaze from one face to another, bending over his plate to see who was speaking at the end of the table, to see who was laughing. The little boy bore his resemblance to his mother like a gift whose value he knew about. His eyes, like his mother's, seemed balanced by serenity, by the trust that all he was to desire of life would be granted, and Ilona called upon reason to rescue her from her archaic view of the world that saw it divided between those who appeared to be blessed and those who appeared to be forsaken, and reason failed. She tried then to imagine at this table a great writer of the past, say a century ago, someone who had observed compassionately women who went unnoticed, but if that figure, whoever he was, were really to be at this table, absorbed again in life, his gaze would be on the beautiful wife, amazingly like a woman who had enthralled him a hundred years ago.

The host at the head of the table was accusing his guests of envy, envy of the man somewhere up in the air. "Severe envy. It's worse than hepatitis. More people die of it. Nausea, insomnia. But the worst symptom is impotence."

"You know that for a fact?" someone asked, and someone else laughed.

"Impotence," the host repeated. "Of the mind. Of the hand that holds your very own little pen. Look at Claud. Claud hasn't written one word in ten years and he'd like you to think he couldn't care less, he's through. But look. Overnight his hair's turned white and the whites of his eyes have turned green. Claud, let everybody see your eyes."

Claud was smiling, smoking a cigarette of his own. His hair was as dark as ever and his eyes as clear as they ever were. "If I'm dying it's not from envy. It's from what that Frenchman, Péguy, said—You die of your whole life. Not just one shock."

The host brought up a Time from under his chair, already open to the photograph of the absent guest of honor, and held up the magazine for all to see. Ilona had read the review weeks ago and the other guests must also have read it then, but everybody complyingly raised their eyes. Except the wife, who was placing tidbits from her own plate onto her son's plate, while the child gazed up anxiously at the picture, afraid of missing something so important to his father.

"One of those faces that haven't been lived in yet," the host said. "He's thirty-four and he looks nineteen and he'll look nineteen when he's ninety, God help him."

"I think . . ." A girl, afraid to contest with the host, appeared to be talking to her plate. "I think he deserves all the praise he's been getting."

Down came the magazine, down beside his plate, and his hand came down flat on the small picture. "I agree, I agree. That's why I've called you all together. To sing his praises. We'll practice every night, we'll gather here every night, and the night he walks in the door a heavenly choir shall greet him."

Like falsely obedient children who've bested a parent they took up their forks and wineglasses again, complacently silent. When the array of delicatessen delights on each plate was one or two bites less, the chatter began again—nothing about the novel itself but everything about those persons who were welcoming Martin Vandersen into the world: critics, and the movie producer who had bought the screen rights to the novel, and the director at whose villa on the Costa del Sol Martin had been a guest, and the actor who was sought for the lead. "Sought," cried the host, staring wildly upward. "One lousy actor sought like in 'they sought God,' like in 'they sought justice.'" But though they pleasurably interrupted one another with details about the lives of those legendary persons who were surrounding Martin at this birth, they appeared to be baffled over why they were so affected by somebody else's recognition, somebody else's entry into the light. She saw the bafflement in their eyes and heard it in their voices.

Out in the living room the host sat down at Ilona's feet, took off his boots, and attempted the lotus position. Apart from them, the others were talking loudly and his wife was upstairs, putting the child to bed.

"She had a lover in Italy last year," he said, low. "A good man. A fine sculptor. American, living in Florence. We would have been great friends if he hadn't been her lover. Your Martin reminds me of him. I met Martin a couple of days before he left, ran into him and Claud, and his resemblance to her last year's lover was remarkable. The looks, the wit." His glance slipped sideways on its way up to her face. "What's he like? I mean when you get to know him."

Bearing a tray of decanters and goblets, his wife came into the room, and the question seemed asked for her. They would have to answer the question themselves, each with a secret answer.

The man at her feet rocked back and forth, gripping his ankles. "How long have you known him?"

"Oh, four years." The number of years for lovers was supposed to mean something, a measurement of depth or truth, but numbers were revelations only for scientists. The things she knew about the lovers she'd never tell this man, and one was that love was never certain—who but herself thought it could be?—but that under the uncertainty of love lay the certainty of comradeness. What else wouldn't she tell? That when Martin had reminded her a time was to come when he would be elsewhere, she had listened reasonably and amenably, but they had pained her, those reminders, and once, afraid that if their time together was without love it was a wasted time, she had gone so far as to quote Camus. "You enrich the future by giving all to the present." Because she disparaged her own words, because her own words lacked persuasion, she relied on time-honored words. After that heavy-laden quote he did give up his warnings and reminders, perhaps believing that she already knew about endings and about elsewhere. But he was not persuaded to give all to the present.

Massaging his calves as though easing a cramp, the host asked, "Ah, you live together?"

"Yes, we live together." Her answer appeared to soothe him, he seemed to accept it as assurance that they would continue to live together and his wife and himself also continue to live together, with no outside interference. "Though sometimes we lived apart."

The man at her feet knew very little, probably, about makeshift dwellings that weren't your own and that convinced you of a destiny to be always without possessions and never even to desire them. So he might be unable to see that the way they lived together was another bond that made them kindred even apart. Six weeks ago, when Martin was in Spain or somewhere in Europe, the house across the bay, in the little town at the foot of the mountain, the house where they had lived together with her child, was sold, and she had found a small apartment in the city, hoping that when Martin returned they would find a larger one together.

"Claud tells me Martin used to live in a basement out by the ocean. Claud says the house was riddled with termites and their eggs or turds rained down on your friend's manuscripts. He said that in the flat upstairs the fleas were like a living carpet and when Martin went up there once to use the phone the fleas were all over him as soon as he stepped inside. He turned and ran."

Any creature, she thought, a flea, a fly, no matter how microscopically small, that's on or near a person who's become famous, joins in the celebration.

"Claud says Martin had only two plates and he put the cooking pot on the table. Claud says he kept his manuscripts in a grocery box and a mouse made herself a nest in there and gave birth, and he didn't know it and kept piling up the pages." A pause. "Was it deliberate? I mean, was it a show of poverty, like 'See, I was poor and now I deserve the rewards'?"

"It's what's called necessary poverty," she said. If it was an attempt at saintly asceticism so that when recognition came along nobody would want to deny him its rewards, she didn't want to know about it. She didn't want to know his superstitions, just as she didn't want to know her own. Superstitions, like clues to dark confusions, were too much to know about anyone and yourself.

"Claud says they've torn down the house and put up a motel. Too bad. What they should have done—the city, I mean, or the state, or even the federal government—was buy the house, restore it, and put up a bronze plaque that says Martin Vandersen lived here, and the dates. If they'd only known. And turn the basement into a museum. The pot and the two plates on the table, a stuffed mouse in the manuscripts, the bed made, the covers turned back like he's away on a journey but he's coming home any day now. You've seen pictures of Tolstoy's study? Everything just where it was when the great man died."

If Martin were present, and if she were to take him aside and point out to him this man's fear of him, this ridicule in the guise of praise, then Martin, who wanted never to suspect anybody, would say What's there to fear about me?

Over across the blue Persian carpet the wife was pouring brandy, and Ilona saw again how each particular of beauty, the beauty of any person, of any object, of anything on earth or in the heavens, leads you on, mesmerized, to all particulars, and she saw again how a woman's beauty seems to pardon that woman in advance for any betrayal, any transgression, for grief brought to others.

"If he's got no place to go," the man at her feet was saying, "he can stay with us until he finds a place. Plenty of room here," pointing heavenward. "Come on, I'll show you," leaping up, leaving his boots behind.

Climbing the stairs at his side, she saw how eager his feet in socks appeared, eager to run and prepare the way for an invasion of his privacy by the man up in the night sky.

On the middle floor they passed the half-open door of the master bedroom and she kept herself from glancing in. She might glance in on her way down. When you were on your way down you were already on your way out, like a trespasser discovered in the upper regions.

Gently he pushed the door to the boy's room a bit more open, motioning for her to step just inside and no farther. The child in the large bed, the lamp with its rosy shade, the shadows—it was like a very large oil painting with somebody in it preciously small.

"Does he resemble me?"

She had seen no resemblance at the table. It was as if the mother and the child had requested the artist to leave the father out of the picture.

"He isn't mine, you know." A pause. "You know about it? His father was Joseph Neely, the poet. They'd run away. He died of a heart attack in Greece, on one of those idyllic islands. She was in a terrible state. Grief, you know, and pregnant, and I went there. We cried together. My God, we held each other and cried for a whole day and a night." His hoarse whisper, his feet in socks—he was like a trespasser himself.

Up another flight, the last staircase uncarpeted, and the room they entered at the back of this floor contained only a narrow bed, a straight-back chair, a small table. No rug, no shade over the ceiling globe.

"If he lived that way in his basement he'll like this room the way it is. We haven't got to it yet. We'll find him some termites if they'll make him feel at home."

Was he expecting the guest to stay forever? Years later, when one evening she was passing through this neighborhood, the house that she did not want to identify for certain in the row of stolid and stately houses caught her eye and roused again the emotions of that time of loss. The host's fear of this guest who would stay on and on had been realized. The house had become the guest's, though the guest wasn't there anymore and hadn't stayed long at all, and the couple and the child weren't there anymore, and the house belonged to somebody else.

Restlessly he moved around the room, a host expecting one last guest before the festivities can begin, and she thought: He throws open all doors and begs loss to enter. Had he brought her into this almost bare room so that she might give him evidence in advance, just by her presence, of how his life was to be changed by the guest who would soon be lying in the narrow bed, sitting down with them to their meals, reclining on their couches, lying in their tub? The guest would even play the grand piano downstairs, the accomplished musician that he was, and a raconteur besides, whose every word would be given rapt attention. Once you leap out of obscurity so many talents come to light.

Awkwardly, as though embarrassed, he faced her from a corner. "You know I write myself? Claud must have told you. That's my study, the other door."

Was he waiting for her to ask him what his novel was about? She never asked that question of anyone and sidestepped it when it was asked of her, and even if he were pleased to answer she chose not to see in his eyes, as he told her, all that pleading with reality to yield up its meanings.

"It's about them," he said. "It's about this poet who runs off with somebody's wife and it's no bed of roses. Some of them die of joy after twenty years but some of them, like Neely, drop off fast even though she's doing all she can to make him the happiest man in the world.

It might have been too much for his heart, he might have wanted to be free of what he'd wanted so much." He glanced at her sharply to see if he were truly heard. "She doesn't know what my novel's about, she thinks it's about my childhood in Iran. My father was an oil exec. I tell her Scheherazade tales and she thinks that's what it's all about. Something else she doesn't know and that's the guilt I feel, stuck in that room like I'm in solitary for committing some crime, and the crime is what I'm doing in there. I'm not supposed to touch them, I'm not supposed to get all wound up in it. It's like I've been warned to leave them alone. In other words, leave life alone. Die of it if you want to, but don't presume to know how it is with anybody else."

He came toward her so fast, switching off the light so fast, that she was forced to step aside to allow him to leave the room first.

On the way down she glanced into their bedroom. A lamp was on and she saw a wide bed covered over with a pure white spread, she saw a deep red Oriental carpet and an antique chair draped with a black silk Spanish shawl. On the nights when their guest was to lie alone, up there on the top floor, would he know that the woman lying beside her husband longed to lie beside him, instead? Ilona, glancing in, was reminded of herself at twelve, when every night before sleep she imagined a different being for herself from head to foot, and that fervent concentration on every particular (from an actress up on the screen—her eyes; from a girl in school—her mouth; from a woman passed on the street—her hair) was to bring about a miracle. When she woke up in the morning she'd be the girl she'd created the night before. The woman who was embraced in that broad bed, the woman loved by many men—was she someone whom the girl, Ilona, would have chosen to become, back on those nights of dreaming herself up?

When they came down the last stairs and the room with its company was out before them, she was still in the past, the street urchin with the tangled hair and torn dress and the shame over herself, the child gazing at the scene through a window, not wanting in, only wondering why so much light, why so many things reflecting light—silver and mirrors and glass and jewels and eyes—were always on the other side of the pane. The wife looked up at them and seemed to know all that her husband had told Ilona, and the face of the woman imprinted itself in her memory, an infliction, a trial, a dazzling fact of life.

The host brought Ilona a cognac and she stood with the other guests around him. He was lightly drunk, transported by his performance. "Old Fyodor, here's old Fyodor back in Russia. Here he is, knocking his shins on heavy Russian furniture again. He's just come back from the gambling spas, Baden-Baden, linden trees, fountains, roulette wheels, chandeliers like heavenly constellations over his little demented head, and here he is and he's under contract to that swine."

"Paulina lay around naked," Claud interrupted. "She lay around and wouldn't let him touch her. All across Europe. The girl he went gambling with, he couldn't touch her." And someone laughed, a short derisive laugh.

"Anna, I'm talking about Anna, the girl he married. Anna comes after Paulina. I don't know what the hell happened to Paulina. Anna was his second wife. The first wife was insane and then she died. You ever think how many of the greats married insane women? Well, here he is, I'll start over again. Here he is back in Russia and he's under contract to that swine and he's got to hand over another novel or else he forfeits his rights to all his works so far. He's got one month and not one word."

Ilona saw that his wife had wandered away to the stereo and, her back turned to the group, was selecting an album. The low voice of a French male singer was heard, and the woman bowed her head to listen.

"One lousy month and not one word. Then this friend says he knows about this class where the girls are learning some sort of hieroglyphics that's just been invented. Shorthand? What the hell's that?

So old Fyodor asks the instructor to send over a student, and he sends over this girl, twenty years old. . . ." One fast step to the side and he was the girl, gazing in awe at the space vacated by Fyodor. "Are you Mr. Dostoevski?" A girl's tremolo. Jumping back into Fyodor's space, he brought up from his chest a weary bass voice. "My dear Anna, I've got one month, my dear, one lousy month to get this novel together." Then he was himself again, his voice his own. "You ever see pictures of her? Tolstoy told her they were look-alikes, Fyodor and her. They were. You can see for yourself. Same eyes, same stare. Or her eyes got to imitating his, she was looking into them all the time. Anyway, she took it all down in hieroglyphics every day, and every night she went home to Mama. They got it all together. So old Fyodor—everybody was old at forty in those days—asked her to marry him. My God, she loved him for the rest of his life, even when he pawned the baby's shoes for gambling money."

Sweat shone on his face, he was a medium on the verge of collapse after conversing with that couple on the Other Side. His clownish act, his exertion stirred Ilona's sympathy. Was it his way of telling his wife that if only she would stay by him, they too would be remembered by the world? Now that his performance was over, the seductively aloof voice of the French singer was heard by all.

When the guests were putting on their coats, the host, waving his arms, called for silence. "My friends, I'd like to sing a little song for you. It's a song composed especially for the remarkable man who was unable to be with us tonight because he's in demand everywhere else." With a rapturous voice he sang his variation of a song heard everywhere, "Mar-tin in the sky-eye with diamonds," while everyone listened dutifully like children taught a song to sing together. Except his wife, who listened incuriously as if not listening.

It was then, at last, that her eyes met Ilona's—while her husband gazed up through the ceiling at the starry heavens and sang his one line—and Ilona saw the woman's awareness of her, she saw the other woman's curiosity about what she, Ilona, meant or had meant or would mean in the future to the man who was to appear any day now, any moment, out of the sky.

2

Claud caught at Ilona to keep himself from falling down the front steps. The collar of his coat was turned under, his hair, combed so carefully before he pressed the bell, was hanging in limp spirals, and his sight was hiding far inside like that of a nocturnal animal, a predator waiting for deeper night.

On the sidewalk—the lurch, the stagger, while she held his arm to keep him up. If she were to let go he might pitch forward onto his face. But out of sight of their host in the doorway and of the other guests, he was not so drunk for her as for them.

"My mother," he explained, "taught me manners. She said someday you're going to mingle with people who count. So tell them how much you enjoyed their company and they'll invite you back again. That's how I do it. I get stinko drunk."

Except for the seething sound he made by whistling through his teeth and for the rattle under the floor of his car, the drive to their neighborhood was a silent one and careful. They lived a few blocks apart on the north side of a hill above the piers fanning out into the bay.

She had been in Claud's one-room place only with Martin, and when the three of them sat around in there, this man seemed not to see her. Something had changed at the party. He had come to stand by her or sit by her, and he had told her who the others were—that man, an attorney, that woman, a psychologist, that man, a reporter—and he had told her what he knew about them, especially their frailties, and from across the room he had saluted her, and the salute was a puzzling tribute. At last, this night, he was acknowledging her presence.

"Come on in," he said, "and I'll drink yours for the road."

She wanted to stay only a minute and to sit in the straight chair, but he swung that chair aside to give her access to the lumpy, upholstered armchair. He sat down on the bed, leaned over to set an ashtray on the floor between his feet, and stayed in that position to hide the troubling in his eyes.

He was an anonymous man again after the brief recognition for his own novel. She hadn't known him then—ten, twelve years ago—and if she were to have met him she would have lost her voice and run away, wanting not to be counted among all those asking something of someone in the light—Oh, please see me—asking the visible one to make them visible too. Usually now he was out in his old fishing boat, wherever the fish or his restlessness led him, and she remembered dawns when she had stood at the window of the rickety house at the water's edge, over across the bay, the newborn girl in her arms, watching the fishing boats moving out toward the channel and the open sea, a line of dark imprints on the pearly, luminous waters. She remembered thinking It's not just a matter of a livelihood. They're testing to see if they're looked after, out there in deep water.

It was cold in the room. The oven door hung open and some heat was coming out, but not far enough.

"It's a blow upside the head," he said, smacking his temple. "Fame hits you like that. That's how it hit me. Even my dinky fame compared to a very large fame. It's like a comic strip. Whack! The guy's out cold, he sees stars, he's got this silly smile on his face. What it did, it was like I was forgiven for everything in my life which I shouldn't have done and for all those things I didn't do which I ought to have done, just because my past, my life, was exactly as it ought to have been, because if I hadn't lived such a life I wouldn't have got what I got, my dinky fame. It was proved to me that it's an all right world and God is an all right fellow. When I woke up I wiped that smile off my face. It made me look like those used car salesmen up on billboards, like those hearing-aid salesmen and realtors smiling away in the yellow pages of your phone book, like Orville Rednecker on his cartons of ice cream. I thought—Hey! We all got ourselves some homemade immortality."

No matter what their host had said about envy, accusing all his guests, envy wasn't this man's problem and it wasn't her own and it might not be the host's. What was it then? Was it a storm warning when the horizon was clearer than it had ever been, the way they thought Martin Vandersen saw it now? Was it your own longing to be seen on earth while you were still here, and remembered for a while after? Was it only that longing, simple enough? Whatever it was, their host had called them together so that no one would be alone with it. Until now, after the party.

"Let's talk," he said, "about something cheerful. Do you ever think about the end of the world? You think I don't know why I like to think about it, but I know, I know. You've heard about that ecstatic feeling epileptics get before a fit? Well, say you're ecstatic over a friend's good fortune and then you throw a fit."

"Some other time," she said.

"By cataclysm," he began, "and the kind I'm talking about isn't what everybody else is talking about, like what we're doing to the planet. I've got an Old Testament God hanging around in my head and it will be His doing. You've got Him, too. I can see it in your eyes, you always look like you're waiting for an angel to banish you from wherever you are. I was never raised in any religion and I never chose one for my very own, and a certain convert, my ex-wife, used to ask me How are you going to write about a tormented Catholic? And I told her I'll just consult the encyclopedia and find out all about a cathedral, where the hell the nave is or the apse, and then I'll throw him in and torment him. Well, this cataclysm is going to be our hothead God's when He's pissed-off enough. Say He gives a little push with His finger, say it's the same finger He touched Adam with, and the world somersaults. Over we go. The ocean goes bed-hopping. We'll all be swept over to the other side of the world and around again. It's not true you only go round once. Waves of unprecedented fury. If we could see it on television that's what they'd say. 'A wave of unprecedented fury is sweeping over the earth.' Then your set's off and you and yours are swept away the same moment as your anchor man. Fffft."

One foot was turned in, pigeon-toed. It was that way when he walked, too, as if part of him, if only a foot, was at odds with the sardonic rest. "If it happens tonight, if the earth somersaults tonight, you alone in your bed, me alone in mine, that'll take care of any trouble Martin might have caused us. Something bigger than Martin Vandersen will consume us."

3

Out alone in a neighborhood that was now her own but still unfamiliar, out alone in the night, she tried to free herself from the person she was with others, the trespasser who imagined more than she saw and saw more than she ought to see, the person who could not look into their eyes because, if she did, they would look into hers. She tried to rescue herself from this night, from the party, from the couple who lived in that house, from Claud, and from the premonition of loss, and the way to try was to remember two nights ago when she had embraced her daughter at the airport and watched the plane rise into the night sky.

Among a crowd of passengers checking their luggage, their unwieldy backpacks, she stood with her daughter, sixteen, Antonia, going off to Nepal, to the Himalaya, into antiquity. Not yet dawn, deep night still, and she had put her hands to her child's face and kissed her on the mouth, on the brow, on each cheek, and over again.

"Mother?"

"Yes?"

"All you need to do is bless me."

"I bless you."

"Now if you wake up in the night afraid about me, all you need to do is remember that you blessed me."

Only a few pinpoints of light—the plane was only that, and then the lights had disappeared fast, though she had tried to mistake a star for the plane. It had come as a surprise to her that her child, or anyone, believed that she could bless and that the blessing might work.

Ilona, climbing the hill, became someone other than the woman she had been at the party. Alone in the night she became the one she was in solitude, solaced by the delusion that simply because she was given life then some deep mystery was promised her, not any answers, only the experience of mystery, a beneficence unlike that granted to those beings who belonged on earth with ease.

A green globe hung above the narrow passageway that led from the street into the concrete courtyard formed by old frame apartment buildings, where the wind rustled newspapers all night long into corners, and a large but dim globe burned above the flight of concrete stairs that led up from the courtyard, and only the night sky lit the higher flight of shaky, wooden stairs and the landing and her door.

Ilona, remembering how the wife had looked at her that last moment, remembered another moment four years ago when Martin's wife had come out into the night to see who Ilona was, to see who Ilona was in his eyes, divining her own future in Ilona's face.

It was in the time when he lived by the ocean and Ilona would drive across the bridge and through the city, out to the Great Highway where the houses facing the sea appeared shriveled by years of salt and wind, and the dim glow in their windows resembled small lights at sea, ready to disappear. At low tide she caught glimpses of the wide beach beyond the high sand dunes, and when the waves were heavy and close their sound against the rows of houses was like the ocean itself towering over them. He liked it there. Any hour, even in the middle of the night, he would leap up from his work and run along the strip of wet, hard sand, and sometimes she ran with him, over the mirrored sky, over the night clouds gliding along under her feet.

Always, when she was expected, his window lit the passage between the houses. His basement rooms were ground level, once a garage. That night the passage was almost dark. Had she come when he wasn't expecting her, drawn only by her own desire? Once in a while, even when he seemed most grateful for her, another voice of his spoke up, cautioning her to expect a time when he was to be elsewhere, but she hadn't expected to be turned away so soon, after only a summer. She raised her hand and he was there before she knocked, springing up from a chair near the door.

Without a word he closed the door behind him and walked her back to the curb, and there he told her that his wife had tried to drown herself. They had parted a year ago, they had not seen each other in that time, but she had driven up the coast to go into the waves at his doorstep. She had waited on the sand for darkness, and then she had gone beyond the farthest breakers. Out there, overcome by terror, she had struggled back to shore and knocked at his door. She was sleeping now. Early on he had told Ilona about their many partings, that each parting was his wife's decision and that it was expected of him to be always waiting for her to return. Someone, he told Ilona now, must have written to her, a friend must have told her about Ilona, he must have told her himself.

They stood at arm's length from each other, not touching, the distance between them decreed by the woman in his bed. Yet even at that distance Ilona felt the ebbing of strength from his body, as much a loss as there would have been had he gone out into the deep water and brought her back.

"Martin!"

A voice thinned by fear was calling him from the passage, and Ilona thought—You have always to be prepared for a voice like that out of the past, calling the name of the lover.

His wife found her way out from the dark passage and, leaning against the porch, looked at Ilona, the woman who had come to spend the night with him. And how did she appear to his wife? There she stood on the curb—Ilona—quite thin, wearing an old raincoat, her hair in disarray even before the wind off the ocean had got to it, and were all her attempts at beauty futile? The mascara, the necklace of blue glass beads, the high heels? There she stood, her hand over the place just above her breasts, a gesture to protect herself from the pain of not being the one, the incomparable one whom his wife must have imagined.

Without wanting to, Ilona glimpsed them as she drove away. They were going back through the passageway, his arm around her shoulders, her arm across his waist. They must have walked together in just that way to rooms where they lay down to love, and now together again they went back into his rooms that his wife must have wondered about from hundreds of miles away, rooms known to other women, unknown to her. Only the address had been known to her.

Ilona had counted the days, imagining how it was in those rooms by the ocean. His wife must have knocked at his door when he was sweeping the faded rugs that kept off some of the cold of the concrete floor, or when he was spreading clean sheets on the bed, or clearing away from the table his manuscript pages and newspapers and magazines and apple cores and walnut shells, when he was shaping up his rooms for Ilona, the woman who was coming to him that night. Someone knocked at his door. On his doorstep—his wife, streaming ocean water, and all expectation of pleasure for that night, and all desire for pleasure, was swept away. He brought her into the room, he peeled off her wet clothes, he turned on the heater and bundled her in under all his blankets. Then he sat in a chair by the bed, wiping her face lovingly, stroking her wet hair, the cold salt clinging to his fingers. She must have said I got scared out there and he must have imagined her out in the darkening ocean, her body lifted by the swells and swept under all night long while, unknowing, he lay with Ilona.

Seven nights after the night he had turned Ilona away from his door, he phoned her after midnight. He had driven his wife back to

San Diego, where she lived with a lover, where she was enrolled in the university. He had driven his wife's car, taking the route through the valley because she had driven up the coast route, along that precariously high and narrow road above the ocean. Then he had caught a plane back to San Francisco, unlocked his door, and called Ilona. After the last parting a year ago, he told Ilona, his wife had written that all the capitals of the world were open to her now. She had written to him like a girl writing to a brother, and in the year apart she had confided in him just as she had done when they were together, she had told him about her lovers, she had told him about her hopes for herself. But when she heard that another woman might take her place, and be loved above all others, then the world with all its capitals had dwindled down to nothing.

"This time," he said, "this time we convinced each other the world is still out there. It's still out there for both of us"—his voice dimmed by the sound of the heavy waves shaking the air.

When Ilona came to him again and lay down with him where his wife had lain, she felt the other woman's fear of abandonment. While he slept the night seemed a night already in the past. She heard the calls and wails of the little children in the house above and the mother's bare feet across the floor, she heard the man who lived on the other side of the passageway, in rooms like Martin's, wander out and come back again, over and over, and she wondered foolishly if everyone's restlessness was brought on by the man beside her, if it seemed to them that in his basement rooms he was devising a miraculous future for himself, leaving them all behind. They probably weren't thinking about him, they weren't troubled at all about whether or not they were to figure in his memory. Only herself, the woman beside him, was already adrift in his past.

5

There were so many mailboxes fixed to the wall of the passageway between the sidewalk and the courtyard that her own sometimes seemed missing. It couldn't be found, first attempt. While she waited for Martin to return in his own time and from wherever he was in the world, freed at last by the work that had kept him captive, freed by the praise for that work as if those who praised wore rings of keys that opened the doors of cells, a profusion of letters and postcards arrived from Venice, from Madrid, from Amsterdam, from London, and she would climb the first flight of stairs and turn and climb the next flight, reading.

The foreign airmail stationery was of a fine, soft texture and subtle colors, and his handwriting over this weightless paper—careful but not precise, quick but still contemplative—and over all the postcards of paintings in museums enabled her to imagine him among the places he described. She imagined him possessed by all there was to see, euphoric one moment and dazed the next by the realization that he was never to see it all.

One among the many postcards was Rembrandt's portrait of himself when he was a young man, and she gazed at that one for a long time. The face was partly in shadow, the small, black eyes so alive in that shadow, and the rest of the face and each hair of his head radiant, lit by the ruddy gold light of a day four centuries ago or by lamplight on a winter night. The postcard came the same day as the letter from her brother, and her tactic to postpone opening her brother's letter was to gaze for a long time at the portrait. If she gave herself over to the beauty of that face it might reflect itself on all human faces, among them her brother's face. It was a superstitious act, an attempt to redeem her brother, and she had done the same thing with a portrait of Copernicus she'd found in a book on astronomers, and that man's narrow, bony face above the ecclesiastic's collar, his sideways gaze sliding away from the painter's concentration upon him, resembled even more closely her brother's face, and she imagined Copernicus living incognito as a poor, demented soul in a rented room in Chicago just to see how different the universe could look from there.

On coarse tablet paper, her brother's letter was composed in the formal style taught him by his father, who had taught him to read and to write, and the pencil was pressed down hard, key words emphasized in red pencil.

My dear sister,

In order not to beat around the bush I must confess I am afraid. There is a pain in the region of my heart and I intend to find out what it means. In the meantime, please give serious thought to my plea. I assure you I will not be a burden if you allow me to live with you. I will find a job and we can share expenses. You might also consider Chicago. You can rent a room for yourself and your child in the Nestor apartments. It is clean and comfortable here. The landlady will prepare a room for you as I have already told her about this possibility. Since you have never informed me about how you make a living I guess you are a jack of all trades. If that is the case you can rest assured you can always find a job in Chicago.

A child only half his age when he was twenty, she had been his mentor and his guide out in the streets of the city, out in the world of terrors and threats, a child keeping step with his long, erratic steps, her eyes down to hide her shame over him and her shame over that shame, an entanglement of shame, and to hide herself from the wary, fascinated, mocking faces that watched them approach and pass by— the poor young madman in dead men's clothes from salvage stores, clothes too big or too small, and his sister with the snarled hair and the soiled dress that was twisted in places because she had stitched a tear wrong. She had not seen him for almost twenty years, not since the day they parted in the empty bungalow on the edge of Los Angeles, the yellow stucco bungalow that was probably not there anymore. An apartment house was probably there, layer on layer of other families living above a memory they knew nothing about. She had kept from him the way she made a living, by ephemeral stories, a way that often, very often, seemed a cowardly evasion, a dense dreaming, a delusion of omnipotence that enabled others, who were wide awake, who knew what they were doing, to slip the floor out from under her feet. He would be unable to grasp it, she knew, because it was less substantial, less meaningful, with less of a future than the way he made his living, scrubbing pots and pans in hospital kitchens, mopping the floors of restaurants and museums, pushing an ice cream cart through the heat of summer, and if he did grasp it, then his very understanding would convince her that both of them were awry, sister and brother closely resembling each other, both so uncomprehending of the world and so willful about how it was to be imagined.

You will recall I told you about my job in the Cook County Hospital. A steel splinter from a brush got into my finger and caused blood poisoning to set in and I didn't know it. Imagine that! I was visiting an elderly gentleman who has an apart- ment down on the first floor. He used to be a pastry cook at the Palmer House and he has a stove in his room and bakes pastries. He saw the red streak up my arm and escorted me to a doctor who gave me a shot. My friend kept me in his room and applied hot, wet cloths to my arm, day and night.

Although he was happy to be tended by a friend out in the world, wasn't it true that his sister ought to be the one tending him, just as she had protected him from what the world might do to him, the years when she had walked beside him and sat beside him on trolleys and buses, her small presence never enough to keep his fear from breaking out as a cold sweat over his face, never enough to convince him he was not at the world's mercy.

Six, seven years ago he had sent her a snapshot of himself. It might be lost, it must be lost. She found it now where she knew it was, at the bottom of a shoebox of snapshots, and, sitting on the floor of the closet, she examined once more the man in the little picture. He was afraid of the camera—she could see that and she knew why. Who was it on any film but a ghost and who wants to see his own ghost? The one in this snapshot was a man at a picnic in a park in Chicago. You could tell by his stance he was tall and didn't know what to do with his tallness, you could see he was thin because of his fear over his body and how it might trick him and do him harm. The pantslegs of his suit were somewhat short and so were the sleeves. But a tie! White cuffs! His forehead had spread upward into the dark wavy hair to become a likeness of the noble brow, and whoever had taken the picture of this man trying to smile, this childlike eccentric, had no way of knowing who he had been in his youth and what tumult had gone on in that stucco bungalow in the weeds.

She, Ilona Lewis, who had vowed to herself to see that certain persons would not pass by unknown, even if all she could do was imagine with a few faltering words their inaccessible selves, had deliberately forsaken one and that one was her brother.

6

When she opened the door to Martin she asked herself several questions and gave herself answers, all in the space of a moment. Was he taller than before? No, he was always tall and you can't grow several inches in three months if you've reached your full height already. He weighed more? No. Or maybe yes. His face, then? Was it any different? His face was larger, even broader than before. But that was not true either. Was he changed or was he not? The enigma came right along with his familiar presence and with the tears that rise at the appearance of someone who's been away for a long time and whose absence is like a hint of forever. He was the same and yet he was changed in her eyes by the thousands of strangers who saw his face in photographs many times over, a hypnotic repetition, and who, before, had no idea he existed.

In that same moment he appeared to be asking himself why he had come here and who she was. Then he stepped inside and embraced her. He went ahead of her down the little hallway, and in the kitchen he sat down at the table, lifting the lamp to the edge as considerately as he would have moved a sleeping cat. They had spoken only each other's name, nothing else.

"Would you like wine? Would you like tea?" Was her voice lost among the countless other voices from wherever he'd been and wherever he was to go? She had dreamed of him often while he was away, and in one dream he was leaning against a doorjamb, framed by the doorway, just stopping by to tell her he was on his way elsewhere, smiling over the thought of someone who was waiting for him, unseeing of her alarm, of the grief that woke her. The figure in the dream stood between her and the man in the familiar wrinkled raincoat with the twisted belt, the man at her table, the table where they had talked the night away, so many nights, back in that house on the mountainside, the man who had seen in her face, then, a spirit deserving of benevolent curiosity, even of love, the man watching her now.

"It's me," he said. "There's nobody here but me."

Then he stood up and she came to him, and he was not the stranger at the door and not the man in the dream. Their arms around each other, they roamed up and down the hallway and in and out of rooms. They roamed the neighborhood and back without knowing they'd gone out, both of them entertained by the comic adventures of Martin Vandersen out in the real world. Strangers, he told her, strangers on the street, in theater lobbies, in restaurants, on planes, recognized his face and failed to know his name, once giving his face the name of a novelist incomparably more famous and twice his age, and once the name of a young French film star, dead years ago, and she wondered if the famous ones, each undeniably different from the rest, bore a striking resemblance one to the others, even so.

Along the windowsills were the postcards he'd sent, among them the hotel postcard from Los Angeles. On the back he'd written That's me in the lower left corner. See what's become of me? The little figure in the photo of guests around the swimming pool was a bald man whose belly ballooned out over his yellow swim trunks. In that vast pink stucco hotel, he told her now, he'd had a suite of his own, his own postage-stamp-size patio with palm tree, steak and lobster in the restaurants, and the use of a long white convertible, everything paid for by the producer who had bought the screen rights to his novel and for whom he was writing the script. Some rewards, he had written on the postcard, are for something other than what you think you've done. It's a case of mistaken identity.

Spain, after that, and the villa on the Costa del Sol, one of the hideouts of the American director and that was no hideout at all but a mecca for notables from all over the world. A general from Israel, a Zen priest from Kyoto, an Italian novelist, a soprano from Austria, a British historian—all had been guests in the time he was there, some singly, some together. And where did he go when he was alone again?

"That will take years," he said. "I'll keep you awake all night long for a year." But he began, at random. "From Malaga to Seville the road winds up among steep, dry hills, and on the slopes are chalk-white villas, far apart, and when you approach Seville you see great piles of golden wheat and a gold haze over the fields. I went to Avila, too. The town is enclosed in ancient stone walls, immensely high, and outside I saw an old woman in black sitting on the grass, sewing, and she was so small at the foot of those walls and she was so used to them. I came back to Madrid on the evening train, and the moon, the full moon, looked like it must have looked centuries ago when people were in awe of it. So close, alive, just about to say something in a voice that would fill the sky, a marvel of a moon. The train stopped along the way at village stations, and young girls were hanging around, flirting with the civil guards, and the light inside the stations was gold because of the white moonlight outside."

Spain was like the moon to her, Europe was like the moon. She hadn't been there, and when anyone assumed she had, she underwent some confusion, some embarrassment, as if caught in a lie. Because she had sent characters of hers there, they figured she had gone there too, before the imaginary ones could even buy their tickets.

"In Madrid I spent four, five days in the Prado Museum, hours in that room where they've got Goya's paintings from that time toward the end of his life they call his Black Period. When he painted those ghoulish, goatlike creatures. Maybe he was in a black period most of his life. Look at his Disasters of War, the terrible things we do to one another, the atrocities, where else was he but in a black period? I looked at those paintings wishing I could be abysmally true, like him, only with words. No fooling around anymore. What I did with my novel, I think I had to make the tragic palatable, like tell a few jokes, because if you take a long look at what's tragic, it's indescribable. Maybe I'll become like Claud and never write another word."

She had imagined him wandering the museums ecstatic, the praise for his own work persuading him to give up his disparagement of himself and accept a kinship with the great ones, and now, aware of her mistake, she kissed him, and her kiss was a way to impart some of that ecstasy she had imagined for him.

It was ten o'clock at night and they were at the kitchen table again. His raincoat hung on the back of his chair and he reached around into a deep pocket and unfolded on the table a large manila envelope. Several smaller envelopes of various colors slid out—blue, lavender, coral, one decorated with sprigs of flowers. Along with the letters came clippings from newspapers and magazines, some with his picture, and the face that the host had held up high for all to see appeared once again. All this had been given him by his editor in New York, yesterday, and he had read the letters on the plane. They were from strangers, some reminding him that they had met or that they had been fast friends in grammar school or in high school or in college, in cities where he had never been. One man recalled the day they climbed the mountain together, the mountain in Montana that rose above the acres of wheat and the farmhouse where the two brothers were born, the mountain that existed only in the novel. Another man claimed to have been present at the death of the younger brother, a medic in the 1st Infantry Division in Vietnam, but Martin's brother, who had served him as the character, was alive if not well in a veterans' hospital. From out of the envelope decorated with flower drawings— a snapshot of a girl. A lovely face, dark curls, and her letter confessed her hope that someday they would meet because she had recognized him as the man she was to love above all others. Whatever, whomever they wrote about, whether about themselves or about him, all their letters were saying the same thing between the lines. You are someone who sees, so please see me. You are someone who is seen, so please see me and make me visible. His voice unmarred by vanity, he read them aloud, puzzled, like someone learning to read a foreign language, and she saw that he was cured of his talent for witty ridicule; his writing outstripped that lesser talent. Some of the reviews likened his vision to that of the great novelists who wrote about peasants and farmers—Hamsun and Giono and Turgenev. She gazed at his face in the lamplight as he read, and, though his voice was disbelieving, his face was soothed by that resemblance.

When everything was back in the large envelope and back again in his raincoat pocket, he looked around the kitchen and down the hallway, so narrow they had bumped their elbows against the walls the many times they'd gone back and forth, arms around each other. "It's small, isn't it?"—asking and answering. He was not to live there with her.

Above them a quarrel was going on, the voices even more distinct than those upstairs in the house by the ocean. Then he told her that the couple—"What's their name? Jerome? Is that their name?"—had invited him, via a letter from Claud, to stay with them until some friends of theirs left for France, and then he could sublet their friends' house indefinitely. Solitude for each was a sound reason for their living apart for a while longer, a reason Ilona supplied but only in thought, a reason to protect herself against the pain of not hearing him say Come live with me. She was not afraid of solitude, she had weathered it often, she desired it often, but now she wondered what there was to fear in solitude that had not been there before.

"Give me your hand."

She laid her hand on the table, palm down. From a pocket of his jacket he took a small white box, turned her hand up, and placed the box in her palm.

"Open it."

She had never felt a need for gifts from a lover, from anyone, and so she failed to know, at first, what the box meant, and only gazed down at it, waiting for him to tell her.

"Ilona. Open it."

Gold earrings in the shape of a rose, a seed pearl in each one. But when she looked up, something in his large clear eyes said to her, without his knowing, I'll forget I gave you this. If there was a roomful of observers, not one would see the gift as a sign of his departure. They would see it as a token of love, and it was that, too. It was both, and maybe that was why she had never wanted gifts, because they were mementos of love.

A continent and an ocean separated them when they lay down together, and every caress was a failed attempt to bridge the distance, and though he held her as he fell asleep, wanting not to lose her while he slept, he took a sudden fall into sleep and was gone.

7

No light was on behind the bamboo screen at Claud's window, the nights she walked by. She had not seen him since that paroxysm of a party in honor of the man who wasn't there. When, at last, the light was on in his room she could not bring herself to knock. She went on down the hill toward the piers, wishing that his window was dark, and contradicting that wish with another—that he would open the door just as she was passing by again and invite her in and tell her, without her asking, about Martin.

While Martin was still a guest in the couple's house he had come by often to be with her through the night, and in her few small rooms he had seemed to be wandering in a vast space. At night the red and white quilt that had belonged to his grandfather lay over them. He had loved his grandfather dearly, and his leaving the quilt with her seemed a promise that someday they would live together again. The nights she lay alone the quilt over her was like intimate knowledge of him as a child, like proof of kinship, but when he lay beside her, whatever she had imagined about his childhood became an intrusion on his life in the present. One night, while he sat on the bed taking off his shoes, he looked down at the quilt wonderingly, as if he had never seen it before. She was already under the quilt, and from the corner of his eye he saw her watching him and gazed back at her, and recognition of her dearness darkened his eyes. But when he lay down beside her, his caresses were as unseeing of her as they had been since his return. The last time she had heard from him was after he had moved into the house of the couple who had gone to France. He had phoned to tell her where he was, and that was all. After three weeks of silence, a silence she kept because she was afraid to hear again the stranger's voice, she had phoned because of fear over him. If, before his recognition, he had seemed destined to become a venerable old man, in the silent weeks she became deeply mindful of how visible he was now and how vulnerable. It was a reversal of her illusion that if you were recognized for your wisdom, for your art, for whatever was admirable, you became invulnerable, you might even live forever. She had phoned him at last and got no answer, and that was yesterday.

Once more she came by Claud's window on her way up from the piers. Fine as broomstraw, the bamboo screen was made almost transparent by the light in the room. Claud was sitting on the floor, reading. She saw the many books in their orange-crate bookcases and remembered something he'd told Martin—that every time he found a book by one of his own beloved writers in somebody else's house he felt a pang of betrayal, as if that writer had been his alone, his closest friend.

A flicker of embarrassment in his eyes when he saw who it was at his door—a woman who had come to hear something she didn't want to hear. With one arm he gestured toward the lumpy armchair, with the other he offered the bed, and the entire small room was made available to whatever her response was to be when he told her what he knew. Anyone who leads you further into the way things are appears to be an enemy, but, watching him close the curtains, she felt an impulse of gratitude, a crucial last-minute impulse to make a comrade of him before he became an enemy.

"She left her husband," he said.

Then, "Sit down."

She was afraid to move. If she moved she'd fall away from her lodging in Martin's life.

Sparing her his sight of her, he turned his back. "She bought a house over on the mountain, up beyond where you used to live. All you've got to remember is. . . ." He must be groping for some truism that would take care of everything. "She hasn't invited me over so I've never been there myself, but he's pointed it out to me from this side of the bay, more or less where it is. A little closer to heaven."

In the past, when this man had seemed not to see her, he must have known about this moment and avoided the sight of her, even then.

"Sit down, Ilona."

Some closeted figure within her was warning her that if she sat down it would reveal itself, its fragile, cloistered self that was unprepared for assaults common to all. Out in the world there was a terrible prevalence of assaults that put to shame this one.

"All you need to remember," he said, "is that your imagination finds more bliss for them than they find for themselves."

A trembling took her over, and she turned toward the door, wanting to run out. Instead, she stayed where she was, to hear more. He was wrong, this man. He had figured it out in reverse. The bliss of lovers was the reality and your imagination came nowhere near. When she turned back toward him he was sitting on the edge of the bed, watching her, and she saw at once, with surprisingly sharp sympathy, how his face contrasted with that of his friend Martin, whose face always expected great tidings, as if a promise had been made to him at birth. The promise was missing from this man's face, or it had passed before his eyes on its way somewhere else.

"Women with that gaze, you never forget them," he said. "Those melancholy beauties. They look at a man that way and he thinks he's the one she's been waiting for. I used to think it was me she had her eyes on. I imagine Anna Karenina looked that way, and Emma Bovary. Maybe Frieda looked at D. H. that way when he came to visit her husband. Women like that are always waiting for the lover to show up and they don't have to wait long, they just wait over and over. Oh yes, and Helen. Sailed away with Paris, the guest who came to stay just a few days. You've read Seferis? For me the greatest poet alive. So many of his lines—it's like we used to say in school—I know them by heart. She wasn't really there at Troy, but nobody knew that, 'and Paris, Paris lay with a shadow as though it were a solid form, and we slaughtered ourselves for Helen ten long years, and the rivers swelled, the blood bedded in muck, all for a linen undulation, a bit of cloud, a butterfly's flicker, a swan's down, an empty tunic, all for a Helen.' I like the idea she wasn't there, it helps me when a woman looks right through me as if I'm air. I think—You're not there either, baby, you cause trouble but you're not who everybody thinks you are, you're a figment of our dumb imagination. Martin told me it got so strong between them he had to leave. I don't know how long he intended to stay. Maybe he set his suitcase down on that blue rug of theirs and thought he was on the Aegean Sea forever. He moved into a hotel until he could move into that place he's in now. She used to come to the hotel."

Lovers obliterate you. She imagined them in the husband's presence, unable even to glance at each other because a glance would reveal to him how far from them he was, swept way back into the past. And when Martin came to be with her, those nights when he was living with the couple, she too was swept back into the past. A necessary cruelty the lovers mistook for kindness. Oh let's not hurt him, oh let's not hurt her. Let's simply make them disappear.

She began to button her coat and realized she hadn't unbuttoned it. Claude was wrong again. It wasn't melancholy in the eyes of those women, it was serenity, it was like that sweet stun in the eyes of children who've been given a gift they never asked for, a gift too much to ask for.

Lamed by grief she climbed the hill and when she reached her street she turned, and there it was across the bay, across the black waters—the glittering mountain—and facing that spectacle of lights was like facing the lovers, their unseeing eyes.

8

A four in the morning she was
kneeling on the floor of the dark kitchen, dialing his number. She
had taken the phone down from the table because this trespass had to
be done in a crouch, so she could not be seen, so she could protect her
breast from his voice, from his presence on the other side of the city
or from his absence, over there. She expected him not to be home. He
was with the woman in the woman's house. They were lying together
in that depthless sleep after loving, that falling away from the won-
drous balancing of one by the other. Or they were in his bed, and the
ring of the phone was waking them both. If he answered, what would
she ask of him? Something beyond the possible? That he become
himself again, change back into himself?

"I'm afraid."

"Of what?" He must be standing nude, he always slept nude. Or
on his way to the phone he might have wrapped himself in a robe,
he might own one now. Neither of them had a robe when they were
together. Robes belonged to the infirm or to those who preferred
sleeping to waking. But the woman might have given him an elegant
robe that made him even more precious to the giver.

"Ilona? What are you afraid of?"

Every night she slept for an hour or less and was waked by the pounding of her heart, by her heart leaping up in fear of itself.

"Of what? Of what?"

"I'm a good person." It made no sense.

"I know you're a good person."

"I'm dear to some. I'm dear to my child."

"Yes you are."

There was no way to ask him to be her comrade again if only for a few minutes, only long enough to assure her that she was not someone who deserved to be left, not untouchable, not like the millions of untouchables, way over on the other side of the world.

"Ilona?"

"Can I come over? When it's daylight, I mean?" Never had she begged for anything from anybody. Unless, without knowing it, she had begged the very air, all her life.

"So early?"

"I mean in the morning. I need to tell you something." She didn't know yet, herself, what it was she had to tell him.

He was waiting.

"I mean when I come. I need to tell you something when I come."

He said nothing, reluctantly waiting for that something to be laid upon him.

"Please tell me how to get there."

When it was over she bent her head to the floor, covering her eyes to hide herself away from the woman's sight of her, from her sight of the woman lying in his bed, her body covered with that shimmer of bliss that had covered her own in the past.

9

The long view of Market Street on a Sunday morning, the trolleys few and far between and only two and three people in sight, moving slowly through the heat of yesterday and of the day to come and through pale sunlight not yet reflected on glass and metal, an odd light like that of the first minutes of an eclipse. Waiting on the corner for a trolley that would take her into his neighborhood, she was again a trespasser into other people's lives, someone who insists upon saying something about the self regardless of the hour.

The clanging trolley carrying her along was like her own ridiculous will. Unassuming people should always be suspect. Sooner or later, when the time comes, their will takes over, their unanswerable desires take over. She kept her head bent with the shame of this tumult over the end of love. It happened to almost everybody, it was as widespread as other misfortunes, but it was the one to keep quiet about.

When she stepped down from the trolley it was just as he had described it to her—she was facing west, facing a steep hill, and just as expected her heart was a tyrant terrified of itself. The climb up the hill was as tiring as it would be if the day were already over. At the top of the hill, on a corner, there it was—a gray frame house, small among the houses and apartments that covered the hill.

Where was the front door? There, at the end of an archway of dusty, flowering shrubbery, and she imagined the woman passing along under this arbor, coming and going.

"I won't stay long." Not long, only long enough to plunge them into everything unanswerable from where it took forever to rise.

He kissed her on the lips, perhaps to placate her, perhaps to pretend he was glad to see her, unseeing of how his kiss deprived her of him.

Off in a kitchen he fixed tea while she stayed in the living room by a window, afraid to turn toward the room, immobilized by the presence of the woman for whom the house and all its objects were familiar. The woman was the atmosphere of the house. She wondered if she had forgotten to comb her hair or wash her face. Was there some gray in her hair she'd discover when she got home? If you bow your head for so many years over your endless unknowing, over your imagination that substitutes for knowing, then how surprised you are, when you lift your head, to find yourself older than when you began.

The interior of this house was to puzzle her memory for years. It was a small house but like a maze where experiments are carried on with animals—a reward somewhere, you had only to find it. She was never to get the scheme of it straight, where one room belonged in relation to another.

Each waited for the other's first words, one mind in fear of the other, and the moment she sat down to accept a cup the unspeakable self spoke up. "I can't be like her."

"Why do you say that?"

Then she was up and roving, leaving untouched the teacup that the woman drank from. "I can't be like her, I can't be serene like her. You told me I was troubled in my soul, you made me feel like I had something you didn't want to catch, but most of the time I was calm, most of the time we were comrades, most of the time we felt love. If there's trouble in me, and there is trouble, it's the nameless kind that's all right to feel because I'm human and I feel, and it's not just over me, it's over so much more than me."

Her voice was loud and harsh, a voice not her own and yet her own but never heard before. So many times, people had to bend their heads to hear her, afraid they'd been stricken deaf. Then she heard that voice say something she herself would never say. "Oh I wish I were her!"

It was shameful, it should never be said and never even thought— the wish to be somebody else. The wish to be that other woman was a betrayal of everyone in her life whose life seemed entrusted to her for safekeeping, even if only in memory, a betrayal of everyone whose life was more precious to her than her own. The wish to be that other, any other, was to abandon them.

In a corner now, cornered by her own self, she was saying something she couldn't believe she was saying, so archaic, so demented, so lost was its meaning. "You're among the blessed ones now, you know."

Nobody thought that way anymore, and she waited for his denial that would relieve her of the idea, relieve him and herself of the burden of it. She waited for a small, scoffing, uncomfortable laugh, at least.

A wind, stirred up by the heat of the days and nights, swept the curtains out over the sills, and a door in another house slammed shut, a distant sound warning of listeners. That voice of hers saying crazy things might be heard by whoever was in the apartment house across the street, by whoever was passing along the sidewalk. He shut the windows and pulled down the white blinds, and went into other rooms to do the same.

A white glare filled the room now, and she was to remember herself roving through that glare in the heat of the day, trapped by her own self within that house she was never to enter again, within rooms that would puzzle her memory like a maze.

When he came back into the room where she waited in her corner, he had an answer for her. "Maybe I am among the blessed."

At the front door she had seen at a glance that his face was mute, a mask concealing his life from her, and she had avoided glancing at him again. But now she looked to see if he were agreeing with her only because he hadn't heard it right. She had wanted him not to agree with her. Nobody was blessed and nobody abandoned. The world wasn't like that.

"Maybe I belong where I was before."

Where was that? Was it where he had thought he was when he was with her? Was it among all those in the dark?

Though the room was between them, he was too near. A door was open to another room and she went in. A bed covered with a sea-blue spread. A bureau with two silver candlesticks, the white candles burned low. On a chair a woman's silk kimono, pale green and amber and garnet, mingling in exquisite harmony, the woman's own colors. Tonight he would recover from this day. She left the room the moment she entered it.

In the doorway she was caught by him and embraced, and in his body against hers she felt that same ebbing away of his strength, that same bafflement over a woman's coercive need of him just as on that night his wife had gone into the waves at his doorstep, and she longed to embrace him and protect him from herself, the enigma that was herself.

"Sit down with me," he begged.

She went with him to the couch but she would not sit down with him. An unbending will had taken possession of her body. She stood above him, and he drew her between his knees and bowed his head against her. Someone years ago had seen in her some goodness of heart, even some beauty of spirit, and only now was she remembering. Was it this man? And had he told her not in words so much as in his embrace of her?

"My heart wakes me all night long," she told him.

"My heart wakes me too."

She hadn't expected that.

"Nobody but you makes me cry," he said.

What did that mean? If she had come to be told that, yes, she was a good person, yes, comprehending of the lovers despite the trouble she was giving them, if she had come to be told this, was he telling her that her striving to be wise was enough to make him weep, so futile was that striving?

She broke away. Flowering plants, ferns in humid air—a conservatory? No, it was only a small room next to the kitchen. A bare table, a mug of cold coffee, a few crumbs. The windowpanes were rattling in the warm wind and a fly was crawling along the sills and tapping against the hot glass. It was really a modest kind of house. But when the woman sat here at this table, the flow of morning sun, patterned with the shadows of leaves, must appear like a lovely scarf floating around her, and he would paint her as Bonnard would have painted her, her hair ablaze with sun, and summer fruit on the table. Back in his rooms by the ocean the walls had glowed with museum prints— portraits of women who had mesmerized the artists years ago, centuries ago, and when he had lain asleep beside her those women had seemed to be the women in his dreams or all icons of one woman.

A door led to the backyard, and Martin stepped out into the wind and the sun. She watched him through the window as he knelt to set a plant upright. One sundown, out on the cold stretch of beach, they had come upon a shorebird whose wings were covered with oil. A few days before, fuel oil spilled from a tanker and hundreds of birds were dying. He had knelt and clasped the bird in his strong, gentle hands though it pecked at his hands with its long sharp beak, and they had taken it to a bird refuge to be cleansed. Watching him kneeling now to attend to a living thing, she saw how he could be mesmerized by a woman's desire for more of life, for him, and by his own desire for more life.

The boughs of a tree in the next yard hung over the high fence between the yards, and she sat down in their shadows that were swept back and forth across the grass. She was always surprised by gardens in the city. This one was a tangle of dry grass, tomato plants, and geraniums. From over the fence drifted the sweet, lulling music of glass windchimes hanging from a branch. Years back, in her neighborhood of bungalows on the edge of Los Angeles, glass windchimes hung on the front porch of a bungalow where something violent had gone on, the nature of it kept from her, a child. The bungalow was empty, no one lived there after that, but the windchimes went on tinkling, stirred by the slightest breeze.

Martin sat down beside her in the confusion of sun and shade, and stroked her hands. "Your hands are beautiful." They were not, the knuckles and fanlike bones too visible. Some caresses of hers that had conveyed to him her sight of beauty in his own being—he might mean that.

"Who are the ones you say are blessed?"—his voice carried away by the wind and back again.

"I just suppose they are"—her voice her own again. "You have to see that my mind isn't altogether gone."

"Who do you suppose they are?"

She lay down on the coarse, dry grass. "Nobody is."

But something comic about his request for simple answers freed her to consider who they might be. Once again she let herself believe that simple answers were always hovering around and she had only to catch one on the wing.

"Explorers, I guess. Where nobody's been before, each one in his chosen territory. Even though they go so high or so deep they can't breathe anymore. They might be."

She didn't know what she was talking about and she didn't want to look up and see his listening face. She could see only his shirt and how the shadows and sun moved across it in quick succession.

"Go on."

"I guess great singers." They would do as well as any.

"Could you speak a little louder?"

"I said great singers."

"I heard that so far."

"Say a great soprano, and the audience stands up and applauds for a long time, and you're standing up with the rest and as the applause goes on and on you notice you've got tears in your eyes. Say you're up in the balcony and you can see the rest of the audience below and you can see the little figure on the stage, and her head is bowed."

No answer, no comment. He must be giving it serious thought.

"Or say a great composer. What if you'd heard Beethoven play the piano, his own music? A friend of his said that his bearing was masterfully quiet, noble, and beautiful. You'd feel you were in the presence of someone blessed, wouldn't you?"

"I hear," he said.

"But if he was blessed he didn't know it. In one of his bad times he wrote to a friend 'A man may not voluntarily part with his life so long as a good deed remains for him to perform.' Maybe he didn't know his good deed was his music. Or maybe he knew it but not all the time."

She glanced up to see him nod because she knew he wasn't going to do more than nod.

After a while, "Who else?"

Who else? Who else? The number had to be small.

"I missed that one."

"No, I said nothing." Lost as it was out there in the wind, her voice wanted to retreat still farther to its usual refuge that was silence.

"Maybe those desert fathers. They stayed in their caves, they starved themselves. When one of them was given a gift of sweet grapes, he passed it on. It went all around and came back to the giver, not one grape missing. They wanted nothing, they wanted nobody around but God. Maybe they were blessed. Or maybe they just wanted to be. I don't know. I never tried to name any before."

"Go on anyway."

Go on anyway. "Would you say those persons who give their lives for others? The ones who spend their whole lives that way because it is their life. Even though they die for others, even though they're executed or assassinated. Would you say they are?"

No answer. Only a waiting silence.

"A while ago I was looking at a book about the Spanish architect, Antonio Gaudí. Could he be one?"

Almost impatiently, "How do I know?"

"Everybody loved him. The whole country. He was like a saintly child, he was so deeply religious. One evening he was on his way home from the cathedral he'd designed and he was struck down by a trolley car and he lay there in the street, an old man in old clothes, and nobody knew who he was, and no taxi driver would take him to the hospital. They thought he was just a derelict. Somebody got him to a hospital and he was put in the paupers' ward, where he died. By then friends had gone in search of him and then everybody knew who he was, this poor old man with snow-white hair, and cries of sorrow went up all over Spain."

"Anybody else?"

"Astronomers?"

"You're the one who's picking."

"Astronomers, I guess. Like Galileo, like Copernicus. Can you imagine how they felt? Their heads filled with those great aerial charts? The planets spinning around the sun in there? When you see their portraits all you see is their faces, but when you think about what was going on inside their heads, they must have felt blessed, don't you think so?"

The rough grass against her face was suddenly unbearable. "I remember something Michelangelo said about human beauty, how it seemed to him that God revealed his beauty that way and so it's an outward sign of spiritual beauty. No matter that I know for sure it's not so, it seems so. It seems true because it's so simple and because Michelangelo said it. But isn't it a terrible blindness to everyone else in the world?" She sat up. "No, I can't anymore. I don't know who is blessed or who isn't. It's a waste."

"No great writers? The long dead ones?"

"They could be."

"They wouldn't agree they were blessed."

"No, I guess they wouldn't agree. I remember an old German book of pictures of the death masks of great artists and composers and writers from all over Europe, and the faces of the composers and the sculptors seemed serene, as if they were on their way to Paradise, but the faces of the writers were tormented."

She brought her knees up and bent her head to them, closing her eyes, wanting not to see him. It was absurd, this pursuit of something always elusive—an answer to why there was so much light around the few, even centuries after they were last seen on earth, and why the rest went down in the dark.

"Ilona?"

"I hear you."

"Do you think they were blessed?"

"Maybe everybody thought they were just because they tried to rescue people—us, everybody—from oblivion. Maybe the rescue was an ordeal for them because they knew in their hearts it wouldn't work after all. I remember about Chekhov, his long, long journey across Russia and Siberia to that island, Sakhalin, where the czars sent convicts. He was tubercular, he was already coughing blood, but he made that journey—floods, awful rains, cold—to record what went on there, who they were. He wrote that the street noise there was the clanking of leg irons."

Silence. Then, "No more?"

At last, and against the most resistance. "Lovers. In the beginning."

"Ilona, where do you come from?"

He began to stroke her hair consolingly as if she were a lunatic quieted down, and she wished she had kept her cumbrous delusion from this man who no longer cared to hear even the lighter ones.

10

The blinds changed from sunstruck white to mauve to gray. A streetlamp on the corner came on and the blinds changed to silver. In those hours the woman he loved now, the woman who resembled those portraits on the walls of night, back in his basement rooms by the ocean, seemed to be wandering the street, away and near again, and some moments so far away she might be lost out there forever. The kimono had been put away, he had slipped it away without her seeing how. Instead of a lessening of desire for him because she had become less, she felt desire as intense as in the beginning of their time together, a desire that was like the desire for life that flares up and takes possession in moments of danger.

They slept, and when she woke she was certain it was late, almost midnight. It was only evening. Seven, by the clock on the bureau. Martin was awake, lying on his back, very still.

"Does it seem she's always known you?" It was a question she ought to have left behind in sleep, where she must have heard it clearly spoken.

"I don't know what you mean."

Neither did she. Unless she meant that the woman he loved now must seem to him to have known him back in the years of his obscurity, when no one else had known he was already the man he was to become, when only he had known.

"She loves me, that's all I know," he said, and the longing in his voice confirmed his love for the other. "She would have loved me when I was a nobody, if that's what you want me to doubt."

She got up and with her back to him began to dress, wanting to destroy the tormentor in herself, wanting to give in to the way things were in the world, wanting to regain an innocence from years ago, that receptive innocence to which all things offered themselves.

She heard him get up and begin to dress. Somewhere in the house a phone rang. Over in her aerie the woman must be wondering why he hadn't appeared, suspecting he was caught in the maelstrom stirred up by the woman he'd left. He closed the door to the small room where Ilona had seen a desk and books, and she heard no words, only the resonance of his voice against the door. She imagined the compulsion of love that brought the woman to phone him. More than compulsion—the conviction that she was loved and her voice always welcomed and waited for, and Ilona imagined his pleasure, his relief, hearing the voice that rescued him from his tormentor, if only for a brief moment.

When he came back she begged him, "Don't tell her what I'm feeling. Never tell her."

"She's compassionate," he said.

Compassion from the woman he loved for the woman he left— what an unbearable offering! It was a blow to her very center. Why didn't he know this? It was the simplest thing in the world to know. She tried to get past him in the doorway. She was dressed and she tried to get past him and go out into the world and leave him forever.

"Wait, wait, wait, Ilona."

With both fists she struck him on the chest. He caught her wrists and she struggled to be free, twisting her arms, trying to bite his hands. The woman must be watching from over there in her aerie, that serene, that knowing face watching her, Ilona, whose compassion was only a tenuous little virtue, and who had none at all for these lovers. It was as if he had taken it away from her and given it to the other, who had already so many virtues to be loved for.

"Wait, Ilona, wait. I don't know where I am."

It calmed her a bit, his confession. If he didn't know where he was, then neither did the woman know for sure and neither did she.

Then they were wandering together through unlit rooms, arms around each other, locked in silence. After a time he began to switch on lamps, and after a time she sat down at the table in the room with the flowering plants and he began to prepare supper for them and, watching him moving about in the kitchen light, she saw him as the ultimate stranger, someone proving to her how little she knew about anyone, almost nothing about the feel of his life to him, about the desperation of his desires, and she saw herself as a censor of his life, substituting herself for life's deepenings.

Martin set plates and silver on the table, sat down across from her and served her.

"Give me your hand"—placing his left hand over her left hand, and they held their forks in their right hands but could not eat.

"I expected you to understand"—touching the tines of his fork to his brow and then to his heart. "Like you feel for your characters."

She shook her head. She understood nothing, and the time was coming—it might already be here—when she wouldn't be able even to pretend in her work to be on the trail of even the slightest clue.

"Ilona, look at me."

No matter how gently he asked she couldn't lift her eyes. Her eyes would be so unseeing he'd wish he had never asked her to meet his eyes.

He kept his hand over hers all through the silent meal, and when they sat on the backporch steps, under faint stars and in the warm wind, he stroked her hand and stroked her hair. Voices and music from the apartments and houses around them were carried toward them and away, and the thrashing of branches was louder in the darkness.

When they lay down together to sleep he kissed her on her forehead and on her lips, lay back, clasped her hand in his hands on his chest and, breathing very quietly, fell asleep, yielding to sleep so it might bear him away. She remembered dreams he had told her about—daring escapes, false accusations that might be true, of being trapped again in the army and running amok, and she remembered a dream about her. He had sat up in sleep and called her name, though she was lying right there beside him, because he was dreaming that she was running down some stairs, away from him forever. She slept and was wakened by the certainty that this night was the last night she would sleep beside him and that no one would question him about her disappearance. No one, because he was absolved of any act, any confounding of himself and others, he was absolved because his life was just as it ought to be. All the strangers out in the world who saw his work as an absolving of them for being so human, all were absolving him of her disappearance from his life.

The streetlamp was dimming out, giving way to dawn. She picked up her clothes to carry them into another room so the rustling as she dressed wouldn't wake him. He was sleeping on his back again, his face upward, and she found no grateful acceptance in his face of that absolution she had granted him. A troubling lay over his face, but lightly, as if whatever was going on in the depths of sleep had a long way to rise to the surface.

A dense fog covered the city, concealing the hills below this one. Only a few patches of neighborhoods could be seen, floating islets, appearing and vanishing in a gray sea. She went down the hill trying not to shiver. Yesterday she had come here in just a skirt and blouse, believing the hot spell was to go on forever or disbelieving she was to stay the night.

11

When her heart waked her in the night she would get up, slip a sweater over her pajamas, sit down at her table, and call up from the past the one who was pleading with her to rescue him, the one she had kept at a distance so that he could never be recognized as her brother. In the middle of the night, every night, she was called out on a rescue mission, fearful over whom she must rescue, not her brother alone but herself along with him. Nobody else in the world was going to get up from bed and sit down at a notebook to rescue them from the dark.

Early on in their time together, Martin had told her about himself and his farm family in Montana in an amused, indulgent way like a father of himself, and that was the way he had told about them in his novel, and when he had asked Ilona about herself she had told him a few things, hesitantly, and then more, and everything she told him seemed to have been waiting to be told just to him. It was only the usual way lovers exchange stories about their lives, hoping, without knowing they were hoping, that years later when they had lost touch with each other, what little each had learned about the other would be remembered with understanding. Once when they were strolling and she glimpsed his reflection in a mirror in a store window she had mistaken his face for her own. They didn't resemble each other. She had entrusted his face, his broad, wide-gazed face, with her own history, her own self, and his face had become so kindred, so dearly familiar, that to see his face as her own had been a natural enough mistake. But now this scribbling away in a dimestore notebook set her among those nocturnal souls who fill their pages—every inch and the margins too—with eternal concerns of no concern at all to anyone else.

Over and over in memory she approached the yellow stucco bungalow in the weeds, afraid to go in and see again the ones unutterably dear, those she could not tell about because to attempt to tell was like an invasion of sacred ground, because something was protecting them from her, from fallacy, from artifice, from failure. But at last she went in, choosing—among all the weathers in which she had approached that bungalow and gone in—a summer twilight, because the sky of that time of day had been filled with promise and the deeper the blue became the more certain she had become of the existence of the world's great cities and far outposts.

She had always come home alone. She had a lover in that time, that last year, but she never brought him home to see her mother fading away in the tiny bedroom where the plaster had fallen in patches and the slats showed through like the bones of the house, and to see her brother in other men's discarded clothes, too small or too large, and to see his excited face and to hear his hollowy voice, like the voice of a desert prophet. Every stranger was the wisest being on earth for him, even the welfare worker who came at intervals since their father died to assure herself they were in need and whose eyes swelled with fear of him, the towering man leaning over her, asking her questions about people in the newspapers and in history, because wasn't it her job to collect data on everyone in the world? If Ilona were to bring a lover home, just for that lover to see who were the ones she was close to, he would have to be someone like Rilke who saw the blind man, the leper, the lunatic, with infinite compassion and whose poetry she read in the back room of the bookstore when there were no customers to wait on and no books to wrap.

Out of high school, seventeen, she had inquired at every bookstore for a job, the secondhand ones, the antiquarian ones, the ones that sold only the latest, because to work in the midst of thousands of books, no matter how cluttered, how musty, how concrete-cold the store might be, was to feel cloistered and concealed from the world and yet in the world. From the edge of the city she had ventured far into its illusory center, into a glamour core, an enclave, where she passed celebrities on the street and persons who desired nothing more devoutly than to be mistaken for celebrities, all of them confusing her eyes and widening her sight. She was hired because her stuttery shyness must have stirred the proprietor's benevolence or because she answered in an unpredictable way his predictable questions.

"Who's your favorite writer?"

"Conrad." Was that a mistake?

"Why him?"

"Because," trying to make a joke that would soften her trying to make a joke that would soften her stiff lips, "because if God could write He'd write like Conrad."

"You mean God took a nom de plume? If He's up to tricks like that, He wouldn't be satisfied with one. Name some more."

Whenever celebrities wandered into the store, figures one hundred times smaller than they were on the screen, then something—pride or a faltering conviction of incomparably more value in the dusted books—protected her from their bedazzling selves. She would look away, and if she had to wait on them she would pretend ignorance of who they were. But sometimes they would see her hands tremble and sometimes she lost her voice.

From the illusory capital that mesmerized the rest of the world, she rode a long way back each night to the bungalow with the stains under the windows from rain on the rusted screens and, stepping from the streetcar, she saw the racing forms, pink, green, yellow, caught in the dry weeds of the yard, tossed there by the throngs on their way back from the racetrack a mile away, the papers thrown away yesterday bleached by this day's sun. The crowds were already gone, inward-bound to the city, except for a few stragglers on foot, except for some elegant cars still coming from the track, bound back to where the faultless beauties lived and those who loved them. In one of these cars—three persons: the bareheaded man at the wheel, another man on the far side, and, between the men, a lovely woman. No one in the car glanced at her, no one in the car suspected her of wondering how it felt to be so highly visible for beauty and how it felt to bring that beauty like a gift to lovers. If that face in the center were to glance out, the girl on the sidewalk might be extinguished by the secret, ideal life in the depths of that glance and by the way the eyes would slide away as if they'd seen nobody out there.

Night in that little house low to the ground, the last night, and Ilona awake in the bed that had been both hers and her mother's, and her brother calling to her from his bedroom across the hall that was not really a hall but only a cubicle of space, his voice startling her from sorrow over her mother, a sorrow like a dark, cradling sleep. It was a few nights after their mother's strong will to live had left her body, taking all traces of grace and beauty meant to charm death into giving up its own inexorable will.

"Ilo?"

"Yes?"

"Ilo, let me come with you."

"Let me find out first."

"You need a man to protect you."

"Nobody's going to hurt me."

She was already twenty but for him she was the child who had protected him from terrible possibilities waiting for him everywhere, inside the city, out in vast space, and in the narrow confines of buses and streetcars, and now if she would only allow him to repay that kindness he would be grateful for the rest of his life. In the tentative silence after he went back to his bed, she sensed the imploring going on in his shallow sleep where he must be offering up incontestable reasons, down on his knees. The tempest that possessed him when she was a little girl spent itself when their father died, though the furrows in his brow got deeper, and the sweat in his hair and the agitated walk and the fear in his eyes remained.

"Ilo?"

Near dawn, and he was in the doorway again, a tall wraith in faded, shrunken pajamas, closely resembling an asylum inmate in an old etching she had come upon in the bookstore, and the likeness was an anointing of him, as if across a century the artist rescued him from his solitary, forsaken condition. At seven he had almost been forsaken by life, consumed by fever for days, and after that he was not who he had been, not anymore the little boy who drew intricate pictures of trains and passengers, someone in each window unlike anyone else in all the other windows.

"Ilo, we won't see each other again."

"Don't think that way."

Then from his lonely throat dry sobs rose. A few only, because he must be afraid they would turn her against him since he was not the most reliable of protectors. Like an admonition his very loneliness closed up his throat, and he went back to bed.

They sat at the table trying to eat their breakfast of dry toast, the table where their father had taught him to read and to write, where their father, the times he was home, ate his supper in a slow, reflective way like a man far from home, where she, Ilona, had scratched away at her stories, each story a refuge into which she escaped and where no one recognized her. This table was to be taken away with the rest of the furniture by the mailman, with whom he had made friends and who was to pay him a few dollars.

"Ilo, you won't have to work. I'll find a job and take care of you."

It was like an offer to lame her for life, an offer to imprison her within his own benighted being forever.

"Wherever I go," she said, "let me get settled first." And this denial to him of the future he was begging from her was a cruelty that was to strike back at her when she was to write at all the many tables of her life, roaming her imagination with the hope of finding her own future there. No latent beauty was to be revealed in her work, only the cruelty of forsaking him that confessed itself in the emptiness of each story.

"I'll go to Aunt Sarah's, I'll go to Seattle and live with her." He was striding around the room in a frenzy of helplessness. "If she can't take me in I'll get a room near her and I'll help her, I'll do her shopping for her and I'll go with her on the streetcar if she's afraid of going out alone and I'll mop the floors for her."

The old woman who was their father's sister had come down to console them when their father died and to pay for the funeral, and she had tucked her purse under her pillow at night, afraid the two demented children might steal from her while she slept.

"Then I'll know where to reach you," she said, "when the time comes for you to be with me."

He thanked her profusely for that. "If you don't do well where you go," he said, "you can come and live with me."

"If I don't do well," she promised.

Eagerly, on the run, he helped the mailman's two sons carry the furniture out to the open truck. He hoisted up his father's ancient black suitcase of heavy, pebbled leather, with straps and buckles. Up it went and over. Their father was gone most of the time, on the road, searching for work on newspapers in other cities, soliciting ads. He was on the edge of oldness when she was born, and the Sundays he took her to hear the soapbox orators in Pershing Square, people would ask him if she were his grandchild. So his suitcase was old-fashioned even then. On the run, her brother carried out grocery boxes filled with salvage-store clothes, with paraphernalia of inestimable value, each box tied with twine, and, last, the wooden box with handle, containing his shoemaker's tools.

They were alone in the empty house. The mailman's sons waited, one in the driver's seat, the other on a chair in the truckbed. The seat beside the driver was to be his, like a seat of honor. He wore a black suit that some larger man, years ago, must have worn to his own significant events. He was to spend the night, or even a few nights, at the mailman's house, and she was to board a bus to San Francisco, where she had never been. It was time to part. When he bent his head to kiss her on the cheek, his loneliness struck him across the face and left him pale and shaken. He was already lost in the world he was to enter as soon as this embrace was over. He would never again be even halfway sure she loved him, though she kissed his trembling cheek and his brow filmed with sweat.

Then he climbed up into the truck and, wearing a departed man's dapper Panama hat and hunched over in fear of this exciting time, he waved to her, an exaggerated wild waving, as they drove off.

Ilona, alone at her table, raised her head and saw that it was a dark four o'clock. If it was six o'clock in Chicago, was he already on his way to his job through cold half-dark streets or was he on his way home from a hospital's steamy basement kitchen after scrubbing pots and pans all night, a tall figure, head sunk forward, hat pulled down over his ears, overcoat flapping in the wind? Or was he still asleep in that city closer than this one to the hour of waking, and if he was still asleep, his sleep was not deeper than hers had been all her waking life.

12

Uncertain about which door was the right one, someone was bungling along the landing, knocking at all of them. The dog inside the apartment next to Ilona's clawed at the door, banging against it, and its bellowing bark caused the walls of her room to vibrate. Then the caller knocked at her door.

"Ah, it's you," Claud said, surprised he had found her. "I want you to join me in an act of supreme cruelty. You remember Jerome, our host? If not his name at least his suffering face? We're going out to the ocean and we're going to make a bonfire and we're going to burn his manuscript. His only one, that one about his wife and Neely in the coils of a boa constrictor passion."

One second of perverse pleasure—it sprang so fast to her eyes she had no way of concealing it from him. If all those pages, all those years of labor were to go up in smoke, then the woman herself might end up unremembered, her life unknown.

"That's an awful thing to do," she said, "burning up all that labor," her dismay as true as that shameful pleasure a moment ago.

"It's cold out there at the ocean," he warned. "Dress warm."

"I don't want to see him."

She wanted to back away, close the door. They were two of a kind, herself and that husband. There was a shame about them both for their fear of loss and for the loss that had come about.

"Oh, but he looks great. He's skinny and he's got a haircut and he's wearing suits again, and he's got himself a big desk in the trust department at the Bank of America or Bank of the Cosmos. One little thing left to do, burn up his obsession, and he'll soar like a big pink flamingo."

He found her raincoat and held it up for her and she slipped it on. At the foot of the stairs he took out a black knit cap from his jacket pocket, a watch-cap like the one he was wearing, and drew it over her head, down to the eyebrows.

"You and me," he said "I'm the executioner and you're the priest. Say a prayer over the ashes."

The time was midafternoon, but their host was lying asleep on Claud's bed. He sat up, hampered by the blankets over him, struggling up from the exhaustion that precedes an act of finality. Ilona would not have recognized him in a crowd. He was somebody else or more truly himself than on the night of his party. His face, that night, must have been padded with hope that everything would stay the same, the tolerable same, despite the man up in the air.

Claud pushed a chair firmly against the backs of her knees. "Sit down, sit down." And to the host, "Sit up, sit up. I'll brew something bitter."

Jerome sat on the edge of the bed, head down. "How've you been?" he asked his shoes.

"I've been fine," she said.

"Me too."

She had wanted never to see this man again. The night of the party, his prophetic fear of losing his wife to Martin had diminished her, Ilona. His confession had been direct as a statement that she, Ilona, was not one to keep a lover when that lover was to come into the presence of his beautiful wife. He diminished her further, now, by the loss of his flesh, by the grief and rage that had brought him here and entangled him in his friendly enemy's blankets. She was not loved beyond reason, as his wife was loved. She was not loved anymore within reason.

"You want to tell Ilona what you did? What he did," Claud went on, "was hide out by her house and wait for them to come out. He bought himself a Triumph because it's easily hidden under a bush, the sort of car a rodent can drive. He told himself he wasn't going to hurt anybody, he just wanted to see them together. Maybe he hoped the sight of them would bring on a heart attack and he'd collapse and die, like those primitives who fall down dead at the sight of a sacred person even if it's their own cousin. But when they showed up he began to shake, like this. He was shaking so hard he thought he was going to shake himself right out of his car and across the street on his hands and knees. They didn't see him and he got away. He got back across the bridge all right because those Triumphs drive themselves. Then he came over here. I thought he came to kill me because it was me who brought Martin Vandersen into his life. I was afraid he had a weapon on his person, like a lady's ivory-handled revolver that belonged to his grandmother, maybe with a blood-red ruby in the handle. The rich kill you with the very best, it's a matter of noblesse oblige. So I pleaded with him for my life, I said 'Martin Vandersen's relieved you of a life-threatening wife.' I said, 'Unless that's what you want, an early death with her kneeling by you, floor, street, wherever, so the last thing you see is her beloved face.' That was too much to think about so he toppled over. But before he fell asleep he told me his manuscript was in his car and he was going out to the beach to burn it. I said, 'Why don't you do it in your fireplace?' and he said, 'The smell of human flesh. The neighbors will call the cops.' If he talks that way in his novel it's good he's burning it."

The bitter brew fumed up over the percolator lid.

"You ever see that painting Paradiso?" he asked them, bringing black coffee in chipped mugs. "Where everybody's dressed up in their Renaissance best, finding each other again, falling into each other's arms? Well, the people in that Paradise are forever in the shape in which they were last seen on earth. There're people of all ages, kids and middle-aged ones and old, old ones. I've always puzzled over that painting, it wakes me up in the middle of the night. I think, Well, it's all right for the young, it's real nice to spend the rest of eternity look-ing the same. But what about the older ones? I bet when they get a little time to be alone up there and to think, maybe the old ones say to themselves 'It was me at six years old and it was me at twenty and it was me at forty, so why does it have to be me forever when I was ninety-one? Why ninety-one forever even if my arthritis is all gone?' Myself, if I could have a word with God, I think I'd tell him 'Look at me, God. I'd hate to go through eternity like I am now at forty or like I'm going to be, even worse. I resemble a bullfrog now, my chin is adhering to my chest because you took my neck away, and look at my sad froggy eyes. I used to be good-looking, God. I was good-looking for a long enough time to give you time, God, to think about keeping me that way forever.'" And to the host, who had scalded his mouth with the hot coffee and was bent over in pain, head down to his knees. "I'm telling you this as an argument for an early death. You ought to make it up there before you look any worse. Maybe all you need to do to get there fast is persuade your wife to come back to you."

No one spoke, not even Claud, on the drive to the ocean. They went in Claud's rattling car and, by a trick of his, the manuscript lay in Ilona's lap. Its weight was impressive. She guessed there must be close to a thousand pages in the brown wrapping paper tied with string. No matter if he had revealed nothing more than how trapped he was in his own life and how oblivious to the rest of the world—his pages ought not to be burned. Why, then, was she riding along with the manuscript in her lap?

Claud slowed down along the Great Highway, selecting the site with care. On the landward side of the highway the old houses and the new stucco motels faced the sea, and on the seaward side the high sand dunes, some ten feet high with purple iceplant clinging to their slopes, belonged somewhere else on the earth, an ancient port on a desert coast.

Claud parked before a green stucco motel aglitter with specks of gold. She was about to say No, not here and said nothing. Martin's house had stood there, and she knew that when the pages had all gone up in smoke and they were climbing back over the dune, Claud would pause at the top and say You know, I think Martin's basement was along about here. In fact, right there. You see that green motel? And the specks of gold would be flashing and sparkling in the rays of the setting sun.

"Somewhere else," she said, "might not be so windy."

"No wind anywhere," Claud said, and got out first.

They climbed the dunes and were met by a fitful wind, the ragtag end of a storm yesterday. The wind, though not strong enough to break up the glaring overcast sky, was lifting foam high off the breakers. A fisherman in hip-high rubber boots was casting his line into the breakers, a very small figure in the glare of sky and water. Far down the beach a few lone persons and a dog were either approaching or retreating in the mist along the water's edge.

Claud led the way down the slope, past three seated figures facing the sea. It was obvious in their calmness, the disciplined erectness of their backs, that they were meditating. Ilona, trudging down last, saw that they did not move a muscle. It was as if no one passed by. Up ahead, Claud stopped at the foot of the slope, turned, and waved his arms. The spot he had chosen was only a few yards from the three figures who were seated in an arc, above.

"Why here?" Jerome asked. "Look, there's nobody for miles."

"These dudes don't see a thing," Claud assured him. "They won't laugh at you, they won't cry. They're above it all, they're floating above all human suffering. You used to be into it yourself."

The figure in the middle was a girl, her long hair drawn back, her face blanched by the cold, her heavy clothes shapeless. The young man to the south of her was bearded, his dark hair hanging thickly to his shoulders, and the young man to the north was beardless, his wisps of thin blond hair lifted and laid down by the wind, his eyes closed. The other two held a steady gaze on the horizon.

"We're disturbing them," she said.

"We can't. Nothing can." Claud took the package from her and dropped it straight down at his feet. The package scooped a shallow place for itself, scattering sand over his boots.

They searched a long way, up and down the beach, for enough dry sticks and driftwood. From far Ilona saw Jerome moving about, a figure in an excellent suit a shade darker than the sand. He stumbled over a mound, and she expected to see him drop to his knees and stay there. A dog, running along the beach in zigzags and loops, stopped to nose the package and dig furiously with its hind legs, throwing sand over it. They came back with their arms full.

With a show of expertise, Claud arranged wood and newspapers and set the pile ablaze with Jerome's cigarette lighter. "The rest is up to you. Don't throw it all in at once, you'll smother the fire. A few pages at a time and don't try to read them."

Kneeling, Jerome untied the string, unfolded the wrapping. The wind lifted the top page and began to slip it away, left it to riffle through the pages just underneath. Then, leaping up, waving his arms, he was shouting at the three figures above them. "Look what's going on here, fellas!"

He took off running, he ran in circles, searching for something he must have seen earlier, and swooped down on it at last—a yellow plastic pail, or part of a pail. Waving it above his head, he ran down to the water, waded in, filled the pail, ran back and past the fire, and stopped before the girl.

"Fellas, look!" he shouted, holding the pail over his head. "I'm going to burn myself up. I'm like your Buddhist monk over in Saigon. See! I'm pouring this gasoline over myself. See, fellas?"

Ilona saw no change in the faces of the three, no smiles, not even annoyance. The one with his eyes closed did not open them, and the other two continued to gaze out to sea.

Jerome tipped the pail and the water splashed over the crown of his head and streamed down his face. He threw the pail away, leaped down the slope, ripped off his shoes and socks, and thrust his bare foot into the fire. He kept his foot in the fire beyond the limits of even Claud's endurance.

Claud shoved him off, and he went hopping away. Hopping back, he picked up the entire manuscript and dropped it into the fire. The fire was almost extinguished. Sparks, burning bits of wood shot out all around. Claud handed him a long stick, and he stirred the fire to life again. The flames flared up, the corners of the pages turned brown, curled up, the words in black ink turned brown and lost their meanings. The top pages rippled, rose up and fell back and vanished, and the pages below, facing suddenly the vast white sky, shriveled into evanescent shards. The bulk of the manuscript remained almost untouched, too heavy and dense for the air to enter and lead the way for the flames.

Jerome limped away fast and Ilona followed him. For a long way he waded through shallow water, cooling his burned foot. His trousers were wet to the knees. She could tell by his back, by his lifted shoulders and bent head, that he was crying. In the white glare of sky and ocean she lost sight of him. When she found him again he was sitting on the sand, up away from the water, gripping his ankle.

She sat beside him. The skin on the sole of his foot was burned away. "That monk," he said. "I wasn't ridiculing him. God no. I wish I were him. The man had something to burn himself up for. The world's over there, that's where it's at, and I thought it was waiting to hear what's going on inside my head. The rot up here, up here. What I did in that novel to her and old Neely, Willy Nilly Neely, poor old cocksman! You look at your pages, you look at the type, it's like barbed wire. You've got your victims, your prisoners inside there. Years ago I read about what those syndicates down in Mexico do to the prostitutes who try to escape. They roll them up in barbed wire. I was doing that to her. Elisa."

The wind was colder, it seemed colder. It stung her face, hung back, slipped by, came around and struck her face again. She could say that the ones he thought he'd imprisoned behind barbed wire were not there, that he had imprisoned only himself and not forever, and someday he would forgive himself for the attempt on their lives and his own, but the roar of the ocean filled the sky and her voice would be unheard.

"Well, I guess I set them free," he said. "I guess I'm free myself, free of her, free of her boy. He always reminded me of his father. I think I loved that boy, I think he loved me, but I'm glad he's gone. I loved his father, too, but he shook me up, the son of a bitch. But I can't say I'm free of Martin Vandersen. Maybe I'll never get rid of him, maybe I'll become one of those nighttime teeth-gnashers, and if I ever get married again my wife will sleep in a separate bed. The only way I can ease myself of him is to imagine him when he's old, you know what I mean? When he's old and his fame gone, and all those seraphic curls gone, all those red curls shining under all my goddamn lamps, maybe we'll embrace in Paradise. 'Goddamn, Martin, glad to see you again!' Maybe that's where we were in a dream I had a couple of nights ago, but I didn't know that's where until Claud reminded me there's a Paradise. Joe Neely was there, too, and we were standing on a sort of balcony, the three of us, me and Neely and Martin. We had on white robes like angels or maybe they were hospital nightgowns, but we weren't old yet, we were like we are, or Neely was, and all the pain and envy and anger were gone, and there were all these women down below, women and children looking up at us, and I said to Martin or he said to me or Neely said to him or to me, one of us said it anyway, 'Which one did you say was Elisa?' We didn't know and it didn't matter. Maybe that dream made me decide to burn the stuff."

It was a long way back to the fire. He walked all the way in the shallow water, limping. The three meditators were gone, the fishermen gone. The only ones left were a lone figure far down the beach and Claud, poking the fire.

"It's got to be ashes," Claud said. "You don't want somebody to come along and read a fragment and take it home. It could trouble him the rest of his life—What came before and what came after?" At the end of his stick the last page burst into flame.

They climbed the sand dunes, Claud in the lead, and at the top he paused. The green motel was flashing a million promises of glamour and ecstasy to the overcast day. No blazing sunset was necessary.

"Claud, don't say it," she begged.

Jerome came up the dune last, shoes in hand. His hair was wet, his trousers wet, his face pinched closed by the cold wind and the loss of his captives. A white line, like salt, sealed his lips.

They went down the sand dune together, no one leading, no one straggling, and all the way back into the city they spoke not one word.

13

One night she heard Martin's footsteps on the stairs. She knew they were his footsteps, always light, rather slow, those of someone led by a reason not yet known to him. The room where she slept and where she wrote faced the landing. The lamp was on, the curtains closed. He tapped at the window.

"Ilona? It's me."

It began, the trembling of desire and resistance to it. Her hand was trembling so much she had trouble with the simple lock.

Avoiding the room where the lamp was lit, he went on into the kitchen.

"You're working late."

She was wrong about his footsteps. He knew why he had come. He was troubled over what she was doing in her own way about the end of love. Or, as usual, she was only imagining what went on in someone else's eyes.

"It's not about us," she said.

Relief in his eyes, and then a doubt, and then, perhaps because he chose not to doubt her, his eyes accepted her words. "Some say it's best to wait ten years before you say anything about any experience.

If you did that you'd give me time to escape and yourself, too, if you want to escape."

Was he cautioning her to wait until balance was restored by time, to wait until the memory of love would suffice to soothe her and redeem her? She had only to wait and wait.

"What's it about, then?"

"It's about my brother."

"I forgot," he said. "I forgot you had a brother."

Strange that this man by leaving her was leading her more deeply into herself than he had when he was with her in those few years of love. Like a guide who has no idea where he leads.

"That's what I tried to do," she said. "I tried to forget him, but I couldn't. I was always afraid he would appear, knock at my door just as it was getting dark, when we were sitting down to supper or when it was just getting light and the air was cold, and I would be left alone with him because everyone would leave me, even you, not my child but maybe even her, and my friends, my few friends. He'd knock and I'd open the door and I'd see his face again, his face that never knew how it looked to the world. It's about him, even if it's just for myself to see, because now he breaks my heart."

"Ilona." He came no closer. She wanted him to come closer but he stayed where he was, across the room. "Ilona, can you see me that way? Not like everybody else sees me. Not like you see me now. You think I'm blessed, you think Somebody out there loves me, and sometimes I go along with that because it feels good. But I'll tell you something. Someday I'm going to be back with everybody else again, you won't be able to tell me apart. Me, just a lowly human being again, maybe even lowlier than the rest, and what if I knock at your door, the real Martin Vandersen, Old Mortal Martin? Would I break your heart?"

When he came to her she put her hands over her face to hide her desire for him. He kissed her hands hiding her face and led her back down the hall that was not wide enough for two abreast, and drew her down onto her bed. She had imagined herself far in his past, faded from his memory, and she was engaged, day and night, in a desperate rescue of herself, a rescue by thought, by words, but all the time she had known the rescue required something more—his body over hers, his hands over her, his mouth over her, his desire moving over those secret places where proof of love seems to lie.

Apart, each facing upward in that rapt position memory places you in years later: "Ilona, did I tell you I dreamed about you? The other night? You knew where underground rivers ran and where trees could be planted and thrive."

Nights to come, when she was to be wakened by her fear of belonging nowhere, by despair over who she was, so lacking in the virtues that make your presence, your time on earth so precious to some others, it was to calm her like a deep persuasion of his love.

At dawn when the phone rang she was lying against his back, curved to him as she had been curved to him countless times before, and in the first moments of waking the loss of him had not yet come about. Wrapping his shirt around her—it was closest to hand—she ran down the hall, praying that all was well with everyone.

The sound of distance like little waves, and within the waves a voice asking to speak to Ilona Lewis.

"That's me," she said. "I'm here."

Washed over by distance, the voice—a man's voice or the grainy voice of an elderly woman clerk—told her that her brother, Albert Lewis, had died at six that morning. A voice in a vast hospital told her that her brother had been brought there in the night, suffering a heart attack.

"I'll come on the earliest plane," she said, and when she put down the phone her cries were the ones her brother kept down in his throat that last morning when he came to the bedroom door to beg her to allow him to protect her from the world.

Martin sat on the rim of the tub and bathed away the sheen over her body. He drove her to the airport and, waiting in line to board the plane, she rested her head against his chest and he kissed her on the brow, and to everyone else he must have appeared to be someone who would be waiting for her when she returned.

14

A glass door to a dim vestibule, and the landlady peering out at the woman on the porch who had pressed the bell so early in the morning.

"I'm Albert's sister." At last. And when she was let in she said it again, repeating it to exonerate herself from the years of her denial of it.

A second, inner vestibule, dim also, a black pay phone on the wall and a black leather discard chair before it. So this was where he sat waiting for her to call at the time they had agreed upon by letter, and always he had waited half an hour in advance, afraid he would miss her call or another tenant would have claimed the phone. So this was the small space wherein he waited for her voice.

"Come in. You like cuppa tea?" I have a Greek landlady who knows how to make repairs like a man.

Ilona followed her into the flat and down the long hallway and into the kitchen. The presence of the night still lay heavily in the rooms off the hallway, they were so solidly crowded with massive furniture and the drapes were closed, but the light of day came through the kitchen window.

"Your brother a nice guy. Nice guy. He always like cuppa tea. Sit down."

Ilona sat at the table, in the chair where her brother had sat. A large dog dropped a red ball at Ilona'a feet and backed away, head cocked, a bright anticipation in the corners of its eyes. Its black and white fur lay in tidy, tended layers.

"Your brother, he like Hector. He always throw the ball. Nice guy."

The sister, too, threw the ball. She threw it the length of the hall and the dog was back in no time, dropping the ball at her feet again. She threw the ball again, keeping her eyes on the dog to avoid the landlady's eyes. This woman's two sons, both in their teens when her brother moved in, became doctors while her brother went on living in the same room, observing their transformation with a tenant's pride.

"He talk alla time about his sister. Come in, have cuppa tea, I say. He say, Thank you, thank you, and talk alla time about his sister. He want you to come here so he can take care of you. You got no husband?"

"Not now."

"How you make a living?"

Not very well—she could say that if the time were appropriate to smile. Not very well, but enough of a living to keep a roof over herself and her child, and the pitcher of milk was always full, surprisingly, as if by a benediction, the same as that bestowed on the couple in the myth whose wine jug or milk jug was miraculously full for the rest of their lives because they'd shared their meager fare with a couple of strangers.

"Albert tells me you write alla time."

"That was a long time ago"—lying to clear away the scornful curiosity trembling in the landlady's eyes, the derision of this sister who failed to attend to reality. But some lies, like riptides, sweep you out into a dangerous truth. If she had hoped to go on dreaming up enough stories to keep the pitcher full or partway full for the rest of her life, that hope, fragile anyway, must have left her when Martin left.

"The sweet ladies, you know about them? Bernice and Harmonia? Oh, they got sweet voices. Lady angels. They come to visit him, they take him for nice rides. They tell me Albert loves the Lord. They talk alla time about Lord Jesus. They smile at me like I got a pain."

"He told me." His voice a loud whisper, he had told her about the two ladies. Though it was unthinkable, his whisper implied, the ladies might be closer to God than she was. Sunday dinners at their house, reading aloud from the Bible, each taking a turn, and she had imagined his voice—portentous, hollowy, shaky with awe.

Ilona, like a bird that leads the predator away from her nest, eluded the landlady's eyes prying after an incontrovertible sign of sorrow. The sweet ladies had borne him in their angel arms, but where was his sister? The sister had kept her distance, hoping that her sorrow over him, already deep when she was a child, when she had no name for it, would serve as her presence near him, and knowing that it would not.

"Where's Al now?"

She mistook it for a superstitious query and looked into the woman's eyes to see where her brother was in the woman's own scheme of the world. Did this landlady think he was still in this room where he drank his tea and threw the ball and talked about his sister?

"What you going to do with his body?"

She had always to gather her strength to answer any questions, the ones asked and the ones unasked, and this one required of her a strength to overcome the shame of her failure to appear before he became only a body. "Yesterday afternoon," she began, knowing the landlady was listening to the shame stumbling around in her voice and not to the words, "as soon as the plane got in I went out to the hospital and tried to find the doctor who was on duty when he was brought in. Somebody said he'd be back soon and I waited but he didn't come back and then I walked for miles up and down the corridors, trying to find somebody who could tell me how to get my brother out of there." Up and down the corridors—it had the sound of pity for herself, but she had felt none. Some fault of hers, like a lack of foresight, kept her in narrow corridors, unable to escape, unable to suggest a way of escape for anybody she might run into there.

"What you going to do with him?"

The same question. It had to be answered with a word of such terrible finality she could barely hear herself saying it. But the landlady heard.

"The Greeks, we bury our dead."

It must seem to this woman that what she, the sister, was to do with her brother's body would be her final failing of him—this complete vanishing as if he had never lived. But the ancient Greeks built pyres, didn't they? Isn't that what all peoples did, in ancient times? And the ones who became ashes were remembered, weren't they? The millions who vanished into ashes in the concentration camps were remembered, weren't they, and the ones everywhere in the world who were dragged away in the night were remembered, weren't they, though they disappeared without a trace? Each one by someone or all by someone?

"Alla time, your brother walk, walk alla time," the landlady said. "Restless, always walk. I tell him he going to wear out all those shoes he got. He laugh at me, he tell me he got enough shoes to last one hundred twenty years."

With the key to her brother's room in her hand, a dimestore key that might open any door in this place except the landlady's door, Ilona climbed the rubber-tread stairs to the second floor, passed along a gray-walled hallway, by several doors close together, and unlocked her brother's door. She left the door open, to breathe.

The room was a cell and the smallness gripped her heart, confirming for her, once and for all, how small it had always been, her heart.

She had imagined the room larger, of course. You always imagine comforts for someone you fail to comfort. Above his cot a cardboard sign, printed with blue pencil:

Turquoise Bulletin Board
Third Revised Notice
as of May 14, 1969
In an Emergency Please
Notify my Sister
Ilona Lewis

Over the erasures of previous numbers, her present phone number was printed in red.

If the above number proves to be
in error, the correct number can
be located in my wallet.
Signed, Albert L. Lewis

The odor of sweat, the lingering odor of life. The cot and dingy blankets, a kitchen chair, a dresser, and half the cell, the back part, taken up by clothes on hangers hooked over lines that stretched from wall to wall. Only the top of a grimy window and the upper part of a closet door were visible above the lines of clothes. Always, his desire for clothes imbued with the lives of other men, garments that must have been, for him, like gifts left for a son by many kindly fathers, left for a nephew by generous uncles. He must have imagined them watching over him from high windows, so pleased their clothes were being put to further use by this sensible and grateful man.

Long gray underwear over the back of the chair, and on the seat of the chair a box filled with ties in a snakepit twining. Under the dresser, oxblood oxfords, black moccasins, a pair of white buck shoes that must have belonged to a church-going man, three hundred pounds. She remembered his slender bare feet, the tendons, the tension, the unpredictability of those bare feet on the bare floorboards at night.

"Throw everything over the railing."

With an armload of plastic bags the landlady moved swiftly around her, dropping the bags on the cot, and, into one, stuffing the tenant's long underwear, a large bundle of socks from the dresser drawer, the ties, a suit and four sweaters along with their wire hangers, exposing behind the first row of clothes a portion of the second row.

"Follow me."

Down the narrow hallway and out onto a railed porch, a balcony of sorts. The stairs down to the yard were boarded up, the drop to the earth, to the damp, bare yard was twenty feet or so. The landlady lifted the heavy bag to the rail and gave it a push. Over and down. The bag split on impact with the hard earth and the clothes leaped forth. A shoe kicked out, a sleeve and a pantsleg jerked once.

"Throw everything over. Is okay. I go down and make a pile."

Briskly the landlady went back along the hall toward the front of the house. On the ground floor there would be a rear door to her flat and she would emerge into the yard. In an unknowable maze you have to imagine an exit.

Under the cot, four pairs of overshoes, elaborately large and all readily available for the coming winter that he was not to enter. She gathered them up from the strings of dust and placed them in the bottom of a plastic bag. Flannel pajamas, thin as gauze in spots, from the foot of the cot, and from the first row of hanging clothes an apple green cardigan sweater, a stained winecolor robe, steelgray trousers crudely darned, three gaudy shirts that once belonged to a racetrack buff, and three suits for summer. The bag was too heavy to lift from the top. She lifted it from the bottom and carried it down the hallway to the porch.

Below in the yard the landlady was gathering the scattered clothes into a pile. Seen from above, she was even more plump, shorter, and the weak sunlight showed the black dye in her twisted-back hair. She looked up to see if the sister had appeared, their eyes met, and the quick, wavering light in the landlady's eyes was an accusatory question: Since you failed to come and see him, can you see at all? Ilona rested the bulging bag on the rail and pushed it over.

The bag plummeted in an instant, smacking the hard earth and flying apart. Up to that moment her abandonment of her brother had been a secret unknown in its extent even to herself. Now it became a public act, though no one looked out from the windows of the tenement next door, not from any grimy window of the four stories nor from the basement windows whose sills were level with the earth. No face stared out from the shreds of curtains. She knew the place had tenants, she had seen pale children playing in the entrance. But no one came to a window to see someone's earthly possessions strike the ground. Only the goad, the landlady, saw.

Up and down the hall, carrying out to the rail bags filled with sweaters, shirts, towels, brushes, combs, empty coin purses, half a hundred of them filled only with hope, and carrying over her arms suits for summer and suits for winter, and when all the hanging garments were cleared away and the clotheslines taken down, the closet was accessible.

Someone in an adjacent room was watching television or listening to the radio; she heard the boxed-in voices. The man struck the air; she heard the rustle of his arm and the shout of rage. Other persons so close around her brother—had their sounds comforted him, even the sound of someone endangered by his own self?

On the closet floor, her father's black leather suitcase, familiar as a repetitive dream. Along with the cardboard boxes tied with twine, the suitcase had gone aboard the mailman's truck, then aboard the train to Seattle, and when their aunt died it was loaded aboard the train to Chicago. He had gone east when everyone else was going west. He had gone back into the city of his mother's childhood, transforming it into the city of his future, imagining his mother a little girl again in a doorway not far from his own. What a sight he must have been on that train! Trembling with courage, loudly sociable with the person next to him in the coach like a jocular, seasoned traveler. The passengers must have been warily entertained by him, by his voice, by his clothes, by his anxious, excited face, by the way he bent low over his meal, guarding it from the covetous. If she had accompanied him on that train, obliged by her heart to sit next to him, her dear, dread companion, how she would have longed to sit far away from him, denying him even a brief acquaintance, her face turned toward the passing sights.

Down on her knees she opened the suitcase. The figured paper lining was a dry brown like the manuscript pages before they flamed up. The world atlas, here again, already old when she was a child, its maps even then in wrong shapes, and here again was his geography textbook, and the arithmetic textbook, and the grammar, and the dimestore tablet over which he had bent his head so low, his face so close to his hand erasing an error, erasing one small letter into extinction, leaving a hole where the offender had been. Over the tablet pages his pencil, sent along the blue lines at his father's command, pressed factual information of extreme importance to the world:

The earth turns on its axis from west to east once every twenty-four hours, giving us the impression that the sun moves around the earth from east to west. The earth completes one rotation of 360 degrees in a day; hence in one hour it must rotate $\frac{1}{24}$ of 360 degrees or 15 degrees.

The Bible, here again, in its flexible leather cover, with its red silk cord to slip between the pages. They belonged to no church, no temple, but their father had made them read the Bible, and was it to blame for her delusion that everything that happened on earth was taken into a divine memory? There was no memory like that.

Objects both strange and familiar, the way sacred objects seem. The gray photograph folder, here again, embossed with the name of the studio and Chicago. If she opened it she'd find a full-length portrait of a young woman before she became their mother. The pale, pure oval face, the eyes bravely meeting the camera's eye, dark hair drawn up and her dress outgrown, lace cuffs barely concealing thin wrists. If she were to look into that face would she find there the secret disquiet that must have come later to the mother's face, the forbidden wondering over the end of her children's lives—when and where? Here again, the pocket planetarium her father had invented, a square of cardboard folded in sections and tied with a string. If she were to unfold it, the sun and the planets would spring into existence, surprisingly white on the black background of space. Once or twice he had mused over a desire to visit Einstein, and when he died away from home she wondered if he were on his way to pay that visit and to unfold his modest design of the heavens under that great man's gaze. They were small enough, these possessions, to fit into her purse and small enough to be hidden away when she got home, where she would promise them to take them out later.

Only the dingy blankets, the flat sepia pillow, and the limp sheets that would be sure to rip were he to lie down on the cot one more night, only these were left to throw over the rail. His last night on this cot—he hadn't known it was his last, and this unknowing was like a trick played on him, a humiliation, the last, the deepest, the most mysterious of all the deprivations of his life, the ones known to him and the ones he could never even suspect.

On the porch for the last time she looked out over the neighborhood at the roofs, the few, low trees, the mist that indicated where the lake must be. The landlady was in the kitchen, fixing supper for her husband, who would be home soon. It had taken a day to clear out the accumulation from almost twenty years in that room and the things from the stucco bungalow. Her brother had brought her here at last to this high porch above a damp yard where his possessions lay in a large, darkening heap.

The dust of the room over her clothes, her hair, her hands, she locked his door. There was no use in trying to rid herself of the dust before she went out into the city. Her hands refused to do anything about it anyway. Back along the hallway, past flimsy, narrow doors close together, through fumes of menthol from behind one door, down the rubber-tread stairs and into the vestibule with the pay phone on the wall and the chair with a broken leather seat. She would come back tomorrow, to bid the landlady good-bye and to find the pastry cook and thank him for caring for her brother.

Out on the sidewalk the cold of early evening got through her raincoat, the advance cold of the coming winter. She had no heavy coat, she had never owned one or wanted one, nor any clothes other than a couple of skirts, a couple of blouses, a sweater, wanting no more than a few things easily carried to the capitals of the world and its far outposts, everywhere she had never been. She had wanted to be invisible—that was another reason for only the few possessions. Invisible, moving among people everywhere, observing all particulars and no one able to observe her.

On the bus she looked out at the streets familiar to her brother, at the cafés where he sat at counters, friendly to proprietors and waitresses, imagining himself a man of the world always on the verge of a momentous occasion. The bus entered the park, a prosperous section where lamps were already lit in the entrances of high apartment buildings, the glimmering lights restoring shades of gold to the twilight trees, and she imagined him striding through this park like someone on a mission of historical consequence, or like a large skimming bird keeping up with the bus. Unless he had slowed down toward the end, lamed by the pain in his heart, and then she saw that his face was not a young face anymore, that his vision of the world belonged to the face of an older man whom she might not recognize at first glance.

Along by the lake, the bus moved slowly through the glare and glitter of heavy traffic, and she saw him hurrying to a night job or homeward bound, a figure in several layers of other men's clothes, his heavy overcoat flapping in the wind, and a fedora, with a high-class firm's name on the silk lining, down low to his eyebrows. On the bridge over the dark waters reflecting the gold and silver lights of this downtown, he paused, imagining his sister beside him at the railing. There, you see? It's Lake Michigan, you see? pointing to make sure she wasn't looking for it in another direction.

15

Up in her unlit room on the hotel's fifteenth floor she drew apart the drapes to see a little more of this city at dusk. The gray building across the street seemed a surprising reflection of the one she was standing in, but, locating the window at a level with hers, she found no reflection of herself. An adamantine sightlessness was in all things and in all creatures, and she was probably the last one to learn this. For too long a time, when even a moment was perilous, she had allowed herself the delusion that there was sight everywhere, in everything.

She closed the drapes and lay down, face up, raincoat on, and exhausted as a penitent after a journey across a continent on foot, she wept and the tears streamed down her temples. For years, what a mighty struggle had gone on in her brother's room! All the clothes of other men taking up the space that fear over his abandonment would have claimed, the fear that if given a chance would have filled up that cell completely.

She slept in her clothes on top of the spread and was wakened by her desire to see her child and to hear her voice that, just by its sweet vivacity, would assure the mother she was a good person after all, despite any evidence to the contrary, and was even someone who could bestow a blessing. But even if she were able to put in a call to so far a place, to India, to Nepal, wherever the girl was now, her child had heard of the mother's brother only once or twice, not enough times to know he truly existed. The only way she could tell about him now was to say Antonia, I wanted to tell you I love you, and the child would think the mother was nowhere else but home, waiting for her to come home. Unless she heard the sorrow under those words of love and would be a little afraid of what was kept quiet when love was voiced. She could call a friend, a woman back in San Francisco, a friend who had confided in her for years, but she had told that friend nothing about her brother. Martin was her confidant and one confidant was enough. She could tell only Martin about this entanglement of grief, but he was not at home, he was over on the mountain, lying in love through the afternoon.

She bathed and lay down again, wanting to sleep until morning, wanting not to wake up in the middle of the night and set Martin's phone to ringing in an empty house.

Footsteps along the corridor wakened her. She heard a door being unlocked and heard a woman's voice, buoyant, and heard a man's voice, low, and then the closing of the door. It was two o'clock in the room, it was midnight on the coast, and the imagined bliss of lovers brought on again the dying away of herself. It lasted only a few moments, because the dying away of her brother forbade her to die away over such a trivial reason as the loss of a lover. Even if she were surrounded by lovers, even if every room was intended for lovers, if in all the rooms around her lovers were lying together now for the first time, loving through the night, inseparable, she was forbidden to die away from their midst.

She brought her hand before her eyes, trying to see it as Martin had seen it that day, out in the sun and wind. Maybe he had called it beautiful just for its striving to form something of beauty, no matter how meager the results, how riddled with faults, and maybe he had known that the striving would save her from himself. If, for a time, you weren't a lover, there were other ways to belong in life. Like her brother in his cell filled with the clothes of a hundred other men, in the cell of her mind she'd striven to become so many others, and in that way belong.

16

The fortress like an old-time gangster's mansion where her brother lay—she went there again in the morning. She waited again at the heavy door with its high, round, opaque window like a blind eye. He must have passed this fortress countless times on errands of utmost importance for his future. Her first visit, the evening of the day she arrived, a man had peered out at her through the blind eye before he let her in. He wasn't expecting anyone and he wore a green shirt and green plaid trousers. This morning he was attired in a black suit, clothes for a busy day.

She told him her brother's name in case he had forgotten she had signed a permission for him to claim her brother's body at the hospital. He asked now, "Is he a tall fellow?" and then he remembered. Again she went up the wide, carpeted staircase, past empty, shaded chapel rooms. She wished to live.

Upstairs at his desk he asked her, "Where do you wish to scatter the ashes?"—a whisper of false sympathy. "By the lake?" She shook her head. The lake waters were lead gray, miasmic, though people fished along its banks. "We often scatter the ashes over the cemetery."

There was something absurdly futile about that. "The forest pre-serve?" She had seen no forest preserve anywhere near this scorched and moldy city, but she nodded.

Then she waited while the man flurried around behind a door to a small room. She hadn't yet seen her brother, and when the door was opened for her and the man stepped aside and she went in.

Under a sheet, only his head and feet exposed. Sparse black and gray tendrils of hair lay over his head, the dark curls gone. His nose was more curved, the nostrils more flared as if by all the odors and fragrances of his life. His feet, pointing outward, were very pale, the nails like discolored ivory, and the loneliness she had underestimated to save herself was now in its pure state. She kissed his brow to tell him that in the years apart she had loved him deeply despite the obstacle that was himself. Expecting the film of sweat, the same as the day they parted, she was surprised to find his brow cold and dry. Whatever her kiss meant to her, for him it was of no consequence, placed on his brow an eternity ago.

Out in the sun again, she went on toward his street, assailed by the memory she had tried to keep away, of her brother striking their mother to the floor, and of herself, a child at the window watching him stride away, and wishing—afraid to pray for so awful a thing— that he would die someway, out there away from home. Yet they had loved him and he had wept and they had not sent him away, and as the years went by the turbulent youth gave way to the childlike man, but always the pariah, futilely camouflaged by all those clothes of all those other men who seemed to belong in the world.

The closer she got to his street, the more articles of clothing lay along the curbs and in empty lots. They may have been there yester-day, even always, but she hadn't seen them, just as yesterday she hadn't seen the many persons tenaciously adrift in these few mild days.

The landlady was in the vestibule, chatting with a white-haired woman coming slowly down the inside stairs, her cane feeling the way.

"Dr. Muller," the landlady said, introducing the woman and neglecting to name Ilona, simply "Albert's sister." Since the brother was gone, there was no necessity to ask or to remember the name of the sister. Like a calm, worldly physician, the woman smiled a half-smile of sympathy over the facts of life. *A wise old woman lives down the hall from me. She revealed to me that Franklin D. Roosevelt, also known as F. D. R., had seven illegitimate daughters. She is the youngest. Nobody knows about this, so please keep it under your hat.*

"The Salvation Army, they tell me 'No, thank you,'" the landlady said to Ilona. "They got too much stuff already. So we take Al's stuff to the corner. Lots of people like free stuff."

Ilona asked her where she could find the man who had taken care of her brother, and the man who answered her knock was graciously quick, uncritical of whoever it was on the other side of the door. Slight, he stood very erect as if his spirit drew him upward while age shrank his body, two opposing forces.

"I'm Albert's sister," she said. "I want to thank you for taking care of him."

"Please come in."

Ilona stepped into the room where her brother had lain and been tended, a room larger than her brother's, tidy, with flowered curtains at the clean windows, a crocheted spread over the double bed, an armchair, small rugs, a cookstove.

"I am so sorry about Albert," he said. "Always a good morning, always polite. We will all miss him."

The odd, solitary figure of her brother was always to be expected, around a corner, down a corridor, on the seat next to you, any place, and this man was telling her, without his knowing, that she was not to blame for her brother's aloneness, that her brother was not unlike all the solitary others, everywhere and always, each one odd in the way his own loneliness dictated.

"Sit down, please."

She sat in the armchair and he told her he had been a pastry cook. He described the varieties of pastries and recalled the number baked each day for the guests of the hotel, and she saw that even such airy concoctions as pastry spirals in memory can sustain your esteem for yourself to the very end.

"Did you know," he asked, "that Ho Chi Minh was a pastry cook in Paris? I've followed his career with great interest. I suppose I, too, could have been a general under the right circumstances."

At the door they shook hands. His hand was small and smooth and warm, and he told her how he had admired her brother for his good cheer and consideration of others and told her again that all the tenants would miss him.

She left the house then, the house whose atmosphere was her brother's presence and her own, together. She had been one among the tenants because of his constant longing to see her again, because of his voice confiding and pleading over the pay phone in the dim vestibule, because of the countless times he must have imagined her at his side, entering the house with him, this place he had found for himself courageously in a city halfway across the country.

The sky was overcast. It had been clear earlier in the day. Out in the street a man's large white shoe lay on its side. Along the sidewalk, before a row of grime-dark apartment buildings, she passed a rubber overshoe, a belt, a man's black shoe. A shirt hung over a stair-rail. Farther on, a mound of earth and rocks in a vacant lot changed into a tangle of clothes as she passed by, and to save her reason she thought: If they had not been there yesterday, all these scattered clothes, it didn't mean they were his for sure. In a puddle of water by the curb a tie floated, partly blackened by the water, partly shiny blue, the blue an inducement to the overcast sky to show its true color.

17

The rain began while she waited by the hotel for the airport bus, a cold drizzle after the spell of warm weather. Three months later she was to see a newspaper item about the record cold in this city, and she was to picture the ice and snow over the earth of the forest preserve. Do you know where the forest preserve is? she had asked the landlady in the vestibule, and the landlady had answered If they say so, it's there, suspecting perhaps that the sister doubted its existence even as she had wanted to doubt the existence of her brother.

The plane rose into the rain darkening the sky before twilight. The rain was left behind and the sky was alight again for a little while, and then night took over.

Up on the small screen, way forward in the cabin, a short documentary began. She watched without benefit of sound. A famous photographer in a large fur coat and hat to match was telling anecdotes about the celebrated ones whose photographs were as famous as the persons themselves. One after the other their faces appeared. The rotund face of a Pope whose name Ilona failed to remember, an old man's face lively with a little boy's pleasure over having his picture taken. The bland face of Eisenhower, gone before she could count the stars on his general's cap. Hemingway's face above a thick turtleneck sweater, like a sacrificial head on a platter. And oh! the very large sadness in Einstein's moist old eyes, the white strands of hair drawn up in cosmic amazement. The forever young head of John Kennedy, an earnest university debater. Then the lion head of Albert Schweitzer, like a marble sculpture of a god both animal and man. And then the coveted face of Bardot—All is dross that is not Helen. Churchill's old toad face, a toad vexed by the weight of the jewel in its head. Claud would look like that in another twenty years. Again, the photographer in his grand fur coat, relating interesting things she couldn't hear, and in a moment he, too, vanished and the screen was white and empty, and then it, too, vanished.

She gazed out at the night, but the faces on the screen remained before her eyes. They were always there before your eyes, whether you were awake or asleep, so highly visible were they. You could even assume they were among the blessed of the earth, if you wanted to, if that was your favorite delusion.

Across the aisle, the three close-cropped soldiers began a laughing jag together, shouts and spurts of laughter, waking her from shallow sleep. Then in the calm after, only murmurs here and there in the dim cabin, a dream began to surface, a dream from several nights ago, or weeks ago, that shocked her now with its meaning. She was with Martin in a small room and she was whispering Don't let him in but the door was open and her brother entered. Nothing could keep him away. He was a young man again but oh so different. A white skull-cap was on his head, his eyes were lucidly dark, seeing beyond them, and he was calm as he had never been, his being infinitely resigned to the journey. No tumult anymore, no frightful suppositions. He sat down in a chair against the wall, placed on the floor a portmanteau of a past century, and the room became a waiting room. He was on his way elsewhere.

THE LIGHTS OF EARTH

Far below lay the endless bas-relief mountains, lead color, iron color. There must be a moon, ravine shadows were sharp, and she thought—If some people were in the light, like the ones up there on the small screen, like Martin, like the woman he loved, like all those who were embraced wherever they went, it didn't follow that all the rest were lost to the dark.

18

It was after midnight when she climbed the stairs to her apartment. She had heard Martin's footsteps on these stairs that last night, and now she wished he was hearing hers and was drawn up from his chair or up from his bed and over to the phone, so that, when she turned the key in the lock, her phone would be ringing. The apartment was silent and remained silent.

On the kitchen table a little book lay face down, as if the lamplight had placed it there on the instant. Almost weightless in her hand, Madeleine, by André Gide. Martin must have left it that last night when he came to be with her. Something would be underlined, a passage meant as a message to her. Often he, too, relied on the wiser ones of the world to describe his dilemmas. Ah, here it was, his borrowed message. She sat down, blaming her weariness on the days past, on the hours gazing down from a great height on the depthless solitude of earth, but knowing that the weariness was over messages offered in words. Everything uttered, everything written was a message she failed to comprehend and failed to act upon.

Her vision slipped here and there, first to the last passage and then to the first, her eyes trembling with all they had seen away from home.

It was a day like all the other days. I had need to look up a date for the memoirs I was then writing. I had asked her for the key to the secretary in her room where my letters were put away. . . . Suddenly I saw her become very pale. In an effort that made her lips tremble, she told me that the drawer was empty and that my letters had ceased to exist.

What did his wife say then?

After you left, I found myself all alone again in the big house you were forsaking, with no one on whom to lean, without knowing what to do, what to become. . . . I first thought that nothing remained but to die. Yes, truly, I thought that my heart was ceasing to beat. . . . I burned your letters in order to do something. Before destroying them I reread them all, one by one. . . . They were my most precious belonging.

And he, what did he do then?

For a solid week I wept.

Ilona laid her head down on the open book. What did Martin hope for these underlined passages? Did he hope to persuade her not to forget or deform or destroy whatever he had entrusted to her of himself? Did he hope to persuade her of his love though he wasn't around anymore to confirm it? If she fell asleep where she was, not moving a muscle, without any objection from any part of her body, would her sleep be like a promise to him that she would do no harm, neither to him nor to herself nor to love, and would her promise be sensed by him, enabling him to sleep through the night beside the woman, serenely?

19

Every day, the entire day, she wandered the city, walking miles through neighborhoods where she had never been, hoping that when she returned to the apartment the lovers would be gone and she would be alone again, alone with all those beings in her imagination who were waiting to exist, waiting to be given faces, desires, personal trinkets, foibles, failings, aches and pains, waiting to be given voices, sacred silences, waiting to rescue her, their rescuer. But the lovers were always there when she returned, and out in the city, wherever she went, she was afraid that by some trick of fate she would encounter them, they would appear, strolling out from a shop, from a café, and she would be face to face with them, inescapably.

One day she saw the woman again. It happened in an Italian café not far from her apartment. Ilona was inside, sitting at one of the small round tables and facing the door. She chose to sit facing the door because if she sat with her back to the door the lovers might enter without recognizing her. The place was fragrant with coffee and steamed milk and pastries. The day was warm, the door open, and she began to hear the voices around her after so long a time of hearing only his voice and her own in memory, repeating their last words to each other. Obsession wears itself out or wears out its prey, the self—one and the same, and then the world around begins to make itself known again like a person returning after twenty years away, brimming with his own life. Then the woman was in the doorway, her little boy at her side, the woman she had seen only one evening and who, since then, she saw everywhere.

The patrons in the café faded away, along with their voices, along with the world. Then the woman saw her, their eyes met, and the wound opened unbearably wide because the woman's eyes must look into his while they loved, the woman's eyes were like a stage where all her life went on for him to see. The man who came up beside her wasn't Martin, but the wound was not to be healed simply because Martin was elsewhere, even if he were never to lie in love again with this woman, even if he were to love a thousand others and forget this one. Ilona saw the man frown when the woman told him she had changed her mind about this café. Only a fraction of a minute had passed, he had locked the car in that time or stopped to glance into a shop window, and what could have caused her in so short a time to refuse to enter this place? He glanced around at the patrons, at Ilona, and found no one to suspect, no one he had seen before and no one to remember.

When Ilona looked up again they were gone. So close a resemblance between the woman and the man beside her—she saw it clearly now. The man was the brother whom Claud had told her about, a sculptor living in Italy, in Florence, and on his rapid way to fame. They were brother and sister reflecting each other's beauty. Years later, when Martin and the woman were married and living in Florence, Ilona was to dream of the three, the woman, her brother, and Martin, sitting side by side on a bench in a marble rotunda, the woman between the men, precious to them, protected by their love. They were troubled, they were waiting for a verdict, a parting—Ilona didn't know what. She was barred from their lives. She saw only that Martin and the woman were holding hands, fingers entwined, she saw that their love was deepened by sorrow, and she tried to pry their fingers apart, waking herself with a harsh cry of despair over herself, over who she had become—desirous denier, scourge.

Before she went out into the streets she gave them enough time to leave the neighborhood, and then she found the streets as unfamiliar as those in another city. It was as if she belonged nowhere, as if this city, this part of the earth was no longer accessible, as if the earth itself belonged now to the woman and to her brother and to Martin. She got lost deliberately, wandering until evening, afraid to enter the apartment because the lovers, waiting there, would seem more enduring than ever.

Above the narrow passageway the little green globe was lit, casting a patina over the bank of mailboxes all alike. A letter from her child was waiting for her. Climbing the stairs, she began to read by the light of the large, dim globe that hung above the courtyard, fascinated by the foreign envelope, by the handwriting, like a provincial who has never received a letter in her whole life.

Dearest Mother,

First of all I am perfectly well and hope you will tell me you are too. If you ever wake up in the middle of the night, I hope you remember to tell yourself you blessed me, so you can go back to sleep. One night you must have done just that. It was when we got lost, John and I, because he was in so much of a rush to start up into the mountains before the monsoons came. He got careless about the trails, he was in such a hurry, and we ended up high in the mountains but not where we should have been. It was beautiful even though we were lost. We camped on the shore of a Hindu sacred lake. There was a mist over the lake until sunset when the mist lifted and we saw how incredibly blue it was. It's hard to describe that blue. It was either a deep blue or a light blue, because the lake was so clear and reflective and deep. We were camped in a stone hut and we'd been out of food for three days. We built a fire and got rid of the leeches on us. We took off our clothes and hung them on a pole over the smoke, and the leeches dropped off, and we stood close to the fire and pulled the leeches off each other. That night I thought We're going to be all right because my mother just woke up and remembered she blessed me. Of course the time was different because of the time zones, but that didn't matter. The next day we hiked over the pass and weak, weak, weak, we came down through a forest fragrant with vanilla and into a valley covered with mist, where we heard bells and knew we were safe. We came to a hut and two boys were in there and they gave us eggs and yogurt and yak-butter tea. They directed us to their aunt's house in the village, where we could stay for the night. On our way down to the village we met a hippie washing his clothes in the stream. "Hi," he said. "I'm Harvey. I'm from New York." So you see, we weren't lost anymore.

When we were up in the mountains we couldn't see the farther mountains because a mist was over everything, the way it is before the monsoons, but for about five minutes the mist parted and we saw those terribly high peaks far in the distance, and the wind was whipping long snow banners off the tops. We were really high, we had to take slow steps, the oxygen was so thin.

I am back now in Swayambhu in our little house, two stories, with a view of the Kathmandu valley as the storms blow in. The windows are only latticework and open to the night air, and I burn Chinese mosquito coils to keep the monsters out. Below the window is a water buffalo and I brush my teeth

and spit on his back. He doesn't seem to mind. I walk around
the hill to the springs for our water, which I carry in an earth-
enware jug. Except Tuesdays when it's men's day. Nearby is a
Buddhist temple on top of a mount, with the eyes of Buddha
painted on the walls. Sacred temple monkeys with crazy faces
live in the trees on the mount. The priests wear orange robes
and walk around the mount, spinning their prayer wheels. The
prayer wheels are silver cylinders and inscribed on them are
the words Om Mane Padme Hum, something like that, and
the priests say these words as they go around, and the words go
up to heaven.

Mother, you ought to come here. You said it would be like
a rite of passage for me and you made it possible for me to
come here. You said you weren't ready yet for your rite of passage. You said you'd have to invent your own. Mother, you are
a contrary person, like you used to call me. But I love you with
all my heart, whoever you are.

I guess Martin is back by now, so kiss him for me and ask
him how it feels to be a celebrity.

Your blessed child,

Antonia

On the landing she finished reading the letter by the light from the
evening sky and then it seemed that the same light, the same hour
lay over the entire world, just as it had seemed on those summer evenings when she had taken the deepening blue as a promise that someday she would find herself far away from the stucco bungalow. For
a moment now the earth was hers to know, even as it was known to
everyone to whom the earth with all its wonders appeared to belong.
A child out in the world can do that for you, can bring you to belong
in the world yourself. With the key in the lock, with her hand on the
key, she bowed her head against the door that she must open.

20

Like Martin's place by the ocean, this cottage on the sand trembled with resonance from the deep waters at its doorstep. She felt it at once. If the ocean were to rise up suddenly, a level rising with no warning, or if it were to come thundering over, the way Claud had described it that night of the party, not much of a house would be lost. Years after her year in that little house it was washed out to sea, the first house to go because it was the farthest out, and no trace was left, no fragments were swept up against the other houses built on sand. High tides, high winds, the winds piling up the water, a full moon at its closest point to earth, a point called perigee, and the earth at its closest approach to the sun—all forces joined together to sweep it away.

Claud carried in her possessions from his car. Offering the cottage to her for the year his former wife was to be away, he had described Ilona's move as a step into the world, but anyone who had ever roamed the world or crossed an ocean would laugh at the distance she'd come, only twenty miles north from the city, around the same mountain whose one side at night was ornamented with lights and whose side facing the sea was densely dark.

Wandering the small rooms through the horizontal light from the setting sun, she knew she had chosen to come to this place so that the constant presence of the lovers in her being, as implacable as figures in a dream and who would demolish her if she stayed any longer in that dream, might be overcome by the reality of the ocean. And she knew that her fear of the night ocean was to wake her even on calm nights and that she would switch on a lamp by her bed and lie in light for a little while. Lamplight in the middle of the night always seemed to emanate from the other side of the earth, come from elsewhere to keep her safe.

Claud came into the bedroom where she was sitting on the floor, glancing through the record albums she had found in the closet. The music was opera, the faces of the celebrated singers on the covers like masks laden with cosmetics and fate.

"She thinks she's an opera singer," he said. "I mean she is an opera singer but she's usually in the chorus. Once in a while she gets to sing a few words by herself. She likes it out here, she strolls along the sand singing above the din and everybody thinks she's crazy. Her voice isn't beautiful enough to compensate for everything that's wrong in her life. I wish it were."

The bedroom was almost bare, the bed not quite a full bed, too narrow for a husband also but just right for a lover, a night or two. On the chest of drawers was a framed snapshot of Claud at the age of twenty or so—barefoot on a lawn, thumbs hooked in the front pockets of his jeans.

"Some of my stuff is here," he said. "There's a little bit of me under the bed. When I left I thought if my valuables were under there it would be like I was there, and if she had a lover in her bed, I could hear them. She'd like that."

From under the bed he pulled out the same sort of grocery box she'd found in her brother's room, the universal grocery box, and the grating sound of sand came along with it. He sat down on the floor beside her and brought up a pair of bronze-plated baby shoes.

"They don't do this anymore," he said, weighing the shoes in one hand. "It's like I died at the age of one."

A wristwatch, the crystal badly scratched, his initials and the year of his graduation from high school engraved on the back. A battered book next.

"The name of the kid in here is Diamond. He sleeps in a stable loft and he has spells of delirium, and every time he's delirious he goes off in the arms of the north wind, who's a great big woman. That's the way I remember it, but it might not be that way." Over the inside of the cover, a drawing of a marvelously large woman, her hair flowing and rippling across the sky, and in her arms a very small, very thin boy. "She carries him off on excursions and the last time she doesn't bring him back. See, here's my name in the properly rounded letters, and my age. Claud McCormack, nine years old. This stuff, this watch, this book, these adorable shoes, I found in my mother's garage. The rest of the stuff, I'm to blame."

Up from the box a blue shirt, mottled with sweat and fuel oil. A pair of unwashed gray socks, holes in the toes and heels. A black wallet, split along the seams, and another wallet, yellow leather embossed with the Aztec calendar. A jockstrap. A half-smoked cigarette in an empty box of matches.

"My last cigarette."

A dozen and more ballpoint pens in a bundle, bound around with a rubber band. A mailbox, the kind that hangs on a wall, its coat of green paint flaked away. A red toothbrush, bristles flattened.

"All this junk, I've been saving it with a purpose in mind. It's for that librarian who used to beg me for mementos of my life. Unless he's forgotten how he used to desire me. Some university library—Sore Neck, Nebraska, or Hang Dog, Georgia, I can't remember which. Anybody who's ever got one paltry word in print hears from him. He wants to embalm the writer's spirit. That's his word, embalm, not mine. You've sent him something?"

"I need it myself."

"Ilona, send him something. It might be the only way you'll be remembered. He stashes it away—manuscripts, underwear, prostheses, bounced checks, pisspots, empty bottles of sleeping pills, empty bottles of booze, condoms, he stashes it all away in a sort of a tomb. No earwigs, no moths, no maggots, no mice, no rats, nothing ravenous. And think of it, Ilona—every hundred years your stuff gets set out on a revolving shelf in a glass case and round and round you go. I can't see how he can promise us that hundred years slot. Writers proliferate like rabbits. We'll be lucky to get on that merry-go-round every seven thousand years. What do you think, do you think seven thousand years from now when this junk goes around, along with my one novel and my picture on it, some beautiful girl will fall in love with me? Maybe by that time girls will have three eyes, but it won't matter how she looks as long as she falls in love with me. Like Anna for Dostoevski, only seven thousand years too late. Not just in love with my soul, but me, me, driving her wild in bed."

A pair of shoes, a grayed, rundown pair of canvas shoes, the shoestrings knotted together.

"They're not mine. I'll let him think they're mine. They belonged to a friend of mine, a fairly decent poet. The son of a bitch stepped out of these shoes and over the edge of a cliff, up in Mendocino. A couple of guys fishing on the rocks found his body. I was living on my boat at Fort Bragg and I went over to the cliff and found his shoes."

Swiftly he bent his head away, then he got up and drew her up. "Ilona, come to bed with me. Come in under with me."

That longing for another lover, that longing she confessed to herself reluctantly because the desire was like a betrayal of Martin, because it was an accusation that she was the deserter, that longing for a lover who would bring her to the bliss she imagined for those other lovers, who would take her down into that deep communion with all lovers, now that longing confessed itself to this man.

It was night when they lay apart. The ocean was louder. The sound of a breaking wave began at one end of the beach and traveled its length, and before the sound reached the other end another wave began to break. There was no silence between the waves.

"At night," he said, "I'll tell you how it is out there at night. Out there the clouds pile up on the horizon like that wave I told you about and I figure that's just what it is and everybody else has got the message over their crackly radios and they're already climbing the nearest mountain with their loved ones. But me, I'm sticking it out, smoking my dope, singing at the top of my voice. I can't keep a tune like my wife but I sing anyway. I sing what my father used to sing when he was shaving in the morning. 'Throw out the lifeline, someone is drifting away.' Or I sing, 'Kansas City, here I come, they got some crazy little women there and I'm gonna get me one.' The cabin's a mess, my bunk stinks like I pulled up a drowned man and hoped to revive him by warming him up, but I'm singing away. Some nights I'm so high I tend to neglect the rules of the road. The other night a freighter passed so close I saw the guy up in the pilot house, I saw him so close I'd recognize him in a crowd if I was ever to be in a crowd again. They don't see you way down there, your running lights are the farthest stars in the universe. Ilona," kissing her brow, "I'll tell you a dream. Not mine but my friend's, the one who stepped off the cliff. He used to go out on the boat with me, he used to help me out. One morning he comes up on deck—I'd been on watch while he slept—and he says, 'Oh, you still here?' And he told me he dreamed he woke up and came up on deck and I'm not there. Morning clear and brilliant, without me."

Lying close beside him, she knew he was telling her about his friend's dream to waken her even more to his presence, to the preciousness of his life.

Then, in the deceptive calm of strangers surprising themselves as lovers, "Ilona, tell me what you mean by blessed. Who is?"

So Martin had told him about that day she'd raved on and on, berserk. What Martin knew about her worst moments—shouldn't he have kept it secret out of respect for her, someone who appears to be balanced most of the time?

"My mind's way back in the Dark Ages."

He was stroking her hair, waiting just as Martin had waited, out in the sun and the wind. "The reason I asked, I thought if I was going to go around on that shelf every seven thousand years, maybe I'd be certified as blessed. I'd be remembered forever, more or less, and my picture was going to keep me the same age I was then, thirty and a goodlooker. But what the hell. One day out of seven thousand years guarantees me nothing. I'm going to take that stuff down to the boat and throw it over. Something's bound to wash ashore. Somebody, say in Patagonia, is going to pick up a shoe and wonder who it belonged to. Did you know the ocean currents can take a shoe around the world? See, this guy's standing on this desolate shore, way down there, he's standing there with my shoe in his hand, thinking 'Who the hell did this belong to?' I like that idea. I could be anybody."

His hand stroking her face came to rest over her mouth, where no answer was waiting, nor any further speculation as to who was blessed and who was not.

"Ilona, you suffer from delusions of the other fellow's grandeur. Whoever they may be—saints of all sorts, Nobel Prize winners, Jesus, Tolstoy, maybe Garbo, anybody in the hands of what you think is a great destiny. Ilona, I struggle with that delusion myself, all my life, and that's why I stay out there at night, because out there we're all in the same boat. I've got them all jammed into my smelly little boat that's going to spring a leak any minute. Ilona"—kissing her brow. "Come out with me some night."

As he fell asleep his hand slipped down from her mouth, his arm stretched out, and his hand opened palm up.

21

Claud slept, and she lay listening to the waves breaking. She had never fallen asleep before the man beside her slept, and it had been that way with her child. She hadn't slept until the child slept. Long ago she had been charged to observe the drifting away of the spirit and just by her waking presence protect the sleeper in that transition. She slept, then. Startled awake, she lay waiting to learn just what it was that had waked her but it would not let itself be known. All she knew was that there was more space out in the heavens for it to swoop down and farther depths in the ocean for it to rise up and surge toward the ledge on which they lay.

She dressed in the room that faced the ocean and lit the lamp. The light would tell her where the house was when she made her way out from the waves. It would tell her where Claud was. His sleeping presence would guide her out just as Martin, without his knowing, had drawn his wife out from the ocean at his doorstep. The lights of earth are all the beings who draw you out from the dark, and are they everyone in your life?

One step down, and her bare feet sank into cold sand. The wind off the ocean snapped strands of hair across her eyes. She went down toward the water at a diagonal, struggling against the wind, wanting to give herself over—only for a moment—to that engulfing embrace, wanting to immerse herself in the element that was to wake her in the night, all the nights of that year. Above the sound of deep water spunglass notes sprang up, almost like voices. Out before her now lay the vast surface glazed over by the stars' light. The ocean was a great eye, turbulent over its blindness.

Even in the cold sweep of the shallows there was such a merciless draw. The sand under her feet yielded to it and yielded her over. She stepped down the slope until the water rose to her breasts, and in that rocking expanse, in that rising mound before the first big wave broke, she turned and looked back to shore. The unlit houses along the sand were unseeable and the few lights were dimmed by the turmoil of distance and mist. The waters surging around her shifted her sight and jumbled the lights about and the light in the little house where Claud slept jumped sideways. The tremendous wave broke over her, knocking her under, dragging her down, and when she fought her way up and was almost standing again, the wave that followed struck her down again, and within that raging blindness she beat her way toward shore or toward where the shore was last seen.

"Ilona!"

Ilona. Her name came over the din like a stone skipped over a calm lake, and in that voice was an intensity of need for her presence on earth. Against the waters sweeping her back she found her footing and made her way toward the little figure running along the sand.

Conference
of
Victims

We are created from and with the world
To suffer with and from it day by day:
Whether we meet in a majestic world
Of solid measurements or a dream world
Of swans and gold, we are required to love
All homeless objects that require a world.

W. H. AUDEN, *Canzone*

1

The day was election day but Hal O. Costigan, candidate for Congress, was nowhere around to have his picture taken as the winner or the loser. By his own choice he was nowhere around to care. The day was warm and windless, the large flags at the polling places rustling a little toward evening. Inside garages swept clean and living rooms tidied up, women with an official look appropriate to the day sat at card tables and checked off the names of the voters. Everything was as it should be, except one: a dead man's name was on the ballot.

Naomi Costigan did not vote. Her brother was dead and she had no use for all the other men whose names were on the ballot. Whatever they had promised to do meant nothing to her. She went to work at the county recorder's office and was deaf to the prophetic voices in the portable radios that some men carried with them to the counter and along the courthouse corridors. The only thing she heard that day was what she expected to hear that night, her mother's grief over the loss of the son.

They sat at the kitchen table facing each other, the bereft mother and her forty-year-old daughter, dipping their spoons into their bowls of soup. The mother wore her son Hal's high school cardigan sweater, its emerald green dulled by the years but the emblem still secure above a pocket. Maybe old women should never comb their hair, Naomi thought. They look worse when their hair is parted and smoothed down, like children keeping themselves neat so life will love them.

"Cort," said her mother, "I told Cort, 'You're his brother. It's your duty to find out who killed him. That's why a mother has more than one son, so they'll protect each other. If one is murdered, the brother never rests until he finds out who did it.' But Cort's a coward. He's got a birthmark on his back looks like a little eel."

"It always looked like nothing to me," said Naomi.

"An eel. He was always slippery."

Naomi did not defend her younger brother. Their mother loved him and that was his defense.

"Isobel," said her mother, "I said to her, 'Isobel, you're his wife. You go to the mayor, you tell him they killed Hal. The man he was running against got the police to do it.' The mayor would have listened to her, but she ran away. First she sent the boy off on a plane, alone, and then she runs away herself."

Elbows on the table, the mother crumpled the pink paper napkin under her cheekbone, into the sagging flesh, and Naomi thought, betrayingly, that she had never seen a face so intricately wrinkled, like a puzzle God presented to the daughter's gaze for her to figure out, like a warning to the daughter to act, to run, before it was too late. But how could you escape if love and conscience were your jailers?

"Can you imagine her sending him off like that? A little boy? On the plane alone. Suppose her aunt, who was going to meet him, didn't get there, something happened, and there he'd be, alone. Any degenerate could of got hold of him. They walk around everywhere, and whores, the lowest of the low."

"I walk around, too," said Naomi, and saw that her mother

couldn't tell whether the daughter was lowering herself to belong among the lowest or elevating herself to belong among the virtuous ones who were also present in the world.

"Why didn't they ask that girl if *she* murdered him? They hired a little whore to do it. They hired a little whore to say he slept with her."

"Mama, cut it out."

"They didn't find any note because the girl did it. No note."

"No note!" Naomi gripped the table edge. "Mama! He didn't need to leave a note. He said it loud, Mama, like they told him to speak up in debating class. He told us everything just by what he did to himself."

"What's everything?"

"Mama, I don't know what it is. How can *I* know?" How could his dimwit, homely, job-bound sister, Naomi, know what *everything* was? If she lived to be a hundred, she'd never know.

Naomi shook out a cigarette from the package by her plate. "Who's President?" she asked brightly. "Eisenhower, I bet."

"Hal would of won," her mother said.

"Oh, he had it in the palm of his hand." Was it something called privilege her brother had, right from the day of his birth, and thrown away? Maybe she, too, Naomi, had been granted a privilege of sorts. Maybe you had to think so in order to live, and what was hers? A long time ago she had got herself a job, in the time of the jobless when sad-eyed men came to the back door to ask if they could earn a bite to eat. She had begun to support her mother and her brothers, and was that her privilege? That must have been it, and, though times had changed, forever after she had clung to it, that astounding privilege, as if it were her very life.

The unlit cigarette on her lip, she leaned to the radio on the counter, twirling the dial from music to audience laughter. A comedian's voice, falsely modest, falsely hesitant, insinuated its way into the expectant laughter and capped the joke. Louder laughter and the crackle of applause tumbled out into the kitchen.

"It's your friend," Naomi said. "The Great Goofball. He should've run for President. I would've voted for him."

The announcer's voice cut into the laughter and applause, switching the listeners, Naomi and her mother among them, to cities where counting was in progress, the microphone moving westward from New York to Chicago to San Francisco, the nearest large city to their own small city in the interior of the state. Excited voices rattled off the names of the candidates and the number of votes for each, so far, but the name of Hal Costigan was never spoken, as if the name had never appeared on a ballot or the man had never appeared on earth.

2

On the front page of the evening newspaper her father brought home, there was a photo of her under the headline COSTIGAN KILLS SELF OVER SCHOOLGIRL. That morning when she had left the sheriff's office, her father had tried to put his jacket around her, but, alarmed by this closing-in from behind her of a garment that wasn't hers, she had thrust it away, and the camera caught her with her elbow lifted in a way that twisted her body and exaggerated her breasts in the cotton dress. *Dolores Lenci, 17-year-old paramour,* the caption said. She had never seen that word before.

They had come to the house in the morning, after a farmer's children, going down their dirt road to the highway to catch the school bus, had come upon his car parked among the willows. They knew, the sheriff's deputies, that she had been the last person with him that night. They knew because a deputy, cruising the outskirts of the city and surprising lovers in cars parked off country roads, had surprised them, had contemptuously asked her her name and her age, and contemptuously not asked the name of the man with her because he was recognizable in the flashlight as the young, respectable attorney, father, husband, and candidate for U.S. Congress. In the sheriff's office they had questioned her about what he had said that night, whether he had told her anything about the campaign, about money, about enemies, whether he had threatened to kill himself, whether her father had threatened to kill him, whether she had threatened, and though they asked their questions as if they knew what they were after, she felt that they were asking for no answer, only enjoying themselves, titillating themselves with the presence of the girl whose lips could barely move.

Dolores's mother came in after the cafe was closed and sat down on the bed, but the girl pushed away the hand that was dear to her and covered her face again with the blanket. Whenever her mother came to her, that evening and again in the morning, her mother was the stranger, her hand was not *his* hand and could not go to the parts of her body where his had gone; but in the hours she was alone, *he* was the stranger. Her body bore the impress of the stranger. At times his strangeness, intensified by his act of suicide—who was he?—bore down upon her and, with hands, with mouth, with whispers, set all the places astir again, each place desiring, until all was clamor. By his dying he had made the demand upon her to *know* him.

At noon, the next day, alone in the house, she sat at the kitchen table and read the two days of newspapers and gazed at the photographs of him, Hal Costigan, and his wife and his son and even his sister, who stared at the camera from among the record books and filing cabinets in the county recorder's office. She gazed at herself on the front page and saw nothing in that girl to warrant the man's risking anything for, and the thought that he might already have known what he would do if they were caught and had risked his life for her—that thought was a burden. She fed herself tasteless toast and wept, not for him and not for herself, but in fear of all the things she knew nothing about, until the newspaper pictures between her elbows grew damp and dark and the type showed through from the page underneath.

"What did he do it for?" She asked it of her father as he was taking off his shoes in the kitchen.

"What you got to learn," he said, pulling at a dusty boot, "is that everybody is a little bit crazy."

He glanced at her sideways, a secret glance of satisfaction that said the most respected, the most popular, the ones on their way up, as Costigan, were no better than the dolts, than himself, a maintenance man in an oil refinery, and, in this glance that was without any sympathy for the dead man, he revealed a stoniness of heart she had not glimpsed before. It was not that way all the time, his heart. Only now, and was it his own little bit of craziness? She opened a can of beer for him and set it on the table with a glass, and when he glanced up, his fatherly love for her had returned to his eyes.

After a week she went back to school. She told herself not to keep her eyes down, but they went down anyway, there were so many eyes looking at her. She had always met the eyes of the men who came into her mother's cafe because it was her way of telling them that she was somebody else beside the girl they were appraising. She was somebody who could appraise them, but always in this exchange was the excitement, concealed or unconcealable, of joining in the discovery of herself. Now she was unable to return anyone's gaze because the discovery of herself was public knowledge. A man had died and told them all about her. She wore a buttoned sweater that was too large and a bulky pleated skirt, but under these garments was the girl who had lain with the man.

When she came into the cafeteria, the voices went silent, the clatter dimmed down. When she went along the halls from class to class, clusters of boys would fall silent and watch her walk by, the more nervous among them laughing. The girls in the lavatories stopped their chattering or their languid conversations, and she did not look at herself in the mirror or stay long enough to comb her hair. The teachers were as respectful of her as though she had lain sick for a month, but they were self-conscious before their students, and all lectures and all formulae pointed to on the blackboard seemed as trivial to the teachers as they were to the students. In the home economics class where, a month ago, the teacher had singled her out as an example of a "neat-minded" girl, she sat in her commendable style and embarrassed the teacher by confronting her with her teacher's superficiality, for within the nice clothes was the body that was not, and within the candidate's suit from the best men's store in the city, behind the smile, the wit, the eloquence, the respectability, everything that had charmed the teacher, was the man who had lain with the girl.

The newspaper photos of the funeral troubled her, in the days after. The women in black, a color incriminating of her, had known him better than she had known him, and they mourned the man they knew, while she went around the house in her pastel cotton dresses or in her sky-blue bathrobe. The figures in black accused her of ignorance of him and of destroying him, and she could not turn the blame on him because his suicide seemed to be an act of expiation. The girl with her long brown hair, which she had let grow long because it was exciting to men to see it hanging down her back, the girl alive and aware of her tantalizing self, *she* was to blame. She accepted the blame because the mystery of her lifted her above the sordid and, after a time, above the blame, and, without blame, she called up the times on the blanket in the back of the station wagon parked among the yellow willows by the creek. She became the girl desired beyond any risk, and the memory of herself and the man overcame her as she sat in study hall, her head bowed over a book, as she walked home, as she lay in her bed at night. All the details of love, the entwining of bodies, everything was recalled, and the time she had drawn herself upon him and loosened her hair into a dark silken enclosure for their faces and in that enclosure drawn upon his mouth until, with a sudden knotting of his body, he had thrust her under him. Again the willow branches scratched the windows, stirred by the night wind that moved like a creek above the creek; again the yellow-smoke trees surrounded them as she lay in the blanket he had wrapped her in to cover her nakedness, which he had explored and still explored; and again she lifted her head from his chest because his heart was beating under her ear—an overwhelmingly secret sound, the heartbeat of a stranger.

On election day her father came home early, bringing another worker from the refinery. They had been given an hour off at the end of the day and had gone to vote, and they sat in the kitchen, making jokes about the election. She was peeling potatoes at the sink, carefully so the peeler wouldn't nick the pink polish on her fingernails, aware of her long back and broad hips in the schoolgirl skirt and sweater and of the man's shy curiosity about her, notorious daughter of his co-worker.

"What the hell anybody want a change for?" her father asked his friend. One foot was up on a chair, and he lifted his foot to give the chair a push with it. "It's always the same bullshit, both sides the same bullshit, and when they get in themselves, where's the change?"

"There's a difference," the friend said, his arms leisurely on the table. "With the Democrats you get war, and with the Republicans you get a depression."

She had heard conversations like this before and they had meant little to her, but now she felt a rising resistance, an alarm that she tried to stop with the deadening sound of her hair falling across her ears as she bent her head lower. They recalled government scandals, bribery, and every name they spoke and every acquittal and conviction deprived her of her mystery, brought her down into the arms of a petty politician who had gone berserk with the idea that everything was due him, with wanting everything.

3

As Cort Costigan prepared himself to meet his girl, as he showered, shaved, brushed his teeth, shined his shoes, and then resented his being forced to make himself as handsome and as clean as possible when, after all, he was a plain fellow not always scrupulously clean, as he fretted over his falsified self but was pleased by the sight of himself at his best, he was preparing also the revelation of his inward self. He was not preparing the revelation in words because he was afraid of words. Words had a life of their own beyond him. Once when the words *great guy, oh, he was a great guy* spoke themselves inside his ears, startling him, he clamped his hands down over his head in a desperate stifling reflected in his bathroom mirror.

Pauline was already at the door when he drove up to her sister's house, already down the stairs and opening the car door, and was already sitting close to him before he was ready for the transition from the woman of his fantasies to the solid woman animated not by his wishes but by her own, a tall, big-boned, large-breasted girl with a sullen, bony face and straight blond hair to her shoulders. She sat against him, her skirt flaring over his knee, dispelling with her closeness the two days since he had seen her last and in which time his need for her had struggled with his doubts about his need. When she sat by him, he needed her, and this need increased through the evening along with his need to unburden himself of his brother. Now that he had found this girl, it seemed to him that he had been searching for her ever since his brother died, through the winter and into the summer, but he was reluctant to admit to himself his desire to exploit the tragedy of his brother for the benefits he hoped to get from it, the comforting and the passion that he hoped the story would arouse in her.

After the movie, they wandered around the library grounds, over grass illumined by the neon signs of the theater and the bar across the street, pausing to embrace in the shadows under the trees. It was a warm night in the middle of summer. They circled the old, cream-colored, two-story library, its high stone steps lit by a large white globe on each side, and found a bench at the back, under the windows of the basement reading room. They watched other couples crossing the grounds to their cars slowly, as if wading through the short grass, heard their voices carrying far in the quiet night, heard car doors slam and motors start, and a wakened bird complaining among the thick branches above their heads. Then he heard the words begin, as adroitly fumbled as if he had permitted himself to rehearse them that way.

"Pauline, Pauline, I want to tell you about my brother...," and the use of his grief to persuade here to love him deepened his grief. "He was a great guy, a great guy."

"I know he was, Cort."

"No, I'm not saying it like in the obituary. That's not what I'm saying."

"I know what you're saying," she told him, stretching her fingers between his fingers.

"No you don't. You can't know until I tell you because I'm the one it happened to. I mean, my mother and Naomi, they cried and they still cry, my mother does, but it didn't shake them. My mother cries and goes right on watching television, and Naomi goes to work and goes home and talks about nothing and eats half a berry pie and drinks twelve cups of coffee up to the time she goes to bed. I don't drop by much anymore. That's the way women are, they survive. The men get killed in a war and the women put ashes on their heads and fight over the men who come back. Mama and Naomi, they got each other. But *me*," he said. "It did me in."

"It didn't do you in." She was stroking his sleeve. "You got a job, you got me, you laughed so hard tonight, the time the guy was holding onto the balloon."

"You ever look up to anybody? I looked up to him like he was my father. He was nine years older than me, and my father died when I was four, so it was easy for me to look up to him. I learned from him. He was my brother and my father, he was the man in the family. You know what I thought when I heard he was dead? I thought—somebody did it to him. All these years he's been showing me how to live. But after a while I had to admit he did it to himself. I had to admit it. I had to admit you don't do something like that to yourself without saying it's the thing to do. Jesus Christ, why did he tell me that?"

A man, standing on the curb before the bar, way across the grounds, glanced toward them, hearing Cort's faraway voice rising.

"You've heard the old saw about the good die young? It's true, they're killed off in the scramble to get to the top. What I mean, they're stepped on because they can't step on anybody because they don't like the goddamn war that goes on all the time. Or they do themselves in like my brother did. I look around me, I look at the other salesmen, and I think to myself—Jesus Christ, is that what we're put on this earth for, to sell goddamn refrigerators, hop-skip up to a customer before the other guy gets to him, make a big production out of a bloated piece of tin with an electric wire coming out of it?"

She was scratching his scalp with her long, strong fingers, her pointed fingernails. "But everybody said it was the girl," her voice low, curious.

"You sound like my mother, you sound like Naomi. Naomi asked me, 'You ever seen her, Cort?'" imitating his sister's grainy, whispery voice. "Mama wanted me to go over there and shoot her, she had this crazy idea about me avenging my brother, maybe something she picked up from a soap opera. If the girl was the reason, he made her the reason on purpose. He wasn't a kid, he didn't get all worked up like a kid does, you know how it was in high school, can't eat, can't sleep, can't live if you can't have the girl. Once he took me in there, bought me lunch there at her mother's joint, and she was there. It was a couple months before. She was there, it was Saturday, and he treated her like he treated any other waitress, considerate, kind of indifferent, too. I don't think he knew her name. She was just like any other good-looking high school girl, tall, long hair in a pony tail, used her hips like they do. You see them all the time, everywhere. But he said something to me I remember, he said something out of the Bible. He said, 'King David was old and stricken in years and his servants covered him with robes, but the old man was still cold. So his servants found a fair young virgin for him, and she ministered to him and lay down on his breast.' He quoted the Bible word for word, he was always good at that, and he said, 'That's an idea, isn't it? Bring in a young girl to warm up an old man in his last days. That's what I need.' And I said, 'You aren't old.' And he said, 'They call me young. Young Costigan. The young can act, the young can change things, there's nothing the young can't do, it takes a young man for the job. But I'm not young, I'm nine hundred and sixty-seven years and I'm cold. They cover me with campaign posters, I got this nice English suit, I got wool blankets and my wife Isobel and my son and life insurance, I got all that to keep me warm. But how does the Bible say it? He 'gat no heat?'" The tenor ring of his brother's voice—he heard it again, and he remembered that his brother had laughed, shifting in his seat in the booth, so unaware of the girl that if he were to choose some handmaiden she would not be the one.

Pauline was comforting him, stroking his shirt, unbuttoning one button to slip her hand inside and stroke his chest, and he drew her face to his, a swift claiming of her. "Come home with me," he begged her. "You want to come home with me, don't you?"

When he returned alone to his apartment and lay down alone where both had lain, the sorrow he had made use of to bring her to his bed, and that she had soothed away with her embrace, reclaimed him. Pauline's embrace, her long, strong arms and legs around him, had claimed him for only part of the night. As he was falling asleep, he was wakened by a clear convincing of his own self with the story he had told her. His brother had tried to link himself with life, one last attempt, just as the old king had tried, but the cold was already in the marrow of his bones. But *himself?* Cort Costigan? The younger brother wanted to live more than he wanted to die, and the girl who had embraced him an hour ago had more power over death than the girl who had lain in his brother's arms, and he drew her back again, Pauline, young woman fragrant with life, odorous with life.

4

Naomi, following her friend Athena into the bar's blue-glass entry, was reminded of a black-fig tree on a summer day, of the smell of the figs fallen to the ground and beaten to a fermenting pulp by the hot sun. The summers of her childhood were surprisingly contained in this unfamiliar bar one step from the cold street of late October.

"Smells like old figs. You know, old fruit," she said, tittering, stumbling because it was so dark inside, only the mirror behind the row of bottles lit by an amber light.

"That's everybody's breath you smell," Athena said, the lifting of her voice like a greeting to the bartender. "They never air the place. Everybody's old whisky breath stays in here."

"Some people need it like oxygen," said the bartender, a tall old man, bald. He was turned to the mirror, fussing with something, and Naomi saw his face and the back of his head at the same time. The double image heightened her wariness.

Athena dropped her purse on the small round table and pulled out a spindly chair. Naomi, in imitation, pulled out the other spindly chair and sat down. Her knees, as she crossed them, kicked up the table and joggled the amber glass ashtray.

"It's so damn dark in here," Athena said, explaining away Naomi's clumsiness. "Over at the Executive they got two sixty-watts going day and night."

"They can afford it," said the bartender.

A young man at the end of the bar turned his face toward them, taking them in and disgorging them at the same time. "That's where the bigshots hang out," he said. "The D.A., the mayor, those guys. Every time I go in there I see big money passed under the table."

"You're crazy, boy," the bartender said. "They do that kind of thing in privacy." He lifted his eyebrows at the women. "What'll it be?"

"A martini for me," Athena said.

"Privacy!" The young man blew his lips out to make an obscene noise. "Who's private? Everybody writes their mem-wahs about who they screwed, all the movie stars write their mem-wahs. Big swindlers, big gamblers, they all write their mem-wahs. Privacy ain't natural."

"He sounds like my dad," Athena said, bowing her shoulders with a secret laugh.

"Sounds like Mama," Naomi said, and she too bowed, laughing.

The bartender, deaf to the young man at the bar, was tipping his head toward Naomi, his eyebrows still lifted queryingly.

"Oh, it'll be the same for me," Naomi said. She was familiar with martinis. Her brother Hal had taken her into the Executive a few times and she had liked martinis best, and this possession of a preference made her feel at home now.

"My old dad hates everybody," Athena said. "I got it figured out that the closer you get to dying, see, the closer you get to being alone the rest of eternity, the more you want to be alone. It's kind of like nature preparing you."

"My mother's not that bad," Naomi said. "She's got pity for orphans. One time there was a piece in the paper about five kids left in a room by their mother. She went out with some guy and there they were with no food, no fire, nothing, and one kid real sick."

Athena shrugged off her coat with a nervous, coquettish movement that went from her shoulders down her arms to her dry,
wrinkled hands and their nails heavy with red polish. "There was
this father who was shot by his boy scout son. You remember, up in
Lassen County? My dad says, 'Must of been a mean bastard, guess he
deserved it.' Then he says, 'Boy must be crazy, whole family crazy.'
Course me," she said, twisting her red beads, "I feel sorry for the
father, you know, but I feel even worse for the boy. There in one
minute his whole life is ruined. The father, he lived his life and maybe
he didn't live it right and maybe he shouldn't of brought kids into
the world. Or maybe he lived it right, they say he was a church elder.
Who knows? You never know what goes on inside a house. But I
feel sorrier for the boy. You think, someday he'll wake up and realize
what he did, and then you think, he's never going to wake up because
when he pulled the trigger he done himself in, too. You know what I
mean? Unless these psychologists they got working on criminals like
that, I mean kids in jail because they're too young to go to the gas
chamber, unless the psychologist makes him feel not too bad about
what he did. I mean, bad enough, bad enough, that's the first step,
and then not too bad, so he'll be able to redeem himself."

Athena pushed away the money Naomi was trying to place on the
bartender's tray. "When I was sixteen," she said, sipping, "I had it
all plotted out to get rid of my dad. He hated everybody even then.
There was some people he liked, he wasn't as bad as now but bad
enough for me because I felt like I had to grow up to hate people and
I didn't want to hate people. I had it all plotted out. Now he's seventy-
six, I make custard for him and kiss him and tuck him in at night."

Naomi's eyes began to water from the drink and the embarrassment
of hearing a confession.

"Sometimes I think that maybe I should've done it. They would've
sent me to Tehachapi Prison for Women. I'd have had a little patch
of garden, maybe, and listened to other tales of woe over the sewing

machines or the jute mill or whatever they put you to work on. I would've been out by now, if it was twenty years. But I mean, there's something about doing something like that that lifts you out of the rut. While you're young, I mean." She laughed a long laugh, buoyed up by the pleasure of being in the bar. "It doesn't mean anything when you're fifty. No purpose in it. The old man's not long for this world anyway."

Athena stirred the martini with the toothpick. "That's why I never had kids. I could have, I was married eleven years, but I figured they'd grow up to hate me. No, maybe that wasn't the reason, maybe I just didn't have the courage. Is it courage? What is it? Maybe I was selfish, but when I look back on those years, I wonder what I had to be selfish about. You like kids?"

"My brother Hal, his wife's got a boy, thirteen years old now. I haven't seen him for a year. Yeah, I like *that* kid." She sipped. "My brother Cort's going to have himself some kids. Got married this summer. Met this girl, love at first sight, got married a month after. He's the baby of the family. I always think of him as the baby of the family."

"I feel sorry for kids," Athena mused. "So damn much to learn. Sometimes you almost snap your cap, like my own plot."

Naomi found it very hard to lift her gaze to the tired face across the table. Athena had come to work in the assessor's office six weeks ago, and this was the first time they had gone out together after work, and Naomi was unable to combine in one person the friendly, joking woman and the woman confessing a plot to murder her father.

Three young men came in, bareheaded, wearing jackets, and hoisted themselves up in a row at the bar, talking loudly, carrying on a humorous argument. One, at the end, leaned around the one in the middle and punched low in the back the one at the other end. The punched one gave a half-laugh, half-moan, jerking his back inward.

"If kids could only see beyond the hump," Athena said. "If they could see that pretty soon they're going to be helping the old man out of the tub. When you're a kid, you couldn't see them with no clothes on and you wouldn't let them see you, your father I mean, and now I help him out of the tub." She laughed through closed lips because she'd put the olive in her mouth.

"Cort married a nice girl," Naomi said, wanting to drop this talk about the terrible things that could have happened when they were young. "Her name's Pauline. She's a typist at the Bon Marché. One time Cort brought her over to meet Mama and she hardly said two words. She wouldn't let Cort hold her hand."

"I got no brother," Athena said. "Got a kid sister, used to have two but one died a couple of years ago, left three kids. The sister I got left lives in Tulsa." She took another sip, began to laugh before she had swallowed it. "I remember one time we were living in Louisville, Kentucky. My dad was working in the tobacco company there, and one night my mom and dad had this awful fight, he said the kid she was pregnant with wasn't his. My sister and me, we held each other in bed. I guess I was about eleven or so. Then he comes in and orders us girls to get up and get our clothes on. Our mom began to beat on his back, and he let her because it wasn't hurting him any, he was a big guy. He piled my sister and me into his Chevy and drove us a hundred miles to some little town where we'd never been and he knocked on a door there. To this day I don't know if he knew those people or not. He won't answer me when I ask, I think he's forgot. He says to the woman who answered the door, he says that 'we hadn't no breakfast and hadn't no money,' and would she give us some breakfast while he looked around for work in that town. She gave us oatmeal, my sister and me. It was the first time I ever ate oatmeal."

"What happened after that?" Naomi asked.

"Oh, after that they got together again and we had another little sister and we all moved out West. Los Angeles."

A warmth came over Naomi, a feeling like love. The woman across the table had become her sister, and nothing was secret between them and nothing was unforgivable. "Our family was real close," she said, carefully because the words wanted to mix themselves up.

"Some families are." Athena looked irritated.

Naomi wondered if what she had said about her own family was taken as a criticism of Athena's family. I ought to be going home, she thought. Mama's alone. What am I doing, sitting here laughing with this woman who almost murdered her father?

"My father was a barber," she heard herself say. "Had a shop where they've got Rich's Cafeteria now. He died of a heart attack when Cort was still almost a baby." Her tongue and lips got in the way of her words. She wanted to say that he was a small man and meticulously neat, she wanted to describe his face and the way he walked and his gentle hands that smelled of cologne, but she couldn't form the words right, and even if she could, respect would prevent her from describing his physical aspects. The memory of him bloomed up here in this place where she ought not to be, and she was a delinquent child whom he had come into the bar for, to fetch home. Hal had gone into bars and Cort went into bars, and that was all right. But what was *she* doing here when she ought to be home with her mother, especially on this day, the day a year ago her brother had died?

"How old's your mother?" Athena asked, and began to laugh again. One of the three young men in a row at the bar turned his head to watch her. "The reason I asked, I had this idea about your mother and my dad. Maybe they could get together."

Naomi watched the young man watching Athena laughing. Athena could not see him. Her friend might be pleased with his interest, Naomi thought, but to her it was not interest in Athena as a woman, it was a contemptuous interest, because the woman was not young, because her sagging throat moved with the laughter, and the gold particles in her teeth shone in the amber light. As she watched the young man watching—a man with a crew cut over his flattish head and wide eyes in a small face—a desire rose up in her to protect her friend with love, to protect even the young punk, to protect everybody with a love that would submerge all contempt. He saw her watching him and turned his gaze on her, and a many-fingered lightning raced across her belly.

"We ought to arrange it so they'd get married," Athena was saying. "One time I tried to get him to go into a rest home. I told him he'd have lots of friends, but he wouldn't budge. So I thought, what the hell, let him have his own way, take care of him, give me something to do in the evening besides file my fingernails."

A seeking look in Athena's large eyes shocked Naomi, and she fumbled around in her conscience for the right response. In her friend's eyes was a desperate need to be instructed in the rigors of her own old age coming, a need to be solaced even by the picayune face of Naomi, by Naomi, who was ignorant of what everybody else knew. But Naomi could console only her own, only Mama and Cort. She heard herself laughing, she bent her head down to the rickety table, laughing at the joke that Athena had already left far behind. "Oh, they'd make a couple all right!" she agreed.

"You girls think of something funny?" the young punk asked.

"We just arranged a marriage," Athena said.

"For you?"

"Oh, yes, for me!" Athena, laughing, almost choked on the smoke of her cigarette.

"Well, why not?" he asked, his eyes closing for an instant to hide the taunting in them, his mouth smiling acceptingly. "Why not?"

Athena was pounding her chest to bring up the smoke. "Don't ask me why not so many times or I'll tell you why not!"

Naomi, impressed by her friend's rejection of the young punk's ridicule, bowed her head to the table again, laughing, taken over by pleasure with her own life. She was who she had chosen to be, a county courthouse clerk, unmarried, going home in a minute to her mother.

The sky was dark when she got off the bus and walked the three blocks to home. "Mama," she called, unlocking the door, accidentally kicking a small sample box of cereal left on the porch. With the door open, her hand on the knob, she stooped to pick up the box. On it was the face of a happy squirrel wearing a bow tie. "Mama," she called, "somebody left something for you."

Her mother was lying on the sofa, covered by the afghan, her face pale in the flicker and waves of blue light from the television screen. No light was on anywhere in the rest of the house. "Where you been?"

"I did some shopping."

"Today's the day he died." Her mother lifted her arms, and Naomi sank down and gathered up the old body grown so thin in the past year. But her mother thrust her away. The smell of the bar was on her.

Naomi pushed herself up and stood unsteadily, took off her hat, took off her coat, stepped out of her high-heeled shoes. She had been reminded for over a month that this Friday was the date he had died a year ago. She had known it herself without reminders. Without any warning in herself, a wail came up, and more wails, sounding like wails of remorse to appease her mother. Unable to do anything about them, she could only wonder. They weren't over her brother, nor over her mother, and she didn't know what they were over, unless they were over herself.

5

Dolores left the city a few days after high-school graduation exercises, boarding the bus to San Francisco. She found a place to live in an apartment shared by three other girls. It was a first-floor apartment, old, heavily carpeted, the living room full of potted plants, the mantelpiece laden with dime-store china figures. They took turns cleaning the kitchen and vacuuming the living room that nobody used. Above them lived more girls, and on the third floor, the top, lived the landlady, a Frenchwoman who came down to investigate complaints and to make complaints of her own. Her rooms for girls were known to agencies for immigrants, to the French consul, and were advertised in the "For Rent" columns, and no more than a day passed between the vacating of a room and the renting of it. At the time Dolores moved into the front bedroom that faced the street, two French girls were living in the bedrooms down the hall, one a secretary at the consulate and the other a typist for an importer, and the fourth bedroom was rented to a girl from Chicago, a cocktail waitress, who made use of the extra closet in the living room to hang up the clothes her own closet couldn't hold and to set out shoes in a row, shoes with heels fantastically high—lucite heels and gilt heels and electric-blue suede heels and red lacquered heels.

"Oh, you are so *attracteef*!" Janine, the consular secretary, told Dolores the first day. Chatting over coffee in the small kitchen, Dolores began to sense sharply the appraising that women do of one another. Janine was observing Dolores's womanness, everything about her—her skin, her features, her hands, her legs, her hair, particulars even more meaningful than they had been to the men in her mother's cafe back home, and Dolores felt the presence of the thousands of women in the city, the women by whom she would be measured and against whom she would measure herself. The eyes of this woman showed a degree more of keenness than that in men's eyes, a desperation, a touch of despair, and Dolores felt trapped by this woman across the table, this flattering woman constantly pushing up the sleeves of her soiled pongee kimono, tossing back her short dark hair.

Dolores found a job as waitress in a small restaurant serving expensive lunches on white tablecloths, and in her third week there accepted an invitation to take a ride around the city from a gray-haired, bustling man, a contractor who joked with her almost every day, snuffling his laughter down his nose. Back home, small-time contractors came into her mother's cafe in clothes the color of concrete dust and complained about unions, lumberyards, architects, owners, and banks. This one wore tailored suits and parked his red and white Corvette at the foot of a hill and pointed out to her an apartment building at the top, its windows hot gold in the setting sun, or parked before a modern house, square, a great reflective expanse of glass facing the bay, or before a stark, concrete church, a neon cross dividing its triangular front. Once, when they were parked on a hill that gave a view of the Embarcadero, she expected him to say that the white ship alongside a pier was his, like an exuberant child would say to an adult in tow. But she saw that *she* was the child, believing that a city grew up by itself, magically. Not only did he alter the skyline, change the views of the city, he knew about scandals in city politics, and those involved in the scandals were friends or enemies of his; he patronized the best restaurants and the jazz clubs, and pointed out to her which innocuous houses had once been famous houses of prostitution.

Her first time out with him he had explained that his wife was away for a couple of weeks and he needed to hear a woman laughing and to help her put on her coat, and she laughed at the comedy they saw and gracefully moved her shoulders for the coat. The evening was his way of telling her he missed his wife. The following night he parked his car in the Marina, and while the masts of the sailboats swayed across the windshield, he spent two hours caressing her. She prepared for the third evening by dropping scented balls of oil, like somber-colored jewels, into her bath water, by changing earrings three times and lipstick twice, by drawing mascara lines around her eyes, fascinated by the effect of each artifice.

"You are stunning!" Janine clapped her hands, muttering something in French, like a prayer. "Who is he? Who is the man? Is he a movie star?"

Dolores sat at the kitchen table and, over a cup of black coffee, told Janine about him while the woman muttered prayers in French and allowed her pongee kimono to fall open at her breasts.

"Oh, he is a man of distinction," Janine said. "That is the kind of man you deserve. You have an *expenseef* look," laughing with an excess of pleasure that proved the laughter false.

The flattery was demanding something of Dolores. She couldn't reject it because she needed even flattery's imitation of praise. It demanded that she confirm the truth of it and surprise this woman with the truth. Toying with her teaspoon, her voice low, she said, "There was a man back home, he was an attorney, he was running for Congress. I mean he was very intelligent and everybody liked him, and he killed himself over me. I mean he was in love with me. He had a wife and child."

Janine lifted her dark eyes to stare, and a tangle of noises came into her throat, a seductive laugh entangled with a moan. "Ah, no, that is *terrible*! Poor man! Poor man! I could tell when I saw you. Whenever you see a beautiful girl who is sad, you can say to yourself, 'Some man has wounded her, he is tied to his wife's apron strings and he did not have the courage to untie himself.' That is the way it is. But with you I saw something more, something tragic. I said to myself, 'There was violence. The man shot his wife.' And then it came to me, 'No, he shot himself. That girl has that look of losing what she can *nevair* get back.'"

"You knew about me?"

"I looked and I knew."

"You mean I didn't even have to tell you?"

"That is *why* you told me. Because I knew already. You could see in my face that I knew. All my life I have this intuition. It has *nevair* disappointed me. *Nevair*. Have you also felt intuition? *They* do not have it, men do not have it. Only women. It is mysterious, who knows where it comes from? That is why they look up to us. When a man takes a woman out, as tonight this man will take you out, he will be in awe of you. Because you have the intuition. They envy us for it. We have this gift while *they*," and she clapped a hand to her head, "they *think* and they *think* how to figure out somebody, who to trust and who not to trust, but the woman, *she* has the answer just like that," snapping her fingers. "You have intuition about this man?"

"George, you mean?"

"That is his name? You have intuition there will be trouble?"

"He's married, if that's what you mean."

"Married or not! Sometime there is no trouble at all with the married ones. I am talking about how you *feel* . . ."

"You mean am I in love with him?"

"No, no, no! I am asking—do you feel trouble is coming?"

"Not exactly."

"Well, good then. That is good. You have a nice time and do not worry." Janine's eyes were luminous—she had revealed herself. She was a seeress, she knew about Dolores's past and future, and her thin mouth smiled a false apology for her intrusion into another person's life.

Dolores's heels, clicking sharply on the sidewalk from the Corvette to the door of his apartment building, were silenced by the thick carpet of the foyer. Silence now, like the unspeaking moment before the embrace. They hurried in silence up the stairs and past the doors of other tenants, doors he must have entered with his wife for an evening's visit, and came at last to his door.

A lamp was on in the small entry. He went before her into the living room, switching on another lamp. "Come on, come in, don't stand there like a country cousin," he called back to her. He did not help her take off her coat, as he had done in restaurants and theaters, and she dropped it on the long beige couch. "Want some coffee?" he asked, drawing curtains together across the expanse of glass, closing out the reflection of the large white lamp he had lit. The moment's reflection of the lamp had intrigued her—the lamp itself was his, but the reflection of it, like a lamp out in the night, was hers. "Come on, let's have some coffee. Something else, see what we can find. Usually some fish eggs around, put 'em on crackers."

Her heels still silenced by carpet, this one the color of sand and that sent up a thick, stuffy feeling into her legs, she followed him toward the kitchen. At the kitchen doorway he turned, impetuously, fitfully, to watch her cross the room, a nervous, embarrassed smile in his eyes. "Come on," he said, taking in how she looked in his apartment, a girl whose face was excitingly unfamiliar and whose body he was to know in a little while.

She followed him into the small, gleaming kitchen, and sat down at the glass-top table. Through the glass she saw her legs and how her short black dress slipped up past her knees as she crossed them. He tossed his cigarettes onto the table. Every time, before, he had brought out the pack gracefully, a wordless, confidential, insinuating offer. She did not touch them. She put her elbows on the table and her chin in her hands and watched him opening jars, stooping to look for crackers in a low cupboard, measuring coffee for the tall chromium percolator.

"That thing looks like a rocket," she said, and he laughed, a quick, eager laugh to make them both feel at home.

"It does, it does," he agreed, talking so fast as he counted spoonfuls that his teeth caught at the words. He's fifty, she thought, and he talks as fast as a kid. Some coffee grounds scattered over the top of the stove, and he glanced at her sideways to see if she had noticed.

"You nervous?" she asked, laughing.

"Naw, naw, I hate this teaspoon stuff. I hate little bitsy stuff. I'm a mountain mover, like to move big things fast. You know what I've always had in mind to do? Move New York to San Francisco and vice versa. Lots of people I know in New York are never going to get out here, so I could do that little favor for them. No more blizzards in winter, no more steam baths in summer."

"I like this city where it is," she said, implying that she was already rooted there, making the entire strange, confusing city her own so that she might feel less homeless now in his apartment, less vulnerable to him.

"What's the matter with you, you don't like to move around?" He was glancing at her derisively. "You come up from Fresno? San Bernardino? and that's the big move in your life? Got no ambition?" He set out a jar of caviar, crackers on a plate, little silver knives, and jerked out the other chair. "Go ahead, eat," he said, biting a cracker in two. The black caviar slid down his tongue. "I like women with ambition. The only trouble with my wife, it made her kind of shrill, you know what I mean? When I first met her it was fine, she was restless, she had to be the best in everything and that meant bed, too, and that was fine. But after a while the ambition destroyed the woman in her. What you've got to remember is not to let it destroy you but you've got to have it in you. You just want to be a waitress all your life?"

She had no answer. Why should she drag up wishes enmeshed in her life, unformed wishes that were a part of her being, and give them as answers to his nervous hounding of her? She sensed that he was talking so fast and so compulsively, jamming crackers and caviar into his mouth, because he felt on the spot and wanted her there instead.

"Is that it?" he persisted.

"I don't know what I want," she said.

"You want to marry a fry cook and get yourself six kids?"

"Maybe," she said. The caviar was too fishy and black. She had never eaten the stuff before and could not make herself like it while beset by his heckling in this kitchen that belonged to his wife.

"Don't you like it?"

"Not much."

"You marry a fry cook and eat french fries and fried eggs every meal. You like that better?"

"No."

The suspense, the desire for him was fading from her face, from her gestures. She saw his face go blank with confusion He laid his fingertips over hers, attempting a delicate approach. "Come on, smile," he said. "Ah, that's great, the sun is shining again. My wife's in Palm Springs," supping up his coffee. "She went down to L.A. to push accounts down there and took a little vacation afterwards. I think she got somebody with her, some guy from San Diego. How I can tell, I phoned her tonight and she sounded happy. When she's alone anywhere she sounds like a kid. Cries."

"She must be awfully smart to run a business. My mother has this cafe, but that's nothing compared to what your wife does. How many people work for your wife?"

"She runs that business like a man. I set her up with the capital, and in seven years she's made it into a big thing. Galatea, Inc. That's a lousy name, I said. What about Linda Lou? What about Dolores Dee? That's what I said—what about Dolores? But she wanted that Galatea. So the best shops in the country carry Galatea lingerie. She was my secretary but she turned out to be so smart I had to marry her. I guess she's got about fifty people in the factory." He took off his glasses to wipe them with the yellow linen napkin, holding them down on his stomach, farsightedly. "See? She's got a business, she's got a name, but she's unhappy because she figures she's not woman enough. She'd take one look at you, she'd be envious."

He wanted her to believe that he *knew* women, she saw that. He wanted her to believe he knew *her,* the girl across the table, and that if there was anything she didn't know about herself she had only to ask him and he'd tell her. He was wiping his glasses on and on, gazing at her with exposed eyes, the exposed face without glasses bringing instantly nearer the time of exploring and exposure.

"She was miserable in Mexico," he said. "The women there are so voluptuous, Jesus. She's built like a sparrow. She had to do something to attract attention so she went into a beauty shop and had her hair colored pink. Pink. That got her the stares. Someday how'd you like to go down there with me? There's a motel in Hermosillo, got a swimming pool like a harem pool, beautiful tile, outdoors, pillars in the water, and all lit up at night. You swim in there at midnight, warm, feel like you're living. They got a deer that wanders around on the grass, eats out of your hand." He slipped on his glasses, got up. The time was near. "Come on, you want to hear some music? You like jazz? Stravinsky?"

She got up, holding her small gold leather purse under her breasts, and followed him, puzzled now by his nervous delaying.

"Got a Giuffre record here," he said, twirling knobs on a long, low, blond wood cabinet, setting down record and needle, all with his back to her. "You like him? You ever heard him?" The music began to ricochet around the room. "Sit down," he said. "Listen to this guy on the bass. Listen." Over his shoulder he was watching her. "What's the matter, you think you're a cat or something, got to think about every chair? Sit on the couch. Listen, they're good, uh?" Leaning back against the cabinet, he watched her sit down. "They're good, uh?" he said, coming to her, at last, sitting down by her, laying his hand on the black silk over her stomach, running his lips around the rim of her ear. "Come on, come on, it's bedtime."

Awkwardly, because he was holding her against him, she entered the bedroom, a room of pale colors and rich and various textures, a room that, though it was shared by him, was a woman's room. Lustrous chalk-white curtains hung in pure stillness from ceiling to curly beige carpet. The headboard of the bed was a great whorl of gilded plaster with a gilded cherub's head in the center, and gold threads gleamed here and there in the heavy white silk spread. She was afraid of the woman's wrath. She was afraid and felt sympathy, yet found pleasure in her own desirability, herself so coveted that he had brought her here to the bed he shared with his wife. She stepped out of her shoes and came down to his height. At the same moment he embraced her, she felt a trembling begin at the core of him.

"Sit here, sit here," he said, and sat her down on the bench before the oval mirror in an ornate frame, and, standing behind her, he fumbled the hairclasp out and, when her hair was down, slipped her dress off her shoulders. She could not glance at herself in the mirror because the mirror was not hers and had held the image of his wife, but she could glance up at his reflection as he went about undressing her, his gray head bowed toward the mirror, and in that moment her dislike of him overcame her. Who was he but a blundering, trembling, fast-talking fifty-year-old man whose gray hair was bouncing lifelessly as he bent forward toward the mirror to lift in his hand the breast he had uncovered and watch how it moved in his moving fingers. But her dislike of him frightened her, she saw him as she did not want to see him. The signs of his weakness laid her down again beside Hal Costigan, now knowing beforehand that he was to take his life. She wanted to see this man as he had been before this night, when his gray hair had a life to it, and the body in its fine suit a strength to it, and his face a cleverness and an assurance of all he had accomplished. With sudden urgency she turned to him and took his face in her hands and kissed him. She heard a moan come into his mouth and stay baffled there because it had no escape.

When his wife returned, three days later, he came to Dolores's room for the first time. All was quiet at midnight, the other girls asleep. She switched on the light in her room before she dropped the Venetian blinds, and anyone glancing out a window across the street or up from the sidewalk could have seen him there in her room, and that possibility annoyed him. The girls had men of their own sometimes: the cocktail waitress had opened her door for a departing lover at five in the morning at the same moment Dolores had opened hers to go to the bathroom, and Janine on Saturday nights had her slight, sad-faced American lover. But the stories she had told him of the other girls and their lovers must have contributed to his discomfort. He said the place had a "transient atmosphere." He made love to her quickly, smoked half a cigarette, and left. She did not see him for a week, and then one day as she was climbing the stairs after work she heard the phone ringing on the table in the hallway.

Within an hour he came by, and drove for another hour to Sonoma, over the bridge and north. They ate supper in a flashy res-taurant that she knew was not the best in the town, and two blocks away they found a motel. Its green neon sign blinked on and off around the edges of the blind in the small dark room. He was more curious, more experimental than he had been in his own bed, and she felt that he was living a lascivious dream, materialized for him by the cheap motel and the girl who complied with his dream. But on the long ride home through the stretch of darkness, he seemed not to remember or to be grateful for his dream come true. He talked about city politics, labor racketeers. She was afraid that they meant nothing to each other, after all. His talk, now, about events in which she did not figure, told her clearly that he did not require her in his life. The night she had gone up to his apartment, she had felt that she was entering some opulent state—his mistress, more beloved than his wife, set up in an apartment of her own and adorned by couturier dresses, by real jewels. The fact that the motel was not high class, that the room smelled of disinfectant, that silverfish raced over the bathroom tile, and that he talked to her now of things that cut all threads with the intimacy in the motel—these facts, she told herself, had no bearing on their future. She lifted his right hand from the steering wheel and kissed the back of it and between the fingers.

But three more weeks went by, and he did not suggest that she look for an apartment of her own, and he brought no gifts. Instead, he drove her habitually to a motel on the beach, south of the city. Up a short dirt road off the highway, a small white frame motel and a row of cabins stood isolated by the rocky cliffs and the sea and sky. They returned each time to the same cabin and plugged in the electric heater for warmth. The orange glow of the wires in the battered cylindrical heater filled the room with a dim, coppery light, and the sound of the sea struck a great echo, far out. Across the highway, a seed company's acres of flowers were blooming, and their fragrance was blown in through the cracks, permeating the cabin when the wind was still, and in those times of being with him there, she longed to be in love with him. Her resentment of him for bringing no gifts had to be banked down because if he suspected that she wanted more of him than himself making love to her, he might drop her. The loving was enough. All she needed she had in these nights in the sand-shifted shack.

Some nights the music from the jukebox in the motel bar blew down

Gina Berriault

past the row of cabins. A man's voice singing took her by surprise, and she lay afraid of intrusion, convinced the singer himself was coming down the path. Or the muted notes of a saxophone, heard above the subsiding sound of the waves, was the voice of a lover in another cabin, amplified by a mystical trick. The music was a reminder to her of the closeness of others at the bar who knew by the red car parked behind the cabin that a couple was inside. When a man and woman came along the row one night, the woman muffling a high laugh, it seemed to Dolores, lying on the rented bed in the dim, wire-lit room, that at last the curious were stealing down the path to peer in under the curtains.

"What you scared of?" he asked in her ear. "You close up like a little ol' morning glory when it isn't time yet."

But the couple on the path had intruded, bringing with them her complaints against him. If she asked for gifts, it was only because she wanted them as evidence that she was more than a pretty waitress taken out to a shack on the beach. But if she asked, he might turn cold and cruel instantly, take his face from her face, his body from her body, and leave her alone and ashamed of her need for anything more than the few hours, the few nights with him.

"Come on, what you scared of? They don't rent the same cabin to two couples. They went in already."

She closed her eyes against his impatient eyes that could not take a moment to wonder. She lifted her mouth to his as a way of asking him to stay with her, and she asked his forgiveness for her complaints by drawing from his mouth all his anger, every cruel word that he might say, and by being as he wanted her to be for the rest of the time; and when they lay apart, what she was asking for changed back again. If she brought him pleasure, wasn't it natural that he tell her so with gifts? It must be natural, so many women were given gifts by the men who loved them for the pleasure they gave. If she never complained, then she was cheap. She was nothing but a dumb waitress who went to bed with him for nothing.

270

"I guess you think I'm a fool," she said.

"A fool?" He was already sitting with his back to her, rubbing the sole of his foot before he pulled on his sock.

"Because I come here for nothing."

"What do you mean for nothing?" so swiftly she suspected his answer had been ready for weeks. "Don't you like it? You act like you like it."

How would other women say, *that's not enough*? With what words, in what way? "That's not enough," she said.

"I'm not man enough for you? What you want, some nature boy? Jack Biceps?"

"That's not what I mean." Was he trying to cuff her away from her real meaning by pretending to be hurt by what she didn't mean? "What I mean is, you never bring me anything." But, spoken at last, it wasn't what she meant, either.

"Like what? Like what?"

Her fear of being discarded by this man who was more to her now than any man had ever been, even more than Hal, took away her wishes, leaving her only a trace of a complaint. "Like little things."

"What little things?"

"Like big things."

"What then? Big things or little things? Make up your mind." Though he continued with his dressing, his clothes appeared not to be his own. With distaste he examined his shirt as if suspecting someone of borrowing it and returning it unclean.

"It depends on how much you like me. If you like me a lot, they're little things." She was shameless, forcing him to weigh and measure her value to him.

"Give me an example."

"Like a place, like an apartment . . ."

"Anything else?"

"You shouldn't ask me to list them."

"Why not? Don't you like to list them?"

"No." She had made a mistake. She didn't need anything more from him, not anything more than her numb, kneaded mouth whose lipstick was gone, its color, chosen with care for its promise of love, now a barely present coloring over the rest of her face, not anything more than the clamoring of her body for him, waking her up in the night, back in her own room.

"Go on."

"No."

"You sorry you started it?"

She stuffed some ends of her hair into her mouth and began to cry, confused by her contradictory wishes.

"What's the crying for?" patting her stomach.

She twisted a strand of hair around her fingers, close to her face. "There was a man who killed himself over me," she wept. "You think I'm nobody, but there was a man who fell in love with me."

"No, hell, I don't think you're nobody," patting. "What do you mean, he killed himself?"

"Just what I said."

"All right, all right. But I'm a little deaf. I don't get it."

"You want me to say it again?"

"If it doesn't hurt too much."

"I said he killed himself."

"How did that happen?"

"It happened, it happened."

"Sure it did, sure it did. Just tell me how."

"He was married, and he had a little boy," covering her mouth with her hair.

"Yuh, go on," patting.

"He knew we were going to be found out but he didn't care."

"Yuh?"

"He didn't care."

"Listen, sweetie, listen, doll," he said. "You must have left something out."

"What?"

"You tell *me* what. I don't want to hurt your tender feelings, but it doesn't seem like that's enough reason for a man to kill himself over."

"You don't know the whole story!"

"That's exactly what I'm saying."

"He was running for Congress," she explained, with as much insulting, indignant enunciation as she could scare up for her small, broken voice, "and we were found out a few days before election day. What I'm saying is he didn't care about the election, I mean if he had to kill himself. What I'm saying is that he couldn't help it if he was in love with me."

"Sounds funny to me," he said. "Oh, you're telling the truth, you're telling the truth as you see it. But a man doesn't do that, I mean go out of his mind for wanting some girl unless he's out of his mind already." He turned his back on her again to tie his shoes. When he straightened up he consulted his wristwatch. "Quarter to twelve," he said. "Time to get up."

She placed a palm over her nipple to hide a spangle of pain that she imagined was detectable by him. He was taking away from her all that she had tried to claim for herself in her story about Hal Costigan, the image of herself as a girl desirable beyond any risk. With his mockery, he was taking that story away just as she was telling it for the first time to any man, and here, under her palm, her nipple's small begging voice was calling him back.

Standing above her, he dropped her underwear and slip over her crossed hands. "Come on, come on. What're you looking like a madonna for? Are you Catholic? You sore at me because I said your story doesn't make sense?" He dropped her dress over her stomach, covering up everything he had wanted uncovered before. Her nylons he dropped on her thighs.

"You're not so great," she heard herself say, low.

"Hell, I know I'm not so great," pretending good humor about his deficiencies.

"You could die, too," she said.

"I know all about it," shrugging on his coat.

"You could shoot yourself."

"Yeah, I could if I got cancer or something."

"You could do it anyway."

"Who knows?" he said, agreeably.

With angry flicks of her hand, she tossed aside the clothes, sat up, and began to dress. "You're not so great."

"Nobody ever told you I was, did they?" He went to the window, drew back the curtain, and, with a hand at each temple, peered out through the glass. "I can see the waves," he said. "The foam, the white part on the breakers. You ever see that old movie where the guy walks out into the ocean? Can't swim, just keeps on walking out into the ocean? Maybe that's the way I'd do it if I was going to do it. If I get to thinking about how not so great I am, like you want me to." He chuckled. "Unless I get worried about sharks."

She glanced up as she dressed and saw her reflection in the window he was peering through, the reflection of the half-clad girl imposing itself between him and the darkness. With her dress held to her breasts she gazed at his back, at his gray head bent forward so his brow touched the glass, and at her almost transparent self in the pane, and shame came over her for asking something of this man who was as vulnerable as Hal Costigan to dying. The girl in the glass stood between him and the night, just as she had between Hal and the night.

He turned and stood waiting, hands in his pockets jingling coins and keys, and she knew when she glanced at his face and saw him gazing at nothing that the bitter taste in her mouth was in his, the same.

6

Toward midnight Cort's wife felt the labor pains come faster. She was walking through the house, and every time the pains came she knelt down. She knelt down by the bed where Cort was lying, and when the pain passed she looked up at him, and he saw the frown, the knot of pain, ease from her face. The contractions had kept her awake the night before and most of the day, and her face was very pale, and he saw in her eyes only a remote need of him. Her fear of the ordeal that was near left him out.

Wrapped in her coat, she leaned against him in the car, and when the cramps came he stroked her thigh. Most of the houses were dark. He had always been disturbed by the presence of so many people asleep, by the blocks and blocks of flimsy houses into which the darkness flowed. Everyone seemed at the mercy of so many things, and again the memory of his brother came to him as it had come so often in the past few weeks. The memory of his brother came to him vividly now as he drove his wife through the streets of the sleeping city. For a moment, a hallucination that his brother was sitting on the other side of his wife caused him to slip his arm around her shoulders and kiss her hair.

She was given a bed in the labor room, in a row of four beds. Down the row, a young woman with pink curlers in her hair was chatting with her husband, who was sitting in a chair by her bed. But Cort's wife, who hadn't slept for almost twenty-four hours, was given a sedative by a tired young doctor. She spoke just a few words to Cort and began to drowse.

Cort went out, under a stucco portico, past a trickling fountain, and around plots of flowers. He walked past the emergency entrance, under its red light, past the wing of the building and its rows of lighted windows. It was the last few hours of their being two, he and his wife, the last hours of a closeness he suspected would never return when the child entered the picture, and he resented the stranger child who was to intrude on the intimacy of the parents and claim some of the love, or even all, from the tall, long-legged woman with her sullen, bony face that could focus on a kiss and draw out of him the brooding left by his brother. He loved her for her healing of him, he loved the woman asleep in that high bed on which other women in labor had lain, and he needed her more than would the stranger of a child. A desperate desire came over him to return with her to the beginning, to take her home with her belly flat and no child anywhere, a desire for her unhindered, undivided, fresh and startling, healing of him as she had been at the beginning, because, contending with her now and with the child, was his brother, following him step for step in the night.

Under an elm tree lit by a lamp hanging high above the street, he waited for his brother to take the last step to him, and, when the presence of the dead man was full upon him, he struck the trunk of the tree to punish himself with pain because he, Cort, was a criminal and nobody knew it. It was a crime to bring a child into the world and not love life yourself. It was a crime to hold out to the child a hand that had no meaning to offer, and to lead the child into life. He stood on the curb, crying noiselessly with fatigue and anxiety and the desire to return his wife alone and without child to the past.

Leaf shadows, enlarged to enormous size by the high globe, lay all around him, intensifying his feeling of unreality, and he sat down on the curb in their midst and lit a cigarette to smoke out the tears from his throat. How often in the past year he had called up his brother! Even in the midst of pleasure, he had brought him into the company and introduced him around to remind them all of the meaninglessness of their existence. Six weeks ago on a Sunday afternoon, Pauline and he were guests at a neighbor's outdoor party; the odor of barbecued meat floated over the yard, smoke swirled out from the brick barbecue, and the fragrance of liquor rose up from the cold glass in his hand. He was sitting by a lattice that cast a striped shadow over him—he liked that puzzling shadow—and his wife was reclining close by on a canvas chair. By him were three men, all with glasses in their hands. He knew none of them, they were friends of the host, but given a lead by a word, by a pause, he had told them about his brother, he had lauded his brother to the smoky sky. No one so sensitive, no one so intelligent, no one with the courage to say what he'd said in his act of suicide, oh, the greatest guy in the world! They had nodded or gazed at him, but one man had wandered away, and later, when the party was breaking up, Cort had caught sight of him. Their eyes met, and the antagonism in the man's eyes had shocked him. On the curb now, in the midst of the giant leaf shadows, he remembered the times when he and his wife had gone to movies with other couples and as they all sat crowded together in a booth in a bar, he had recalled his brother. He told about his brother every chance he got, like a derelict who claims high-class relatives. He had to tell everybody that he, Cort, was different, he was smarter than his listeners, who accepted life without questioning. With knuckles that were still crumpled with pain, he struck the elm tree again, then spread his stinging, jerking fingers over his knee, waiting until they calmed.

He got up, crossed to the other corner, and walked along by the old two-story frame houses that made up this neighborhood where wealthy, elderly women lived, where lawns were hedged in and lace curtains hung in windows that looked out onto high porches and wicker chairs. An exotic tree of waxy white blooms confronted him at the edge of a yard, overbearing in its still, heavy beauty. From somewhere came the fragrance of orange blossoms and from somewhere the fragrance of wisteria, and it seemed to him that fragrances in this neighborhood of the elderly were like children who had wandered over from another part of the city where children slept two and three and four in a bedroom and no bedroom was unused, as bedrooms were unused in these tall houses. Maybe, he thought, the child, the wandering fragrance, would assist the mother in the task of eradicating the image of the dead brother from the heart of the father. Maybe the child would be an ally. But what a job he was assigning the child at the moment of its birth. The child was to give the father a reason for living! It would never be equal to the task. The task was the father's, the task of the father was to give himself and the child a reason. Not love yet, but the possibility of love caused him now to protect the child from the harm the father might do it. He heard in his throat his plea to his brother to go, to stop hounding him, to disappear on this spot, and leave him, younger brother, alone.

Unwilling to go back to the maternity ward and wait there, he walked on, wanting to go instead to his sister, Naomi, wanting to knock on the kitchen door and ask for a cup of coffee. He wanted to know, for the first time, if she felt the same way about Hal that he felt. He had never even wondered before if that which had been done to him had also been done to her. Only Naomi—he wanted to see his sister alone, he wanted his mother to be asleep, so he and his sister could talk very quietly in the kitchen. But what could *she* do for him? Naomi, simple, awkward, skittish woman? What could he say to her when he was convinced beforehand that she would not comprehend? She had idolized their brother, their brother could do no wrong, not even in that final act.

Crying in his throat for a love of life to exorcise the dead man, he wandered out into the street. A dog up on a porch growled at him, growled a late-night threat, safe under a hammock or a chair.

They sat down, tugged off their gloves, took off their hats.

"You girls are getting to be regulars." The bartender clucked his tongue. "Every damn week."

Naomi sat with her back to the entrance. At the table behind Athena a man sat alone, his glass down on an open newspaper. He had lifted his head, slowly alerted, amused by their entrance.

"What do your husbands say when you come home late, no supper, nothing?" the bartender asked.

"That's why we got no husbands. They gripe too much." With elbows resting on the table, Athena ran her fingers through the curls above her ears, bowing her head quickly to do it. "Isn't that right, Naomi?" winking at her.

"Naomi what?" the man at the table asked, gazing at her past Athena, who turned around to see him.

"Costigan," said Athena.

"You from Butte, Montana?" the man asked Naomi. "I had a sister by that name. She left home at sixteen and we never heard a word from her."

"I'm from right here," Naomi said.

"Native daughter," Athena said.

"It ain't often you hear the name Naomi," he said.

"It isn't often you hear my name, either," said Athena. "I think my old man named me after some Greek goddess."

"I got a name everybody else's got," he said. "Or it sounds like that. I'll tell you if you don't laugh."

"We won't laugh." Athena was acting strange, her voice had a crackling sound, and her body seemed rich with pleasure.

"Dan O'Leary," he said. "Do I look like one?"

"Like what?" Athena asked.

"Like a Dan O'Leary."

"If you gave me any other name I'd think you were kidding me," she said.

"You know what his real name is?" the bartender said. "Adolf Hitler. He never really died."

"Yeah, I'm looking for work over here," said Dan O'Leary, and he laughed half a dozen staccato sounds. "Dirty work."

"What kind of work do you do?" Athena asked.

"Well," he said, "I've been a pants presser, ship's steward, I've been a funny man in a burlesque show, and I also barked. You know, stand out in front and bark," and he barked like a dog.

Athena's laugh was loud and crackly.

"That was the most low-down job of all, barking like that," he said. "But a princess rescued me. Princess Nadja. She was the stripper and she fell in love with me. She set me up in business for myself, opened a little bar for me."

"You go broke?" asked Athena.

"Me go broke?" He seemed offended. "It wasn't me that went broke. The bar went broke."

"What happened to Princess Nadja? She get mad at you?" Athena turned her chair so that she could talk to both Naomi and the man, and crossed her legs.

"Nobody gets mad at me," he said. "It ain't in my nature for people to get mad at me. No, she didn't get mad. I just left her. She was loony about white and it gave me the creeps."

"What's white?" asked Athena, puzzled.

"Every goddamn thing white. She got some crazy fixation on white. Is that what you call it?" he asked Naomi, implying that since she spoke less she knew more. "It begun to bug me. Every damn rug in the house was white, every damn lamp, every damn everything, and her hair is also pearly white. It's real nice for a while, feel like you're living on the moon. But after a while it begun to bug me. I said to her, you ain't fooling me, baby, you sit on the toilet like everybody else—excuse me, girls. I said, you trying to look pure or something, and I spilled a gallon of dago wine in the middle of the living room rug. I don't do things like that habitually, you understand." He leaned forward on his elbows, speaking to Naomi. "You follow me or you think I'm bats?"

Athena turned back to their own table, laughing. "You're bats!"

He smiled at Naomi, a pale, lopsided smile, his eyes aware of his mouth's pleading. "That don't hurt me," he said. "As long as I'm bats and funny. If I was bats and sad, you'd have every right to turn me in."

Naomi disliked his singling her out to talk to, a homely woman who had to be treated with respect, who had to be talked to for a few moments to relieve his tension from talking to Athena, the woman he wanted to talk to. But she wondered—was he saying to her, past Athena, that between himself and herself was an unspoken understanding requiring no jokes? You're a crazy woman, she said to herself. He got to sleep with a woman other men pay to see undress herself. You're not a woman to him and Athena's not a woman, and he gets a kick out of making us believe he thinks we're real attractive women. He gets a kick out of hearing a couple of gullible women laugh their cackling, girlish laughs. She pulled on her gloves.

"Hey, you're not going?" he said.

Usually she had a smart remark to make to the men who came into the recorder's office and teased her with their insinuations that she was somebody and that if they had the courage, the recklessness, they'd leave their wives for her. She didn't want to answer that way to this man, but she did. "I'm afraid of the dark," she said.

"Of the dark?" He wagged his head. "God Almighty, she says she's afraid of the dark." His face lapsed into petulant resentment, and she realized that even the dumbest woman, leaving him in the midst of his act, could hurt his feelings. "God Almighty," he said, "something's wrong. Here this woman comes into a bar and she got to leave before it gets dark. Everybody think they're two years old?"

When they left, she saw that he was still wagging his head. It was the first time ever she had hurt a man. She had hurt him inadvertently, but all evening, at home, she was troubled by contending feelings, by a sense of her own power and by a sense of guilt, and, lying in bed, a crazy fear that she had ruined her chances with him took hold of her.

She saw him again the next day. He was at the other side of the horseshoe-shaped lunch counter in the drugstore, and when she looked up from the menu and saw him across the space where the waitress flitted around, he began to shake his head again, unbelievingly, chidingly. He was again the man whom nobody could get mad at because he got mad at nobody. He carried his coffee and sandwich carefully around the counter and sat down by her, and he learned, that noon, who she was because she sat there with her hands trembling on her cup.

A few minutes before it was time to put on her coat, he came into the recorder's office. With his hands in his pockets, he glanced along the shelves of red and gray record books, his manner that of one who finds no place too exclusive for him to enter. She slipped her coat on, buttoning it up to her chin, and he opened the door for her and walked along beside her down the hall, limping.

"You never knew I had a bullet in my knee, did you?" he asked. He had not limped when they walked out of the drugstore together, and she knew he was pretending to limp now.

"I got this hotel room almost in the center of town, so I don't need to ride any buses to get to where the action is. So I figured it'd be interesting just to ride a bus, but I didn't want any old line, like the B or the G. It's got to be your bus with you on it. Then you can point out what you think I ought to see, like the high school, you know? What's the population of this town, would you say?" They stood on the edge of the crowd waiting for the buses across from the courthouse.

"Maybe a hundred thousand," she said.

"They all catch the bus at this hour?"

She laughed, and he bent over to grip his knee. "Don't make me laugh," he said. "My knee buckles."

He limped behind her aboard the bus and half fell into the seat beside her, his leg stiffened out into the aisle. Some passengers, who had ridden the bus every evening for as many years as she had, nodded at her and glanced at him, examining him, she knew, for any resemblance to her, for only a relative would ride home with her after all her years of riding alone. Never out of the clear sky, out of the sky from where mates fell, would a sort of handsome man fall into the seat beside her, Naomi, the woman with a face flat and familiar as the advertisement placards above the bus seats.

"This knee is a good thing," he said. "I don't have to get up to let a lady sit down. You see?" His breath smelled of clove gum or mouthwash. His hand, gripping the horizontal steel rod on the back of the seat ahead, was a pale hand with high blue veins, almost the hand of a convalescent, but so strong in its power over her that she had to glance away. She felt sick with the suspicion that he was playing a trick on her. Only a drunk, only a man without a conscience could play a trick like this on a homely woman.

"You think I'm mean, Naomi, because I don't let a woman sit down?"

It was her chance to say yes. Yes, get up and get off and let somebody else sit down, somebody I'm used to. The only other answer she could give was No, and, by saying No, imply that she liked him sitting there, but if she said No, he'd go back to the bar and tell the bartender about what the scared, silly woman had said, that she liked him sitting by her.

"But I ain't a mean person, Naomi." He spoke so low the passengers in the seat ahead, their ears protruding to catch the conversation, could not hear. "Only I don't like to *prove* I ain't mean by doing something nice. When I have to do something nice, I feel mean." He gave a small, hiccuping laugh to tell her he was only joking. "Naomi sounds like an Indian name," he said. "There used to be a burlesque queen who was a full-blooded Cherokee. Some of them Indian girls are real beauties."

"Was that Princess Nadja?"

"Was who Princess Nadja?"

"The Cherokee girl."

"Hell, Nadja ain't an Indian name. It's Roosian, ain't it?"

"I thought you were married to the Cherokee queen."

"Me? I wasn't married to no Cherokee." He glanced up quickly as a few passengers, wanting out, pressed past the others standing in the aisle, and, when the commotion was over, he continued to gaze up into the faces above him. After a few moments, he suddenly sat up straight. "Three times," he said. "I been married three times, all of them fine women to begin with. I must of been fine to begin with myself or they wouldn't of begun with me." He laughed soundlessly. "There's a beginning and there's an end. Nobody likes endings and that's why they get bogged down in the middle."

"Which one was Princess Nadja?" she asked. That voluptuous

woman with moon-white hair had become a terrible adversary, a woman whose seductiveness was as beyond her as the moon was beyond her. "I bet you made her up," she said, wanting to wound him, wanting to let him know she was not a dupe. "Am I right?"

"Right as rain," he said.

So she destroyed his imaginary princess, and the real ones remained beyond him, this pale, thin barker, pants presser, barman, clown. If she lived alone, she thought, she'd ask him in for supper. She would have no fear that he had come to sponge on her for a meal and then make fun of her afterwards to the bartender. She'd have no fear because she would say right off, tough like Athena, You want to come in for supper? You look like you need some meat on your bones.

He was smiling, maybe over the loss of Princess Nadja, running his hand over his head, scratching at the gray hair that had a mealy look though all his clothes were clean as a whistle, scratching with a monkey's musing curiosity.

"I get off here," she said rising.

"Hey, hey," he said, confused, rising with her, hopping out into the aisle, glancing toward the front of the bus and toward the back, like someone trapped. A string of hair swung out over his forehead as he swung his head from left to right, and she bent her head into his back, laughing at him. She poked her finger in between his shoulder blades to tell him he was blocking her way. At once he lurched down the aisle, jerked forward and backward by the motion of the bus. Tossed out, they stood on the corner before the drugstore's lighted window confronting them with a jumble of hot-water bottles, perfumes, toothpaste tubes, dead flies, and holly wreaths.

Past stucco houses, mottled and faded like the one she was going to, he walked beside her, fast, his narrow shoulders hunched under his rakish sport jacket. It was a cold twilight with a rose-colored light in the sky. "I can't come in," he said. "I got to get back and meet this friend of mine at Rich's Cafeteria. I'm just escorting you home because you're afraid of the dark." After a block of the same houses, he asked her if she lived alone, and then he asked her who she lived with, and then if she had brothers and sisters, and, without any warning to herself to not tell, she was telling him about Hal.

"That's something I'd never do," he said, his voice mingling awe and pity. His small feet in polished old shoes, once stylish, went quickly, dapperly along. "I guess it takes courage, uh? Maybe I ain't got that kind of courage."

Was he praising her brother to ingratiate himself? But she wanted no member of her family around, least of all her dead brother. A man was walking her home. She had laughed with him on the jolting bus, she had been smart enough to see that he talked big, and cruel enough to tell him that she saw. Oh, what a fascinating life she led! The pleasure she had found in this encounter began to desert her now as she heard his praise for her brother, for her brother who was always praised, and praised now for the courage to take his own life.

"Well, so long," he said, the instant she paused by the small lawn worn bare in spots by children's feet. "Naomi sounds like a river," he said, and sang softly, *By the banks of the Naomi, an Indian maiden waits for me.* You think that's a tune that'll catch on? You got a piano?"

"Yes," she said. "We used to play it but nobody's touched it for years."

"We'll work out a tune," he said. "We'll make a million bucks," and he gave a tricky salute, tugging at the brim of an imaginary hat, and went back the way they had come, a man wanting her to feel the loss of him. She could tell that much by the way he walked, briskly, confident of his charm.

That was the way it began. He rode home with her again and made excuses for not coming in before she made excuses for asking him in. He bought her lunch and invited her to a movie. After the movie she went up to his room in the National Hotel and he sat on his bed and she sat in the chair, and he told her about his other marriages. His first wife had died, his second had left him for another man, and his third he had left, and there was no Princess Nadja among them. The serious way he told about his life showed his respect for her. He percolated coffee on a hot plate and gave her some stale cookies to dip. On the sidewalk before her house he kissed her very lightly. The next time she went out with him they did not go to a movie. He met her in the hotel's drab, cold lobby and they went up to his room, and he was gentle in his passion. A delight began to stir in the core of her being, that night. It did not take her by surprise because she had suspected all along that it was waiting there.

Naomi was deserting her mother to go and live with a man who came out of nowhere. That was the way her mother described the change in the daughter. Naomi and her Dan were married by a judge in the county courthouse and moved into a rented duplex, and Naomi interviewed a woman for the job of companion to her mother. Mrs. Wade came into the recorder's office at noon, a plump, uneasy woman who couldn't smile, and Naomi became at once the one to be interviewed, reversing the positions, wanting not to subject the woman to the ordeal, the quivery-faced woman with the dodging eyes. They sat across from each other at the Dairy Lunch, and Naomi apologized for everything at home, the mix-up in the cupboards, the worn linoleum on the kitchen floor, and her mother's mind in captivity to her son's death. "You'll have to listen to all that," she said. "She's never going to give up her suspicions." Naomi told about everything that might displease the woman, wishing the woman would refuse the job now, because, if she walked out on the job later, she'd carry away with her a stranger's unsympathetic knowledge of secret sufferings, both Naomi's and her mother's.

The woman moved in that evening, and Naomi's mother called her at the recorder's office the next morning. *She doesn't answer me,*

Naomi. She was two hours in the bathroom last night. Nobody needs to take a bath that long. I was afraid she'd fainted. Suppose she died in there? She didn't answer me and finally I had to scream at her, and she said she's got a right to privacy. Several nights later Mrs. Wade phoned Naomi at home. *Maybe you better come this one night. Maybe if she knows you come when I call you, she won't feel she needs you so bad. I been with old people like this before. One of 'em slashed his wrist so his daughter'd come back from New York. They think they can stop the sun from going down.* Naomi put on her coat and hat, left the supper dishes in the sink, and took a taxi to the house, and her mother clasped her in her thin arms. "She won't believe me," her mother complained. "I told her they did it to him, but she won't believe me."

It took a while before Naomi's mother and Mrs. Wade began to make balky, grudging moves toward one another, but when a kindly acceptance was found, the familiarity seemed too much for them to handle—what each one knew about the other. Then her mother began to call to her again.

"She went to her room right in the middle of cooking our supper and she won't come out," her mother said, waiting at the table in the kitchen, wearing the quilted satin bathrobe, a present from Cort and Naomi, an extravagant present to impress upon her their love that they knew would never, never compensate for the loss of her son, Hal.

"It's Naomi," she said, knocking at the door of the bedroom that had been her brothers' and then hers and was now Mrs. Wade's.

The woman opened the door after a minute, a quivery-cheeked woman with all her excess flesh that was too much of herself when the self was only a companion to a shrill old woman as deserted as herself. The woman's pale blue eyes were enclosed in pompoms of flesh, but, hidden as they were, they still attempted to slide away.

"Mama's sorry," Naomi said. *Ah, poor woman I ought to know!* she thought. And she was ashamed that she was only Naomi who was to be as deserted soon as this woman in the faded dress and the new apron. *Ah, poor woman! So much like myself and so much like Mama. We are all so much alike, skinny from loneliness or bloated with it.*

After that night, Naomi went across the city though nobody called her and though, often, she found her mother and Mrs. Wade contentedly, querulously watching the brawls and commotions on the television screen. She went because her husband was away in the bars until they closed, and because the nights he stayed home and drank alone, he played cruel jokes on her with words, jokes that ridiculed them both, himself and Naomi, *Na-o-mi,* the greenhorn, the goody-goody, the simple-minded woman who had fallen for him. Naomi sat beside her mother, holding her mother's hand, watching the screen and not remembering much from one second to the next, her soothing fingers sometimes pressing too hard on the bones of the hand she held.

One night he barred her way. "What're you putting your coat on for?" he said. "You ain't going anywhere." He was wonderingly sober.

"I'm going over to Mama's."

"You ain't going to Mama's, girlie," he said, and for a moment, because she was locked in and didn't know the man, she was a child again, her mind was a child's mind, wondering whether *girlie* was an affectionate word or a derisive one. Then she turned and ran down the hall to the back door. He ran after her and caught hold of her coat and threw her down on the kitchen floor. Her hip struck the floor and her face struck the table leg. She pulled her skirt down—it had leaped up past her knees—and attempted no other move, afraid that any move other than the modest one would make him more angry. For a second, as she lay stunned, she felt that he was right, throwing her down. It was such an extreme act, he must be right. Ashamed because she had brought him to violence, she could not look up into his face, she could only stare at his shoes. The great number of times she had left this apartment to find a queasy comfort from her comforting of her mother all added up to a crime. Her coming and going was a crime of futility.

"You're a goddamn saint, Naomi," he said, "but I ain't religious. It makes me sick to see a saint. They don't serve no good example, they just make you feel like a louse. Get up, get up," he said, banging around the coffee pot from one burner to another. The match he struck leaped out of his hand and fell on the table, and he swung after it furiously, and blew it out. With shaking hand, he struck another match. "Get up, get up. Sit down, sit down. Take off your coat, stay awhile."

She reached up to the table and drew herself up, and she sat down. Although she was suffocatingly hot, she left her coat on.

"Fix you some hot coffee," he said. "You should of seen all the coffee we drank over in England, on those cold nights with the V-1's buzzing around. Did I ever tell you about the time the anti-aircraft brought down a V-1 over the airfield? It began to bob around up there, turned around, changed its mind, and fell just half a mile away." He cleared his throat, a loud, raspy, prolonged scraping.

She was afraid to touch her cheekbone and afraid to lay her head in her hand, afraid that any soothing of herself might be mistaken for reproach.

"You going to take your coat off?"

She shook her head. The coat comforted her, the coat gave her dignity, it gave her access to the outdoors and protection against the inside of strange houses, like this one. She was about to draw her coat together when he went down on his knees, encircling her hips, laying his face in her lap, kissing the triangle into her closed thighs.

"Naomi, I wish I was a saint myself. Then it would be impossible for me to be mean."

"Danny, I'm no saint, Danny."

"Yeah, you are, you are, and when I leave that's what's going to make it easier for me because I'm going to say to myself, she's a saint and she knows I'm just human. You see what your trouble is, you saints? You make it easier for us to be human because you make allowances. Am I right? You make allowances?"

"I don't know what you mean."

"All I mean is you forgive people." He laid her hand on the crown of his head, moving her hand back and forth, and, when he took his hand away from hers, she went on stroking his head, thought she felt no love for this man who had come out of nowhere, out of everywhere, and fooled her into thinking she was his woman and fooled her again by elevating her above everybody else, calling her a saint because he was going to leave her and saints always forgive.

"Suppose you lived in Omaha, suppose you had children, suppose you died—your Mama would get along. She lost her precious son, so she's taking it out on you. Because you're just Naomi. What's Naomi doing, still alive? You ever stop to think that over? You ever stop to think?"

You ever stop to think? Stop *what* to think? The heart?

"When are you going?"

"Did I say I was going anywhere?"

"You said you were going."

"Oh, hell, I say that all the time. It keeps me alive."

Wiping her face with the sleeve of her coat, she stood up. She went down the hall to their bedroom and lay down on the bed, still with her coat on, face up. He followed her, sat down by the bed, and removed her shoes, chuckling, attempting his old seductive wit in the sound of it. "I bet you don't believe I ain't mad," he said. "That's a fine thing—you knock a woman down and then you tell her you ain't mad."

She lay weeping openly, uncaring how grotesque her face must be. She knew why he had pushed her down. He had pushed her down, this simple-minded woman, because she had turned her face toward him as toward the sun. Who had ever seen before that Naomi Costigan was a woman with a heart in her breast? He had pushed her down because she had made a mistake, because he was only a pale and shaky itinerant drunk, and she ought to have known. She ought to have known even from the start, even from the nights of love, and at last his contempt for her for not knowing threw her to the floor.

"Don't cry, Naomi," he said, kissing the soles of her feet. "I'm not going, don't cry."

So small his allotment of love! It seemed to her that each person at birth was granted an allotment of love to give to someone, or to two, or to three, or to the world, but how small his allotment of love! She didn't know how to measure other persons' love for her, like her mother's, like Cort's, but this man's was like Hal's. Her brother ran out on everybody, and this man was running out. They had the least to give. The least. Humbly, he was massaging her feet, his hands small and cold and straining to be of help, but her feet were numb to his hands, and her ears were deaf to his voice. She was transforming him into nothing, so that when he was gone no one would be missing.

8

Dolores returned to her parents' house four years after she had left it. When she climbed down from the bus, her father, waiting in the alleyway where the buses came in, embraced her. "Don't look at me," she said.

"Hell," he said, walking her solicitously to his car, arm around her, "you look like you ate too many kumquats. You took sick from kumquats when you were a kid."

The bedroom off the kitchen was waiting for her, curtains, spread, rug all new, all blue, a color she had turned against, along with ruffles. She took off her clothes that were saturated with the bus fumes and the sweat of her illness, slipped on a nightgown, lay down, and slept at once, slept on an immense airy bed of relief and return, wakened over and over by tormenting dreams.

At seven, her mother came home and into the bedroom on the soundless rubber-soled oxfords she wore at work. Dolores had seen her parents several times in the years she had been way, when they had come up to the city to visit her, but her mother's face, this time, was glaringly older. The fever must be doing crazy things to her eyes. Her mother bent over her, covering her face with kisses. "It's all right,

I'm immune," her mother said. "Bugs run the other way."

For weeks she lay in bed, waiting for recovery. Evenings, she watched her parents in the kitchen, an audience of one observing two actors on the stage. They had lived in marriage for twenty-five years and if someone were to ask them to sing just one note, each choosing one, they would sing the same note, she was sure. The girl in the bed denied any accomplishment in their similarity. Two persons, almost fifty years old, who had never lived in any other city, who had never held other lovers in their arms, what did they know? Something more than she knew, or less? One afternoon, sleeping, she heard the vast silence in which the neighborhood was set. Not since those last moments between herself and the man in the shack on the beach had she been surrounded by so much meaningful silence, and she listened for the breaking of the wave. But this silence belonged to a time farther back, this was the silence that surrounded Hal Costigan. Calling for her mother, she woke herself completely to the fact that it was early afternoon in her parents' house with nobody home yet.

When she began to recover, she took short walks to the drugstore and looked into the magazines, and she sat in the shade of the trees in the backyard and knit a sweater for her father, and she planted flowers, day by day, gradually, and when she felt strong enough, a girlfriend got her a job in a cocktail bar, working two hours on weekend evenings. She had her hair cut and curled and tinted red. She wore her filmy blouses and cinched her wide gold-leather belt tight around her waist. After a few weekends of parrying with the customers, she began an affair with a man older than herself and married, like most of the other men she'd been with. She went to meet him in vacant apartments and houses that he, as realtor, was agent for. He was big—football-player size—and that size, along with his deep blue eyes edged by thick black lashes, impressed the women shopping for homes with their husbands. His office chalked up more sales than any other in town, he told her.

Because she knew the affair would end, she began to imagine herself desperately in love with him. As always, there had to be some meaning to the time with a man. The meaninglessness of each time was like a sin for which there was no name. She repeated to him his criticism of his wife, and her caresses were promises to be the wife he ought to have. She held to him on mattresses that he covered with an old, faded spread he kept in his car, and begged him to love her.

On the day that was to be the last day, he was already in the apartment when she arrived. He was at the table in the dining room, reading the evening paper, his coat off, his feet up on a chair. He did not greet her. He was concentrating on something in the news and on the secret use he was going to make of it. She went into the bathroom to see again how her hair was done, cut again and curled again and tinted red again, and the sight of herself in the mirror evoked the many mirrors in the beauty salon, where she had just been, and all the reflected faces, hers among them, seemed, in memory, like participants in a plot that would net them nothing. She went into the kitchen to open the cartons he'd brought.

"You ever see such stupidity?" he called. "God! If you can't do it yourself, then don't do it at all. Here the guy hires a two-bit gangster to do the job for him and not only does he fumble it, he's a witness against him, he sits up there and says Dr. Dick hired me to do it. So it's just like hiring a witness against you, that's what it comes down to." He read on for a minute. "What's crazy about the whole thing is this—here the guy wants to do away with his wife so he won't have to give her half his fortune when he gets a divorce, and now, boy, he won't have a penny left if he goes free. The lawyers'll get it all. That's what I should have been, a criminal attorney, get hired by all the guys who murder their wives." He had a loud, easy laugh that came from down in his chest.

She spooned the delicatessen food onto the paper plates, not answering. His ridicule of the man on trial was another way, a final way, of telling her how impossible it was for a man to free himself of a vengeful wife.

"What's the matter? You sore at me?" he asked.

While they ate, he talked on about the trial. He took his time when he ate, chewing with his big jaw, his mouth closed as his parents had taught him, his blue eyes pleased with the food and with the details of the trial that he was relating between the long, slow bouts of chewing. Over the coffee and cake, he said, "If you had in mind to do something like that, you couldn't ask your wife for a divorce because it would cast suspicion on you. If I'd ask Laurie, she'd tell her mother, she'd tell all her friends, she'd tell her auntie. The best way is to be lovey-dovey, the best way is to leave off seeing the girl for, say, two, three months, maybe a year, get close to your wife again. . . ."

"Go back to her!" she screamed. "You never left her so it won't be so goddamn hard to crawl into her bed again." With the back of her hand she knocked her empty paper cup off the table.

"The tenants," he cautioned.

"Everybody's stunted! Your Dr. Dick is stunted and his mistress is stunted and even the poor wife who got done in because she wanted all she could get, she was stunted, and the goddamn judge who has to sit there and judge, he's stunted, and all the jurors. Everybody is."

"Everybody is," he said, agreeably.

Lying beside him on the bed, knowing that this was the last time, she told him about Hal Costigan. She said that the man had been in love with her and had killed himself because of the scandal. She said that she was seventeen then and beautiful, as if she were old now, a remark to remind him that she was as beautiful now as ever and young enough to be his daughter. Voice breaking, she told the story into his ear, and she knew by the tension in his body that he was listening differently from the man in the beach shack. He was lying on his back, gazing up at the ceiling, listening closely, and when he turned to her she knew that she was as exciting for him as she had been their first night. The shame she felt over her version of the tragic, unknowable story of another man's suicide was effaced by the flaring up of her desire for this one.

When she left, he was sleeping so heavily he seemed to be sleeping away the density of his body, an infinitesimal amount with each exhalation. She covered him with the side of the spread that she had been lying on. The room was warm, the wall heater was on, but she could not leave him exposed in his nakedness. She put on her clothes, and, when she closed the door, she tried the knob over and over to make certain it was locked.

The apartments opened onto a small square court paved with dark red Mexican tile, spikey cactus plants in the corners. She went on tiptoe across the court, her high heels ringing only now and then on the tiles, and walked along the dark street toward her own neighborhood a mile away. On this street with its few dim lamps and overgrown shrubbery, she was back in the city of her childhood. She felt her return more than she had felt it on the day she lay down again in her own bed in her parents' house, because now Hal Costigan was close beside her again. She had called him up, back on the mattress, to make use of him in the living present, and here he was, beside her again and of no use to her at all. What he had done to himself made her all or made her nothing, and she had clung to the belief that it had made her all, because the other belief was unbearable—*to be nothing, to be nothing.* What he had done to himself told her she was nothing and everybody nothing and the world nothing.

A need to be consoled by her parents grew stronger the closer she came to their home. Her suspicions about her parents, about monotony, about each one's loss in the hope of gain, were blotted out by her need to be consoled. The door was left unlocked, sometimes, and tonight she saw a meaning in that negligence. It was natural, strangely natural, to live without fear of harm or loss. She went on to their bedroom, turning on no lights along the way, and paused in the doorway, calling softly to her mother.

"What? Dolores?" her mother called, sitting up.

She fell to her knees by the bed and took her mother in her arms, and her father sat up and switched on the lamp above them.

"Nothing's the matter," she assured them because everything was the matter but no one thing could be named.

9

The evening of the day her mother died, Naomi went for comfort to her brother Cort's house, knowing that no comfort was to be found there. She sat in the living room, she sat in the kitchen, she sat in the boys' room and read to them as they lay in crib and bed, she ate a small supper and drank several cups of coffee and talked with her brother and his wife, but found no comfort. Pauline was downcast and uncomfortable because she had disliked the old woman, Naomi knew, and must be feeling guilty now. Naomi saw the girl as the stranger of five years ago, and the small, forgotten discords of the girl's physical self were apparent again, like Pauline's sunken cheeks at odds with her large, round breasts. Everything, that day, was without a reason and in no need of a reason. Naomi sat on the sofa next to Pauline, and, as the girl bent forward to pour more coffee into the cups on the low table, she wondered if it were dampness that was causing the girl's fingers to curl back at the tips. Was dampness a sign of life? Like the blood, sweat, and tears Churchill had called for during the war? The pockets of Naomi's jacket were stuffed with damp tissues. The boys had come out from the bath wet, leaving wet tracks, dragging wet towels. All day she had sipped tea and coffee, and wept because her mother had grappled with life and it was like grappling with water.

"Yeah, she had a hard life," Cort said, over in the heavy chair. His face was long with sorrow and he couldn't look anybody in the eyes.

That's true and yet it isn't, Naomi thought. She had reminded herself during this day that there were millions of people who spent half their lives in prisons, in the places for the insane, there were men and women and children mutilated by bombings and those mutilated in their souls by cruelties, and that, back in the Depression, before the war, the hungry roamed the streets of every city, and in Europe a death corps rounded up thousands in one night. It might be impossible, she thought, to compare one person's pain with somebody else's.

"Yeah," Naomi agreed, obligingly pondering his remark. "She sure did."

"She had more than her share."

"Yeah, she had more than her share," Naomi agreed, though she didn't know what a share was, how much it was, and why there should be suffering like a law and a sharing of it.

"She expected a lot from Hal," Cort said, his legs stretched out far, elbows close, peering into the aperture that his curled hands formed close to his eye while the other eye was kept shut.

"Yeah, that was the worst thing."

"Jesus," he said, shifting in his chair, his long, thin body jerking with sudden anger. "Then that guy you married! Jesus, you could've picked somebody decent, Naomi."

Her laugh shot up out of her throat and collapsed. "When you get as old as me," she began, twisting her shoulders like a senile coquette.

"Oh, hell," he said. "You're not old. It's just you don't have much experience with men, and the first one who lays his hand on your knee . . ."

The restraints upon sorrowing were too harsh. The shamelessly loud cries she wanted to release would serve as her defense of her husband. They'd combine her sorrow over the loss of him and her mother. But another laugh shot out. "Yeah, that's the way it was. He put his hand on my knee and old stupid Naomi thinks this is it, this is it." She blew her nose.

Pauline's long, agitated fingers pushed strands of hair behind her ears. "Oh, he wasn't that bad," she said, embarrassed by her ambivalence toward Naomi.

The boy in his crib began to cry, a sudden waking-up crying.

"You want to see if you can shut that kid up, or shall I go?" Cort asked his wife.

"Let me go," Naomi said, rising. "I'll tell them goodnight again. Then I got to be running along." With pinching fingers she jerked her skirt straight.

"You got a nice shape, Naomi," he said. "You always did."

"Oh yeah, old knock-em-dead Naomi."

The older boy began to call for his mother to quiet his crying brother.

"You tell them both to shut up," said Pauline, generously giving over to Naomi some authority to wield.

Naomi found the older boy sitting up in his bed and the younger one sitting up in his crib, and in the sudden light from the hallway they quieted down, waiting to be told to be quiet. She hadn't wanted to come in here again, this blue room with its pile of dirty clothes, broken toys, and the humid ammonia smell of diapers. She knew that when they were to be her age she would mean nothing to them, only a speck of an aunt in the past. "Your Aunt Naomi wants to kiss you again. She's going now." Clowning, she gave them loud, smacking kisses.

"You want me to drive you home?" Cort asked her in the hallway.

"You stay right here," she said. "It'll do me good to sit in a bus. People around."

He followed her as she gathered up her coat and hat and gloves and purse, and helped her with her coat, docile, considerate, because he had wounded her. Pauline kissed her on the cheek. Naomi had always felt intimidated by this young woman, by her uneasiness, even by her tallness. Isobel, Hal's wife, had also intimidated her, but Isobel had done it with her prim, schoolteacher ways, and most of all by being Hal's wife. They turned on the porch light for her. She stepped around a toy on the path, wondering crazily why the toy, left where someone could stumble over it, showed their disrespect for her mother's memory.

She sat at the back of the empty bus, and when she got off at the corner where she was to transfer to another bus, she went into a bar instead. In the bar's glowing, watery, slowly swirling colors, she might find what her mother had told her she would never find and that she needed now when her mother was dead—comforting from strangers. A small table by the entrance was empty, and she sat down and gave her order to the waitress, a woman her own age, with bleached hair and dangling earrings. She sipped her drink and felt the warmth spread down to her toes. The music on the jukebox vibrated along the floor. She gazed up at the hanging lamp that was like a metal ostrich egg pricked by holes through which the globe within shot out stings of light. She thought of how the life in her mother had sunk down and away, and fear of this sinking made her hand so shaky she almost knocked over her glass. She drank down the rest in a hurry because its effect was a rich swelling of life in her face and breasts and belly. She was filled now with her own presence, herself, whose eyes must resemble the lamp with the stings of light.

The man's face was at a discreet distance, but its smile brought it as close as a breath touching her face. Something was wrong with his face. The dark eyes were set too deep and one chunky cheek was lopsided, but there was a kindness in his face, elusive but there for sure. "You mind if I sit here?"

She waved him down. "You sure can."

"You crying for your mother?" He set his glass before him.

"How do you know?"

"The waitress told me."

She remembered the waitress's solicitous question, but she hadn't guessed that her answer would be relayed to somebody else.

"What'd she die of?" The slight Mexican accent, the quick, jerky voice—were they tricks to hide his indifference?

"You don't know a person, why do you want to know what they died of?"

"I'm sorry I asked," he said. "A person shouldn't ask. You're right."

She let him buy her another drink. He told her his name was Victor and that he was born in Texas, and he wanted her to guess how old he was. She squinted, guessing thirty-six. He slapped the table. "That comes of hard living," he said. "That comes of lifting sacks of potatoes up in Idaho, comes of being in the army, comes of digging ditches. I'm twenty-seven."

"You're younger than my kid brother."

"Don't treat me like a kid brother," he said, warningly. "I didn't sit down here to get treated like a kid brother."

She listened closely for signs of trickery in the blurry accent, and she examined closely his sidewards face and the shimmery, silvery stripes in his shirt, wanting to find him reliable despite the evidence against him. When they finished their drinks she went out with him into the street, and he put his arm around her and his hand into her armpit, implying that she had to be held up because of her sorrow.

"Have you got sisters and brothers?" she asked.

"I got a kid brother in the army. I got a sister, too. Fifteen."

"Three kids in the family?"

"Yeah," he said.

"That's like us."

"That's a coincidence, uh?"

"Except one of us is dead," she said.

He said nothing, showing no interest in the missing one.

"My brother," she said. "Not the kid brother I was telling you about, but my other brother."

"That's terrible," he said, his voice jerky with desire.

"He was going to be President of the United States," she said.

"Ahhh," he said, exhaling sympathy.

"I could've been sister of the President. They would've given me a filing job in Washington, D.C., for three times as much as I make now. That's the way you do things, you elevate your family and all your relations. I would've been elevated."

"It's too bad he died," he said, giving her a deft push in the small of her back, guiding her toward a doorway.

She began to climb a flight of stairs to a hallway of doors that she saw above. Behind her on the narrow stairs, he lifted up her coat at the back, but before his hand touched her she backed against the wall.

"You know what he did, I'll tell you," she said. Her purse slipped out from under her arm as she lifted her hands to shield her breasts from his heavy face. "You know what he did? He killed himself. Now there's nothing as bad as that, is there? That's what he did to his own mother. He threw his life right back at her."

"Come on, come on," he urged, picking up her purse and swatting her hip with it to make her turn and go up.

"That's what he did to Mama," she said, climbing.

At the top, she was assailed by the picture of her mother waiting at home for the wayward daughter to return sometime in the night, waiting for the daughter who was her bosom friend, her dear slave, waiting in a cold, dark house for the daughter who wasn't coming home this night. The mother would have to stay alone this night because the daughter wasn't fit to come home.

10

On his last day with the company, Cort Costigan came home after work, bringing another employee who had also been weeded out, and two six-packs of beer. He brought the man, who had been barely more than an acquaintance, because the other's presence reminded him that he was not the only one fired, and he wanted his wife to be reminded of it. Pauline was sitting on the front steps in the sun, absorbing sun into her long body for the benefit of the child within her. When both cars drew to the curb she watched, unwelcoming. Cort saw, from afar, her rebuff of the visitor. She must have wanted him to come home alone on this last day of his job, wanting no spectator. She spoke sharply to the kids playing in the water sprinkler on the lawn, and by the time he and the intruder had come up the walk, she had already grabbed up the younger boy and was tugging up his wet shorts, scolding him because she couldn't scold Cort.

Cort introduced the fellow, who was so shy he seemed to bend away from her. They stepped past her and the boy and went through the house to the kitchen. Cort opened two beers, and the intruder sat down only after Cort sat down, and then with a joke and a mumble.

Sprawling in his chair to persuade the intruder to feel at home, Cort wondered why the man's timidity had never been so evident around the insurance office. The loss of his job and the unsmiling woman on the front steps must have caused him to collapse.

"Let's celebrate this promotion, boy," Cort said, and the intruder clutched at his chest, his laugh as painful as a heart attack.

They drank their beer and, in the midst of their first swallowing, began to laugh again. Cort heard his own laugh go high and wild as it used to when he was a boy. "You ever think old Snyder, you ever think old Snyder . . . ," bowing his head to the table, covering his nose to trap the snorts inside, "looks like a fish? Like one of those brute fishes, where their lower jaw comes up to their eyes? If you saw old Snyder lying among the other fish down at the Crystal Market, you wouldn't be surprised, would you?"

The intruder sputtered his beer. "I'd say slice that one for me!" pointing with his pale, stabbing finger that had no job.

"Ah, slice it!" Cort said.

"The girls . . . ," gasped the intruder.

"Go on!"

"The girls, specially Rosalind, the girls, all the girls in the whole goddamn claims department—bitches, bitches! The only one I like is little Susie. She wrote me a note, hey, she wrote me a little note on her typewriter, says—here, read it—says, 'You are one of the nicest people at Fidelity. I hope you find a position you will enjoy.' " He clutched his face, spattering laughter through his fingers. "She's fresh out of high school, she doesn't know what she wrote. What I ought to do is write back, 'Dear Susie, the only position I will enjoy is one with you under me.' Oh, great!"

"You know that machine they got that chews up the old records, old stuff they don't want around anymore? Hell, take the whole damn Fidelity building, take the lunchtime movies, take the roof garden, take the girls and the boys, take 'em all, the long and the short and the tall, take their Fidelity Frolics, run 'em through the masticator, maserator, what's it called?"

"Don't let the efficiency man get away! Anybody who'd train himself for a job like that is queer as an undertaker, queer as a queer," said the intruder.

Cort leaned his chair far back. Once he'd gone over in the shaky metal chair, and, afraid it might embarrass him again, he held to the table's edge with his fingertips. "They had their eyes on me," he said. "Snyder says to me, 'You happy here, Costigan?' I thought he was kidding. I thought, 'You tell *me*, boy. You want me to go around kissing ass?' "

"You're not a smiler."

"But that doesn't mean I was unhappy, man!"

"You never looked unhappier than anybody else. Snyder—he look happy to you?"

"Snyder's the saddest sack this side of . . ." The spindly legs of the chair were slipping away and he gripped the table. "Hell, I'm glad I'm through with the bastards. I think I'll go back to selling refrigerators. Get to walk around. I always felt like a fairy, sitting at a desk. My calf muscles are down to nothing. Lost my elasticity. I'm like an old rubber band—can't snap anymore." He heard a child's footsteps in the living room, and waited. His younger son appeared in the doorway, red shorts wet, face impassive. "You want some little thing?"

Pauline came up behind the boy. "He can have milk and a cracker. It's too close to dinner." Because her words were an inescapable hint to the intruder, she kept her eyes down as she crossed to the refrigerator.

"I guess I'll be going," said the intruder.

"Finish your beer! Finish your beer!" Cort commanded. "We got a long ways to go before dinner. She says that so he doesn't spoil his appetite." He could ask the intruder to stay for dinner. He could do that in spite of his wife. But, pouring more beer, he admitted that he was eager to be rid of him. The man was a reminder of the company, and only after the fellow was gone would the severing be complete. They knew each other too well. At their desks they'd assumed their position of indebtedness, they'd joined in the exhibitive laughter, they'd kept their boredom from their eyes as if it were a crime, something stolen from the company, and now, worst of all, they were hilarious outcasts together. "What am I going to do with all this beer, man? You've got to help me get rid of it."

The child climbed onto a chair and watched the milk pouring into the glass, his fingers laid out flat on the table.

"How old are you?" the intruder asked. "Twenty-one?"

"You think we got a midget here?" Cort went off into his high laugh again.

"You a midget?"

The boy still gazed, forgetting his milk.

"Something funny about my face?" the intruder asked, covering it with his hands and staring back at the boy from between his fingers.

"You've got Fidelity branded on your forehead, man," Cort said. "You got it there as long as you live." He pointed to his own forehead. "See mine? Every place I ever worked got their name branded on me. That's the only way people got of knowing who you are, they read all those company names on you. The more names you got, the less they can trust you. Snyder's got only one name on his—Fidelity."

"Mighty Mouse Snyder," said the intruder.

They gagged on their laughs. The intruder controlled himself sooner than Cort because Cort's wife, unsmiling, was standing by the boy's chair, a long-legged woman in shorts with a pregnant belly, a composite condition that embarrassed the man unmercifully.

"Sit down and have a beer," Cort said to his wife.

She sat between him and the boy, her chin in her hand. Her sun-bleached hair hung in strings to her shoulders—she hadn't curled it for a long time—and her face was blotchy. Her throat was a little thick with the fat that always came with her pregnancies, but no fat ever came to fill out the hollow cheeks, and her eyes appeared lash-less because the lashes were as light as her hair. Cort suspected her of retaliating against him by looking that way. He suspected that the only way she could retaliate against the company for firing him while she was pregnant with their third child, and retaliate against the pregnancy that went on for so long, was to retaliate against him, her husband, closest, handiest, and more imperiled than she had ever expected any man to be. He kneaded her shoulder affectionately, tell-ing her, in that way, that she was the woman for him, and that it was her love for him, not her grimness, that was getting through to him.

The intruder was thrown into a state of confusion by this knead-ing. Cort's hand on his wife's bare shoulder insinuated their intimacy and its result. He shifted in his chair, crossing and recrossing his legs.

"Do you have another job lined up?" she asked him, her voice softer than her face.

"My wife's brother," he said. "My wife's brother's in auto supply, he's going to put me on the floor, selling."

"Your legs won't hold you up," Cort said. "They been bent too long."

The intruder gripped his thigh, massaging it involuntarily in the same way Cort massaged his wife's shoulder. "If I can find something else, I'll take that instead. For the reason that I hate my wife's brother. He's got a knack for making me feel like . . ." For the obscene word in his mouth he substituted "a nobody. You ever meet anybody who made you feel like a nobody? You ought to meet him."

"That's just the kind of guy I shouldn't meet," Cort said.

The obnoxious brother-in-law became an enemy in common. They swallowed down more beer, knocked off the ashes of their ciga-rettes, while the intruder kept shaking his head over his relative, curs-ing in his cheek as if his anger were a fingernail he'd bitten off and wanted out of his mouth.

"Yeah," Cort said, clicking his index finger against his beer glass, "the world's full of bastards. It's a bastard world. Everybody wanting his, spitting in your eye, crossing off your name. If you don't like that stuff, if you don't like it, you might as well do yourself in because you're going to get done in anyway." In the midst of his tirade he heard the click of his nail repeated by his son on his own glass.

"You can say that again," the intruder said.

Cort saw his wife take down the child's hand to stop the tapping and hold it firmly under the table. The boy began to squirm and cry.

"That's what my brother did," he went on. "He said to hell with it."

Pauline lost to the boy's struggles and released his hand. The tapping on the glass began again, the child staring at the visitor, seeking praise of his talent.

"The man had a heart," Cort said, his voice rising. "You're not supposed to have a heart, you're supposed to be ashamed of it, you're supposed to hide it or get rid of it, do something. But he couldn't help it, he had a heart." He narrowed his eyes, probing the visitor's eyes. "You around then?"

"When was it?"

"Six years ago," he said. "Come October."

"No," said the intruder. "I was in L.A. We came up here a year ago. My wife wanted to be near her sister. Then I got this job with Fidelity." He was giving details of his own existence to forestall details from Cort, and Cort, realizing how close to breaking he looked, dropped his gaze but let his story run on.

"He was what you'd call a complete man. You know what I mean? I mean he had everything. He was on his way up because he had a mind, he was smart. God, that man could persuade. But he had a heart, too. That was his trouble. He couldn't stand the dog eat dog. That's the only thing to do if you got a heart, man. Bow out. So he bowed out just before the curtain went up. He was running for Congress, see?"

The child continued to tap the glass, smiling.

"It's no place for a man with a heart," said the intruder solemnly, pushing the ashtray around with his knuckles.

Pauline took the boy's hands again and held them in a hard clamp, and the boy wailed and thrashed around in his chair.

"He's doing all right, leave him alone!" Cort told her, his voice high and breaking.

"That isn't the reason," she said.

"Then why're you holding his hands?"

"I'm talking about your brother. That isn't the reason." A corner of her mouth jerked down.

"You never even knew him!"

"People with hearts, they don't kill themselves. I know people with hearts. I can name you some."

"Name me some!" he shouted. "Name me some!"

The intruder laughed, embarrassed, responding to his host's challenge as to a joke.

"He was weak," she said.

"Oh, Jesus, it takes a hell of a lot of courage to do what he did."

"He was weak."

Cort put his fists to his temples. "What the hell do you know about it? What the hell do you know what goes on in a man?"

The child was crying under the table. He felt the soft body when he moved his feet.

"What I know is you talk too much about messes."

"That's what they are. You going to deny it?"

"No, I don't deny that," she cried. "All I'm saying is you don't have to kill yourself to show you don't want any part of it. All I'm saying is there's lots of people with hearts. They stay alive as long as they can."

He struck the table. "Don't tell me about your people with hearts. Anybody I'll name, it'll be somebody you don't like. You take my sister Naomi. You don't like her. There's somebody with a heart and you don't like her. You say she's a sap, she's a clown."

The boy was climbing up from the floor and she was trying to help him. Then, realizing that she was drawing him onto her lap when she did not want him there, she unclasped his hands from her clothes and held him away.

"Every time you get a friend in here," she was saying, "every time we go anywhere, you've got to bring up about your brother. You make death sound like something to brag about. You talk like death is all there is to life."

"He was my brother!" he shouted, stumbling up from his chair. She had never criticized him before about his brother, she had never complained. Why had she chosen the worst possible time, now in the presence of this loser, who would go on his way convinced that Cort Costigan was the real loser, a man with a monstrous habit, an attachment to a dead man.

The loser stumbled up with him. "I got to be going."

Cort walked him to the door, shook hands, said, "See you around," and closed the door. On his way back to his wife at the table he stopped in the kitchen doorway, his fists straining dangerously down at his sides. This anger, trapping him there, seemed not to be against his wife. Who, then? Who, then? But something was terribly wrong if this anger was against his brother. Unmercifully wrong. He made his way to the table, sat down by his wife, took her hand in both his hands, and lay his head down on the knot their hands made together.

11

Seagulls were flapping along after the ferry, hovering high and low on the wind. "Bigger than most birds, aren't they?" Naomi remarked to the waitress who was sliding the coffee toward her. "Oh, but ostriches, too! I forgot!" and laughed. *"They're* really big!" She gazed out the ferry windows again, her legs crossed, her high heel caught on the rung of the stool. They might not be as big as some, but they're bigger than the sparrows back home. Cold-eyed birds! What else could you expect, with cold, sea-salty crud in their gizzards, fishheads and guts and wet crusts of bread? She was smiling humoringly at them in case anybody was watching her. The whole city was cold, a gray puzzle beyond the windows, beyond the dipping, flapping, mean-eyed birds. The fish-gray water was cold and God knew how deep under this rumbling tub of a ferryboat. "Oh, they're strong birds all right. My, they got strong wings!" trilling her flattery, ducking her head to drink her coffee.

"You sure don't realize how big the world is, do you? No, you sure don't," she answered herself, and asked for a bearclaw to eat with her coffee. The more she purchased, the more the waitress might like her. She cut the pastry into four strips, picked up one daintily, and, with the avid, happy eyes of the enchanted visitor, watched the smoke-brown buildings slide by. The hotel room where she'd slept last night—all night long a bad smell kept waking her. Was it a mouse rotting? Or was it only her own fear of a strange city? "Can't make out which hotel is mine!" She laughed, half expecting the waitress to turn her head and help her find it. *You're over forty yourself,* she said to the waitress. *Is that why you can't smile? But you're in your own city, behind your own little counter on your own chuggling ferry, you chuggle along in the same watery groove every day. You're not far from home. You didn't spend last night in a dead-mouse hotel room.* Was it done in this city, too, like that woman had done a year ago back home, checking into a hotel and the next day found on the bed, dead from an overdose of sleeping pills? What the hell you trying to do? she asked herself. Stir up this woman's sympathy with a threat of what you'll do to yourself if she doesn't smile at you? She can't read your mind, she can't even read your face.

The stale pastry was like a wad of paper in her mouth. She washed it down with the coffee and glanced contentedly around. They keep these ferries clean all right, she thought. Windows clean as sky, long benches varnished with a thick, dark wine of a shine, floors mopped. Over by the door of the ladies' lavatory, two men in white overalls were painting light green paint over the old-fashioned dark green, each man down on a knee, each painting with slow and easy, careful strokes. Everything shipshape, engines rumbling along, hot coffee in the urn, candy machine and popcorn machine standing against the wall like members of the crew. *My those ferryboats are a joy to ride!* That was the first thing she'd say to Isobel. *They keep them so clean!* she'd say, as if Isobel had a hand in it. *My, this part of the country, I bet you can't beat it. Why, Mount Rainier looks just like a dish of ice cream standing up there behind Seattle, and all those mountains, my, they make a pretty background for the city. Just like an oil painting!*

What a shock to the heart to see someone waiting for you who

315

didn't want to be waiting! Isobel. Isobel, wife of her brother, Hal. Once they'd been friends—wife and sister. But in the six years since Isobel and her son had fled, there'd been only a card at Christmas, with that hasty blue-ink signature that said, *You're just one among many,* and the card not even to her, Naomi, only to her mother, with herself understood as sharing, and after her mother died, no cards. The city was far behind them now, most of the seagulls had flapped away, and far out across the gray water was the shore where Isobel waited.

"If you're getting off at Winslow, you'd better get up to the front," the waitress advised after the second cup of coffee. "You can see the ferry put into the slip."

One high-heeled shoe found the floor, her knees stretching her tight skirt. She dug out her coin purse to slip a quarter under the saucer. Pay her to make her like you, she thought, teetering a bit on the black suede heels of her red pumps, drawing her coat around her. Two men in dark suits, facing each other on the face-to-face, back-to-back benches, unrememberable men, reading newspapers, glanced up as she left her perch and glanced down again, uninterested in a woman with a homeless face, anxious eyes way in under painted black eyebrows, and dyed black hair in stiff, chic curls under a red hat. *It doesn't hurt so much any more, thanks,* she said to them. *The older I get the more used to it I get. When the time comes when you don't look up at all, then I won't feel anything.* She knelt to pick up her overnight case, and in that small activity, because they did not watch her, a feeling of immeasurable abandonment came over her. For several moments she could not rise. Clutching her coat together, she went forward toward the bow.

Now through the windows she saw land again, forested hills, narrow beaches with little cottages, sailboats moored to docks, and again the wash of waters against and over things, over broken docks, over logs on the sand, and the merciless rocking of everything on the waters. Close overhead, she saw a seagull borne back on the wind, saw the white breast, saw the light from the sky shining through the wings, saw the beak with the preying knob, saw the crazed eye. There was the slip, its high, slanting timbers rising up out of deep water, there the long black ramp up to the concrete building, and there, on that higher level, a parking lot with tiny cars far away and growing larger. Small figures wandered about up there. Which one was Isobel? But in that moment, seeking out Isobel and avoiding her, she felt the frightening closeness of her mother barring her way in a narrow hallway, Mama in the satin robe. *What've you come to see Isobel for? She never wrote, she never brought Hal's son back for me to see. What Hal did to himself, she's to blame because she was no wife to him.* Naomi put up her gloved hand as though to clear a spot on the window glass.

The engines changed their tune, or did they stop? The rumbling stopped, the ferry struck against a piling, and her hand at the glass helped her to keep her balance. A man in a uniform ran down the narrow iron ladder from the captain's cabin and disappeared around the deck. The cluster of passengers was increasing at the bow, the wind blowing up hair and scarves and coat hems. It must be like docking a big ship, she thought. You haven't come very far in forty-six years, she said to herself. *Isobel,* she begged, *forgive me for being a hick, for coming to visit. I won't stay long, I'll stay just tonight.* A child out on deck, his hand in his mother's, was gazing over his shoulder at her, and she changed her face to the face of a dazedly happy visitor awaited eagerly by someone up there in the town.

They embraced, kissing each other's cheek, each bending to pick up the overnight case and Isobel gripping it first. It was done as it ought to be done, for anybody watching and for themselves, and, arm in arm, they walked to the parking lot.

"If anybody'd asked me, I could have picked it out!" she said as Isobel unlocked the car door. "There's something so neat about it!" Not old, not new, a clean, light green sedan with plaid green seatcovers. "You were always such a neat one!"

"Guy's very cooperative," Isobel said, settling in the driver's seat, smoothing her coat under her, fitting the key with a sure hand. "He uses the car, too, mostly on weekends. Even though he takes his friends with him—they go to the beach or Seattle or Mount Rainier— why, he brings it back in good shape, even the ashtrays emptied."

Naomi doubled over with a disbelieving laugh. "Guy drive? Oh, God, I keep seeing a twelve-year-old boy. He's a man!"

"In September he'll be starting at the university," Isobel said, glancing over her shoulder as she reversed the car out of the line. "Medicine."

"Medicine? Oh, you mean he's going to be a doctor!" Again Naomi bent over, laughing, because she was so dense. She's still Isobel, she thought. She's got her own schoolteacher way of saying things, and she looks more like a teacher now than ever. So vapory kind, like a nun. "Well, isn't that nice! A doctor! There's nobody in the world gets more respect than a doctor."

The houses were far apart in this town. Back in her own neighborhood, they were boxy stuccos of pastel colors, plots of grass in front littered with children's toys and paper. They passed an acre of grass, two horses grazing, then a long row of small houses all alike, gray frame with dark green trim. "Company houses," said Isobel, and Naomi nodded as though she knew the meaning. Then, after more grass, "That one? The white one?" she asked, peering through the windshield, directed by Isobel's pointing finger. "Say, that's sure a cute little house."

"It belonged to my aunt," Isobel said. "She left it to me. She died three years ago. We've got awfully nice neighbors. Another teacher at the high school lives just a couple of houses down, the green one, see? And on the other side of us there's a nice family, he works on a newspaper in the city. They're all nice people around."

Isobel parked the car exactly before the few stone steps to the yard so that, in lieu of an honest welcome, there was a path for the guest's feet directly as the guest stepped out of the car. Naomi thought—Anybody looking out a window would see a smartly dressed visitor, nice figure, nice legs, nice posture, a visitor positive of her welcome, carrying a snappy, round, black and white overnight case. A forever-young woman delighted with small surprises. "Say, look what you got here!" pausing on the concrete path. "Clam shells! Say, don't they make a pretty border!" her voice the voice of Athena, a tough woman with a kind heart.

So this is the house Isobel got for herself! Naomi passed through the little hallway and into the living room, her heels muted by braided rugs. This is the house where Isobel found refuge, protected by distance and silence. "Oh, say, this is cozy, Isobel!"

"Let me take your bag upstairs," Isobel said. "You're welcome to my bedroom."

"No, no!" shaking her head vigorously. "What's the matter with the sofa? I'll sleep on the sofa. Won't be any trouble to anybody, that way," tossing the bag onto the sofa, removing her hat, her coat, and tossing these over the bag. "Wait'll I get my cigarettes," she called after Isobel who was moving on into the kitchen to make tea, and, fishing up the package from her purse, holding it under her breasts, she followed Isobel. At the kitchen table, she hung a cigarette on her lips and struck a match. "I can stay overnight, like I told you, but I got to get back in the morning. I'm staying with friends in Seattle and it wouldn't be polite if I stayed away longer. They drove me to the ferry and I wanted them to come along for the ride, but they said it's nothing new to them. Real nice people. The wife used to work in the recorder's office with me."

She sat down, leaned back, flicking together the nails of thumb and little finger to make a hard, worldly, nervous clicking. "Say, you've got a sweet little kitchen here!" glancing around at the crockery windmill clock on the wall, at the crockery Dutch boy and girl with ivy growing out of their heads, at the yellow and green curtains with ruffles.

"Nobody keeps house like Isobel, that's what Mama always said. You remember?" Her face lapsed. "Mama's dead, you know. I wrote you, didn't I?"

Isobel was setting teacups down, place mats, teaspoons. "We were sorry to hear," she said. "And I thought to myself, wouldn't it be nice if Naomi could come here for a visit, a change of scenery. Last night when you phoned, we were so pleased. Guy said," and she laughed, "he said 'I wonder if she looks like I remember her, in a blue dress.' "

"Mama never did forgive you for taking Guy away," she said, thinking, Why am I making accusations for Mama? "I was always having to explain to her how I figured you felt. But you did do everything so fast, hustled him off on the plane, sent him all that way, a kid alone."

A slice of lemon slid off the saucer Isobel was setting down. She picked it up with hasty fingers. "The stewardess took care of him," her voice flat. "And my aunt met him in Seattle. He was twelve years old already."

"That's what I told Mama," her voice rising with dolorous insistence like that of a child who is seldom listened to. "That's what I said. Oh, I was always defending you, Izzybell. Remember how I used to call you Izzybell? Oh, say, I sure missed you, Izzybell."

Isobel sat down angrily, a teacher fed up with a student's perverse behavior. "One thing, one thing let me ask of you. Not one word to Guy about his father's suicide. Not one word. And for that matter, not to anybody else, if anybody comes by while you're here."

"Oh, God, never!" clasping her throat. "Never. What did you think, that I came all the way here just to bring up old troubles?"

"That's all I ask."

"Well, that's certainly not too much to ask." She laughed. "You don't have to be afraid of me, that's just a little thing to ask."

Isobel pushed herself up as if already unbearably weary of this visitor, and, at the stove, pouring boiling water into the flowered teapot, her back to the visitor, she asked cheerily, "Tell me about *you*. Anything interesting?"

"Me?" Naomi crossed her legs, sliding her palms down along her thighs, and clasping her hands together when they met upon her knees. "I got married. Yes, I did. I was going to write and tell you, but oh, my, it was like the roof falling in. Dan, his name was Dan O'Leary, that's just what it was, and a nice guy, nice as pie, but an alcoholic. One of those real ones. It didn't last long, the marriage I mean, oh, maybe six months. He went back to New York, business stuff. He never wanted me to go and see Mama, I had to fight with him. When he left, I moved back with her." All told with a shrugging of shoulders, with pulls on her cigarette, and a crossing and recrossing of legs.

"What was his business?" Isobel asked.

"Oh, he used to be an engineer, really. He used to be a big time engineer, he was that smart. But then his alcohol craving got the better of him, and he started drifting."

"It's sad, isn't it, what it does?" Isobel, sipping her tea.

Naomi rubbed her knees. "You'd never believe your sister-in-law, old workhorse Naomi, you'd never think she'd start drinking around, now would you? I used to go around to the bars with him, got to like it. Oh, don't get worried!" holding up her hand. "Don't worry about *me*. I'm off it now, haven't had a drink since the night I almost got run over. After Dan left and I moved back with Mama, I used to go out after she was asleep, go visit the bars. Up until the night I almost got it. That sobered me up."

"What about Cort? What's he doing?"

"Cort? Kid brother Cort? He was just twenty-six when you left, wasn't he? Well, now he's married, got himself a nice honey, and they got two boys, yep, two boys, and now they got a baby girl. They don't waste time these days, do they? The oldest boy's the smartest kid you ever saw, four years old and talks like a judge. Mama used to say he was going to grow up to be like his Uncle Hal. But Hal was one in a million. Everybody watching him. Watch that man going nowhere but up! Got out of law school, right away he's in with the biggest lawyer in town. If he'd made that election to Congress, I'll bet he'd be a Senator now. Senator Hal Costigan. It's okay, isn't it, if I tell Guy what a smart father he had?"

"He knows it."

"What did you tell him happened?" she asked, dartingly.

"I told him it was a heart attack."

"That's what *I'll* say, then. Because I've got to talk about Hal, you just can't not talk about him. You can't come and meet the son of a man like Hal and not say something about his father. That's asking too much."

"That's not what I asked."

"I know what you asked. You don't have to tell me twice," a friendly jabbing in her voice, a pretense at being offended.

At four, Guy came home. Naomi, rising, cried, "Look at that boy! It's Guy, I bet!" She stood on tiptoe to kiss him on both cheeks. "Your Mom said you remember your Aunt Naomi," holding his hands, swinging his arms from side to side.

"That's true," he said, trying not to lower his eyes, trying not to shift his feet.

"You sure don't look like your Dad!" roaming her gaze over his broad face, like Isobel's, over the ugly haircut, shorn close, glancing down to the large feet in hiker's boots. Looks like any other teenager, she thought. "Don't get me wrong, you're a good-looking guy, but you don't look like your Dad."

She dropped his hands, rattled by her own effusiveness. Slowed by her behavior, self-conscious, he took off his leather jacket and washed his hands at the kitchen sink. She helped set the table, laying out plates edged in blue and gold, lifting silverware from the wine velvet lining of the case, protesting that she wanted to eat on any old plate with just any old fork. The ornaments for the meal and the meal itself, composedly created by Isobel, an apron across her little bulge of a stomach and a glimmer of sweat on her brow, all were declarations of this guest's imposition. While they ate, Naomi told old family jokes, even joggling Isobel's foot for emphasis, but all the while aware of Guy's sullen face, given grudgingly to a smile. Catch Hal with a face like that when he was a boy, and he'd change quick as a flash. But this one showed it off, as if he'd made it all by himself. Maybe it was the time of life to be sullen, maybe it was natural, she thought. Maybe I wanted to be sullen, too, but Mama wouldn't let me. "You got a girlfriend? I bet you got a girlfriend."

"Up 'til yesterday," he said.

Oh-ho, there's the reason! she thought, as Isobel said, "And tomorrow there'll be another. Guy never has to worry."

"What're you talking about?" he demanded. "You said yourself that Alice was a prize, you said nobody, no other girl, measured up to her. Why do you make it sound so, oh, so damn, oh, like it doesn't matter?" Filling his mouth with peas, he deprived her of the chance to answer, as if it were her mouth he had stopped. His mother ate on neatly, implying that to observe pauses in conversation was an art.

Oh-ho! Naomi thought. His girl's thrown him over. That's why his eyes can't lift up, that's why he looks like a mean bear.

"Alice Ann is a nice girl, prettier than most, lots of personality," Isobel explained to Naomi. "Her father is a physician and her mother comes from a wealthy family, and Alice Ann has been, well, she has that manner of having the advantages."

What's she doing? Telling me that Guy deserves the best things in life? Naomi saw Guy's hands breaking a biscuit and buttering it, callow hands that had petted around the girl's prize body. Like a handshake with a movie star, maybe he'd never wash his hands again to keep the feel of the girl on them, and when he was married to some other girl and had three kids, he'd tell the fellows in the bar about that one who got away.

"They were going to be married," Isobel said. "Her parents like him so much. He was over there twice a week for supper. They were even going to help him with medical school. Then her brother comes back for the summer with this friend of his from Harvard, and the friend, well, he and Alice Ann, well, she fell in love with him. Yesterday she broke it off with Guy. She cried about it."

"All right, tell it all," he grumbled. "She cried. . . ."

"That's what you said!"

There he was, trying not to be pleased with the fact that she'd cried. At least she'd cried, he'd always have that to remember. Naomi ate on, daintily, a guest appreciative of every morsel and their sharing of family matters.

"She cried," he said. "So what?"

They ate on in silence. Naomi shifted in her chair, an involuntarily flirtatious move, flipped her napkin and spread it again over her lap, trying to quiet an odd triumph over his loss. "I guess I better not take seconds," she said, "because I saw that cherry pie."

"They're cherries from the tree in our yard," Isobel said, exaggerating their pride in that bountiful tree.

"Oh, I saw it!" Naomi cried. "Aren't you the lucky ones!"

When the kitchen was tidied, Naomi followed Isobel into the small garden at the front of the house, and while Isobel troweled around the plants, Naomi, in a borrowed sweater, wandered up and down the concrete path, arms crossed to keep herself warm. "The air here sure is different," she said. She gazed up into the branches of the cherry tree, every branch hung with a profusion of red and yellow cherries. The cherries were the colors of sunset, the colors of life and variety, the stems so springy, curving with the weight of the tiny fruit, the sky like large, pale blue leaves intermingling with the green leaves.

The trowel made a dry, rasping sound. She went over to Isobel's squatting figure, her shoes on the gravel between the flower beds sending up a fiery sound. "You mean Guy goes all the way to those mountains just for the snow?" hugging herself, facing the range across the waters and beyond the city, mountains almost transparent, almost air.

The trowel rasped on, clods broke apart. "You know, I never mentioned it to Guy, but there's something about Alice Ann I didn't like. She's calculating. She saw possibilities in Guy. She was the one who made the first move, she invited Guy to go on a hiking trip with her parents. But all the time I kept thinking—If somebody comes along who's a little older than Guy, say, knows more about women . . . "

Isobel unbent, rubbing her gravel-bitten knees on the way up, her trowel with its flakes of dirt held outward. "In a way, I'm glad it happened."

Don't bother me with her hot and cold, Naomi pleaded. *Because the only one I knew was Dan, and a couple more that were hotel-room romances. If I ever go up to a room again, I'll go up every night until I come into the courthouse some morning reeking with the smell of the man and me, and my stockings hanging down in baggy wrinkles, and after that I'll have to live in one of those rooms.* Cozily bowing her shoulders, she went ahead of Isobel to the door. "Say, this sure is a cute sweater. You knit this one yourself?"

Guy was on the hassock, watching television. When they entered the darkening room, he straightened up from his slump.

Naomi collapsed in the center of the sofa, stretching out her legs. "Say, it gets chizzly around here, doesn't it? What we could use right now is a little bitty rum or something."

Isobel knelt to light the oil stove. "We've got a bottle of brandy somewhere. Got it for Christmas a few years ago."

Naomi wiggled the toes of her red shoes to catch the boy's eye. "Excuse me if I'm interrupting."

"Why don't we just turn it off," Isobel said, and did it herself on her way to the kitchen.

In the quiet, the boy was left without a voice, without an excuse for his lack of a voice. Naomi felt for her cigarettes in her purse on the sofa, the small rustling, the scratch of the match loud in the silence. "What's the matter? Cat got your tongue?"

He shifted on the hassock.

"Want a cigarette?" She lifted her arm to aim the package at him.

"Don't smoke," he said. "Thanks."

"Maybe you ought to. Want me to teach you?" A tremor crossed her belly, and she felt again the excitement of the cocktail bar, the anonymous man on the stool beside her, just because the room was dim and he was humped in silence. A young lout over there, denied the facts of life by his mama.

Guy sniggered his appreciation of her humor, unsuspecting of the innuendo because he was unaware of her as a woman whom other men took down into their beds.

"No, you sure ain't your father," she mused, defiantly ungrammatical. "He was smaller than you, for one thing. Wiry, nervous, real nice smile. He kept that boy's smile right to the end. I'm not saying you don't have a nice smile yourself, you just don't use it very often. I was telling Guy here," she said to Isobel, returning, "that there wasn't anybody had a nicer smile than Hal. What'd they call it in high school? A winning smile. Yeah, he was always winning."

Isobel settled down with her knitting. "It wasn't just a matter of being lucky," she said. "He worked hard."

Naomi waved it back at her. "Sure, I know he worked hard, but he had a winning streak going all the time. When you get those two things together," holding up two fingers, "you've got dynamite." She winked at Guy. "There was one time he didn't work hard for something he wanted. When he fell in love with your mother, there, she fell right into his arms. Am I right, over there?"

Isobel crossed her ankles. "I guess you're right."

"I remember when you two got together, you and Hal, just kids in college. He brought you home one day to introduce you around. Say, I thought you were mighty cute, with all that nice curly hair. I remember Mama asking you in that just-asking way, asking you what your father did and you said, a grocery store, and Mama said, a market, and you said, no, a grocery store, and Mama said, oh, a little one, and you said, but he's dead now." Naomi laughed, twenty years late an encouraging laugh for the girl.

Guy scratched his back, trapped in the evening that belonged to the visitor.

"You got someplace else you want to go?" she asked him.

"He wants to visit with you," Isobel said.

The sky in the window was dark, the lamplight brighter, the oil heater purring. "Yeah, I remember I thought to myself—Well, here comes that cute girl to Hal's crummy house, old cheap furniture, rag rugs from Woolworth's, his skinny sister with a frizzy cheap permanent in her hair, smiling like a jack-o'-lantern, like a happy loony, everybody living on her file-clerk salary, and Mama asking *her* what kind of people *she* comes from. You remember that, Izzybell?"

Isobel rocked once, and, almost with fear, Naomi saw that the chair was one of those upholstered rockers for matrons. "She was right, you know," Isobel said, her gaze down on her ticking needles and the dragging sock in her lap. "She didn't want him to ruin his chances."

"You know what I said to myself? I said, that little gal's going to be good for him. And I was right."

"I don't know if I was good for him," Isobel said. "But he acted as if I were. He loved his little family, he was a good father and husband, so maybe I *was* good for him. I can't say he was easy to live with, but that's the way it is with ambitious men."

Naomi got up hastily and elbowed her way around the room in search of an ashtray. *Oh, God, what's she doing? Telling a story to a kindergarten class? Who's she talking about? Storybook animals?* "Just because nobody smokes around here . . . "

327

Isobel was up at once, and came back apologizing, offering the tiny, flowered bowl the guest had used at the kitchen table, and Naomi went on elbowing the room, bowl in one hand, cigarette in the other. "Tell you what," she said, just as Isobel settled into her rocker again. "You go get that brandy. Just a teensy weensy bit, that's all I'll have, I promise. Just to celebrate me being here, how's that?"

Guy brought the brandy, and she took the bottle from him, and the glasses. "Oh, say, this is great! You're sweet." Perched on the sofa arm, she poured the brandy, her wrist perky. "Just a little bitty bit for each. Am I the only one around here who knows how to pour a drink?" *One for the overgrown kid and one for his mother who keeps him a kid.* "Say, this will hit the spot!"

Guy, on the hassock again, held up his glass to catch the lamplight in the amber brandy, and Naomi watched him focus on the wobbling light, transfixed, herself, by his seeking look, a look she had always observed in young faces and that seemed the essence of their beauty. Maybe she'd had that look herself when she was young, but nobody had ever told her.

"They serve all kinds of great stuff over at Alice Ann's," Guy said. "Her father's got a real wine cellar."

"Take me over there sometime!" she whooped, her humor separating her from the boy just as their antennae were touching. "Hey, listen, you mark my words. Someday you're going to have your own wine cellar and you'll be pulling corks for better men than Mr. Doctor-What's-His-Name. Listen, you don't need a doctor's daughter to get ahead, you've got all you need in yourself. The same way with your father. And maybe your luck'll bring you a wife like Hal's, like your Mom over there. You should've seen them, living in a little house in somebody's backyard, both of them studying away hard as they could. Made me want to cry."

"Naomi helped us out," Isobel said. Her glass stood untouched on the chairside table.

"You make it sound like I was going to sponge off her father," Guy said.

"Listen, you think I can't see you were in love with her, I mean *in love*? It's written all over you."

She took a big swallow of brandy. The warmth spread down into her breasts, a burning bush in both of those silly, leftover things. She saw Isobel take a slow sip and sipped slowly herself, mockingly, thinking how like children they all were, the three of them at a make-believe tea party. "That's the best way to do it," she said, instructively. "You sip it slow. You're right, Izzybell."

"It was a gift," Isobel said. "It must be the best."

Naomi gazed down the length of her legs to the toes of her red shoes. "Say, it's good to get away, believe me. I've got two whole weeks off. I've been in that courthouse seems like two hundred years."

"I've always said that clerks are underpaid," Isobel said. "They do an awful lot of routine work that keeps the wheels going around."

"They do! They do!" her voice big enough to discuss politics with and what was going on in the world. "And even when they get everything microfilmed and automated, they're still going to need clerks. Maybe even more. Less room for the papers and more room for the clerks. How do you like that? So I guess I don't have to worry about a job."

"You get to meet nice people that way," Isobel mused. "You're not isolated. Some clerks are, but at the courthouse you've got all those men who come in to consult the records."

"Most of those guys are married," waving her hand. "And if they aren't, they want the young ones. We had a kid under me, twenty, about the same age I was when I started, but pretty. My trouble was I wasn't pretty to begin with. She didn't work there more than six months and she marries the deputy district attorney. She brings her kids in for me to see, a couple of babies. Real sweet girl." She held up her glass. "Empty. No glass is allowed to go empty around here," she proclaimed, pouring.

"But there must be some nice men who come in . . . ," Isobel persisted.

"You want to know who? Creeps. That's who's interested in *me*. There was a creep came in the other day, some farmer looking up a deed, one of those real skinny guys who've got enormous eyes you wonder what they're so big for. And you know what he says to me? He said, didn't they have your picture in the paper? For what, I said, Queen of the Grape Festival? And he said, six years ago, that time your brother killed himself. He was smiling at me like he thought I wanted to talk about it, like it was what I talked about all the time. Then he asked me where was the best place to eat lunch and I said the Wherry Hotel, and he asked me to eat lunch with him and I said, real cold, that I always brought my lunch in a paper bag. That's the kind of creep you meet on this job."

Silence. This panic, was it like stage fright? Because here she was, Naomi acting Naomi's part, indignantly erect at her desk, withering with her stare the hayseed at the counter.

"What brother was that?" Guy asked.

"Never mind," waving the question away. "Everybody's got to forgive me. It's bad taste to pity yourself."

"Was it Cort?"

"Cort? You crazy? Cort's got the soul of a farm horse and me, too, and we're both alive and pulling. It's the sensitive ones who leave early. The party's too rough for them."

The silence wasn't broken yet because the silence was Isobel's, who sat with her head bowed, fingers stopped, her feet in fringed moccasins set severely close together. "You are a vile, insane woman," Isobel said.

Naomi hung a cigarette on her lips, searched for matches in the pockets of the borrowed sweater though she knew none were there, found a packet on the sofa, and scratched one across. The flame shook up and down, eluding the cigarette, and, frightened by her own shaking hand, she almost gave up. She leaned back, crossing her legs, blowing out smoke. "That's okay with me," she said.

"What for?" said Guy.

"What for what?" Naomi snapped.

"I mean why."

"Who knows why?" her voice hard and shaky. "Because there he was, Hal O. Costigan, candidate for U.S. Congress, lots of friends, pals, lots of charm. Who the hell knows why? They said he did it because he ruined his chances by running around with a high school girl and they got found out. But who the hell knows why he was running around with her? It's the same question. A man with a nice wife, cute son, why would he want to do anything like that? Maybe he was in love with the girl and couldn't help himself. I guess that's happened before," laughing a high, mocking laugh.

"You stop it!" Isobel cried.

Guy glanced at his mother, but fear of her, like a violent hand laid on him, twisted his head away, forbidding him to see her rage.

Ashes scattered over her lap. "It ain't easy," Naomi said, frantically brushing the ashes away with her left hand, holding the cigarette high in the other.

"I say don't answer me," Isobel hissed. "Just stop it." Since there was no other place for her to go, she settled back into the rocker, tucking her skirt around her, shooting out one leg to see what was on her foot, a shoe or a slipper.

"It ain't easy," Naomi said, a bad student.

"Guy never did anything to you!"

"What do you mean I never did anything to her? What's she done against me?" Unmovable on his hassock, slow to pick up on anything.

Isobel stood up, catching at the knitting falling to the floor. She knelt to pick it up, her back to him. "You didn't have to know about it."

"So now I know!" he shouted. "Is it going to ruin my life?" He had thrown tantrums, Naomi suspected, and he had slammed doors, and he had shouted, but he had never shouted before with this voice.

He was up on his feet, hitching up his trousers, tugging down his sweater. "No dead man is going to ruin my life. A lot of guys I know don't have a father. Do they cry about it? If he killed himself, it's something people do all the time, you're always reading about it in the papers. How's *he* going to ruin my life?" With a palm to each temple he brushed back his hair, shorn too close for the gesture to make a difference. "I guess I'll take the car," he said.

"What for?" Isobel demanded. "Where you going?"

"You asked me so I'll tell you. I'm going to find Lorraine Forbes. You know her, you had her in your class last year. Well, this Lorraine likes me. She more than likes me, she clings to me."

"You leave her alone!" Isobel was following him. "You want to stay in this town forever, a fool, a fool because you got yourself a kid to support?"

"She never leaves *me* alone," he said. At the front door he remembered his jacket. Leaving the door ajar, night air streaming in, he went into the kitchen and came out again, zipping up his leather jacket, striding past Isobel, who was covering her throat with her sweater to keep her dreadful voice from any neighbor passing by.

Guy's footsteps down the path were quick as Isobel's coming toward her. Naomi stood up, covering her face. The fist struck her wrist and, as she lowered her arms to soothe the place, the fist struck her face. But the shock of pain was nothing compared to the shock of Isobel's face. Naomi gripped the weeping woman's arms, forcing them downward, but partway down their resistance vanished, and Isobel clasped her around the waist. Enraptured, Naomi clasped her in return with all the strength of the young woman, years ago, who had been so spontaneously fond of the red-haired, round-faced girl, Hal's bride, little scholar, just learning. In her arms now was the plump teacher body, as spent as her own and to be left by all. Holding each other, they sat down on the sofa.

"Your mother must have felt this way about Hal," Isobel was saying. "She *was* Hal, she lived in him. Like me, what's life got to do with me? A teacher, what's that? What I know I keep back from them. The awful things, the things that happen, I keep back, and pretty soon they're the ones who know. They find out for themselves and they figure I never did."

Isobel was up, searching for something around the room, a note being passed among the students, about her. "I'm glad he knows. I'm glad and I'll tell him more because I'm the only one who knows about Hal. Everybody else thought—well, here's a man who's got respect for himself, who's got it for the next fellow, who's got enough for everybody. You can say they loved him for that in their hicktown way. But he didn't have it, he was faking it. He should have been an actor. It was like a fever, he'd run around with a fever all day and at night he'd come down with the chills. He said someday he'd get rid of himself, he said it was like a mandate. I came down with the disease myself. The neat little Red Cross nurse out in the jungle with her white shoes on."

Naomi was by the window. Beyond the reflection of the room, a watery cluster of lights floated on the night. She covered her face.

"Isobel," she called through her hands, "do you pity him? I'm supposed to pity him, but I've got no pity in me."

Silence. No pity? It was what she had come to hear, it was what she had come to share so that she wasn't so alone.

"I pity him," Isobel was saying. "Sometimes there's nothing and sometimes there's the pity, and the pity when it comes always makes up for the times I feel nothing. It rushes in where there was nothing."

Naomi heard Isobel catching sharp breaths, heard her go farther away, up the hallway. Alone, she took her hands down from her face. The roof was still over her, the lamp on. Her confession was shaking her heart, her hands, but nothing else was shaken from its harmonious place.

Isobel came back, wiping her eyes on the blanket in her arms.

Together they tossed off the sofa cushions, floated down sheets, unfolded the blanket. Naomi had come a thousand miles from the house where her mother had lain, waiting for her to come home from work. She had come all that way to confess about Hal, and it was an affront to her mother that she, Naomi, was given a bed to lie down in. She ought to be wandering the streets of that cold city across the waters.

"I always tried to keep Mama clean," she said. "Her bed clean and everything. Whenever I see a nice clean bed I think of Mama. Even on television, if I see one. My friend Athena has this bed a mile high. Looks like a cloud, lots of eyelet pillows. Her father died just after Mama. She says she deserves a good night's sleep. She got herself this fancy bed."

The overnight case was found, and Naomi held up her black nylon nightie. "Something special, this is. Got it when I used to go up to Dan's hotel room. He said he liked black lace on a woman, so I got it."

Isobel was kneeling by the heater, turning it off. "That girl," she said, "that girl who Hal . . . "

"Dolores."

"That picture of her, she was lovely, wasn't she? Answer to a prayer or something." She got up, began her search around the room again.

"She came back," Naomi said. "I saw her once. It was on my bus, I was on my way home. She recognized me, too, I could tell. She looks real cheap. At first I thought it wasn't her. She got real thin, and her hair's cut—you remember how it was long?—and you should see the makeup. Before I knew who she was I felt sorry for her, I said to myself, oh, boy, that girl sure thinks she's the cat's pajamas." She took no pleasure now in the girl's change, but she'd taken it then, on the bus, because the change had seemed like punishment, until she admitted what she'd known all along, that the girl warranted none. That bus ride with the girl was the longest ever. There she'd sat, just across the aisle from the girl, clutching her vengeful pleasure to her breast.

Naomi sat down on the sofa and pushed off one pump with the toe of the other. The news she'd brought to Isobel about the girl was a gift like the few others she'd brought. Isobel might be grateful for it, but it wasn't going to last very long.

"Isobel, kiss me goodnight." Lifting her face at the same moment Isobel bent over her, she forced the kiss intended for her hair to come down on her forehead instead.

"Sleep well," said Isobel.

"Don't worry about *me.*"

Naomi, tilting on one hip and then the other, unsnapped her nylons from the garter belt and peeled them down. Barefooted, she crossed the room to turn off the lamp by the rocker, and when she returned to the sofa Isobel was gone. Unzipping her dress, lifting it off, she heard footsteps above her, a secret, surreptitious sound like Isobel's wish that the woman in the dark room below had never come back into her life.

Wrapped in the blanket, Naomi sat on her bed, poured more brandy from the gifty bottle, lifted her feet to the low table, and drank, protected by the blanket as a baby is or a potentate, protected by the brandy against the attempt of the house to expel her, Naomi, who had entered under false pretenses as mute, as deaf, as lacking memory, heart, as a harmless woman climbing up the ramp from the ferry, waving a clean-gloved hand and smiling the ivory-toothed, silver-specked smile of the middle-aged visitor, the past tucked into her overnight case, the past weighing nothing more than the cheap gifts from a drugstore back home, perfume for Isobel and a tie clip for Guy.

The languor from the brandy was spreading all the way down to her feet. She tried to raise her knees, and the languor brought her Dan. "Dan," whispering. She placed a hand each side of him, there at his waist, to form him and to bring him to lie down upon her with the weight of his life, but he denied himself to her and disappeared.

Burdened as he was with himself, he could still turn away from those who would further burden him with themselves.

Left alone again, she summoned up the people on the train to be with her. On the train there had been lots of company, sleeping and awake, curled up and sprawling, in all the seats up and down the coach, and she had drowsed side by side with an old woman whose throat noises in sleep accompanied the mechanical noises of the train. The train swept along, wayside lights flickering, vanishing. Lurching figures to and from the toilets, quiet, deformed elderly women—lumping together of breasts and belly, lumping down of ankles—going dimly by in slippers, hardly there and gone, and their quiet husbands in white shirts cross-marked by suspenders, the cross of morning reprisal that the king's scout leaves on the door at night, figures gentle to their own selves as to children who wake in the night and must be led.

Naomi slept, opened her eyes to a lighted station deep in night, the train stock-still, waiting. Someone was pottering about in a little office of unshaded light. What station was it? What town?

"Isobel?" swallowing down sleep.

Isobel, moving around in the light from the kitchen doorway, her bathrobe hanging open, the sash trailing. "You never should have come," said Isobel.

"What time is it?" Naomi whispered. Was it time to get up and get dressed and go down to the ferry dock?

"Four."

Ah! Guy and the girl! The couple in the car! Naomi sighed a long, anxious sigh, a favor done for sleepless Isobel, a comprehension of this terrible night and who was to blame for it. She lifted her feet off the table, aware that a scolding for one thing leads to a scolding for another.

Isobel yanked up the trailing sash. "You come and tell me a little thing like you can't find pity for Hal. So you can't, so what? Is it a crime? Maybe it is, but if it's justified why make it into such a big thing? Why come all that way to tell *me* about it? There are so many crimes, who can keep track of which are right and which are wrong?"

Naomi sat with the blanket around her, no longer like a potentate or a child but like an invalid with a little commonplace ailment that she'd exaggerated into a consuming one. What was it, little or big?

"The ferry leaves at six," Isobel was saying. "You get dressed and make yourself some coffee and call a taxi. It's daylight then." She left on the kitchen light for the departing guest to dress by.

Naomi in her blanket heard Isobel climb the stairs, and her love trailed after, her early love for Isobel that she had brought along, hoping it would keep her upright, save her from tottering around. But Naomi's love was nothing to Isobel, was of no account, a nuisance, and so love gave up on Isobel, couldn't find her again, she was nowhere, and Naomi was alone in an empty house.

12

Seagulls again, flying against the wind, their scornful laughing like that of a colony of lunatics on an excursion. She sat by a window, on a wine-varnished bench in the ferry's warm interior, comforted by the constant vibrations of the engines. Only one person was out on deck, a portly man in over-coat and hat, passing her window for the second time in his morning round-and-round of exercise, pushing against the wind. The rest of the commuters were reading fresh newspapers, their face content with the routine of crossing deep waters. Her overnight case lay under the bench, in it her black nylon nightgown, the pink panties she hadn't changed into, the toothbrush she hadn't used. What kind of dead-letter depository received suitcases left by persons jumping overboard if the next of kin wasn't as close as the next of kin sounds? Isobel, what would she do with it? Or Cort, back home? Pauline would give her things to a church rummage, and who would buy her black nylon nightie for twenty-five cents and feel her lover's hand come in under? With her heel, she felt for the case under the bench to assure herself that she was still there, in touch with her possessions.

The cup of coffee she'd drunk in Isobel's kitchen seemed to have rinsed out her stomach. She'd left a dirty cup and a dirty spoon, and after Isobel had washed them and put away the blanket, would everything be the same as before? Maybe Naomi was to be around forever. She had dug up a root from the father's body to plant in the son, that root that was a need for a reason to stay on this earth. Not the reason his mother taught him, nor the ones that seemed to work for others, not even the real solemn reason you got for going to church. A need for a reason that she, Naomi, who thought she was so smart, hadn't even known about. Why did you need a reason to stay among the living? You stayed because you'd been put there. But when Hal took his life, out there among the willows in the night, she'd learned for the first time that some people never find a reason good enough.

The sun was concealed behind a blanket of high, gray clouds, but its light was reflected on the open waters—a cold, glittering patch far out, like a drifting island. No next of kin would fall heir to the overnight case under her heel. She'd keep it herself. She'd stay inside the ferry, with the morning faces around her, in the warm, vibrating air. She'd stay with the women like herself, combed, powdered, their faces adjusted to the day, nightmares and resignation wiped off by the washcloth. She'd return on the train and hand up to the conductor the long, folded ticket. (She had expected the ticket to be small, like a movie ticket.) She'd unlock her door, unpack, and toss the overnight case onto the closet shelf, and maybe in a month or two she'd move out, move into a two-room apartment closer to work, a place with a tiny kitchen, and maybe get herself a cat. But this anticipation of a time that was to be her own stirred up a vast need to love someone, to use up that future time with love for someone, and it came to her, as she said *Mama, Mama,* inside her mouth with her lips closed, that her love for someone, for all of them, had been her reason for living, as futile a reason as it seemed now. This past love for them, among them her brother in his life before his death, absolved her now of her sin of no pity, and, absolved, she felt the pity for him come flooding over her, like all the pity in the world.

Again the man out on the deck appeared, coming up alongside her, facing her way, the wind thrusting him back, his glasses misted, his hands rammed into his overcoat pockets. He passed her, going on toward the bow, and for a moment he was a forbidden sight—a struggling man, his back exposed.

The gray mound of the city was separating itself into angular buildings and on the large ships moored below the city an array of minute objects became huge anchors, smokestacks, cranes, men. On the roofs of the wharf sheds and high on the log pilings, seagulls watched the ferry enter the slip. The passengers were folding up newspapers, tucking papers into their briefcases as the city filled all the windows of the ferry, both sides. Naomi rose with them and went down with the pressing crowd, quickstep into the terminal, passing under the high small lights of the vast echoing waiting room.

GINA BERRIAULT was born in Long Beach, California. She was awarded the PEN/Faulkner Award for fiction, the National Books Critics Prize in fiction, and the Rea Prize for lifetime achievement, and many other awards including two O'Henry prizes and the Aga Kahn Fiction Prize. Her several screenplays included "The Stone Boy," made into a film starring Robert Duvall and Glenn Close in 1984. She died in Marin Country, California, in 1999.